NEW YORK REVIEW BOOKS
CLASSICS

PARIS STORIES

MAVIS GALLANT (1922–2014) was born in Montreal and worked as a journalist at the *Montreal Standard* before moving to Europe to devote herself to writing fiction. In 1950, after traveling extensively, she settled in Paris, where she would remain for the rest of her life. Over the course of her career Gallant published more than one hundred stories and dispatches in *The New Yorker*. In 2002 she received the Rea Award for the Short Story and in 2004, the PEN/Nabokov Award for lifetime achievement. In addition to *Paris Stories*, New York Review Books Classics publishes two other collections of Gallant's short stories, *The Cost of Living: Early and Uncollected Stories* and *Varieties of Exile*, and a novel, *A Fairly Good Time*.

MICHAEL ONDAATJE's novels are *Coming Through Slaughter*, *In the Skin of a Lion*, *The English Patient*, and *Anil's Ghost*. His books of poetry include *The Cinnamon Peeler* and *Handwriting*. His most recent novel is *The Cat's Table*. He lives in Toronto, Canada.

PARIS STORIES

MAVIS GALLANT

Selected and with an introduction by
MICHAEL ONDAATJE

NEW YORK REVIEW BOOKS

New York

This is a New York Review Book
Published by The New York Review of Books
435 Hudson Street, New York, NY 10014
www.nyrb.com

Library of Congress Cataloging-in-Publication Data
Gallant, Mavis.
  Paris stories / Mavis Gallant ; selected and with an introduction by
Michael Ondaatje.
    p. cm.
  ISBN 1-59017-022-9 (Paperback : alk. paper)
  1. Paris (France)—Fiction. I. Ondaatje, Michael, 1943– II. Title.
  PR9199.3.G26 A6 2002
  813'.54—dc21

                              2002009790

ISBN 978-1-59017-022-9

Book design by Lizzie Scott
Printed in the United States of America on acid-free paper.
20 19 18 17 16 15 14 13

CONTENTS

INTRODUCTION

A HANDFUL OF SMALL SHIPWRECKS

MAVIS GALLANT was born in Montreal in August of 1922. After a peripatetic childhood (she attended seventeen schools), she found a job with the National Film Board of Canada, and then at the *Montreal Standard* as a journalist. In 1944 she published her first stories, and six years later, determined to become a full-time writer, she moved to Paris, where she has lived ever since. Paris seems to be her home in every way, emotionally, spiritually, physically, although she is still very much a Canadian who is living abroad.

In the last fifty years her publications have included several collections of short stories, two novels, works of nonfiction such as *Paris Notebooks*, which covered the student uprisings of 1968, novellas, plays, and literary essays. Her stories and nonfiction have for years appeared regularly in *The New Yorker*. And she has won many distinguished literary awards. Still, at present in the United States, her work is not even in print, while her reputation and readership are smaller than she deserves, though among writers she is a shared and loved and daunting secret. I know two writers who have told me that the one writer they do *not* read when they are completing a book is Mavis Gallant. Nothing could be more intimidating. "The long career of Marguerite Yourcenar," Mavis Gallant once wrote, "stands among the litter of flashier reputations as testimony to ... the purpose and meaning of a writer's life." One feels the remark is an apt description of Gallant's own accomplishment.

This new selection of stories, drawn from the many she has written, is just a hint of her remarkable literary talent. And *Paris*

Stories, as a title, is more suggestive than exact (though Gallant notes that it's appropriate if only because everything in this collection was written in Paris, either at her desk or in her kitchen). The stories, however, take place all over Europe: in France, Austria, Germany, Switzerland, Italy, and other parts of the Continent. Many of her characters have roots in Canada, or come from Eastern Europe. Her Europe is a place of "shipwrecks"—a word that occurs more than once in the stories. All her characters are seemingly far from home. They belong, to be honest, nowhere. Most of them are permanent wanderers, though a nomadic fate was not part of their original intent. With no land to light on, they look back without nostalgia, and look forward with a frayed hope. So that even the epigraph, from *As You Like It*, that Gallant chose for her early novel *Green Water Green Sky*, seems painfully ironic: "Ay, now am I in Arden, the more fool I. When I was at home, I was in a better place, but travellers must be content."

"All immigration is based on misapprehension," Gallant has written, and she catches or witnesses her subjects in waiting rooms, halfway across bridges, overhead in balloons, in transit— her very titles signal incomplete and transient states. (Only her recurring comic character, Grippes, a writer who happens to be a slum landlord, harassed by neighbors, disturbed by the changing times, is where he wishes to be.) After a while this collection of souls begins to represent for the reader the true state of the world.

The characters who people Mavis Gallant's Europe are complex and various. The same is true of her protean prose. She is light years away from writers who claim a recognizably indelible style and constant landscape, although we as readers *do* become accustomed to her chameleon nature, her quick pace and her sudden swerves, so that we watch and listen carefully for any ground shift of humor or sadness. Her tenderness arrives unexpectedly, while her wit is sly, almost too quick. Comic possibilities are everywhere:

> The Blum-Bloch-Weilers, heavy art collectors, produced statesmen, magistrates, anthropologists, and generals, and were on no account to be confused with the Blum-Weiler-

Blochs, their penniless and mystical cousins, who produced poets, librarians, and Benedictine monks.

"Speck's Idea"

I had not even a nebulous idea of how children sprang to life. I merely knew two persons were required for a ritual I believed had to continue for nine months, and which I imagined in the nature of a long card game with mysterious rules.

"Varieties of Exile"

Gallant is brilliant at tilting a situation or a personality a few subliminal degrees in the mind of the reader so that he discovers himself located in a strange new place, seeing something from a more generous or more satirical position. The stories feel cubist in their angles and qualifications, although the narrator often gives the air of being attached, lazily, almost accidentally, like a burr to some character—an Italian servant perhaps, a tax consultant, an art dealer . . .

Just listing a few of Gallant's characters reveals the range and diversity of her world—lost sons, émigrés, refugees from the nuclear family or the establishment, all trying to scramble back but with no weapons to do so. She catches the behavior of the out-of-place citizen, who carries a single-minded bundle of craft and belief. What she gives us, in fact, is an underground map of Europe in the twentieth century, and what feels like a set of dangerous unauthorized portraits. Even ghosts have their say in "From the Fifteenth District," that sly story of complaint.

The world Gallant depicts is cosmopolitan, and she is a writer of seemingly endless voices and personae, but in these stories she is also regional in the best sense. She has a brilliant sense of place. She speaks, in an essay on Paris, of "a small, dim chapel of gentle ugliness." The city for her constantly shifts and evolves and Gallant will offer a humorous archaeology of Paris that seems to draw together all aspects of it, as we see in this opening to "Speck's Idea":

Sandor Speck's first art gallery in Paris was on the Right Bank, near the Church of St. Elisabeth, on a street too narrow for cars. When his block was wiped off the map to make way for a five-story garage, Speck crossed the Seine to the shadow of Saint-Julien-le-Pauvre, where he set up shop in a picturesque slum protected by law from demolition. When this gallery was blown up by Basque separatists, who had mistaken it for a travel agency exploiting the beauty of their coast, he collected his insurance money and moved to the Faubourg Saint-Germain.

Most of the time though, Gallant's subject is the comic opera of character. She slips into and out of minds and moods so quickly that we often miss the technical craft of that journey. And she often looks into the deepest of motives without, it seems, getting up from her chair. But if we reread her, we see how before we know it she will have circled a person, captured a voice, revealed a whole manner of a life in the way a character avoids an issue or discusses a dress. She meets these characters in the zone between thought and possible action. "Forain" takes place in the mind of a character who seemingly stands in mid-gesture, never quite deciding or moving: to act upon what one would like to do is simply too difficult, the end of that corridor is too far away. The action of the story is that of a Parisian publisher of Eastern European émigré writers going to a funeral, thinking about the deceased, and leaving. But these twenty pages are filled with a crowded and complicated nexus of lives, tactfully and beautifully revealed—of writers and their partners and daughters, their agents and publishers—and the half-ambitious and basically exhausted careers of literary exiles in Europe.

There is always this fraught border between wishful behavior and minimal action. But even though the world Gallant portrays is in shadows, her stories move as quickly and clearly as a glance. They suggest a series of sketches that show every aspect of these incomplete lives. They are often surreally comic, sometimes full of pathos, sometimes vainglorious. We live within them and they show us what we never expected to see about ourselves.

"Writers, I suppose, are like children imagining," Mavis Gallant writes. And in a way what we have in her work is something of a child's strange clarity towards this shadowy, complex world that she is witness to. She studies her characters' behavior with gall, curiosity, with the toughness of a child looking at and studying adults. What results is a wonderful truth and, at the same time, great self-revelation. Many stories suggest a mask or portrait of the artist, or a persona active in the world out there, somewhat the way a writer like Patricia Highsmith invented the amoral Ripley and allowed him action (deceit, bribery, murder, forgery, good restaurant behavior, casual sex), while she herself resided in her small house in Switzerland. This is how writers spin, this is how a self-portrait can be paradoxically achieved by self-effacement. Henry James could turn a *donnée* heard at the dinner table over in his hands and create the intricate choreography of *What Maisie Knew*. Gallant, one suspects, similarly sees and meets people and then invents what becomes a precise landscape of their world. There is no vanity or self-aggrandizement in her process and the portraits are always tough as well as generous. For instance her satire is sharp in "The Ice Wagon Going Down the Street," and yet she will take us beyond that satire to feel compassion for a character we would never have believed could be sympathetic. The tenderness does not replace or override the earlier portrait, Peter is still pathetic, but now there is that one moment where something happened, where the man's awareness of human nature was suddenly profound.

In any case Gallant always surprises us, never bothering with the dramatically obvious. Thus in "Ice Wagon" the possible adultery by the wife is ignored, is *not* the point of that story. These are stories in which you sense a great freedom of creation, the next sentence can bring a complete shift of tone or content, while a quick aside can include whole lives—sometimes halfway through one person's thought you will get another's history. As a writer Gallant seems beholden to no one. And for such a serious writer, one who can be dark and misanthropic, it is remarkable to see how many of her stories are gently and continually funny, even abundant with farce.

In one of the more recent stories in this collection, "Scarves, Beads, Sandals," we see Gallant in her prime, the prose moving at a brisk trot, but somehow still relaxed, utterly casual. Stray thoughts leap from paragraph to paragraph. Does Theo look like Max Ernst or Braque to his ex-wife's new husband, or is it Balthus? And this minor refrain continues to resurface in an off-hand way throughout the tale. The story also has that most remarkable of Gallant's qualities—which is the ability to slip or drop into the thought processes of minor characters, without any evident signaling of literary machinery. And there is also a rare narrative intimacy where the mind of the central female character, Mathilde, at times merges with (possibly) something close to the voice of the narrator *outside* the story. But one could equally be persuaded by a similar intimacy with the ex-husband's memories, or even the wandering thoughts of Henri Grippes in the story "In Plain Sight." Gallant's craft and empathy, with that skill in evoking subtle and obsessive voices, is always ahead of us. She has, after all, what she claims Yourcenar had, "a reflective alliance."

"I had a great, great fear that I was bent on doing something for which I have no ability, and that took years and years to get rid of ... that I was dedicating my life to something I was not fit for," Gallant once told an interviewer. With some writers greatness emerges out of their very tentativeness, their own uncertainty about how they make stories, or if it is even possible to make them. It results perhaps in every word and line being tested for falseness or complacency. It results too in a kind of testing, self-critical humor that lies within the text. "I am uncertain about every line I write and I am uncertain until I get readers." With the arrival of that reader, the uncertainty about "an unsafe life" becomes a shared witnessing. This, for a very few writers, becomes the purpose and meaning of a writer's life. "Like every other form of art," Mavis Gallant has written, "literature is no more and nothing less than a matter of life and death."

—MICHAEL ONDAATJE

PARIS STORIES

To Tess Taconis, en souvenir de notre jeunesse

THE ICE WAGON GOING
DOWN THE STREET

Now THAT they are out of world affairs and back where they started, Peter Frazier's wife says, "Everybody else did well in the international thing except us."

"You have to be crooked," he tells her.

"Or smart. Pity we weren't."

It is Sunday morning. They sit in the kitchen, drinking their coffee, slowly, remembering the past. They say the names of people as if they were magic. Peter thinks, Agnes Brusen, but there are hundreds of other names. As a private married joke, Peter and Sheilah wear the silk dressing gowns they bought in Hong Kong. Each thinks the other a peacock, rather splendid, but they pretend the dressing gowns are silly and worn in fun.

Peter and Sheilah and their two daughters, Sandra and Jennifer, are visiting Peter's unmarried sister, Lucille. They have been Lucille's guests seventeen weeks, ever since they returned to Toronto from the Far East. Their big old steamer trunk blocks a corner of the kitchen, making a problem of the refrigerator door; but even Lucille says the trunk may as well stay where it is, for the present. The Fraziers' future is so unsettled; everything is still in the air.

Lucille has given her bedroom to her two nieces, and sleeps on a camp cot in the hall. The parents have the living-room divan. They have no privileges here; they sleep after Lucille has seen the last television show that interests her. In the hall closet their clothes are crushed by winter overcoats. They know they are being judged for the first time. Sandra and Jennifer are waiting for Sheilah and Peter to decide. They are waiting to learn where these exotic parents will fly to next. What sort of climate will Sheilah consider? What job will Peter consent to accept? When the parents are ready, the children will make a decision of their own. It is just possible that Sandra and Jennifer will choose to stay with their aunt.

The peacock parents are watched by wrens. Lucille and her nieces are much the same—sandy-colored, proudly plain. Neither of the girls has the father's insouciance or the mother's appearance—her height, her carriage, her thick hair and sky-blue eyes. The children are more cautious than their parents; more Canadian. When they saw their aunt's apartment they had been away from Canada nine years, ever since they were two and four; and Jennifer, the elder, said, "Well, now we're home." Her voice is nasal and flat. Where did she learn that voice? And why should this be home? Peter's answer to anything about his mystifying children is, "It must be in the blood."

On Sunday morning Lucille takes her nieces to church. It seems to be the only condition she imposes on her relations: The children must be decent. The girls go willingly, with their new hats and purses and gloves and coral bracelets and strings of pearls. The parents, ramshackle, sleepy, dim in the brain because it is Sunday, sit down to their coffee and privacy and talk of the past.

"We weren't crooked," says Peter. "We weren't even smart."

Sheilah's head bobs up; she is no drowner. It is wrong to say they have nothing to show for time. Sheilah has the Balenciaga. It is a black afternoon dress, stiff and boned at the waist, long for the fashions of now, but neither Sheilah nor Peter would change a thread. The Balenciaga is their talisman, their treasure; and after they remember it they touch hands and think that the years are not behind them but hazy and marvelous and still to be lived.

The first place they went to was Paris. In the early fifties the pick of the international jobs was there. Peter had inherited the last scrap of money he knew he was ever likely to see, and it was enough to get them over: Sheilah and Peter and the babies and the steamer trunk. To their joy and astonishment they had money in the bank. They said to each other, "It should last a year." Peter was fastidious about the new job; he hadn't come all this distance to accept just anything. In Paris he met Hugh Taylor, who was earning enough smuggling gasoline to keep his wife in Paris and a girl in Rome. That impressed Peter, because he remembered Taylor as a sour scholarship student without the slightest talent for life. Taylor had a job, of course. He hadn't said to himself, I'll go over to Europe and smuggle gasoline. It gave Peter an idea; he saw the shape of things. First you catch your fish. Later, at an international party, he met Johnny Hertzberg, who told him Germany was the place. Hertzberg said that anyone who came out of Germany broke now was too stupid to be here, and deserved to be back home at a desk. Peter nodded, as if he had already thought of that. He began to think about Germany. Paris was fine for a holiday, but it had been picked clean. Yes, Germany. His money was running low. He thought about Germany quite a lot.

That winter was moist and delicate; so fragile that they daren't speak of it now. There seemed to be plenty of everything and plenty of time. They were living the dream of a marriage, the fabric uncut, nothing slashed or spoiled. All winter they spent their money, and went to parties, and talked about Peter's future job. It lasted four months. They spent their money, lived in the future, and were never as happy again.

After four months they were suddenly moved away from Paris, but not to Germany—to Geneva. Peter thinks it was because of the incident at the Trudeau wedding at the Ritz. Paul Trudeau was a French-Canadian Peter had known at school and in the Navy. Trudeau had turned into a snob, proud of his career and his Paris connections. He tried to make the difference felt, but Peter thought the difference was only for strangers. At the wedding reception Peter lay down on the floor and said he was dead. He held a white azalea in a brass pot on his chest, and sang, "Oh, hear us when we cry to Thee for those in peril on the sea." Sheilah bent over him and said, "Peter, darling, get up. Pete, listen, every single person who can do something for you is in this room. If you love me, you'll get up."

"I do love you," he said, ready to engage in a serious conversation. "She's so beautiful," he told a second face. "She's nearly as tall as I am. She was a model in London. I met her over in London in the war. I met her there in the war." He lay on his back with the azalea on his chest, explaining their history. A waiter took the brass pot away, and after Peter had been hauled to his feet he knocked the waiter down. Trudeau's bride, who was freshly out of an Ursuline convent, became hysterical; and even though Paul Trudeau and Peter were old acquaintances, Trudeau never spoke to him again. Peter says now that French-Canadians always have that bit of spite. He says Trudeau asked the embassy to interfere. Luckily, back home there were still a few people to whom the name "Frazier" meant something, and it was to these people that Peter appealed. He wrote letters saying that a French-Canadian combine was preventing his getting a decent job, and could anything be done? No one answered directly, but it was clear that what they settled for was exile to Geneva: a season of meditation and remorse, as he explained to Sheilah, and it was managed tactfully, through Lucille. Lucille wrote that a friend of hers, May Fergus, now a secretary in Geneva, had heard about a job. The job was filing pictures in the information service of an international agency in the Palais des Nations. The pay was so-so, but Lucille thought Peter must be getting fed up doing nothing.

Peter often asks his sister now who put her up to it—what important person told her to write that letter suggesting Peter go to Geneva?

"Nobody," says Lucille. "I mean, nobody in the way *you* mean. I really did have this girl friend working there, and I knew you must be running through your money pretty fast in Paris."

"It must have been somebody pretty high up," Peter says. He looks at his sister admiringly, as he has often looked at his wife.

Peter's wife had loved him in Paris. Whatever she wanted in marriage she found that winter, there. In Geneva, where Peter was a file clerk and they lived in a furnished flat, she pretended they were in Paris and life was still the same. Often, when the children were at supper, she changed as though she and Peter were dining out. She wore the Balenciaga, and put candles on the card table where she and Peter ate their meal. The neckline of the dress was soiled with makeup. Peter remembers her dabbing on the makeup with a wet sponge. He remembers her in the kitchen, in the soiled

Balenciaga, patting on the makeup with a filthy sponge. Behind her, at the kitchen table, Sandra and Jennifer, in buttonless pajamas and bunny slippers, ate their supper of marmalade sandwiches and milk. When the children were asleep, the parents dined solemnly, ritually, Sheilah sitting straight as a queen.

It was a mysterious period of exile, and he had to wait for signs, or signals, to know when he was free to leave. He never saw the job any other way. He forgot he had applied for it. He thought he had been sent to Geneva because of a misdemeanor and had to wait to be released. Nobody pressed him at work. His immediate boss had resigned, and he was alone for months in a room with two desks. He read the *Herald Tribune*, and tried to discover how things were here—how the others ran their lives on the pay they were officially getting. But it was a closed conspiracy. He was not dealing with adventurers now but civil servants waiting for pension day. No one ever answered his questions. They pretended to think his questions were a form of wit. His only solace in exile was the few happy weekends he had in the late spring and early summer. He had met another old acquaintance, Mike Burleigh. Mike was a serious liberal who had married a serious heiress. The Burleighs had two guest lists. The first was composed of stuffy people they felt obliged to entertain, while the second was made up of their real friends, the friends they wanted. The real friends strove hard to become stuffy and dull and thus achieve the first guest list, but few succeeded. Peter went on the first list straightaway. Possibly Mike didn't understand, at the beginning, why Peter was pretending to be a file clerk. Peter had such an air—he might have been sent by a universal inspector to see how things in Geneva were being run.

Every Friday in May and June and part of July, the Fraziers rented a sky-blue Fiat and drove forty miles east of Geneva to the Burleighs' summer house. They brought the children, a suitcase, the children's tattered picture books, and a token bottle of gin. This, in memory, is a period of water and water birds; swans, roses, and singing birds. The children were small and still belonged to them. If they remember too much, their mouths water, their stomachs hurt. Peter says, "It was fine while it lasted." Enough. While it lasted Sheilah and Madge Burleigh were close. They abandoned their husbands and spent long summer afternoons comparing their mothers and praising each other's skin and hair. To Madge, and not to Peter, Sheilah opened her Liverpool childhood with the words "rat poor." Peter heard about it later, from Mike. The women's friendship seemed to Peter a bad beginning. He trusted women but not with each other. It lasted ten weeks. One Sunday, Madge said she needed the two bedrooms the Fraziers usually occupied for a party of sociologists from Pakistan, and that was the end. In November, the Fraziers heard that the summer house had been closed, and that the Burleighs were in Geneva, in their winter flat; they gave no sign. There was no help for it, and no appeal.

Now Peter began firing letters to anyone who had ever known his late father. He was living in a mild yellow autumn. Why does he remember the streets of the city dark, and the windows everywhere black with rain? He remembers being with Sheilah and the children as if they clung together while just outside their small shelter it rained and rained. The children slept in the bedroom of the flat because the window gave on the street and they could breathe air. Peter and Sheilah had the living-room couch. Their window was not a real window but a square on a well of cement. The flat seemed damp as a cave. Peter remembers steam in the kitchen, pools under the sink, sweat on the pipes. Water streamed on him from the children's clothes, washed and dripping overhead. The trunk, upended in the children's room, was not quite unpacked. Sheilah had not signed her name to this life; she had not given in. Once Peter heard her drop her aitches. "You kids are lucky," she said to the girls. "I never 'ad so much as a sit-down meal. I ate chips out of a paper or I 'ad a butty out on the stairs." He never asked her what a butty was. He thinks it means bread and cheese.

The day he heard "You kids are lucky" he understood they were becoming in fact something they had only *appeared* to be until now—the shabby civil servant and his brood. If he had been European he would have ridden to work on a bicycle, in the uniform of his class and condition. He would have worn a tight coat, a turned collar, and a dirty tie. He wondered then if coming here had been a mistake, and if he should not, after all, still be in a place where his name meant something. Surely Peter Frazier should live where "Frazier" counts? In Ontario even now when he says "Frazier" an absent look comes over his hearer's face, as if its owner were consulting an interior guide. What is Frazier? What does it mean? Oil? Power? Politics? Wheat? Real estate? The creditors had the house sealed when Peter's father died. His aunt collapsed with a heart attack in somebody's bachelor apartment, leaving three sons and a widower to surmise they had never known her. Her will was a disappointment. None of that generation left enough. One made it: the granite Presbyterian immigrants from Scotland. Their children, a generation of daunted women and maiden men, held still. Peter's father's crowd spent: They were not afraid of their fathers, and their grandfathers were old. Peter and his sister and his cousins lived on the remains. They were left the rinds of income, of notions, and the memories of ideas rather than ideas intact. If Peter can choose his reincarnation, let him be the oppressed son of a Scottish parson. Let Peter grow up on cuffs and iron principles. Let him make the fortune! Let him flee the manse! When he was small his patrimony was squandered under his nose. He remembers people dancing in his father's house. He remembers seeing and nearly understanding adultery in a guest room, among a pile of wraps. He thought he had seen a murder; he never told. He remembers licking glasses wherever he found them—on windowsills, on stairs, in the pantry. In his room he listened while Lucille read Beatrix Potter. The bad rabbit stole the carrot from the good rabbit without saying please, and downstairs was the noise of the party—the roar of the crouched lion. When his father died he saw the chairs upside down and the bailiff's chalk marks. Then the doors were sealed.

He has often tried to tell Sheilah why he cannot be defeated. He remembers his father saying, "Nothing can touch us," and Peter believed it and still does. It has prevented his taking his troubles too seriously. Nothing can be as bad as this, he will tell himself. It is happening to me. Even in Geneva, where his status was file clerk, where he sank and stopped on the level of the men who never emigrated, the men on the bicycles—even there he had a manner of strolling to work as if his office were a pastime, and his real life a secret so splendid he could share it with no one except himself.

In Geneva Peter worked for a woman—a girl. She was a Norwegian from a small town in Saskatchewan. He supposed they had been put together because they were Canadians; but they were as strange to each other as if "Canadian" meant any number of things, or had no real meaning. Soon after Agnes Brusen came to the office she hung her framed university degree on the wall. It was one of the gritty, prideful gestures that stand for push, toil, and family sacrifice. He thought, then, that she must be one of a family of immigrants for whom education is everything. Hugh Taylor had told him that in some families the older children never marry until the youngest have finished school. Sometimes every second child is sacrificed and made to work for the education of the next-born. Those who finish college spend years paying back. They are white-hot Protestants, and they live with a load of work and debt and obligation. Peter placed his new colleague on scraps of information. He had never been in the West.

She came to the office on a Monday morning in October. The office was overheated and painted cream. It contained two desks, the filing cabinets, a map of the world as it had been in 1945, and the Charter of the United Nations left behind by Agnes Brusen's predecessor. (She took down the Charter without asking Peter if he minded, with the impudence of gesture you find in women who wouldn't say boo to a goose; and then she hung her college degree on the nail where the Charter had been.) Three people brought her in—a whole committee. One of them said, "Agnes, this is Pete Frazier. Pete, Agnes Brusen. Pete's Canadian, too, Agnes. He knows all about the office, so ask him anything."

Of course he knew all about the office: He knew the exact spot where the cord of the venetian blind was frayed, obliging one to give an extra tug to the right.

The girl might have been twenty-three: no more. She wore a brown tweed suit with bone buttons, and a new silk scarf and new shoes. She clutched an unscratched brown purse. She seemed dressed in going-away presents. She said, "Oh, I never smoke," with a convulsive movement of her hand, when Peter offered his case. He was courteous, hiding his disappointment. The people he worked with had told him a Scandinavian girl was arriving, and he had expected a stunner. Agnes was a mole: She was small and brown, and round-shouldered as if she had always carried parcels or younger children in her arms. A mole's profile was turned when she said good-bye to her committee. If she had been foreign, ill-favored though she was, he might have flirted a little, just to show that he was friendly; but their being Canadian, and suddenly left together, was a sexual damper. He sat down and lit his own cigarette. She smiled at him, questionably, he thought, and sat as if she had never seen a chair before. He wondered if his smoking was annoying her. He wondered if she was fidgety about drafts, or allergic to anything, and whether she would want the blind up or down. His social compass was out of order because the others couldn't tell Peter and Agnes apart. There was a world of difference between them, yet it was she who had been brought in to sit at the larger of the two desks.

While he was thinking this she got up and walked around the office, almost on tiptoe, opening the doors of closets and pulling out the filing trays. She looked inside everything except the drawers of Peter's desk. (In any case, Peter's desk was locked. His desk is locked wherever he works. In Geneva he went into Personnel one morning, early, and pinched his application form. He had stated on the form that he had seven years' experience in public relations and could speak French, German, Spanish, and Italian. He has always collected anything important about himself—anything useful. But he can never get on with the final act, which is getting rid of the information. He has kept papers about for years, a constant source of worry.)

"I know this looks funny, Mr. Ferris," said the girl. "I'm not really snooping or anything. I just can't feel easy in a new place unless I know where everything is. In a new place everything seems so hidden."

If she had called him "Ferris" and pretended not to know he was Frazier, it could only be because they had sent her here to spy on him and see if he had repented and was fit for a better place in life. "You'll be all right here," he said. "Nothing's hidden. Most of us haven't got brains enough to have secrets. This is Rainbow Valley." Depressed by the thought that they were having him watched now, he passed his hand over his hair and looked outside to the lawn and the parking lot and the peacocks someone gave the Palais des Nations years ago. The peacocks love no one. They wander about the parked cars looking elderly, bad-tempered, mournful, and lost.

Agnes had settled down again. She folded her silk scarf and placed it just so, with her gloves beside it. She opened her new purse and took out a notebook and a shiny gold pencil. She may have written

> Duster for desk
> Kleenex
> Glass jar for flowers
> Air-Wick because he smokes
> Paper for lining drawers

because the next day she brought each of these articles to work. She also brought a large black Bible, which she unwrapped lovingly and placed on the left-hand corner of her desk. The flower vase—empty—stood in the middle, and the Kleenex made a counterpoise for the Bible on the right.

When he saw the Bible he knew she had not been sent to spy on his work. The conspiracy was deeper. She might have been dispatched by ghosts. He knew everything about her, all in a moment: He saw the ambition, the terror, the dry pride. She was the true heir of the men from Scotland; she was at the start. She had been sent to tell him, "You can begin, but not begin again." She never opened the Bible, but she dusted it as she dusted her desk, her chair, and any surface the cleaning staff had overlooked. And Peter, the first days, watching her timid movements, her insignificant little face, felt, as you feel the approach of a storm, the charge of moral certainty round her, the belief in work, the faith in undertakings, the bread of the Black Sunday. He recognized and tasted all of it: ashes in the mouth.

After five days their working relations were settled. Of course, there was the Bible and all that went with it, but his tongue had never held the taste of ashes long. She was an inferior girl of poor quality. She had nothing in her favor except the degree on the wall. In the real world, he would not have invited her to his house except to mind the children. That was what he said to Sheilah. He said that Agnes was a mole, and a virgin, and that her tics and mannerisms were sending him round the bend. She had an infuriating habit of covering her mouth when she talked. Even at the telephone she put up her hand as if afraid of losing anything, even a word. Her voice was nasal and flat. She had two working costumes, both dull as the wall. One was the brown suit, the other a navy-blue dress with changeable collars. She dressed for no one; she dressed for her desk, her jar of flowers, her Bible, and her box of Kleenex. One day she crossed the space between the two desks and stood over Peter, who was reading a newspaper. She could have spoken to him from her desk, but she may have felt that being on her feet gave her authority. She had plenty of courage, but authority was something else.

"I thought—I mean, they told me you were the person . . ." She got on with it bravely: "If you don't want to do the filing or any work, all right, Mr. Frazier. I'm not saying anything about that. You might have poor health or your personal reasons. But it's got to be done, so if you'll kindly show me about the filing I'll do it. I've worked in Information before, but it was a different office, and every office is different."

"My dear girl," said Peter. He pushed back his chair and looked at her, astonished. "You've been sitting there fretting, worrying. How insensitive of me. How trying for you. Usually I file on the last Wednesday of the month, so you see, you just haven't been around long enough to see a last Wednesday. Not another word, please. And let us not waste another minute." He emptied the heaped baskets of photographs so swiftly, pushing "Iran—Smallpox Control" into "Irish Red Cross" (close enough), that the girl looked frightened, as if she had raised a whirlwind. She said slowly, "If you'll only show me, Mr. Frazier, instead of doing it so fast, I'll gladly look after it, because you might want to be doing other things, and I feel the filing should be done every day." But Peter was too busy to answer, and so she sat down, holding the edge of her desk.

"There," he said, beaming. "All done." His smile, his sunburst, was wasted, for the girl was staring round the room as if she feared she had not inspected everything the first day after all; some drawer, some cupboard, hid a monster. That evening Peter unlocked one of the drawers of his desk and took away the application form he had stolen from Personnel. The girl had not finished her search.

"How could you *not* know?" wailed Sheilah. "You sit looking at her every day. You must talk about *something*. She must have told you."

"She did tell me," said Peter, "and I've just told you."

It was this: Agnes Brusen was on the Burleighs' guest list. How had the Burleighs met her? What did they see in her? Peter could not reply. He knew that Agnes lived in a bed-sitting room with a Swiss family and had her meals with them. She had been in Geneva three months, but no one had ever seen her outside the office. "You *should* know," said Sheilah. "She must have something, more than you can see. Is she pretty? Is she brilliant? What is it?"

"We don't really talk," Peter said. They talked in a way: Peter teased her and she took no notice. Agnes was not a sulker. She had taken her defeat like a sport. She did her work and a good deal of his. She sat behind her Bible, her flowers, and her Kleenex, and answered when Peter spoke. That was how he learned about the Burleighs—just by teasing and being bored. It was a January afternoon. He said, "*Miss* Brusen. Talk to me. Tell me everything. Pretend we have perfect rapport. Do you like Geneva?"

"It's a nice clean town," she said. He can see to this day the red and blue anemones in the glass jar, and her bent head, and her small untended hands.

"Are you learning beautiful French with your Swiss family?"

"They speak English."

"Why don't you take an apartment of your own?" he said. Peter was not usually impertinent. He was bored. "You'd be independent then."

"I am independent," she said. "I earn my living. I don't think it proves anything if you live by yourself. Mrs. Burleigh wants me to live alone, too. She's looking for something for me. It mustn't be dear. I send money home."

Here was the extraordinary thing about Agnes Brusen: She refused the use of Christian names and never spoke to Peter unless he spoke first, but she would tell anything, as if to say, "Don't waste time fishing. Here it is."

He learned all in one minute that she sent her salary home, and that she was a friend of the Burleighs. The first he had expected; the second knocked him flat.

"She's got to come to dinner," Sheilah said. "We should have had her right from the beginning. If only I'd known! But *you* were the one. You said she looked like—oh, I don't even remember. A Norwegian mole."

She came to dinner one Saturday night in January, in her navy-blue dress, to which she had pinned an organdy gardenia. She sat upright on the edge of the sofa. Sheilah had ordered the meal from a restaurant. There was lobster, good wine, and a *pièce-montée* full of kirsch and cream. Agnes refused the lobster; she had never eaten anything from the sea unless it had been sterilized and tinned, and said so. She was afraid of skin poisoning. Someone in her family had skin poisoning after having eaten oysters. She touched her cheeks and neck to show where the poisoning had erupted. She sniffed her wine and put the glass down without tasting it. She could not eat the cake because of the alcohol it contained. She ate an egg, bread and butter, a sliced tomato, and drank a glass of ginger ale. She seemed unaware she was creating disaster and pain. She did not help clear away the dinner plates. She sat, adequately nourished, decently dressed, and waited to learn why she had been invited here—that was the feeling Peter had. He folded the card table on which they had dined, and opened the window to air the room.

"It's not the same cold as Canada, but you feel it more," he said, for something to say.

"Your blood has gotten thin," said Agnes.

Sheilah returned from the kitchen and let herself fall into an armchair. With her eyes closed she held out her hand for a cigarette. She was performing the haughty-lady act that was a family joke. She flung her head back and looked at Agnes through half-closed lids; then she suddenly brought her head forward, widening her eyes.

"Are you skiing madly?" she said.

"Well, in the first place there hasn't been any snow," said Agnes. "So nobody's doing any skiing so far as I know. All I hear is people complaining because there's no snow. Personally, I don't ski. There isn't much skiing in the part of Canada I come from. Besides, my family never had that kind of leisure."

"Heavens," said Sheilah, as if her family had every kind.

I'll bet they had, thought Peter. On the dole.

Sheilah was wasting her act. He had a suspicion that Agnes knew it was an act but did not know it was also a joke. If so, it made Sheilah seem a fool, and he loved Sheilah too much to enjoy it.

"The Burleighs have been wonderful to me," said Agnes. She seemed to have divined why she was here, and decided to give them all the information they wanted, so that she could put on her coat and go home to bed. "They had me out to their place on the lake every weekend until the weather got cold and they moved back to town. They've rented a chalet for the winter, and they want me to come there, too. But I don't know if I will or not. I don't ski, and, oh, I don't know—I don't drink, either, and I don't always see the point. Their friends are too rich and I'm too Canadian."

She had delivered everything Sheilah wanted and more: Agnes was on the first guest list and didn't care. No, Peter corrected: doesn't know. Doesn't care and doesn't know.

"I thought with you Norwegians it was in the blood, skiing. And drinking," Sheilah murmured.

"Drinking, maybe," said Agnes. She covered her mouth and said behind her spread fingers, "In our family we were religious. We didn't drink or smoke. My brother was in Norway in the war. He saw some cousins. Oh," she said, unexpectedly loud, "Harry said it was just terrible. They were so poor. They had flies in their kitchen. They gave him something to eat a fly had been on. They didn't have a real toilet, and they'd been in the same house about two hundred years. We've only recently built our own home, and we have a bathroom and two toilets. I'm from Saskatchewan," she said. "I'm not from any other place."

Surely one winter here had been punishment enough? In the spring they would remember him and free him. He wrote Lucille, who said he was lucky to have a job at all. The Burleighs had sent the Fraziers a second-guest-list Christmas card. It showed a Moslem refugee child weeping outside a tent. They treasured the card and left it standing long after the others had been given the children to cut up. Peter had discovered by now what had gone wrong in the friendship—Sheilah had charged a skirt at a dressmaker to Madge's account. Madge had told her she might, and then changed her mind. Poor Sheilah! She was new to this part of it—to the changing humors of independent friends. Paris was already a year in the past. At Mardi Gras, the Burleighs gave their annual party. They invited everyone, the damned and the dropped, with the prodigality of a child at prayers. The invitation said "in costume," but the Fraziers were too happy to wear a disguise. They might not be recognized. Like many of the guests they expected to meet at the party, they had been disgraced, forgotten, and rehabilitated. They would be anxious to see one another as they were.

On the night of the party, the Fraziers rented a car they had never seen before and drove through the first snowstorm of the year. Peter had not driven since last summer's blissful trips in the Fiat. He could not find the switch for the windshield wiper in this car. He leaned over the wheel. "Can you see on your side?" he asked. "Can I make a left turn here? Does it look like a one-way?"

"I can't imagine why you took a car with a right-hand drive," said Sheilah.

He had trouble finding a place to park; they crawled up and down unknown streets whose curbs were packed with snow-covered cars. When they stood at last on the pavement, safe and sound, Peter said, "This is the first snow."

"I can see that," said Sheilah. "Hurry, darling. My hair."

"It's the first snow."

"You're repeating yourself," she said. "Please hurry, darling. Think of my poor shoes. My *hair*."

She was born in an ugly city, and so was Peter, but they have this difference: She does not know the importance of the first snow—the first clean thing in a dirty year. He would have told her then that this storm, which was wetting her feet and destroying her hair, was like the first day of the English spring, but she made a frightened gesture, trying to shield her head. The gesture told him he did not understand her beauty.

"Let me," she said. He was fumbling with the key, trying to lock the car. She took the key without impatience and locked the door on the driver's side; and then, to show Peter she treasured him and was not afraid of wasting her life or her beauty, she took his arm and they walked in the snow down a street and around a corner to the apartment house where the Burleighs lived. They were, and are, a united couple. They were afraid of the party, and each of them knew it. When they walk together, holding arms, they give each other whatever each can spare.

Only six people had arrived in costume. Madge Burleigh was disguised as Manet's "Lola de Valence," which everyone mistook for Carmen. Mike was an Impressionist painter, with a straw hat and a glued-on beard. "I am all of them," he said. He would rather have dressed as a dentist, he said, welcoming the Fraziers as if he had parted from them the day before, but Madge wanted him to look as if he had created her. "You know?" he said.

"Perfectly," said Sheilah. Her shoes were stained and the snow had softened her lacquered hair. She was not wasted: She was the most beautiful woman there.

About an hour after their arrival, Peter found himself with no one to talk to. He had told about the Trudeau wedding in Paris and the pot of azaleas, and after he mislaid his audience he began to look round for Sheilah. She was on a window seat, partly concealed by a green velvet curtain. Facing her, so that their profiles were neat and perfect against the night, was a man. Their conversation was private and enclosed, as if they had in minutes covered leagues of time and arrived at the place where everything was implied, understood. Peter began working his way across the room, toward his wife, when he saw Agnes. He was granted the sight of her drowning face. She had dressed with comic intention, obviously with care, and now she was a ragged hobo, half tramp, half clown. Her hair was tucked up under a bowler hat. The six costumed guests who had made the same mistake—the ghost, the gypsy, the Athenian maiden, the geisha, the Martian, and the apache—were delighted to find a seventh; but Agnes was not amused; she was gasping for life. When a waiter passed with a crowded tray, she took a glass without seeing it; then a wave of the party took her away.

Sheilah's new friend was named Simpson. After Simpson said he thought perhaps he'd better circulate, Peter sat down where he had been. "Now look, Sheilah," he began. Their most intimate conversations have taken place at parties. Once at a party she told him she was leaving him; she didn't, of course. Smiling, blue-eyed, she gazed lovingly at Peter and said rapidly, "Pete, shut up and listen. That man. The man you scared away. He's a big wheel in a company out in India or someplace like that. It's gorgeous out there. Pete, the *servants*. And it's warm. It never never snows. He says there's heaps of jobs. You pick them off the trees like ... orchids. He says it's even easier now than when we owned all those places, because now the poor pets can't run anything and they'll pay *fortunes*. Pete, he says it's warm, it's heaven, and Pete, they pay."

A few minutes later, Peter was alone again and Sheilah part of a closed, laughing group. Holding her elbow was the man from the place where jobs grew like orchids. Peter edged into the group and laughed at a story he hadn't heard. He heard only the last line, which was "Here comes another tunnel." Looking out from the tight laughing ring, he saw Agnes again, and he thought, I'd be like Agnes if I didn't have Sheilah. Agnes put her glass down on a table and lurched toward the doorway, head forward. Madge Burleigh, who never stopped moving around the room and smiling, was still smiling when she paused and said in Peter's ear, "Go with Agnes, Pete. See that she gets home. People will notice if Mike leaves."

"She probably just wants to walk around the block," said Peter. "She'll be back."

"Oh, stop thinking about yourself, for once, and see that that poor girl gets home," said Madge. "You've still got your Fiat, haven't you?"

He turned away as if he had been pushed. Any command is a release, in a way. He may not want to go in that particular direction, but at least he is going somewhere. And now Sheilah, who had moved inches nearer to hear what Madge and Peter were murmuring, said, "Yes, go, darling," as if he were leaving the gates of Troy.

Peter was to find Agnes and see that she reached home: This he repeated to himself as he stood on the landing, outside the Burleighs' flat, ringing for the elevator. Bored with waiting for it, he ran down the stairs, four flights, and saw that Agnes had stalled the lift by leaving the door open. She was crouched on the floor, propped on her fingertips. Her eyes were closed.

"Agnes," said Peter. "*Miss* Brusen, I mean. That's no way to leave a party. Don't you know you're supposed to curtsy and say thanks? My God, Agnes, anybody going by here just now might have seen you! Come on, be a good girl. Time to go home."

She got up without his help and, moving between invisible crevasses, shut the elevator door. Then she left the building and Peter followed, remembering he was to see that she got home. They walked along the snowy pavement, Peter a few steps behind her. When she turned right for no reason, he turned, too. He had no clear idea where they were going. Perhaps she lived close by. He had forgotten where the hired car was parked, or what it looked like; he could not remember its make or its color. In any case, Sheilah had the key. Agnes walked on steadily, as if she knew their destination, and he thought, Agnes Brusen is drunk in the street in Geneva and dressed like a tramp. He wanted to say, "This is the best thing that ever happened to you, Agnes; it will help you understand how things are for some of the rest of us." But she stopped and turned and, leaning over a low hedge, retched on a frozen lawn. He held her clammy forehead and rested his hand on her arched back, on muscles as tight as a fist. She straightened up and drew a breath but the cold air made her cough. "Don't breathe too deeply," he said. "It's the worst thing you can do. Have you got a handkerchief?" He passed his own handkerchief over her wet weeping face, upturned like the face of one of his little girls. "I'm out without a coat," he said, noticing it. "We're a pair."

"I never drink," said Agnes. "I'm just not used to it." Her voice was sweet and quiet. He had never seen her so peaceful, so composed. He thought she must surely be all right, now, and perhaps he might leave her here. The trust in her tilted face had perplexed him. He wanted to get back to Sheilah and have her explain something. He had forgotten what it was, but Sheilah would know. "Do you live around here?" he said. As he spoke, she let herself fall. He had wiped her face and now she trusted him to pick her up, set her on her feet, take her wherever she ought to be. He pulled her up and she stood, wordless, humble, as he brushed the snow from her tramp's clothes. Snow horizontally crossed the lamplight. The street was silent. Agnes had lost her hat. Snow, which he tasted, melted on her hands. His gesture of licking snow from her hands was formal as a handshake. He tasted snow on her hands and then they walked on.

"I never drink," she said. They stood on the edge of a broad avenue. The wrong turning now could lead them anywhere; it was the changeable avenue at the edge of towns that loses its houses and becomes a highway. She held his arm and spoke in a gentle voice. She said, "In our house we didn't smoke or drink. My mother was ambitious for me, more than for Harry and the others." She said, "I've never been alone before. When I was a kid I would get up in the summer before the others, and I'd see the ice wagon going down the street. I'm alone now. Mrs. Burleigh's found me an apartment. It's only one room. She likes it because it's in the old part of town. I don't like old houses. Old houses are dirty. You don't know who was there before."

"I should have a car somewhere," Peter said. "I'm not sure where we are."

He remembers that on this avenue they climbed into a taxi, but nothing about the drive. Perhaps he fell asleep. He does remember that when he paid the driver Agnes clutched his arm, trying to stop him. She pressed extra coins into the driver's palm. The driver was paid twice.

"I'll tell you one thing about us," said Peter. "We pay everything twice." This was part of a much longer theory concerning North American behavior, and it was not Peter's own. Mike Burleigh had held forth about it on summer afternoons.

Agnes pushed open a door between a stationer's shop and a grocery, and led the way up a narrow inside stair. They climbed one flight, frightening beetles. She had to search every pocket for the latchkey. She was shaking with cold. Her apartment seemed little warmer than the street. Without speaking to Peter she turned on all the lights. She looked inside the kitchen and the bathroom and then got down on her hands and knees and looked under the sofa. The room was neat and belonged to no one. She left him standing in this unclaimed room—she had forgotten him—and closed a door behind her. He looked for something to do—some useful action he could repeat to Madge. He turned on the electric radiator in the fireplace. Perhaps Agnes wouldn't thank him for it; perhaps she would rather undress in the cold. "I'll be on my way," he called to the bathroom door.

She had taken off the tramp's clothes and put on a dressing gown of orphanage wool. She came out of the bathroom and straight toward him. She pressed her face and rubbed her cheek on his shoulder as if hoping the contact would leave a scar. He saw her back and her profile and his own face in the mirror over the fireplace. He thought, This is how disasters happen. He saw floods of seawater moving with perfect punitive justice over reclaimed land; he saw lava covering vineyards and overtaking dogs and stragglers. A bridge over an abyss snapped in two and the long express train, suddenly V-shaped, floated like snow. He thought amiably of every kind of disaster and thought, This is how they occur.

Her eyes were closed. She said, "I shouldn't be over here. In my family we didn't drink or smoke. My mother wanted a lot from me, more than from Harry and the others." But he knew all that; he had known from the day of the Bible, and because once, at the beginning, she had made him afraid. He was not afraid of her now.

She said, "It's no use staying here, is it?"

"If you mean what I think, no."

"It wouldn't be better anywhere."

She let him see full on her blotched face. He was not expected to do anything. He was not required to pick her up when she fell or wipe her tears. She was poor quality, really—he remembered having thought that once. She left him and went quietly into the bathroom and locked the door. He heard taps running and supposed it was a hot bath. He was pretty certain there would be no more tears. He looked at his watch: Sheilah must be home, now, wondering what had become of him. He descended the beetles' staircase and for forty minutes crossed the city under a windless fall of snow.

The neighbor's child who had stayed with Peter's children was asleep on the living-room sofa. Peter woke her and sent her, sleep-walking, to her own door. He sat down, wet to the bone, thinking, I'll call the Burleighs. In half an hour I'll call the police. He heard a car stop and the engine running and a confusion of two voices laughing and calling good night. Presently Sheilah let herself in, rosy-faced, smiling. She carried his trench coat over her arm. She said, "How's Agnes?"

"Where were you?" he said. "Whose car was that?"

Sheilah had gone into the children's room. He heard her shutting their window. She returned, undoing her dress, and said, "Was Agnes all right?"

"Agnes is all right. Sheilah, this is about the worst . . ."

She stepped out of the Balenciaga and threw it over a chair. She stopped and looked at him and said, "Poor old Pete, are you in love with Agnes?" And then, as if the answer were of so little importance she hadn't time for it, she locked her arms around him and said, "My love, we're going to Ceylon."

Two days later, when Peter strolled into his office, Agnes was at her desk. She wore the blue dress, with a spotless collar. White and yellow freesias were symmetrically arranged in the glass jar. The room was hot, and the spring snow, glued for a second when it touched the window, blurred the view of parked cars.

"Quite a party," Peter said.

She did not look up. He sighed, sat down, and thought if the snow held he would be skiing at the Burleighs' very soon. Impressed by his kindness to Agnes, Madge had invited the family for the first possible weekend.

Presently Agnes said, "I'll never drink again or go to a house where people are drinking. And I'll never bother anyone the way I bothered you."

"You didn't bother me," he said. "I took you home. You were alone and it was late. It's normal."

"Normal for you, maybe, but I'm used to getting home by myself. Please never tell what happened."

He stared at her. He can still remember the freesias and the Bible and the heat in the room. She looked as if the elements had no power. She felt neither heat nor cold. "Nothing happened," he said.

"I behaved in a silly way. I had no right to. I led you to think I might do something wrong."

"*I* might have tried something," he said gallantly. "But that would be my fault and not yours."

She put her knuckle to her mouth and he could scarcely hear. "It was because of you. I was afraid you might be blamed, or else you'd blame yourself."

"There's no question of any blame," he said. "Nothing happened. We'd both had a lot to drink. Forget about it. Nothing *happened*. You'd remember if it had."

She put down her hand. There was an expression on her face. Now she sees me, he thought. She had never looked at him after the first day. (He has since tried to put a name to the look on her face; but how can he, now, after so many voyages, after Ceylon, and Hong Kong, and Sheilah's nearly leaving him, and all their difficulties—the money owed, the rows with hotel managers, the lost and found steamer trunk, the children throwing up the foreign food?) She sees me now, he thought. What does she see?

She said, "I'm from a big family. I'm not used to being alone. I'm not a suicidal person, but I could have done something after that party, just not to see anymore, or think or listen or expect anything. What can I think when I see these people? All my life I heard, Educated people don't do this, educated people don't do that. And now I'm here, and you're all educated people, and you're nothing but pigs. You're educated and you drink and do everything wrong and you know what you're doing, and that makes you worse than pigs. My family worked to make me an educated person, but they didn't know you. But what if I didn't see and hear and expect anything anymore? It wouldn't change anything. You'd all be still the same. Only *you* might have thought it was your fault. You might have thought you were to blame. It could worry you all your life. It would have been wrong for me to worry you."

He remembered that the rented car was still along a snowy curb somewhere in Geneva. He wondered if Sheilah had the key in her purse and if she remembered where they'd parked.

"I told you about the ice wagon," Agnes said. "I don't remember everything, so you're wrong about remembering. But I remember telling you that. That was the best. It's the best you can hope to have. In a big family, if you want to be alone, you have to get up before the rest of them. You get up early in the morning in the summer and it's you, you, once in your life alone in the universe. You think you know everything that can happen. . . . Nothing is ever like that again."

He looked at the smeared window and wondered if this day could end without disaster. In his mind he saw her falling in the snow wearing a tramp's costume, and he saw her coming to him in the orphanage dressing gown. He saw her drowning face at the party. He was afraid for himself. The story was still unfinished. It had to come to a climax, something threatening to him. But there was no climax. They talked that day, and afterward nothing else was said. They went on in the same office for a short time, until Peter left for Ceylon; until somebody read the right letter, passed it on for the right initials, and the Fraziers began the Oriental tour that should have made their fortune. Agnes and Peter were too tired to speak after that morning. They were like a married couple in danger, taking care.

But what were they talking about that day, so quietly, such old friends? They talked about dying, about being ambitious, about being religious, about different kinds of love. What did she see when she looked at him—taking her knuckle slowly away from her mouth, bringing her hand down to the desk, letting it rest there? They were both Canadians, so they had this much together—the knowledge of the little you dare admit. Death, near death, the best thing, the wrong thing—God knows what they were telling each other. Anyway, nothing happened.

When, on Sunday mornings, Sheilah and Peter talk about those times, they take on the glamour of something still to come. It is then he remembers Agnes Brusen. He never says her name. Sheilah wouldn't remember Agnes. Agnes is the only secret Peter has from his wife, the only puzzle he pieces together without her help. He thinks about families in the West as they were fifteen, twenty years ago—the iron-cold ambition, and every member pushing the next one on. He thinks of his father's parties. When he thinks of his father he imagines him with Sheilah, in a crowd. Actually, Sheilah and Peter's father never met, but they might have liked each other. His father admired good-looking women. Peter wonders what they were doing over there in Geneva—not Sheilah and Peter, *Agnes* and Peter. It is almost as if they had once run away together, silly as children, irresponsible as lovers. Peter and Sheilah are back where they started. While they were out in world affairs picking up microbes and debts, always on the fringe of disaster, the fringe of a fortune, Agnes went on and did—what? They lost each other. He thinks of the ice wagon going down the street. He sees something he has never seen in his life—a Western town that belongs to Agnes. Here is Agnes—small, mole-faced, round-shouldered because she has always carried a younger child. She watches the ice wagon and the trail of ice water in a morning invented for her: hers. He sees the weak prairie trees and the shadows on the sidewalk. Nothing moves except the shadows and the ice wagon and the changing amber of the child's eyes. The child is Peter. He has seen the grain of the cement sidewalk and the grass in the cracks, and the dust, and the dandelions at the edge of the road. He is there. He has taken the morning that belongs to Agnes, he is up before the others, and he knows everything. There is nothing he doesn't know. He could keep the morning, if he wanted to, but what can Peter do with the start of a summer day? Sheilah is here, it is a true Sunday morning, with its dimness and headache and remorse and regrets, and this is life. He says, "We have the Balenciaga." He touches Sheilah's hand. The children have their aunt now, and he and Sheilah have each other. Everything works out, somehow or other. Let Agnes have the start of the day. Let Agnes think it was invented for her. Who wants to be alone in the universe? No, begin at the beginning: Peter lost Agnes. Agnes says to herself somewhere, Peter is lost.

IRINA

ONE OF Irina's grandsons, nicknamed Riri, was sent to her at Christmas. His mother was going into hospital, but nobody told him that. The real cause of his visit was that since Irina had become a widow her children worried about her being alone. The children, as Irina would call them forever, were married and in their thirties and forties. They did not think they were like other people, because their father had been a powerful old man. He was a Swiss writer, Richard Notte. They carried his reputation and the memory of his puritan equity like an immense jar filled with water of which they had been told not to spill a drop. They loved their mother, but they had never needed to think about her until now. They had never fretted about which way her shadow might fall, and whether to stay in the shade or get out by being eccentric and bold. There were two sons and three daughters, with fourteen children among them. Only Riri was an only child. The girls had married an industrial designer, a Lutheran minister (perhaps an insolent move, after all, for the daughter of a militant atheist), and an art historian in Paris. One boy had become a banker and the other a lecturer on Germanic musical tradition. These were the crushed sons and loyal daughters to whom Irina had been faithful, whose pictures had traveled with her and lived beside her bed.

Few of Notte's obituaries had even mentioned a family. Some of his literary acquaintances were surprised to learn there had been any children at all, though everyone paid homage to the soft, quiet wife to whom he had dedicated his books, the subject of his first rapturous poems. These poems, conventional verse for the most part, seldom translated out of German except by unpoetical research scholars, were thought to be the work of his youth. Actually, Notte was forty when he finally married, and Irina barely nineteen. The obituaries called Notte the last of a breed, the end of a Tolstoyan line of moral lightning rods—an extinction which was probably hard on those writers who came after him, and still harder on his children. However, even to his family the old man had appeared to be the very archetype of a respected European novelist—prophet, dissuader, despairingly opposed to evil, crack-voiced after having made so many pronouncements. Otherwise, he was not all that typical as a Swiss or as a Western, liberal, Protestant European, for he neither saved, nor invested, nor hid, nor disguised his material returns.

"What good is money, except to give away?" he often said. He had a wife, five children, and an old secretary who had turned into a dependent. It was true that he claimed next to nothing for himself. He rented shabby, ramshackle houses impossible to heat or even to clean. Owning was against his convictions, and he did not want to be tied to a gate called home. His room was furnished with a cot, a lamp, a desk, two chairs, a map of the world, a small bookshelf—no more, not even carpets or curtains. Like his family, he wore thick sweaters indoors as out, and crouched over inadequate electric fires. He seldom ate meat—though he did not deprive his children—and drank water with his meals. He had married once—once and for all. He could on occasion enjoy wine and praise and restaurants and good-looking women, but these festive outbreaks were on the rim of his real life, as remote from his children—as strange and as distorted to them—as some other country's colonial wars. He grew old early, as if he expected old age to suit him. By sixty, his eyes were sunk in pockets of lizard skin. His hair became bleached and lustrous, like the scrap of wedding dress Irina kept in a jeweler's box. He was photographed wearing a dark suit and a woman's plaid shawl—he was always cold by then, even in summer—and with a rakish felt hat shading half his face. His wife still let a few photographers in, at the end —but not many. Her murmured "He is working" had for decades been a double lock. He was as strong as Rasputin, his enemies said; he went on writing and talking and traveling until he positively could not focus his eyes or be helped aboard a train. Nearly to the last, he and Irina swung off on their seasonal cycle of journeys to Venice, to Rome, to cities where their married children lived, to Liège and Oxford for awards and honors. His place in a hotel dining room was recognizable from the door because of the pills, drops, and powders lined up to the width of a dinner plate. Notte's hypochondria had been known and gently caricatured for years. His sons, between them, had now bought up most of the original drawings: Notte, in infant's clothing, downing his medicine like a man (he had missed the Nobel); Notte quarreling with Aragon and throwing up Surrealism; a grim female figure called "Existentialism" taking his pulse; Notte catching Asian flu on a cultural trip to Peking. During the final months of his life his children noticed that their mother had begun acquiring medicines of her own, as if hoping by means of mirror-magic to draw his ailments into herself.

If illness became him, it was only because he was fond of ritual, the children thought—even the hideous ceremonial of pain. But Irina had not been intended for sickness and suffering; she was meant to be burned dry and consumed by the ritual of him. The children believed that the end of his life would surely be the death of their mother. They did not really expect Irina to turn her face to the wall and die, but an exclusive, even a selfish, alliance with Notte had seemed her reason for being. As their father grew old, then truly old, then old in mind, and querulous, and unjust, they observed the patient tenderness with which she heeded his sulks and caprices, his almost insane commands. They supposed this ardent submission of hers had to do with love, but it was not a sort of love they had ever experienced or tried to provoke. One of his sons saw Notte crying because Irina had buttered toast for him when he wanted it dry. She stroked the old man's silky hair, smiling. The son hated this. Irina was diminishing a strong, proud man, making a senile child of him, just as Notte was enslaving and debasing her. At the same time the son felt a secret between the two, a mystery. He wondered then, but at no other time, if the secret might not be Irina's invention and property.

Notte left a careful will for such an unworldly person. His wife was to be secure in her lifetime. Upon her death the residue of income from his work would be shared among the sons and daughters. There were no gifts or bequests. The will was accompanied by a testament which the children had photocopied for the beauty of the handwriting and the charm of the text. Irina, it began, belonged to a generation of women shielded from decisions, allowed to grow in the sun and shade of male protection. This flower, his flower, he wrote, was to be cherished now as if she were her children's child.

"In plain words," said Irina, at the first reading, in a Zurich lawyer's office, "I am the heir." She was wearing dark glasses because her eyes were tired, and a tight hat. She looked tense and foreign.

Well, yes, that was it, although Notte had put it more gracefully. His favorite daughter was his literary executor, entrusted with the unfinished manuscripts and the journals he had kept for sixty-five years. But it soon became evident that Irina had no intention of giving these up. The children adored their mother, but even without love as a factor would not have made a case of it; Notte's lawyer had already told them about disputes ending in maze-like litigation, families sundered, contents of a desk sequestered, diaries rotting in bank vaults while the inheritors thrashed it out. Besides, editing Notte's papers would keep Irina busy and an occupation was essential now. In loving and unloving families alike, the same problem arises after a death: What to do about the widow?

Irina settled some of it by purchasing an apartment in a small Alpine town. She chose a tall, glassy, urban-looking building of the kind that made conservationist groups send round-robin letters, accompanied by incriminating photographs, to newspapers in Lausanne. The apartment had a hall, an up-to-date kitchen, a bedroom for Irina, a spare room with a narrow bed in it, one bathroom, and a living room containing a couch. There was a glassed-in cube of a balcony where in a pinch an extra cot might have fitted, but Irina used the space for a table and chairs. She ordered red lampshades and thick curtains and the pale furniture that is usually sold to young couples. She seemed to come into her own in that tight, neutral flat, the children thought. They read some of the interviews she gave, and approved: She said, in English and Italian, in German and French, that she would not be a literary widow, detested by critics, resented by Notte's readers. Her firm diffidence made the children smile, and they were proud to read about her dignified beauty. But as for her intelligence—well, they supposed that the interviewers had confused fluency with wit. Irina's views and her way of expressing them were all camouflage, simply part of a ladylike undereducation, long on languages and bearing, short on history and arithmetic. Her origins were Russian and Swiss and probably pious; the children had not been drawn to that side of the family. Their father's legendary peasant childhood, his isolated valley-village had filled their imaginations and their collective past. There was a sudden April lightness in her letters now that relieved and yet troubled them. They knew it was a sham happiness. Nature's way of protecting the survivor from immediate grief. The crisis would come later, when her most secret instincts had built a seawall. They took turns invading her at Easter and in the summer, one couple at a time, bringing a child apiece—there was no room for more. Winter was a problem, however, for the skiing was not good just there, and none of them liked to break up their families at Christmastime. Not only was Irina's apartment lacking in beds but there was absolutely no space for a tree. Finally, she offered to visit them, in regular order. That was how they settled it. She went to Bern, to Munich, to Zurich, and then came the inevitable Christmas when it was not that no one wanted her but just that they were all doing different things.

She had written in November of that year that a friend, whom she described, with some quaintness, as "a person," had come for a long stay. They liked that. A visit meant winter company, lamps on at four, China tea, conversation, the peppery smell of carnations (her favorite flower) in a warm room. For a week or two of the visit her letters were blithe, but presently they noticed that "the person" seemed to be having a depressing effect on their mother. She wrote that she had been working on Notte's journals for three years now. Who would want to read them except old men and women? His moral and political patterns were fossils of liberalism. He had seen the cracks in the Weimar Republic. He had understood from the beginning what Hitler meant. If at first he had been wrong about Mussolini, he had changed his mind even before Croce changed his, and had been safely back on the side of democracy in time to denounce Pirandello. He had given all he could, short of his life, to the Spanish Republicans. His measure of Stalin had been so wise and unshakably just that he had never been put on the Communist index—something rare for a Western Socialist. No one could say, ever, that Notte had hedged or retreated or kept silent when a voice was needed. Well, said Irina, what of it? He had written, pledged, warned, signed, declared. And what had he changed, diverted, or stopped? She suddenly sent the same letter to all five children: "This Christmas I don't want to go anywhere. I intend to stay here, in my own home."

They knew this was the crisis and that they must not leave her to face it alone, but that was the very winter when all their plans ran down, when one daughter was going into hospital, another moving to a different city, the third probably divorcing. The elder son was committed to a Christmas with his wife's parents, the younger lecturing in South Africa—a country where Irina, as Notte's constant reflection, would certainly not wish to set foot. They wrote and called and cabled one another: What shall we do? Can you? Will you? I can't.

Irina had no favorites among her children, except possibly one son who had been ill with rheumatic fever as a child and required long nursing. To him she now confided that she longed for her own childhood sometimes, in order to avoid having to judge herself. She was homesick for a time when nothing had crystallized and mistakes were allowed. Now, in old age, she had no excuse for errors. Every thought had a long meaning; every motive had angles and corners, and could be measured. And yet whatever she saw and thought and attempted was still fluid and vague. The shape of a table against afternoon light still held a mystery, awaited a final explanation. You looked for clarity, she wrote, and the answer you had was paleness, the flat white cast that a snowy sky throws across a room.

Part of this son knew about death and dying, but the rest of him was a banker and thoroughly active. He believed that, given an ideal situation, one should be able to walk through a table, which would save time and round-about decisions. However, like all of Notte's children he had been raised with every awareness of solid matter too. His mother's youthful, yearning, and probably religious letter made him feel bland and old. He told his wife what he thought it contained, and she told a sister-in-law what she thought he had said. Irina was tired. Her eyesight was poor, perhaps as a result of prolonged work on those diaries. Irina did not need adult company, which might lead to morbid conversation; what she craved now was a symbol of innocent, continuing life. An animal might do it. Better still, a child.

Riri did not know that his mother would be in hospital the minute his back was turned. Balanced against a tame Christmas with a grandmother was a midterm holiday, later, of high-altitude skiing with his father. There was also some further blackmail involving his holiday homework, and then the vague state of behavior called "being reasonable"—that was all anyone asked. They celebrated a token Christmas on the twenty-third, and the next day he packed his presents (a watch and a tape recorder) and was put on a plane at Orly West. He flew from Paris to Geneva, where he spent the real Christmas Eve in a strange, bare apartment into which an aunt and a large family of cousins had just moved. In the morning he was wakened when it was dark and taken to a six o'clock train. He said good-bye to his aunt at the station, and added, "If you ask the conductor or anyone to look after me, I'll—" Whatever threat was in his mind he seemed ready to carry out. He wore an RAF badge on his jacket and carried a Waffen-S.S. emblem in his pocket. He knew better than to keep it in sight. At home they had already taken one away but he had acquired another at school. He had Astérix comic books for reading, chocolate-covered hazelnuts for support, and his personal belongings in a fairly large knapsack. He made a second train on his own and got down at the right station.

He had been told that he knew this place, but his memory, if it was a memory, had to do with fields and a picnic. No one met him. He shared a taxi through soft snow with two women, and paid his share—actually more than his share, which annoyed the women; they could not give less than a child in the way of a tip. The taxi let him off at a dark, shiny tower on stilts with granite steps. In the lobby a marble panel, looking like the list of names of war dead in his school, gave him his grandmother on the eighth floor. The lift, like the façade of the building, was made of dark mirrors into which he gazed seriously. A dense, thoughtful person looked back. He took off his glasses and the blurred face became even more remarkable. His grandmother had both a bell and a knocker at her door. He tried both. For quite a long time nothing happened. He knocked and rang again. It was not nervousness that he felt but a new sensation that had to do with a shut, foreign door.

His grandmother opened the door a crack. She had short white hair and a pale face and blue eyes. She held a dressing gown gripped at the collar. She flung the door back and cried, "Darling Richard, I thought you were arriving much later. Oh," she said, "I must look dreadful to you. Imagine finding me like this, in my dressing gown!" She tipped her head away and talked between her fingers, as he had been told never to do, because only liars cover their mouths. He saw a dark hall and a bright kitchen that was in some disorder, and a large, dark, curtained room opposite the kitchen. This room smelled stuffy, of old cigarettes and of adults. But then his grandmother pushed the draperies apart and wound up the slatted shutters, and what had been dark, moundlike objects turned into a couch and a bamboo screen and a round table and a number of chairs. On a bookshelf stood a painting of three tulips that must have fallen out of their vase. Behind them was a sky that was all black except for a rainbow. He unpacked a portion of the things in his knapsack—wrapped presents for his grandmother, his new tape recorder, two school textbooks, a notebook, a Bic pen. The start of this Christmas lay hours behind him and his breakfast had died long ago.

"Are you hungry?" said his grandmother. He heard a telephone ringing as she brought him a cup of hot milk with a little coffee in it and two fresh croissants on a plate. She was obviously someone who never rushed to answer any bell. "My friend, who is an early riser, even on Christmas Day, went out and got these croissants. Very bravely, I thought." He ate his new breakfast, dipping the croissants in the milk, and heard his grandmother saying, "Well, I must have misunderstood. But he managed. . . . He didn't bring his skis. Why not? . . . I see." By the time she came back he had a book open. She watched him for a second and said, "Do you read at meals at home?"

"Sometimes."

"That's not the way I brought up your mother."

He put his nose nearer the page without replying. He read aloud from the page in a soft schoolroom plainchant: " 'Go, went, gone. Stand, stood, stood. Take, took, taken.' "

"Richard," said his grandmother. When he did not look up at once, she said, "I know what they call you at home, but what are you called in school?"

"Riri."

"I have three Richard grandsons," she said, "and not one is called Richard exactly."

"I have an Uncle Richard," he said.

"Yes, well, he happens to be a son of mine. I never allowed nicknames. Have you finished your breakfast?"

"Yes."

"Yes who? Yes what? What is your best language, by the way?"

"I am French," he said, with a sharp, sudden, hard hostility, the first tense bud of it, that made her murmur, "So soon?" She was about to tell him that he was not French—at least, not really—when an old man came into the room. He was thin and walked with a cane.

"Alec, this is my grandson," she said. "Riri, say how do you do to Mr. Aiken, who was kind enough to go out in this morning's snow to buy croissants for us all."

"I knew he would be here early," said the old man, in a stiff French that sounded extremely comical to the boy. "Irina has an odd ear for times and trains." He sat down next to Riri and clasped his hands on his cane; his hands at once began to tremble violently. "What does that interesting-looking book tell you?" he asked.

" 'The swallow flew away,' " answered Irina, reading over the child's head. " 'The swallow flew away with my hopes.' "

"Good God, let me look at that!" said the old man in his funny French. Sure enough, those were the words, and there was a swallow of a very strange blue, or at least a sapphire-and-turquoise creature with a swallow's tail. Riri's grandmother took her spectacles out of her dressing-gown pocket and brought the book up close and said in a loud, solemn way, " 'The swallows will have flown away.' " Then she picked up the tape recorder, which was the size of a glasses case, and after snapping the wrong button on and off, causing agonizing confusion and wastage, she said with her mouth against it, " 'When shall the swallows have flown away?' "

"No," said Riri, reaching, snatching almost. As if she had always given in to men, even to male children, she put the book down and the recorder too, saying, "Mr. Aiken can help with your English. He has the best possible accent. When he says 'the girl' you will think he is saying 'de Gaulle.' "

"Irina has an odd ear for English," said the old man calmly. He got up slowly and went to the kitchen, and she did too, and Riri could hear them whispering and laughing at something. Mr. Aiken came back alone carrying a small glass of clear liquid. "The morning heart-starter," he said. "Try it." Riri took a sip. It lay in his stomach like a warm stone. "No more effect on you than a gulp of milk," said the old man, marveling, sitting down close to Riri again. "You could probably do with pints of this stuff. I can tell by looking at you you'll be a drinking man." His hands on the walking stick began to tremble anew. "I'm not the man I was," he said. "Not by any means." Because he did not speak English with a French or any foreign accent, Riri could not really understand him. He went on, "Fell down the staircase at the Trouville casino. Trouville, or that other place. Shock gave me amnesia. Hole in the stair carpet—must have been. I went there for years," he said. "Never saw a damned hole in anything. Now my hands shake."

"When you lift your glass to drink they don't shake," called Riri's grandmother from the kitchen. She repeated this in French, for good measure.

"She's got an ear like a radar unit," said Mr. Aiken.

Riri took up his tape recorder. In a measured chant, as if demonstrating to his grandmother how these things should be done, he said, " 'The swallows would not fly away if the season is fine.' "

"Do you know what any of it means?" said Mr. Aiken.

"He doesn't need to know what it means," Riri's grandmother answered for him. "He just needs to know it by heart."

They were glassed in on the balcony. The only sound they could hear was of their own voices. The sun on them was so hot that Riri wanted to take off his sweater. Looking down, he saw a chalet crushed in the shadows of two white blocks, not so tall as their own. A large, spared spruce tree suddenly seemed to retract its branches and allow a great weight of snow to slip off. Cars went by, dogs barked, children called—all in total silence. His grandmother talked English to the old man. Riri, when he was not actually eating, read *Astérix in Brittany* without attracting her disapproval.

"If people can be given numbers, like marks in school," she said, "then children are zero." She was enveloped in a fur cloak, out of which her hands and arms emerged as if the fur had dissolved in certain places. She was pink with wine and sun. The old man's blue eyes were paler than hers. "Zero." She held up thumb and forefinger in an O. "I was there with my five darling zeros while he . . . You are probably wondering if I was *ever* happy. At the beginning, in the first days, when I thought he would give me interesting books to read, books that would change all my life. Riri," she said, shading her eyes, "the cake and the ice cream were, I am afraid, the end of things for the moment. Could I ask you to clear the table for me?"

"I don't at home." Nevertheless he made a wobbly pile of dishes and took them away and did not come back. They heard him, indoors, starting all over: " 'Go, went, gone.' "

"I have only half a memory for dates," she said. "I forget my children's birthdays until the last minute and have to send them telegrams. But I know *that* day. . . ."

"The twenty-sixth of May," he said. "What I forget is the year."

"I know that I felt young."

"You were. You *are* young," he said.

"Except that I was forty if a day." She glanced at the hands and wrists emerging from her cloak as if pleased at their whiteness. "The river was so sluggish, I remember. And the willows trailed in the river."

"Actually, there was a swift current after the spring rains."

"But no wind. The clouds were heavy."

"It was late in the afternoon," he said. "We sat on the grass."

"On a raincoat. You had thought in the morning those clouds meant rain."

"A young man drowned," he said. "Fell out of a boat. Funny, he didn't try to swim. So people kept saying."

"We saw three firemen in gleaming metal helmets. They fished for him so languidly—the whole day was like that. They had a grappling hook. None of them knew what to do with it. They kept pulling it up and taking the rope from each other."

"They might have been after water lilies, from the look of them."

"One of them bailed out the boat with a blue saucepan. I remember that. They'd got that saucepan from the restaurant."

"Where we had lunch," he said. "Trout, and a coffee cream pudding. You left yours."

"It was soggy cake. But the trout was perfection. So was the wine. The bridge over the river filled up slowly with holiday people. The three firemen rowed to shore."

"Yes, and one of them went off on a shaky bicycle and came back with a coil of frayed rope on his shoulders."

"The railway station was just behind us. All those people on the bridge were waiting for a train. When the firemen's boat slipped off down the river, they moved without speaking from one side of the bridge to the other, just to watch the boat. The silence of it."

"Like the silence here."

"This is planned silence," she said.

Riri played back his own voice. A tinny, squeaky Riri said, " 'Go, went, gone. Eat, ate, eaten. See, saw, sen.' "

" 'Seen'!" called his grandmother from the balcony. " 'Seen,' not 'sen.' His mother made exactly that mistake," she said to the old man. "Oh, stop that," she said. He was crying. "Please, please stop that. How could I have left five children?"

"Three were grown," he gasped, wiping his eyes.

"But they didn't know it. They didn't know they were grown. They still don't know it. And it made six children, counting him."

"The secretary mothered him," he said. "All he needed."

"I know, but you see she wasn't his wife, and he liked saying to strangers 'my wife,' 'my wife this,' 'my wife that.' What is it, Riri? Have you come to finish doing the thing I asked?"

He moved close to the table. His round glasses made him look desperate and stern. He said, "Which room is mine!" Darkness had gathered round him in spite of the sparkling sky and a row of icicles gleaming and melting in the most dazzling possible light. Outrage, a feeling that consideration had been wanting—that was how homesickness had overtaken him. She held his hand (he did not resist—another sign of his misery) and together they explored the apartment. He saw it all—every picture and cupboard and doorway—and in the end it was he who decided that Mr. Aiken must keep the spare room and he, Riri, would be happy on the living-room couch.

The old man passed them in the hall; he was obviously about to rest on the very bed he had just been within an inch of losing. He carried a plastic bottle of Evian. "Do you like the bland taste of water?" he said.

Riri looked boldly at his grandmother and said, "Yes," bursting into unexplained and endless-seeming laughter. He seemed to feel a relief at this substitute for impertinence. The old man laughed too, but broke off, coughing.

At half past four, when the windows were as black as the sky in the painting of tulips and began to reflect the lamps in a disturbing sort of way, they drew the curtains and had tea around the table. They pushed Riri's books and belongings to one side and spread a cross-stitched tablecloth. Riri had hot chocolate, a croissant left from breakfast and warmed in the oven, which made it deliciously greasy and soft, a slice of lemon sponge cake, and a banana. This time he helped clear away and even remained in the kitchen, talking, while his grandmother rinsed the cups and plates and stacked them in the machine.

The old man sat on a chair in the hall struggling with snow boots. He was going out alone in the dark to post some letters and to buy a newspaper and to bring back whatever provisions he thought were required for the evening meal.

"Riri, do you want to go with Mr. Aiken? Perhaps you should have a walk."

"At home I don't have to."

His grandmother looked cross; no, she looked worried. She was biting something back. The old man had finished the contention with his boots and now he put on a scarf, a fur-lined coat, a fur hat with earflaps, woolen gloves, and he took a list and a shopping bag and a different walking stick, which looked something like a ski pole. His grandmother stood still, as if dreaming, and then (addressing Riri) decided to wash all her amber necklaces. She fetched a wicker basket from her bedroom. It was lined with orange silk and filled with strings of beads. Riri followed her to the bathroom and sat on the end of the tub. She rolled up her soft sleeves and scrubbed the amber with laundry soap and a stiff brush. She scrubbed and rinsed and then began all over again.

"I am good at things like this," she said. "Now, unless you hate to discuss it, tell me something about your school."

At first he had nothing to say, but then he told her how stupid the younger boys were and what they were allowed to get away with.

"The younger boys would be seven, eight?" Yes, about that. "A hopeless generation?"

He wasn't sure; he knew that his class had been better.

She reached down and fetched a bottle of something from behind the bathtub and they went back to the sitting room together. They put a lamp between them, and Irina began to polish the amber with cotton soaked in turpentine. After a time the amber began to shine. The smell made him homesick, but not unpleasantly. He carefully selected a necklace when she told him he might take one for his mother, and he rubbed it with a soft cloth. She showed him how to make the beads magnetic by rolling them in his palms.

"You can do that even with plastic," he said.

"Can you? How very sad. It is dead matter."

"Amber is too," he said politely.

"What do you want to be later on? A scientist?"

"A ski instructor." He looked all round the room, at the shelves and curtains and at the bamboo folding screen, and said, "If you didn't live here, who would?"

She replied, "If you see anything that pleases you, you may keep it. I want you to choose your own present. If you don't see anything, we'll go out tomorrow and look in the shops. Does that suit you?" He did not reply. She held the necklace he had picked and said, "Your mother will remember seeing this as I bent down to kiss her good night. Do you like old coins? One of my sons was a collector." In the wicker basket was a lacquered box that contained his uncle's coin collection. He took a coin but it meant nothing to him; he let it fall. It clinked, and he said, "We have a dog now." The dog wore a metal tag that rang when the dog drank out of a china bowl. Through a sudden rainy blur of new homesickness he saw that she had something else, another lacquered box, full of old canceled stamps. She showed him a stamp with Hitler and one with an Italian king. "I've kept funny things," she said. "Like this beautiful Russian box. It belonged to my grandmother, but after I have died I expect it will be thrown out. I gave whatever jewelry I had left to my daughters. We never had furniture, so I became attached to strange little baskets and boxes of useless things. My poor daughters—I had precious little to give. But they won't be able to wear rings any more than I could. We all come into our inherited arthritis, these knotted-up hands. Our true heritage. When I was your age, about, my mother was dying of . . . I wasn't told. She took a ring from under her pillow and folded my hand on it. She said that I could always sell it if I had to, and no one need know. You see, in those days women had nothing of their own. They were like brown paper parcels tied with string. They were handed like parcels from their fathers to their husbands. To make the parcel look attractive it was decked with curls and piano lessons, and rings and gold coins and banknotes and shares. After appraising all the decoration, the new owner would undo the knots."

"Where is that ring?" he said. The blur of tears was forgotten.

"I tried to sell it when I needed money. The decoration on the brown paper parcel was disposed of by then. Everything thrown, given away. Not by me. My pearl necklace was sold for Spanish refugees. Victims, flotsam, the injured, the weak—they were important. I wasn't. The children weren't. I had my ring. I took it to a municipal pawnshop. It is a place where you take things and they give you money. I wore dark glasses and turned up my coat collar, like a spy." He looked as though he understood that. "The man behind the counter said that I was a married woman and I needed my husband's written consent. I said the ring was mine. He said nothing could be mine, or something to that effect. Then he said he might have given me something for the gold in the band of the ring but the stones were worthless. He said this happened in the finest of families. Someone had pried the real stones out of their setting."

"Who did that?"

"A husband. Who else would? Someone's husband—mine, or my mother's or my mother's mother's, when it comes to that."

"With a knife?" said Riri. He said, "The man might have been pretending. Maybe he took out the stones and put in glass."

"There wasn't time. And they were perfect imitations—the right shapes and sizes."

"He might have had glass stones all different sizes."

"The women in the family never wondered if men were lying," she said. "They never questioned being dispossessed. They were taught to think that lies were a joke on the liar. That was why they lost out. He gave me the price of the gold in the band, as a favor, and I left the ring there. I never went back."

He put the lid on the box of stamps, and it fitted; he removed it, put it back, and said, "What time do you turn on your TV?"

"Sometimes never. Why?"

"At home I have it from six o'clock."

The old man came in with a pink-and-white face, bearing about him a smell of cold and of snow. He put down his shopping bag and took things out—chocolate and bottles and newspapers. He said, "I had to go all the way to the station for the papers. There is only one shop open, and even then I had to go round to the back door."

"I warned you that today was Christmas," Irina said.

Mr. Aiken said to Riri, "When I was still a drinking man this was the best hour of the day. If I had a glass now, I could put ice in it. Then I might add water. Then if I had water I could add whiskey. I know it is all the wrong way around, but at least I've started with a glass."

"You had wine with your lunch and gin instead of tea and I believe you had straight gin before lunch," she said, gathering up the beads and coins and the turpentine and making the table Riri's domain again.

"Riri drank that," he said. It was so obviously a joke that she turned her head and put the basket down and covered her laugh with her fingers, as she had when she'd opened the door to him— oh, a long time ago now.

"I haven't a drop of anything left in the house," she said. That didn't matter, the old man said, for he had found what he needed. Riri watched and saw that when he lifted his glass his hand did not tremble at all. What his grandmother had said about that was true.

They had early supper and then Riri, after a courageous try at keeping awake, gave up even on television and let her make his bed of scented sheets, deep pillows, a feather quilt. The two others sat for a long time at the table, with just one lamp, talking in low voices. She had a pile of notebooks from which she read aloud and sometimes she showed Mr. Aiken things. He could see them through the chinks in the bamboo screen. He watched the lamp shadows for a while and then it was as if the lamp had gone out and he slept deeply.

The room was full of mound shapes, as it had been that morning when he arrived. He had not heard them leave the room. His Christmas watch had hands that glowed in the dark. He put on his glasses. It was half past ten. His grandmother was being just a bit loud at the telephone; that was what had woken him up. He rose, put on his slippers, and stumbled out to the bathroom.

"Just answer yes or no," she was saying. "No, he can't. He has been asleep for an hour, two hours, at least. . . . Don't lie to me—I am bound to find the truth out. Was it a tumor? An extrauterine pregnancy? . . . Well, look. . . . Was she or was she not pregnant? What can you mean by 'not exactly'? If you don't know, who will?" She happened to turn her head, and saw him and said without a change of tone, "Your son is here, in his pajamas; he wants to say good night to you."

She gave up the telephone and immediately went away so that the child could talk privately. She heard him say, "I drank some kind of alcohol."

So that was the important part of the day: not the journey, not the necklace, not even the strange old guest with the comic accent. She could tell from the sound of the child's voice that he was smiling. She picked up his bathrobe, went back to the hall, and put it over his shoulders. He scarcely saw her: He was concentrated on the distant voice. He said, in a matter-of-fact way, "All right, good-bye," and hung up.

"What a lot of things you have pulled out of that knapsack," she said.

"It's a large one. My father had it for military service."

Now, why should that make him suddenly homesick when his father's voice had not? "You are good at looking after yourself," she said. "Independent. No one has to tell you what to do. Of course, your mother had sound training. Once when I was looking for a nurse for your mother and her sisters, a great peasant woman came to see me, wearing a black apron and black buttoned boots. I said, 'What can you teach children?' And she said, 'To be clean and polite.' Your grandfather said, 'Hire her,' and stamped out of the room."

His mother interested, his grandfather bored him. He had the Christian name of a dead old man.

"You will sleep well," his grandmother promised, pulling the feather quilt over him. "You will dream short dreams at first, and by morning they will be longer and longer. The last one of all just before you wake up will be like a film. You will wake up wondering where you are, and then you will hear Mr. Aiken. First he will go round shutting all the windows, then you will hear his bath. He will start the coffee in an electric machine that makes a noise like a door rattling. He will pull on his snow boots with a lot of cursing and swearing and go out to fetch our croissants and the morning papers. Do you know what day it will be? The day after Christmas."

He was almost asleep. Next to his watch and his glasses on a table close to the couch was an Astérix book and Irina's Russian box with old stamps in it. "Have you decided you want the stamps?"

"The box. Not the stamps."

He had taken, by instinct, the only object she wanted to keep. "For a special reason?" she said. "Of course, the box is yours. I am only wondering."

"The cover fits," he said.

She knew that the next morning he would have been here forever and that at parting time, four days later, she would have to remind him that leaving was the other half of arriving. She smiled, knowing how sorry he would be to go and how soon he would leave her behind. "This time yesterday . . . ," he might say, but no more than once. He was asleep. His mouth opened slightly and the hair on his forehead became dark and damp. A doubled-up arm looked uncomfortable but Irina did not interfere; his sunken mind, his unconscious movements, had to be independent, of her or anyone, particularly of her. She did not love him more or less than any of her grandchildren. You see, it all worked out, she was telling him. You, and your mother, and the children being so worried, and my old friend. Anything can be settled for a few days at a time, though not for longer. She put out the light, for which his body was grateful. His mind, at that moment, in a sunny icicle brightness, was not only skiing but flying.

THE LATEHOMECOMER

W HEN I came back to Berlin out of captivity in the spring of 1950, I discovered I had a stepfather. My mother had never mentioned him. I had been writing from Brittany to "Grete Bestermann," but the "Toeppler" engraved on a brass plate next to the bellpull at her new address turned out to be her name, too. As she slipped the key in the lock, she said quietly, "Listen, Thomas. I'm Frau Toeppler now. I married a kind man with a pension. This is his key, his name, and his apartment. He wants to make you welcome." From the moment she met me at the railway station that day, she must have been wondering how to break it.

I put my hand over the name, leaving a perfect palm print. I said, "I suppose there are no razor blades and no civilian shirts in Berlin. But some ass is already engraving nameplates."

Martin Toeppler was an old man who had been a tram conductor. He was lame in one arm as the result of a working accident and carried that shoulder higher than the other. His eyes had the milky look of the elderly, lighter round the rim than at the center of the iris, and he had an old woman's habit of sighing, "Ah, yes, yes." The sigh seemed to be his way of pleading, "It can't be helped." He must have been forty-nine, at the most, but aged was what he seemed to me, and more than aged—useless, lost. His mouth hung open much of the time, as though he had trouble breathing through his nose, but it was only because he was a chronic talker, always ready to bite down on a word. He came from Franconia, near the Czech border, close to where my grandparents had once lived.

"Grete and I can understand each other's dialects," he said— but we were not a dialect-speaking family. My brother and I had been made to say "bread" and "friend" and "tree" correctly. I turned my eyes to my mother, but she looked away.

Martin's one dream was to return to Franconia; it was almost the first thing he said to me. He had inherited two furnished apartments in a town close to an American military base. One of the two had been empty for years. The occupants had moved away, no one knew where—perhaps to Sweden. After their departure, which had taken place at five o'clock on a winter morning in 1943, the front door had been sealed with a government stamp depicting a swastika and an eagle. The vanished tenants must have died, perhaps in Sweden, and now no local person would live in the place, because a whole family of ghosts rattled about, opening and shutting drawers, banging on pipes, moving chairs and ladders. The ghosts were looking for a hoard of gold that had been left behind, Martin thought. The second apartment had been rented to a family who had disappeared during the confused migrations of the end of the war and were probably dead, too; at least they were dead officially, which was all that mattered. Martin intended to modernize the two flats, raise them up to American standards— he meant by this putting venetian blinds at the windows and gas-heated water tanks in the bathrooms—and let them to a good class of American officer, too foreign to care about a small-town story, too educated to be afraid of ghosts. But he would have to move quickly; otherwise his inheritance, his sole postwar capital, his only means of getting started again, might be snatched away from him for the sake of shiftless and illiterate refugees from the Soviet zone, or bombed-out families still huddled in barracks, or for latehomecomers. This last was a new category of persons, all one word. It was out of his mouth before he remembered that I was one, too. He stopped talking, and then he sighed and said, "Ah, yes, yes."

He could not keep still for long: He drew out his wallet and showed me a picture of himself on horseback. He may have wanted to substitute this country image for any idea I had of him on the deck of a tram. He held the snapshot at arm's length and squinted at it. "That was Martin Toeppler once," he said. "It will be Martin Toeppler again." His youth, and a new right shoulder and arm, and the hot, leafy summers everyone his age said had existed before the war were waiting for him in Franconia. He sounded like a born winner instead of a physically broken tram conductor on the losing side. He put the picture away in a cracked celluloid case, pocketed his wallet, and called to my mother, "The boy will want a bath."

My mother, who had been preparing a bath for minutes now, had been receiving orders all her life. As a girl she had worked like a slave in her mother's village guesthouse, and after my father died she became a servant again, this time in Berlin, to my powerful Uncle Gerhard and his fat wife. My brother and I spent our winters with her, all three sleeping in one bed sometimes, in a cold attic room, sharing bread and apples smuggled from Uncle Gerhard's larder. In the summer we were sent to help our grandmother. We washed the chairs and tables, cleaned the toilets of vomit, and carried glasses stinking with beer back to the kitchen. We were still so small we had to stand on stools to reach the taps.

"It was lucky you had two sons," Uncle Gerhard said to my mother once. "There will never be a shortage of strong backs in the family."

"No one will exploit my children," she is supposed to have replied, though how she expected to prevent it only God knows, for we had no roof of our own and no money and we ate such food as we were given. Our uniforms saved us. Once we had joined the Hitler Jugend, even Uncle Gerhard never dared ask, "Where are you going?" or "Where have you been?" My brother was quicker than I. By the time he was twelve he knew he had been trapped; I was sixteen and a prisoner before I understood. But from our mother's point of view we were free, delivered; we would not repeat her life. That was all she wanted.

In captivity I had longed for her and for the lost paradise of our poverty, where she had belonged entirely to my brother and to me and we had slept with her, one on each side. I had written letters to her full of remorse for past neglect and containing promises of future goodness: I would work hard and look after her forever. These letters, sent to blond, young, soft-voiced Grete Bestermann, had been read by Grete Toeppler, whose graying hair was pinned up in a sort of oval balloon, and who was anxious and thin, as afraid of things to come as she was of the past. I had not recognized her at the station, and when she said timidly, "Excuse me? Thomas?" I thought she was her own mother. I did not know then, or for another few minutes, that my grandmother had died or that my rich Uncle Gerhard, now officially de-Nazified by a court of law, was camped in two rooms carved out of a ruin, raising rabbits for a living and hoping that no one would notice him. She had last seen me when I was fifteen. We had been moving toward each other since early this morning, but I was exhausted and taciturn, and we were both shy, and we had not rushed into each other's arms, because we had each been afraid of embracing a stranger. I had one horrible memory of her, but it may have been only a dream. I was small, but I could speak and walk. I came into a room where she was nursing a baby. Two other women were with her. When they saw me they started to laugh, and one said to her, "Give some to Thomas." My mother leaned over and put her breast in my mouth. The taste was disgustingly sweet, and because of the two women I felt humiliated: I spat and backed off and began to cry. She said something to the women and they laughed harder than ever. It must have been a dream, for who could the baby have been? My brother was eleven months older than I.

She was cautious as an animal with me now, partly because of my reaction to the nameplate. She must have feared there was more to come. She had been raised to respect men, never to interrupt their conversation, to see that their plates were filled before hers—even, as a girl, to stand when they were sitting down. I was twenty-one, I had been twenty-one for three days, I had crossed over to the camp of the bullies and strangers. All the while Martin was talking and boasting and showing me himself on horseback, she crept in and out of the parlor, fetching wood and the briquettes they kept by the tile stove, carrying them down the passage to build a fire for me in the bathroom. She looked at me sidelong sometimes and smiled with her hand before her mouth—a new habit of hers—but she kept silent until it was time to say that the bath was ready.

My mother spread a towel for me to stand on and showed me a chair where, she said, Martin always sat to dry his feet. There was a shelf with a mirror and comb but no washbasin. I supposed that he shaved and they cleaned their teeth in the kitchen. My mother said the soap was of poor quality and would not lather, but she asked me, again from behind the screen of her hand, not to leave it underwater where it might melt and be wasted. A stone underwater might have melted as easily. "There is a hook for your clothes," she said, though of course I had seen it. She hesitated still, but when I began to unbutton my shirt she slipped out.

The bath, into which a family could have fitted, was as rough as lava rock. The water was boiling hot. I sat with my knees drawn up as if I were in the tin tub I had been lent sometimes in France. The starfish scar of a grenade wound was livid on one knee, and that leg was misshapen, as though it had been pressed the wrong way while the bones were soft. Long underwear I took to be my stepfather's hung over a line. I sat looking at it, and at a stiff thin towel hanging next to it, and at the water condensing on the cement walls, until the skin of my hands and feet became as ridged and soft as corduroy.

There is a term for people caught on a street crossing after the light has changed: "pedestrian-traffic residue." I had been in a prisoner-of-war camp at Rennes when an order arrived to repatriate everyone who was under eighteen. For some reason, my name was never called. Five years after that, when I was in Saint-Malo, where I had been assigned to a druggist and his wife as a "free worker"—which did not mean free but simply not in a camp—the police sent for me and asked what I was doing in France with a large "PG," for "*prisonnier de guerre*," on my back. Was I a deserter from the Foreign Legion? A spy? Nearly every other prisoner in France had been released at least ten months before, but the file concerning me had been lost or mislaid in Rennes, and I could not leave until it was found—I had no existence. By that time the French were sick of me, because they were sick of the war and its reminders, and the scheme of using the prisoners the Americans had taken to rebuild the roads and bridges of France had not worked out. The idea had never been followed by a plan, and so some of the prisoners became farm help, some became domestic servants, some went into the Foreign Legion because the food was better, some sat and did nothing for three or four years, because no one could discover anything for them to do. The police hinted to me that if I were to run away no one would mind. It would have cleared up the matter of the missing file. But I was afraid of putting myself in the wrong, in which case they might have an excuse to keep me forever. Besides, how far could I have run with a large "PG" painted on my jacket and trousers? Here, where it would not be necessary to wear a label, because "latehomecomer" was written all over me, I sensed that I was an embarrassment, too; my appearance, my survival, my bleeding gums and loose teeth, my chronic dysentery and anemia, my craving for sweets, my reticence with strangers, the cast-off rags I had worn on arrival, all said "war" when everyone wanted peace, "captivity" when the word was "freedom," and "dry bread" when everyone was thinking "jam and butter." I guessed that now, after five years of peace, most of the population must have elbowed onto the right step of the right staircase and that there was not much room left for pedestrian-traffic residue.

My mother came in to clean the tub after I was partly dressed. She used fine ash from the stove and a cloth so full of holes it had to be rolled into a ball. She said, "I called out to you but you didn't hear. I thought you had fallen asleep and drowned."

I was hard of hearing because of the anti-aircraft duty to which I'd been posted in Berlin while I was still in high school. After the boys were sent to the front, girls took our places. It was those girls, still in their adolescence, who defended the grown men in uniform down in the bunkers. I wondered if they had been deafened, too, and if we were a generation who would never hear anything under a shout. My mother knelt by the tub, and I sat on Martin's chair, like Martin, pulling on clean socks she had brought me. In a low voice, which I heard perfectly, she said that I had known Martin in my childhood. I said I had not. She said then that my father had known him. I stood up and waited until she rose from her knees, and I looked down at her face. I was afraid of touching her, in case we should both cry. She muttered that her family must surely have known him, for the Toepplers had a burial plot not far from the graveyard where my grandmother lay buried, and some thirty miles from where my father's father had a bakery once. She was looking for any kind of a link.

"I wanted you and Chris to have a place to stay when you came back," she said, but I believed she had not expected to see either of us again and that she had been afraid of being homeless and alone. My brother had vanished in Czechoslovakia with the Schörner army. All of that army had been given up for dead. My Uncle Gerhard, her only close relative, could not have helped her even if it had occurred to him; it had taken him four years to become officially and legally de-Nazified, and now, "as white as a white lilac," according to my mother, he had no opinions about anything and lived only for his rabbits.

"It is nice to have a companion at my age," my mother said. "Someone to talk to." Did the old need more than conversation? My mother must have been about forty-two then. I had heard the old men in prison camp comparing their wives and saying that no hen was ever too tough for boiling.

"Did you marry him before or after he had this apartment?"

"After." But she had hesitated, as if wondering what I wanted to hear.

The apartment was on the second floor of a large dark block—all that was left of a workers' housing project of the 1920s. Martin had once lived somewhere between the bathroom window and the street. Looking out, I could easily replace the back walls of the vanished houses, and the small balconies festooned with brooms and mops, and the moist oily courtyard. Winter twilight must have been the prevailing climate here until an air raid let the seasons in. Cinders and gravel had been raked evenly over the crushed masonry now; the broad concourse between the surviving house—ours—and the road beyond it that was edged with ruins looked solid and flat.

But no, it was all shaky and loose, my mother said. Someone ought to cause a cement walk to be laid down; the women were always twisting their ankles, and when it rained you walked in black mud, and there was a smell of burning. She had not lost her belief in an invisible but well-intentioned "someone." She then said, in a hushed and whispery voice, that Martin's first wife, Elke, was down there under the rubble and cinders. It had been impossible to get all the bodies out, and one day a bulldozer covered them over for all time. Martin had inherited those two apartments in a town in Franconia from Elke. The Toepplers were probably just as poor as the Bestermanns, but Martin had made a good marriage.

"She had a dog, too," said my mother. "When Martin married her she had a white spitz. She gave it a bath in the bathtub every Sunday." I thought of Martin Toeppler crossing this new wide treacherous front court and saying, "Elke's grave. Ah, yes, yes." I said it, and my mother suddenly laughed loudly and dropped her hand, and I saw that some of her front teeth were missing.

"The house looks like an old tooth when you see it from the street," she said, as though deliberately calling attention to the very misfortune she wanted to hide. She knew nothing about the people who had lived in this apartment, except that they had left in a hurry, forgetting to pack a large store of black-market food, some pretty ornaments in a china cabinet, and five bottles of wine. "They left without paying the rent," she said, which didn't sound like her.

It turned out to be a joke of Martin Toeppler's. He repeated it when I came back to the parlor wearing a shirt that I supposed must be his, and with my hair dark and wet and combed flat. He pointed to a bright rectangle on the brown wallpaper. "That is where they took Adolf's picture down," he said. "When they left in a hurry without paying the rent."

My father had been stabbed to death one night when he was caught tearing an election poster off the schoolhouse wall. He left my mother with no money, two children under the age of five, and a political reputation. After that she swam with the current. I had worn a uniform of one kind or another most of my life until now. I remembered wearing civilian clothes once, when I was fourteen, for my confirmation. I had felt disguised, and wondered what to do with my hands; from the age of seven I had stuck my thumbs in a leather belt. I had impressions, not memories, of my father. Pictures were frozen things; they told me nothing. But I knew that when my hair was wet I looked something like him. A quick flash would come back out of a mirror, like a secret message, and I would think, There, that is how he was. I sat with Martin at the table, where my mother had spread a lace cloth (the vanished tenants') and over which the April sun through lace curtains laid still another design. I placed my hands flat under lace shadows and wondered if they were like my father's, too.

She had put out everything she could find to eat and drink—a few sweet biscuits, cheese cut almost as thin as paper, dark bread, small whole tomatoes, radishes, slices of salami arranged in a floral design on a dish to make them seem more. We had a bottle of fizzy wine that Martin called champagne. It had a brown tint, like watered iodine, and a taste of molasses. Through this murk bubbles climbed. We raised our glasses without saying what we drank to, other than my return. Perhaps Martin drank to his destiny in Franconia with the two apartments. I had a plan, but it was my own secret. By a common accord, there was no mutual past. Then my mother spoke from behind the cupped hand and said she would like us to drink to her missing elder son. She looked at Martin as she said this, in case the survival of Chris might be a burden, too.

Toward the end of that afternoon, a neighbor came in with a bottle of brandy—a stout man with three locks of slick gray hair across his skull. All the fat men of comic stories and of literature were to be Willy Wehler to me, in the future. But he could not have been all that plump in Berlin in 1950; his chin probably showed the beginnings of softness, and his hair must have been dark still, and there must have been plenty of it. I can see the start of his baldness, the two deep peninsulas of polished skin running from the corners of his forehead to just above his ears. Willy Wehler was another Franconian. He and Martin began speaking in dialect almost at once. Willy was at a remove, however—he mispronounced words as though to be funny, and he would grin and look at me. This was to say that he knew better, and he knew that I knew. Martin and Willy hated Berlin. They sounded as if they had been dragged to Berlin against their will, like displaced persons. In their eyes the deepest failure of a certain political authority was that it had enticed peace-loving persons with false promises of work, homes, pensions, lives afloat like little boats at anchor; now these innocent provincials saw they had been tricked, and they were going back where they had started from. It was as simple to them as that—the equivalent of an insurance company's no longer meeting its obligations. Willy even described the life he would lead now in a quiet town, where, in sight of a cobbled square with a fountain and an equestrian statue, he planned to open a perfume-and-cosmetics shop; people wanted beauty now. He would live above the shop—he was not too proud for that—and every morning he would look down on his blue store awnings, over window boxes stuffed with frilled petunias. My stepfather heard this with tears in his eyes, but perhaps he was thinking of his two apartments and of Elke and the spitz. Willy's future seemed so real, so close at hand, that it was almost as though he had dropped in to say good-bye. He sat with his daughter on his knees, a baby not yet three. This little girl, whose name was Gisela, became a part of my life from that afternoon, and so did fat Willy, though none of us knew it then. The secret to which I had drunk my silent toast was a girl in France, who would be a middle-aged woman, beyond my imagining now, if she had lived. She died by jumping or accidentally falling out of a fifth-floor window in Paris. Her parents had locked her in a room when they found out she was corresponding with me.

This was still an afternoon in April in Berlin, the first of my freedom. It was one day after old Adolf's birthday, but that was not mentioned, not even in dialect or in the form of a Berlin joke. I don't think they were avoiding it; they had simply forgotten. They would always be astonished when other people turned out to have more specific memories of time and events.

This was the afternoon about which I would always say to myself, "I should have known," and even "I knew"—knew that I would marry the baby whose movements were already so willful and quick that her father complained, "We can't take her anywhere," and sat holding both her small hands in his; otherwise she would have clutched at every glass within reach. Her winged brows reminded me of the girl I wanted to see again. Gisela's eyes were amber in color, and luminous, with the whites so pure they seemed blue. The girl in France had eyes that resembled dark petals, opaque and velvety, and slightly tilted. She had black hair from a Corsican grandmother, and long fine lashes. Gisela's lashes were stubby and thick. I found that I was staring at the child's small ears and her small perfect teeth, thinking all the while of the other girl, whose smile had been spoiled by the malnutrition and the poor dentistry of the Occupation. I should have realized then, as I looked at Willy and his daughter, that some people never go without milk and eggs and apples, whatever the land-scape, and that the sparse feast on our table had more to do with my mother's long habit of poverty—a kind of fatalistic incompe-tence that came from never having had enough money—than with a real shortage of food. Willy had on a white nylon shirt, which was a luxury then. Later, Martin would say to me, "That Willy! Out of a black uniform and into the black market before you could say 'democracy,' " but I never knew whether it was a com-mon Berlin joke or something Martin had made up or the truth about Willy.

Gisela, who was either slow to speak for her age or only lazy, looked at me and said, "Man"—all she had to declare. Her hair was so silky and fine that it reflected the day as a curve of mauve light. She was all light and sheen, and she was the first person—I can even say the first *thing*—I had ever seen that was unflawed, without shadow. She was as whole and as innocent as a drop of water, and she was without guilt.

Her hands, released when her father drank from his wineglass, patted the tablecloth, seized a radish, tried to stuff it in his mouth.

My mother sat with her chair pushed back a few respectful inches. "Do you like children, Thomas?" she said. She knew nothing about me now except that I was not a child.

The French girl was sixteen when she came to Brittany on a holiday with her father and mother. The next winter she sent me books so that I would not drop too far behind in my schooling, and the second summer she came to my room. The door to the room was in a bend of the staircase, halfway between the phar-macy on the ground floor and the flat where my employers lived. They were supposed to keep me locked in this room when I wasn't working, but the second summer they forgot or could not be bothered, and in any case I had made a key with a piece of wire by then. It was the first room I'd had to myself. I whitewashed the walls and boxed in the store of potatoes they kept on the floor in a corner. Bunches of wild plants and herbs the druggist used in pre-scriptions hung from hooks in the ceiling. One whole wall was taken up with shelves of drying leaves and roots—walnut leaves

for treating anemia, chamomile for fainting spells, thyme and rose-
mary for muscular cramps, and nettles and mint, sage and dandelions. The fragrance in the room and the view of the port from the
window could have given me almost enough happiness for a lifetime, except that I was too young to find any happiness in that.

How she escaped from her parents the first afternoon I never
knew, but she was a brave, careless girl and had already escaped
from them often. They must have known what could happen when
they locked that wild spirit into a place where the only way out
was a window. Perhaps they were trying to see how far they could
go with a margin of safety. She left a message for them: "To teach
you a lesson." She must have thought she would be there and not
there, lost to them and yet able to see the result. There was no
message for me, except that it is a terrible thing to be alone; but I
had already learned it. She must have knelt on the windowsill.
The autumn rain must have caught her lashes and hair. She was
already alien on the windowsill, beyond recognition.

I had made my room as neat for her as though I were expecting
a military inspection. I wondered if she knew how serious it
would be for both of us if we were caught. She glanced at the view,
but only to see if anyone could look in on us, and she laughed,
starting to take off her pullover, arms crossed; then stopped and
said, "What is it—are you made of ice?" How could she know that
I was retarded? I had known nothing except imagination and solitude, and the preying of old soldiers; and I was too old for one and
repelled by the other. I thought she was about to commit the sacrifice of her person—her physical self and her immortal soul. I had
heard the old men talking about women as if women were dirt,
but needed for "that." One man said he would cut off an ear for
"that." Another said he would swim the Atlantic. I thought she
would lie in some way convenient to me and that she would feel
nothing but a kind of sorrow, which would have made it a pure
gift. But there was nothing to ask; it was not a gift. It was her decision and not a gift but an adventure. She hadn't come here to
look at the harbor, she told me, when I hesitated. I may even have
said no, and it might have been then that she smiled at me over
crossed arms, pulling off her sweater, and said, "Are you made of
ice?" For all her jauntiness, she thought she was deciding her life,

though she continued to use the word "adventure." I think it was the only other word she knew for "love." But all we were settling was her death, and my life was decided in Berlin when Willy Wehler came in with a bottle of brandy and Gisela, who refused to say more than "Man." I can still see the lace curtains, the mark on the wallpaper, the china ornaments left by the people who had gone in such a hurry—the chimney sweep with his matchstick broom, the girl with bobbed orange hair sitting on a crescent moon, the dog with the ruff around his neck—and when I remember this I say to myself, "I must have known."

We finished two bottles of Martin's champagne, and then my mother jumped to her feet to remove the glasses and bring others so that we could taste Willy Wehler's brandy.

"The dirty Belgian is still hanging around," he said to Martin, gently rocking the child, who now had her thumb in her mouth.

"What does he want?" said my stepfather. He repeated the question; he was slow and he thought that other people, unless they reacted at once and with a show of feeling, could not hear him.

"He was in the Waffen-S.S.—he says. He complains that the girls here won't go out with him, though only five or six years ago they were like flies."

"They are afraid of him," came my mother's timid voice. "He stands in the court and stares. . . ."

"I don't like men who look at pure young girls," said Willy Wehler. "He said to me, 'Help me; you owe me help.' He says he fought for us and nobody thanked him."

"He did? No wonder we lost," said Martin. I had already seen that the survivors of the war were divided into those who said they had always known how it would all turn out and those who said they had been indifferent. There are also those who like wars and those who do not. Martin had never been committed to winning or to losing or to anything—that explained his jokes. He had gained two apartments and one requisitioned flat in Berlin. He had lost a wife, but he often said to me later that people were better off out of this world.

"In Belgium he was in jail," said Willy. "He says he fought for us and then he was in jail and now we won't help him and the girls won't speak to him."

"Why is he here?" my stepfather suddenly shouted. "Who let him in? All this is his own affair, not ours." He rocked in his chair in a peculiar way, perhaps only imitating the gentle motion Willy made to keep Gisela asleep and quiet. "Nobody owes him anything," cried my stepfather, striking the table so that the little girl started and shuddered. My mother touched his arm and made a sort of humming sound, with her lips pressed together, that I took to be a signal between them, for he at once switched to another topic. It was a theme of conversation I was to hear about for many years after that afternoon. It was what the old men had to say when they were not boasting about women or their own past, and it was this: What should the Schörner army have done in Czechoslovakia to avoid capture by the Russians, and why did General Eisenhower (the villain of the story) refuse to help?

Eisenhower was my stepfather's left hand, General Schörner was his right, and the Russians were a plate of radishes. I turned very slightly to look at my mother. She had that sad cast of feature women have when their eyes are fixed nowhere. Her hand still lay lightly on Martin Toeppler's sleeve. I supposed then that he really was her husband and that they slept in the same bed. I had seen one or two closed doors in the passage on my way to the bath. Of my first prison camp, where everyone had been under eighteen or over forty, I remembered the smell of the old men—how they stopped being clean when there were no women to make them wash—and I remembered their long boasting. And yet, that April afternoon, as the sunlight of my first hours of freedom moved over the table and up along the brown wall, I did my boasting, too. I told about a prisoner I had captured. It seemed to be the thing I had to say to two men I had never seen before.

"He landed in a field just outside my grandmother's village," I told them. "I was fourteen. Three of us saw him—three boys. We had French rifles captured in the 1870 war. He'd had time to fold his parachute and he was sitting on it. I knew only one thing in English; it was 'Hands up.' "

My stepfather's mouth was open, as it had been when I first walked into the flat that day. My mother stood just out of sight.

"We advanced, pointing our 1870 rifles," I went on, droning, just like the old prisoners of war. "We all now said, 'Hands up.'

The prisoner just—" I made the gesture the American had made, of chasing a fly away, and I realized I was drunk. "He didn't stand up. He had put everything he had on the ground—a revolver, a wad of German money, a handkerchief with a map of Germany, and some smaller things we couldn't identify at once. He had on civilian shoes with thick soles. He very slowly undid his watch and handed it over, but we had no ruling about that, so we said no. He put the watch on the ground next to the revolver and the map. Then he slowly got up and strolled into the village, with his hands in his pockets. He was chewing gum. I saw he had kept his cigarettes, but I didn't know the rule about that, either. We kept our guns trained on him. The schoolmaster ran out of my grand-mother's guesthouse—everyone ran to stare. He was excited and kept saying in English, 'How do you do? How do you do?' but then an officer came running, too, and he was screaming, 'Why are you interfering? You may ask only one thing: Is he English or American.' The teacher was glad to show off his English, and he asked, 'Are you English or American?' and the American seemed to move his tongue all round his mouth before he answered. He was the first foreigner any of us had ever seen, and they took him away from us. We never saw him again."

That seemed all there was to it, but Martin's mouth was still open. I tried to remember more. "There was hell because we had left the gun and the other things on the ground. By the time they got out to the field, someone had stolen the parachute—probably for the cloth. We were in trouble over that, and we never got credit for having taken a prisoner. I went back to the field alone later on. I wanted to cry, for some reason—because it was over. He was from an adventure story to me. The whole war was a Karl May adventure, when I was fourteen and running around in school holidays with a gun. I found some small things in the field that had been overlooked—pills for keeping awake, pills in trans-parent envelopes. I had never seen that before. One envelope was called 'motion sickness.' It was a crime to keep anything, but I kept it anyway. I still had it when the Americans captured me, and they took it away. I had kept it because it was from another world. I would look at it and wonder. I kept it because of *The Last of the Mohicans*, because, because."

This was the longest story I had ever told in my life. I added, "My grandmother is dead now." My stepfather had finally shut his mouth. He looked at my mother as if to say that she had brought him a rival in the only domain that mattered—the right to talk everyone's ear off. My mother edged close to Willy Wehler and urged him to eat bread and cheese. She was still in the habit of wondering what the other person thought and how important he might be and how safe it was to speak. But Willy had not heard more than a sentence or two. That was plain from the way the expression on his face came slowly awake. He opened his eyes wide, as if to get sleep out of them, and—evidently imagining I had been talking about my life in France—said, "What were you paid as a prisoner?"

I had often wondered what the first question would be once I was home. Now I had it.

"Ha!" said my stepfather, giving the impression that he expected me to be caught out in a monstrous lie.

"One franc forty centimes a month for working here and there on a farm," I said. "But when I became a free worker with a druggist the official pay was three thousand francs a month, and that was what he gave me." I paused. "And of course I was fed and housed and had no laundry bills."

"Did you have bedsheets?" said my mother.

"With the druggist's family, always. I had one sheet folded in half. It was just right for a small cot."

"Was it the same sheet as the kind the family had?" she said, in the hesitant way that was part of her person now.

"They didn't buy sheets especially for me," I said. "I was treated fairly by the druggist, but not by the administration."

"Aha," said the two older men, almost together.

"The administration refused to pay my fare home," I said, looking down into my glass the way I had seen the men in prison camp stare at a fixed point when they were recounting a grievance.

"A prisoner of war has the right to be repatriated at administration expense. The administration would not pay my fare because I had stayed too long in France—but that was their mistake. I bought a ticket as far as Paris on the pay I had saved. The druggist sold me some old shoes and trousers and a jacket of his.

My own things were in rags. In Paris I went to the YMCA. The YMCA was supposed to be in charge of prisoners' rights. The man wouldn't listen to me. If I had been left behind, then I was not a prisoner, he said; I was a tourist. It was his duty to help me. Instead of that, he informed the police." For the first time my voice took on the coloration of resentment. I knew that this complaint about a niggling matter of train fare made my whole adventure seem small, but I had become an old soldier. I remembered the police commissioner, with his thin lips and dirty nails, who said, "You should have been repatriated years ago, when you were sixteen."

"It was a mistake," I told him.

"Your papers are full of strange mistakes," he said, bending over them. "There, one capital error. An omission, a grave omission. What is your mother's maiden name?"

"Wickler," I said.

I watched him writing "W-i-e-c-k-l-a-i-r," slowly, with the tip of his tongue sticking out of the corner of his mouth as he wrote. "You have been here for something like five years with an incomplete dossier. And what about this? Who crossed it out?"

"I did. My father was not a pastry cook."

"You could be fined or even jailed for this," he said.

"My father was not a pastry cook," I said. "He had tuberculosis. He was not allowed to handle food."

Willy Wehler did not say what he thought of my story. Perhaps not having any opinion about injustice, even the least important, had become a habit of his, like my mother's of speaking through her fingers. He was on the right step of that staircase I've spoken of. Even the name he had given his daughter was a sign of his sensitivity to the times. Nobody wanted to hear the pagan, Old Germanic names anymore—Sigrun and Brunhilde and Sieglinde. Willy had felt the change. He would have called any daughter something neutral and pretty—Gisela, Marianne, Elisabeth—anytime after the battle of Stalingrad. All Willy ever had to do was sniff the air.

He pushed back his chair (in later years he would be able to push a table away with his stomach) and got to his feet. He had to tip his head to look up into my eyes. He said he wanted to give me advice that would be useful to me as a latehomecomer. His advice was to forget. "Forget everything," he said. "Forget, forget. That was what I said to my good neighbor Herr Silber when I bought his wife's topaz brooch and earrings before he emigrated to Palestine. I said, 'Dear Herr Silber, look forward, never back, and forget, forget, forget.' "

The child in Willy's arms was in the deepest of sleeps. Martin Toeppler followed his friend to the door, they whispered together; then the door closed behind both men.

"They have gone to have a glass of something at Herr Wehler's," said my mother. I saw now that she was crying quietly. She dried her eyes on her apron and began clearing the table of the homecoming feast. "Willy Wehler has been kind to us," she said. "Don't repeat that thing."

"About forgetting?"

"No, about the topaz brooch. It was a crime to buy anything from Jews."

"It doesn't matter now."

She lowered the tray she held and looked pensively out at the wrecked houses across the street. "If only people knew beforehand what was allowed," she said.

"My father is probably a hero now," I said.

"Oh, Thomas, don't travel too fast. We haven't seen the last of the changes. Yes, a hero. But too late for me. I've suffered too much."

"What does Martin think that he died of?"

"A working accident. He can understand that."

"You could have said consumption. He did have it." She shook her head. Probably she had not wanted Martin to imagine he could ever be saddled with two sickly stepsons. "Where do you and Martin sleep?"

"In the room next to the bathroom. Didn't you see it? You'll be comfortable here in the parlor. The couch pulls out. You can stay as long as you like. This is your home. A home for you and Chris." She said this so stubbornly that I knew some argument must have taken place between her and Martin.

I intended this room to be my home. There was no question about it in my mind. I had not yet finished high school; I had been taken out for anti-aircraft duty, then sent to the front. The role of adolescents in uniform had been to try to prevent the civilian population from surrendering. We were expected to die in the ruins together. When the women ran pillowcases up flagpoles, we shinnied up to drag them down. We were prepared to hold the line with our 1870 rifles until we saw the American tanks. There had not been tanks in our Karl May adventure stories, and the Americans, finally, were not out of *The Last of the Mohicans*. I told my mother that I had to go back to high school and then I would apply for a scholarship and take a degree in French. I would become a schoolmaster. French was all I had from my captivity; I might as well use it. I would earn money doing translations.

That cheered her up. She would not have to ask the ex-tram conductor too many favors. "Translations" and "scholarship" were an exalted form of language, to her. As a schoolmaster, I would have the most respectable job in the family, now that Uncle Gerhard was raising rabbits. "As long as it doesn't cost *him* too much," she said, as if she had to say it and yet was hoping I wouldn't hear.

It was not strictly true that all I had got out of my captivity was the ability to speak French. I had also learned to cook, iron, make beds, wait on table, wash floors, polish furniture, plant a vegetable garden, paint shutters. I wanted to help my mother in the kitchen now, but that shocked her. "Rest," she said, but I did not know what "rest" meant. "I've never seen a man drying a glass," she said, in apology. I wanted to tell her that while the roads and bridges of France were still waiting for someone to rebuild them I had been taught how to make a tomato salad by the druggist's wife; but I could not guess what the word "France" conveyed to her imagination. I began walking about the apartment. I looked in on a store cupboard, a water closet smelling of carbolic, the bathroom again, then a room containing a high bed, a brown wardrobe, and a table covered with newspapers bearing half a dozen of the flowerless spiky dull green plants my mother had always tended with so much devotion. I shut the door as if on a dark past, and I said to myself, I am free. This is the beginning of life. It is also the start of the good half of a rotten century. Everything ugly and corrupt and vicious is behind us. My thoughts were not exactly in those words, but something like them. I said to myself, This apartment has a musty smell, an old and dirty smell that sinks into clothes. After a time I shall probably smell like the dark parlor. The smell must be in the cushions, in the bed that pulls out, in the lace curtains. It is a smell that creeps into nightclothes. The blankets will be permeated. I thought, I shall get used to the smell, and the smell of burning in the stone outside. The view of ruins will be my view. Every day on my way home from school I shall walk over Elke. I shall get used to the wood staircase, the bellpull, the polished nameplate, the white enamel fuses in the hall—my mother had said, "When you want light in the parlor you give the center fuse in the lower row a half turn." I looked at a framed drawing of cartoon people with puffy hair. A strong wind had blown their umbrella inside out. They would be part of my view, like the ruins. I took in the ancient gas bracket in the kitchen and the stone sink. My mother, washing glasses without soap, smiled at me, forgetting to hide her teeth. I reexamined the tiled stove in the parlor, the wood and the black briquettes that would be next to my head at night, and the glass-fronted cabinet full of the china ornaments God had selected to survive the Berlin air raids. These would be removed to make way for my books. For Martin Toeppler need not imagine he could count on my pride, or that I would prefer to starve rather than take his charity, or that I was too arrogant to sleep on his dusty sofa. I would wear out his soap, borrow his shirts, spread his butter on my bread. I would hang on Martin like an octopus. He had a dependent now—a ravenous, egocentric, latehomecoming high school adolescent of twenty-one. The old men owed this much to me—the old men in my prison camp who would have sold mother and father for an extra ounce of soup, who had already sold their children for it; the old men who had fouled my idea of women; the old men in the bunkers who had let the girls defend them in Berlin; the old men who had dared to survive.

The bed that pulled out was sure to be all lumps. I had slept on worse. Would it be wide enough for Chris, too?

People in the habit of asking themselves silent useless questions look for answers in mirrors. My hair was blond again now that it had dried. I looked less like my idea of my father. I tried to see the reflection of the man who had gone out in the middle of the night and who never came back. You don't go out alone to tear down election posters in a village where nobody thinks as you do—not unless you *want* to be stabbed in the back. So the family had said.

"You were well out of it," I said to the shadow that floated on the glass panel of the china cabinet, though it would not be my father's again unless I could catch it unaware.

I said to myself, It is quieter than France. They keep their radios low.

In captivity I had never suffered a pain except for the cramps of hunger the first years, which had been replaced by a scratching, morbid anxiety, and the pain of homesickness, which takes you in the stomach and the throat. Now I felt the first of the real pains that were to follow me like little dogs for the rest of my life, perhaps: The first compressed my knee, the second tangled the nerves at the back of my neck. I discovered that my eyes were sensitive and that it hurt to blink.

This was the hour when, in Brittany, I would begin peeling the potatoes for dinner. I had seen food my mother had never heard of—oysters, and artichokes. My mother had never seen a harbor or a sea.

My American prisoner had left his immediate life spread on an alien meadow—his parachute, his revolver, his German money. He had strolled into captivity with his hands in his pockets.

"I know what you are thinking," said my mother, who was standing behind me. "I know that you are judging me. If you could guess what my life has been—the whole story, not only the last few years—you wouldn't be hard on me."

I turned too slowly to meet her eyes. It was not what I had been thinking. I had forgotten about her, in that sense.

"No, no, nothing like that," I said. I still did not touch her. What I had been moving along to in my mind was: Why am I in this place? Who sent me here? Is it a form of justice or injustice? How long does it last?

"Now we can wait together for Chris," she said. She seemed young and happy all at once. "Look, Thomas. A new moon. Bow to it three times. Wait—you must have something silver in your hand." I saw that she was hurrying to finish with this piece of nonsense before Martin came back. She rummaged in the china cabinet and brought out a silver napkin ring—left behind by the vanished tenants, probably. The name on it was "Meta"—no one we knew. "Bow to the moon and hold it and make your wish," she said. "Quickly."

"You first."

She wished, I am sure, for my brother. As for me, I wished that I was a few hours younger, in the corridor of a packed train, clutching the top of the open window, my heart hammering as I strained to find the one beloved face.

IN TRANSIT

AFTER THE Cook's party of twenty-five Japanese tourists had
departed for Oslo, only four people were left in the waiting room
of the Helsinki airport—a young French couple named Perrigny,
who had not been married long, and an elderly pair who were
identifiably American. When they were sure that the young people two benches forward could not understand them, the old
people went on with a permanent, flowing quarrel. The man had
the habit of reading signs out loud, though perhaps he did it only
to madden his wife. He read the signs over the three doors leading
out to the field: " 'Oslo.' 'Amsterdam.' 'Copenhagen.' . . . I don't
see 'Stockholm.' "

She replied, "What I wonder is what I have been to you all
these years."

Philippe Perrigny, who understood English, turned around, pretending he was looking at Finnish pottery in the showcases on
their right. He saw that the man was examining timetables and
tickets, all the while muttering "Stockholm, Stockholm," while
the woman looked away. She had removed her glasses and was
wiping her eyes. How did she arrive at that question here, in the
Helsinki airport, and how can he answer? It has to be answered
in a word: everything/nothing. It was like being in a country
church and suddenly hearing the peasant priest put a question
no one cares to consider, about guilt or duty or the presence of
God, and breathing with relief when he has got past that and on
to the prayers.

"In the next world we will choose differently," the man said.
"At least I know you will."

The wild thoughts of the younger man were: They are chained

for the rest of this life. Too old to change? Only a brute would leave her now? They are walking toward the door marked AM-STERDAM, and she limps. That is why they cannot separate. She is an invalid. He has been looking after her for years. They are going through the Amsterdam door, whatever their tickets said. Whichever door they take, they will see the circular lanes of suburbs, and the family cars outside each house, and in the backyard a blue pool. All across northern Europe streets are named after acacia trees, but they may not know that.

Perrigny was on his wedding trip, but also on assignment for his Paris paper, and he assembled the series on Scandinavia in his mind. He had been repeating for four years now an article called "The Silent Cry," and neither his paper nor he himself had become aware that it was repetitious. He began to invent again, in the style of the Paris weeklies: "It was a silent anguished cry torn from the hearts and throats..." No. "It was a silent song, strangled..." "It was a silent passionate hymn to..." This time the beginning would be joined to the blue-eyed puritanical north; it had applied to Breton farmers unable to get a good price for their artichokes, to the Christmas crowd at the Berlin Wall, to Greece violated by tourists, to Negro musicians performing at the Olympia music hall, to miserable Portuguese fishermen smuggled into France and dumped on the labor market, to poets writing under the influence of drugs.

The old man took his wife's hand. She was still turned away, but dry-eyed now, and protected by glasses. To distract her while their tickets were inspected he said rapidly, "Look at the nice restaurant, the attractive restaurant. It is part outside and part inside, see? It is inside *and* outside."

Perrigny's new wife gently withdrew her hand from his and said, "Why did you leave her?"

He had been expecting this, and said, "Because she couldn't concentrate on one person. She was nice to everybody, but she couldn't concentrate enough for a marriage."

"She was unfaithful."

"That too. It came from the same lack of concentration. She had been married before."

"Oh? She was old?"

"She's twenty-seven now. She was afraid of being twenty-seven. She used to quote something from Jane Austen—an English writer," he said as Claire frowned. "Something about a woman that age never being able to hope for anything again. I wonder what she did hope for."

"The first husband left her, too?"

"No, he died. They hadn't been married very long."

"You *did* leave her?" said the girl, for fear of a possible humiliation—for fear of having married a man some other woman had thrown away.

"I certainly did. Without explanations. One Sunday morning I got up and dressed and went away. I came back when she wasn't there and took my things away—my tape recorder, my records. I came back twice for my books. I never saw her again except to talk about the divorce."

"Weren't you unhappy, just walking out that way? You make it sound so easy."

"I don't admire suffering," he said, and realized he was echoing his first wife. Suffering was disgusting to her; the emblem of dirt was someone like Kafka alone in a room distilling blows and horror.

"Nobody admires suffering," said the girl, thinking of aches and cramps. "She had a funny name."

"Yes, terrible. Shirley. She always had to spell it over the phone. Suzanne Henri Irma Robert Louis Émile Yvonne. It is not pronounced as it is spelled."

"Were you really in love with her?"

"I was the first time I saw her. The mistake was that I married her. The mystery was why I ever married her."

"Was she pretty?"

"She had lovely hair, like all the American girls, but she was always cutting it and making it ugly. She had good legs, but she wore flat shoes. Like all the Americans, she wore her clothes just slightly too long, and with the flat shoes . . . she never looked dressed. She was blind as a mole and wore dark glasses because she had lost the other ones. When she took her glasses off, sometimes she looked ruthless. But she was worried and impulsive, and thought men had always exploited her."

Claire said, "How do I know you won't leave me?" but he could tell from her tone she did not expect an answer to that.

Their flight was called. They moved out under COPENHAGEN, carrying their cameras and raincoats. He was glad this first part of the journey was over. He and Claire were together the whole twenty-four hours. She was good if he said he was working, but puzzled and offended if he read. Attending to her, he made mistakes. In Helsinki he had gone with her to buy clothes. Under racks of dresses he saw her legs and bare feet. She came out, smiling, holding in front of herself a bright dress covered with suns. "You can't wear it in Paris," he said, and he saw her face change, as if he had darkened some idea she'd had of what she might be. In a park, yesterday, beside a tall spray of water, he found himself staring at another girl, who sat feeding squirrels. He admired the back of her neck, the soft parting of her hair, her brown shoulder and arm. Idleness of this kind never happened in what he chose to think of as real life—as if love and travel were opposed to living, were a dream. He drew closer to his new wife, this blond summer child, thinking of the winter honeymoon with his first wife. He had read her hand to distract her from the cold and rain, holding the leaf-palm, tracing the extremely shallow head line (no judgment, he informed her) and the choppy life—an American life, he had said, folding the leaf. He paid attention to Claire, because he had admired another girl and had remembered something happy with his first wife, all in a minute. How would Claire like to help him work, he said. Together they saw how much things cost in shopwindows, and she wrote down for him how much they paid for a meal of fried fish and temperance beer. Every day had to be filled as never at home. A gap of two hours in a strange town, in transit, was like being shut up in a stalled lift with nothing to read.

Claire would have given anything to be the girl in the park, to have that neck and that hair *and* stand off and see it, all at once. She saw the homage he paid the small ears, the lobes pasted. She had her revenge in the harbor, later, when a large group of tourists mistook her for someone famous—for an actress, she supposed. She had been told she looked like Catherine Deneuve. They held out cards and papers and she signed her new name,

"Claire Perrigny," "Claire Perrigny," over and over, looking back at him with happy, triumphant eyes. Everything flew and shrieked around them—the seagulls, the wind, the strangers calling in an unknown language something she took to mean "Your name, your name!"

"They think I am famous!" she called, through her thick flying hair. She smiled and grinned, in conspiracy, because she was not famous at all, only a pretty girl who had been married eight days. Her tongue was dark with the blueberries she had eaten in the market—until Philippe had told her, she hadn't known what blueberries were. She smiled her stained smile, and tried to catch her soaring skirt between her knees. Compassion, pride, tenderness, jealousy, and acute sick misery were what he felt in turn. He saw how his first wife had looked before he had ever known her, when she was young and in love.

THE MOSLEM WIFE

IN THE south of France, in the business room of a hotel quite near to the house where Katherine Mansfield (whom no one in this hotel had ever heard of) was writing "The Daughters of the Late Colonel," Netta Asher's father announced that there would never be a man-made catastrophe in Europe again. The dead of that recent war, the doomed nonsense of the Russian Bolsheviks had finally knocked sense into European heads. What people wanted now was to get on with life. When he said "life," he meant its commercial business.

Who would have contradicted Mr. Asher? Certainly not Netta. She did not understand what he meant quite so well as his French solicitor seemed to, but she did listen with interest and respect, and then watched him signing papers that, she knew, concerned her for life. He was renewing the long lease her family held on the Hotel Prince Albert and Albion. Netta was then eleven. One hundred years should at least see her through the prime of life, said Mr. Asher, only half jokingly, for of course he thought his seed was immortal.

Netta supposed she might easily live to be more than a hundred—at any rate, for years and years. She knew that her father did not want her to marry until she was twenty-six and that she was then supposed to have a pair of children, the elder a boy. Netta and her father and the French lawyer shook hands on the lease, and she was given her first glass of champagne. The date on the bottle was 1909, for the year of her birth. Netta bravely pronounced the wine delicious, but her father said she would know much better vintages before she was through.

Netta remembered the handshake but perhaps not the terms.

When the lease had eighty-eight years to run, she married her first cousin, Jack Ross, which was not at all what her father had had in mind. Nor would there be the useful pair of children—Jack couldn't abide them. Like Netta he came from a hotelkeeping family where the young were like blight. Netta had up to now never shown a scrap of maternal feeling over anything, but Mr. Asher thought Jack might have made an amiable parent—a kind one, at least. She consoled Mr. Asher on one count, by taking the hotel over in his lifetime. The hotel was, to Netta, a natural life; and so when Mr. Asher, dying, said, "She behaves as I wanted her to," he was right as far as the drift of Netta's behavior was concerned but wrong about its course.

The Ashers' hotel was not down on the seafront, though boats and sea could be had from the south-facing rooms.

Across a road nearly empty of traffic were handsome villas, and behind and to either side stood healthy olive trees and a large lemon grove. The hotel was painted a deep ocher with white trim. It had white awnings and green shutters and black iron balconies as lacquered and shiny as Chinese boxes. It possessed two tennis courts, a lily pond, a sheltered winter garden, a formal rose garden, and trees full of nightingales. In the summer dark, *belles-de-nuit* glowed pink, lemon, white, and after their evening watering they gave off a perfume that varied from plant to plant and seemed to match the petals' coloration. In May the nights were dense with stars and fireflies. From the rose garden one might have seen the twin pulse of cigarettes on a balcony, where Jack and Netta sat drinking a last brandy-and-soda before turning in. Most of the rooms were shuttered by then, for no traveler would have dreamed of being south except in winter. Jack and Netta and a few servants had the whole place to themselves. Netta would hire workmen and have the rooms that needed it repainted—the blue cardroom, and the red-walled bar, and the white dining room, where Victorian mirrors gave back glossy walls and blown curtains and nineteenth-century views of the Ligurian coast, the work of an Asher great-uncle. Everything upstairs and down was soaked and wiped and polished, and even the pictures were relentlessly washed with soft cloths and ordinary laundry soap. Netta also had the boiler overhauled and the linen mended and new monograms embroidered and the looking glasses resilvered and the shutters taken off their hinges and scraped and made spruce green again for next year's sun to fade, while Jack talked about decorators and expert gardeners and even wrote to some, and banged tennis balls against the large new garage. He also read books and translated poetry for its own sake and practiced playing the clarinet. He had studied music once, and still thought that an important life, a musical life, was there in the middle distance. One summer, just to see if he could, he translated pages of Saint-John Perse, which were as blank as the garage wall to Netta, in any tongue.

Netta adored every minute of her life, and she thought Jack had a good life too, with nearly half the year for the pleasures that suited him. As soon as the grounds and rooms and cellar and roof had been put to rights, she and Jack packed and went traveling somewhere. Jack made the plans. He was never so cheerful as when buying Baedekers and dragging out their stickered trunks. But Netta was nothing of a traveler. She would have been glad to see the same sun rising out of the same sea from the window every day until she died. She loved Jack, and what she liked best after him was the hotel. It was a place where, once, people had come to die of tuberculosis, yet it held no trace or feeling of danger. When Netta walked with her workmen through sheeted summer rooms, hearing the cicadas and hearing Jack start, stop, start some deeply alien music (alien even when her memory automatically gave her a composer's name), she was reminded that here the dead had never been allowed to corrupt the living; the dead had been dressed for an outing and removed as soon as their first muscular stiffness relaxed. Some were wheeled out in chairs, sitting, and some reclined on portable cots, as if merely resting.

That is why there is no bad atmosphere here, she would say to herself. Death has been swept away, discarded. When the shutters are closed on a room, it is for sleep or for love. Netta could think this easily because neither she nor Jack was ever sick. They knew nothing about insomnia, and they made love every day of their lives—they had married in order to be able to.

Spring had been the season for dying in the old days. Invalids who had struggled through the dark comfort of winter took fright as the night receded. They felt without protection. Netta knew about this, and about the difference between darkness and brightness, but neither affected her. She was not afraid of death or of the dead—they were nothing but cold, heavy furniture. She could have tied jaws shut and weighted eyelids with native instinctiveness, as other women were born knowing the temperature for an infant's milk.

"There are no ghosts," she could say, entering the room where her mother, then her father had died. "If there were, I would know."

Netta took it for granted, now she was married, that Jack felt as she did about light, dark, death, and love. They were as alike in some ways (none of them physical) as a couple of twins, spoke much the same language in the same accents, had the same jokes—mostly about other people—and had been together as much as their families would let them for most of their lives. Other men seemed dull to Netta—slower, perhaps, lacking the spoken shorthand she had with Jack. She never mentioned this. For one thing, both of them had the idea that, being English, one must not say too much. Born abroad, they worked hard at an Englishness that was innocently inaccurate, rooted mostly in attitudes. Their families had been innkeepers along this coast for a century, even before Dr. James Henry Bennet had discovered "the Genoese Rivieras." In one of his guides to the region, a "Mr. Ross" is mentioned as a hotel owner who will accept English bank checks, and there is a "Mr. Asher," reliable purveyor of English groceries. The most trustworthy shipping agents in 1860 are the Montale brothers, converts to the Anglican Church, possessors of a British *laissez-passer* to Malta and Egypt. These families, by now plaited like hair, were connections of Netta's and Jack's and still in business from beyond Marseilles to Genoa. No wonder that other men bored her, and that each thought the other both familiar and unique. But of course they were unalike too. When once someone asked them, "Are you related to Montale, the poet?" Netta answered, "What poet?" and Jack said, "I wish we were."

There were no poets in the family. Apart from the great-uncle who had painted landscapes, the only person to try anything peculiar had been Jack, with his music. He had been allowed to study, up to a point; his father had been no good with hotels—had been a failure, in fact, bailed out four times by his cousins, and it had been thought, for a time, that Jack Ross might be a dunderhead too. Music might do him; he might not be fit for anything else.

Information of this kind about the meaning of failure had been gleaned by Netta years before, when she first became aware of her little cousin. Jack's father and mother—the commercial blunderers—had come to the Prince Albert and Albion to ride out a crisis. They were somewhere between undischarged bankruptcy and annihilation, but one was polite: Netta curtsied to her aunt and uncle. Her eyes were on Jack. She could not read yet, though she could sift and classify attitudes. She drew near him, sucking her lower lip, her hands behind her back. For the first time she was conscious of the beauty of another child. He was younger than Netta, imprisoned in a portable-fence arrangement in which he moved tirelessly, crabwise, hanging on a barrier he could easily have climbed. He was as fair as his Irish mother and sunburned a deep brown. His blue gaze was not a baby's—it was too challenging. He was naked except for shorts that were large and seemed about to fall down. The sunburn, the undress were because his mother was reckless and rather odd. Netta—whose mother was perfect—wore boots, stockings, a longsleeved frock, and a white sun hat. She heard the adults laugh and say that Jack looked like a prizefighter. She walked around his prison, staring, and the blue-eyed fighter stared back.

The Rosses stayed for a long time, while the family sent telegrams and tried to raise money for them. No one looked after Jack much. He would lie on a marble step of the staircase watching the hotel guests going into the cardroom or the dining room. One night, for a reason that remorse was to wipe out in a minute, Netta gave him such a savage kick (though he was not really in her way) that one of his legs remained paralyzed for a long time.

"*Why* did you do it?" her father asked her—this in the room where she was shut up on bread and water. Netta didn't know. She loved Jack, but who would believe it now? Jack learned to walk, then to run, and in time to ski and play tennis; but her life-long gift to him was a loss of balance, a sudden lopsided bend of a knee. Jack's parents had meantime been given a small hotel to run at Bandol. Mr. Asher, responsible for a bank loan, kept an eye on the place. He went often, in a hotel car with a chauffeur, Netta perched beside him. When, years later, the families found out that the devoted young cousins had become lovers, they separated them without saying much. Netta was too independent to be dealt with. Besides, her father did not want a rift; his wife had died, and he needed Netta. Jack, whose claim on music had been the subject of teasing until now, was suddenly sent to study in England. Netta saw that he was secretly dismayed. He wanted to be almost anything as long as it was impossible, and then only as an act of grace. Netta's father did think it was his duty to tell her that marriage was, at its best, a parched arrangement, intolerable without a flow of golden guineas and fresh blood. As cousins, Jack and Netta could not bring each other anything except stale money. Nothing stopped them: They were married four months after Jack became twenty-one. Netta heard someone remark at her wedding, "She doesn't need a husband," meaning perhaps the practical, matter-of-fact person she now seemed to be. She did have the dry, burned-out look of someone turned inward. Her dark eyes glowed out of a thin face. She had the shape of a girl of fourteen. Jack, who was large, and fair, and who might be stout at forty if he wasn't careful, looked exactly his age, and seemed quite ready to be married.

Netta could not understand why, loving Jack as she did, she did not look more like him. It had troubled her in the past when they did not think exactly the same thing at almost the same time. During the secret meetings of their long engagement she had noticed how even before a parting they were nearly apart—they had begun to "unmesh," as she called it. Drinking a last drink, usually in the buffet of a railway station, she would see that Jack was somewhere else, thinking about the next-best thing to Netta. The next-best thing might only be a book he wanted to finish reading, but it was enough to make her feel exiled. He often told Netta, "I'm not holding on to you. You're free," because he thought it needed saying, and of course he wanted freedom for himself. But to Netta "freedom" had a cold sound. Is that what I do want, she would wonder. Is that what I think he should offer? Their partings

THE MOSLEM WIFE · 85

were often on the edge of parting forever, not just because Jack had said or done or thought the wrong thing but because between them they generated the high sexual tension that leads to quarrels. Barely ten minutes after agreeing that no one in the world could possibly know what they knew, one of them, either one, could curse the other out over something trivial. Yet they were, and remained, much in love, and when they were apart Netta sent him letters that were almost despairing with enchantment.

Jack answered, of course, but his letters were cautious. Her exploration of feeling was part of an unlimited capacity she seemed to have for passionate behavior, so at odds with her appearance, which had been dry and sardonic even in childhood. Save for an erotic sentence or two near the end (which Netta read first) Jack's messages might have been meant for any girl cousin he particularly liked. Love was memory, and he was no good at the memory game; he needed Netta there. The instant he saw her he knew all he had missed. But Netta, by then, felt forgotten, and she came to each new meeting aggressive and hurt, afflicted with the physical signs of her doubts and injuries—cold sores, rashes, erratic periods, mysterious temperatures. If she tried to discuss it he would say, "We aren't going over all that again, are we?" Where Netta was concerned he had settled for the established faith, but Netta, who had a wilder, more secret God, wanted a prayer a minute, not to speak of unending miracles and revelations.

When they finally married, both were relieved that the strain of partings and of tense disputes in railway stations would come to a stop. Each privately blamed the other for past violence, and both believed that once they could live openly, without interference, they would never have a disagreement again. Netta did not want Jack to regret the cold freedom he had vainly tried to offer her. He must have his liberty, and his music, and other people, and, oh, anything he wanted—whatever would stop him from saying he was ready to let her go free. The first thing Netta did was to make certain they had the best room in the hotel. She had never actually owned a room until now. The private apartments of her family had always been surrendered in a crisis: Everyone had packed up and moved as beds were required. She and Jack were hopelessly untidy, because both had spent their early years moving down hotel corridors, trailing belts and raincoats, with tennis shoes hanging from knotted strings over their shoulders, their arms around books and sweaters and gray flannel bundles. Both had done lessons in the corners of lounges, with cups and glasses rattling, and other children running, and English voices louder than anything. Jack, who had been vaguely educated, remembered his boarding schools as places where one had a permanent bed. Netta chose for her marriage a south-facing room with a large balcony and an awning of dazzling white. It was furnished with lemonwood that had been brought to the Riviera by Russians for their own villas long before. To the lemonwood Netta's mother had added English chintzes; the result, in Netta's eyes, was not bizarre but charming. The room was deeply mirrored; when the shutters were closed on hot afternoons a play of light became as green as a forest on the walls, and as blue as seawater in the glass. A quality of suspension, of disbelief in gravity, now belonged to Netta. She became tidy, silent, less introspective, as watchful and as reflective as her bedroom mirrors. Jack stayed as he was, luckily; any alteration would have worried her, just as a change in an often-read story will trouble a small child. She was intensely, almost unnaturally happy.

One day she overheard an English doctor, whose wife played bridge every afternoon at the hotel, refer to her, to Netta, as "the little Moslem wife." It was said affectionately, for the doctor liked her. She wondered if he had seen through walls and had watched her picking up the clothing and the wet towels Jack left strewn like clues to his presence. The phrase was collected and passed from mouth to mouth in the idle English colony. Netta, the last person in the world deliberately to eavesdrop (she lacked that sort of interest in other people), was sharp of hearing where her marriage was concerned. She had a special antenna for Jack, for his shades of meaning, secret intentions, for his innocent contradictions. Perhaps "Moslem wife" meant several things, and possibly it was plain to anyone with eyes that Jack, without meaning a bit of harm by it, had a way with women. Those he attracted were a puzzling lot, to Netta. She had already catalogued them—elegant elderly parties with tongues like carving knives; gentle, clever girls who flourished on the unattainable; untouchable-daughter types, canny about their virginity, wondering if Jack would be father enough to justify the sacrifice. There was still another kind— tough, sunburned, clad in dark colors—who made Netta think in the vocabulary of horoscopes: Her gem—diamonds. Her color— black. Her language—worse than Netta's. She noticed that even when Jack had no real use for a woman he never made it apparent; he adopted anyone who took a liking to him. He assumed—Netta thought—a tribal, paternal air that was curious in so young a man. The plot of attraction interested him, no matter how it turned out. He was like someone reading several novels at once, or like someone playing simultaneous chess.

Netta did not want her marriage to become a world of stone. She said nothing except, "Listen, Jack, I've been at this hotel busi- ness longer than you have. It's wiser not to be too pally with the guests." At Christmas the older women gave him boxes of expen- sive soap. "They must think someone around here wants a good wash," Netta remarked. Outside their fenced area of private jokes and private love was a landscape too open, too light-drenched, for serious talk. And then, when? Jack woke up quickly and early in the morning and smiled as naturally as children do. He knew where he was and the day of the week and the hour. The best mo- ment of the day was the first cigarette. When something bloody happened, it was never before six in the evening. At night he had a dark look that went with a dark mood, sometimes. Netta would tell him that she could see a cruise ship floating on the black hori- zon like a piece of the Milky Way, and she would get that look for an answer. But it never lasted. His memory was too short to let him sulk, no matter what fragment of night had crossed his mind. She knew, having heard other couples all her life, that at least she and Jack never made the conjugal sounds that passed for conversation and that might as well have been bowwow and quack quack.

If, by chance, Jack found himself drawn to another woman, if the tide of attraction suddenly ran the other way, then he would discover in himself a great need to talk to his wife. They sat out on their balcony for much of one long night and he told her about his Irish mother. His mother's eccentricity—"Vera's dottiness," where the family was concerned—had kept Jack from taking anything seriously. He had been afraid of pulling her mad attention in his direction. Countless times she had faked tuberculosis and cancer and announced her own imminent death. A telephone call from a hospital had once declared her lost in a car crash. "It's a new life, a new life," her husband had babbled, coming away from the phone. Jack saw his father then as beautiful. Women are beautiful when they fall in love, said Jack; sometimes the glow will last a few hours, sometimes even a day or two.

"You know," said Jack, as if Netta knew, "the look of amazement on a girl's face . . ."

Well, that same incandescence had suffused Jack's father when he thought his wife had died, and it continued to shine until a taxi deposited dotty Vera with her cheerful announcement that she had certainly brought off a successful April Fool. After Jack's father died she became violent. "Getting away from her was a form of violence in me," Jack said. "But I did it." That was why he was secretive; that was why he was independent. He had never wanted any woman to get her hands on his life.

Netta heard this out calmly. Where his own feelings were concerned she thought he was making them up as he went along. The garden smelled coolly of jasmine and mimosa. She wondered who his new girl was, and if he was likely to blurt out a name. But all he had been working up to was that his mother—mad, spoiled, devilish, whatever she was—would need to live with Jack and Netta, unless Netta agreed to giving her an income. An income would let her remain where she was—at the moment, in a Rudolph Steiner community in Switzerland, devoted to medieval gardening and to getting the best out of Goethe. Netta's father's training prevented even the thought of spending the money in such a manner.

"You won't regret all you've told me, will you?" she asked. She saw that the new situation would be her burden, her chain, her mean little joke sometimes. Jack scarcely hesitated before saying that where Netta mattered he could never regret anything. But what really interested him now was his mother.

"Lifts give her claustrophobia," he said. "She mustn't be higher than the second floor." He sounded like a man bringing a legal concubine into his household, scrupulously anxious to give all his women equal rights. "And I hope she will make friends," he said. "It won't be easy, at her age. One can't live without them." He probably meant that he had none. Netta had been raised not to expect to have friends: You could not run a hotel and have scores of personal ties. She expected people to be polite and punctual and to mean what they said, and that was the end of it. Jack gave his friendship easily, but he expected considerable diversion in return.

Netta said dryly, "If she plays bridge, she can play with Mrs. Blackley." This was the wife of the doctor who had first said "Moslem wife." He had come down here to the Riviera for his wife's health; the two belonged to a subcolony of flat-dwelling expatriates. His medical practice was limited to hypochondriacs and rheumatic patients. He had time on his hands: Netta often saw him in the hotel reading room, standing, leafing—he took pleasure in handling books. Netta, no reader, did not like touching a book unless it was new. The doctor had a trick of speech Jack loved to imitate: He would break up his words with an extra syllable, some words only, and at that not every time. "It is all a matter of stu-hyle," he said, for "style," or, Jack's favorite, "Oh, well, in the end it all comes down to su-hex." "Uh-hebb and flo-ho of hormones" was the way he once described the behavior of saints—Netta had looked twice at him over that. He was a firm agnostic and the first person from whom Netta heard there existed a magical Dr. Freud. When Netta's father had died of pneumonia, the doctor's "I'm su-horry, Netta" had been so heartfelt she could not have wished it said another way.

His wife, Georgina, could lower her blood pressure or stop her heartbeat nearly at will. Netta sometimes wondered why Dr. Blackley had brought her to a soft climate rather than to the man at Vienna he so admired. Georgina was well enough to play fierce bridge, with Jack and anyone good enough. Her husband usually came to fetch her at the end of the afternoon when the players stopped for tea. Once, because he was obliged to return at once to a patient who needed him, she said, "Can't you be competent about anything?" Netta thought she understood, then, his resigned repetition of "It's all su-hex." "Oh, don't explain. You bore me," said his wife, turning her back.

Netta followed him out to his car. She wore an India shawl that had been her mother's. The wind blew her hair; she had to hold it back. She said, "Why don't you kill her?"

"I am not a desperate person," he said. He looked at Netta, she looking up at him because she had to look up to nearly everyone except children, and he said, "I've wondered why we haven't been to bed."

"Who?" said Netta. "You and your wife? Oh. You mean me." She was not offended; she just gave the shawl a brusque tug and said, "Not a hope. Never with a guest," though of course that was not the reason.

"You might have to, if the guest were a maharaja," he said, to make it all harmless. "I am told it is pu-hart of the courtesy they expect."

"We don't get their trade," said Netta. This had not stopped her liking the doctor. She pitied him, rather, because of his wife, and because he wasn't Jack and could not have Netta.

"I do love you," said the doctor, deciding finally to sit down in his car. "Ee-nee-ormously." She watched him drive away as if she loved him too, and might never see him again. It never crossed her mind to mention any of this conversation to Jack.

That very spring, perhaps because of the doctor's words, the hotel did get some maharaja trade—three little sisters with ebony curls, men's eyebrows, large heads, and delicate hands and feet. They had four rooms, one for their governess. A chauffeur on permanent call lodged elsewhere. The governess, who was Dutch, had a perfect triangle of a nose and said "whom" for "who," pronouncing it "whum." The girls were to learn French, tennis, and swimming. The chauffeur arrived with a hairdresser, who cut their long hair; it lay on the governess's carpet, enough to fill a large pillow. Their toe- and fingernails were filed to points and looked like a kitten's teeth. They came smiling down the marble staircase, carrying new tennis racquets, wearing blue linen skirts and navy blazers. Mrs. Blackley glanced up from the bridge game as they went by the cardroom. She had been one of those opposed to their having lessons at the English Lawn Tennis Club, for reasons that were, to her, perfectly evident.

She said, loudly, "They'll have to be in white."

"End whayt, pray?" cried the governess, pointing her triangle nose.

"They can't go on the courts except in white. It is a private club. Entirely white."

"Whum do they all think they are?" the governess asked, prepared to stalk on. But the girls, with their newly cropped heads, and their vulnerable necks showing, caught the drift and refused to go.

"Whom indeed," said Georgina Blackley, fiddling with her bridge hand and looking happy.

"My wife's seamstress could run up white frocks for them in a minute," said Jack. Perhaps he did not dislike children all that much.

"Whom could," muttered Georgina.

But it turned out that the governess was not allowed to choose their clothes, and so Jack gave the children lessons at the hotel. For six weeks they trotted around the courts looking angelic in blue, or hopelessly foreign, depending upon who saw them. Of course they fell in love with Jack, offering him a passionate loyalty they had nowhere else to place. Netta watched the transfer of this gentle, anxious gift. After they departed, Jack was bad-tempered for several evenings and then never spoke of them again; they, needless to say, had been dragged from him weeping.

When this happened the Rosses had been married nearly five years. Being childless but still very loving, they had trouble deciding which of the two would be the child. Netta overheard "He's a darling, but she's a sergeant major and no mistake. And so *mean.*" She also heard "He's a lazy bastard. He bullies her. She's a fool." She searched her heart again about children. Was it Jack or had it been Netta who had first said no? The only child she had ever admired was Jack, and not as a child but as a fighter, defying her. She and Jack were not the sort to have animal children, and Jack's dotty mother would probably soon be child enough for any couple to handle. Jack still seemed to adopt, in a tribal sense of his, half the women who fell in love with him. The only woman who resisted adoption was Netta—still burned-out, still ardent, in a manner of speaking still fourteen. His mother had turned up meanwhile, getting down from a train wearing a sly air of enjoying her own jokes, just as she must have looked on the day of the April Fool. At first she was no great trouble, though she did complain about an ulcerated leg. After years of pretending, she at last had something real. Netta's policy of silence made Jack's mother confident. She began to make a mockery of his music: "All that money gone for nothing!" Or else, "The amount we wasted on schools! The hours he's thrown away with his nose in a book. All that reading—if at least it had got him somewhere." Netta noticed that he spent more time playing bridge and chatting to cronies in the bar now. She thought hard, and decided not to make it her business. His mother had once been pretty; perhaps he still saw her that way. She came of a ramshackle family with a usable past; she spoke of the Ashers and the Rosses as if she had known them when they were tinkers. English residents who had a low but solid barrier with Jack and Netta were fences-down with his mad mother: They seemed to take her at her own word when it was about herself. She began then to behave like a superior sort of guest, inviting large parties to her table for meals, ordering special wines and dishes at inconvenient hours, standing endless rounds of drinks in the bar.

Netta told herself, Jack wants it this way. It is his home too. She began to live a life apart, leaving Jack to his mother. She sat wearing her own mother's shawl, hunched over a new, modern adding machine, punching out accounts. "Funny couple," she heard now. She frowned, smiling in her mind; none of these people knew what bound them, or how tied they were. She had the habit of dodging out of her mother-in-law's parties by saying, "I've got such an awful lot to do." It made them laugh, because they thought this was Netta's term for slave-driving the servants. They thought the staff did the work, and that Netta counted the profits and was too busy with bookkeeping to keep an eye on Jack—who now, at twenty-six, was as attractive as he ever would be.

A woman named Iris Cordier was one of Jack's mother's new friends. Tall, loud, in winter dully pale, she reminded Netta of a blond penguin. Her voice moved between a squeak and a moo, and was a mark of the distinguished literary family to which her father belonged. Her mother, a Frenchwoman, had been in and out of nursing homes for years. The Cordiers haunted the Riviera, with Iris looking after her parents and watching their diets. Now she lived in a flat somewhere in Roquebrune with the survivor of the pair—the mother, Netta believed. Iris paused and glanced in the business room where Mr. Asher had signed the hundred-year lease. She was on her way to lunch—Jack's mother's guest, of course.

"I say, aren't you Miss Asher?"

"I was." Iris, like Dr. Blackley, was probably younger than she looked. Out of her own childhood Netta recalled a desperate adolescent Iris with middle-aged parents clamped like handcuffs on her life. "How is your mother?" Netta had been about to say "How is Mrs. Cordier?" but it sounded servile.

"I didn't know you knew her."

"I remember her well. Your father too. He was a nice person."

"And still is," said Iris, sharply. "He lives with me, and he always will. French daughters don't abandon their parents." No one had ever sounded more English to Netta. "And your father and mother?"

"Both dead now. I'm married to Jack Ross."

"Nobody told me," said Iris, in a way that made Netta think, Good Lord, Iris too? Jack could not possibly seem like a patriarchal figure where she was concerned; perhaps this time the game was reversed and Iris played at being tribal and maternal. The idea of Jack, or of any man, flinging himself on that iron bosom made Netta smile. As if startled, Iris covered her mouth. She seemed to be frightened of smiling back.

Oh, well, and what of it, Iris too, said Netta to herself, suddenly turning back to her accounts. As it happened, Netta was mistaken (as she never would have been with a bill). That day Jack was meeting Iris for the first time.

The upshot of these errors and encounters was an invitation to Roquebrune to visit Iris's father. Jack's mother was ruthlessly excluded, even though Iris probably owed her a return engagement because of the lunch. Netta supposed that Iris had decided one had to get past Netta to reach Jack—an inexactness if ever there was one. Or perhaps it was Netta Iris wanted. In that case the error became a farce. Netta had almost no knowledge of private houses. She looked around at something that did not much interest her, for she hated to leave her own home, and saw Iris's father, apparently too old and shaky to get out of his armchair. He smiled and he nodded, meanwhile stroking an aged cat. He said to Netta, "You resemble your mother. A sweet woman. Obliging and quiet. I used to tell her that I longed to live in her hotel and be looked after."

Not by me, thought Netta.

Iris's amber bracelets rattled as she pushed and pulled everyone through introductions. Jack and Netta had been asked to meet a young American Netta had often seen in her own bar, and a couple named Sandy and Sandra Braunsweg, who turned out to be Anglo-Swiss and twins. Iris's long arms were around them as she cried to Netta, "Don't you know these babies?" They were, like the Rosses, somewhere in their twenties. Jack looked on, blue-eyed, interested, smiling at everything new. Netta supposed that she was now seeing some of the rather hard-up snobbish— snobbish what? "Intelligum-hen-sia," she imagined Dr. Blackley supplying. Having arrived at a word, Netta was ready to go home; but they had only just arrived. The American turned to Netta. He looked bored, and astonished by it. He needs the word for "bored," she decided. Then he can go home, too. The Riviera was no place for Americans. They could not sit all day waiting for mail and the daily papers and for the clock to show a respectable drinking time. They made the best of things when they were caught with a house they'd been rash enough to rent unseen. Netta often had them then *en pension* for meals: A hotel dining room was one way of meeting people. They paid a fee to use the tennis courts, and they liked the bar. Netta would notice then how Jack picked up any accent within hearing.

Jack was now being attentive to the old man, Iris's father. Though this was none of Mr. Cordier's business, Jack said, "My wife and I are first cousins, as well as second cousins twice over."

"You don't look it."

Everyone began to speak at once, and it was a minute or two before Netta heard Jack again. This time he said, "We are from a family of great..." It was lost. What now? Great innkeepers? Worriers? Skinflints? Whatever it was, old Mr. Cordier kept nodding to show he approved.

"We don't see nearly enough of young men like you," he said.

"True!" said Iris loudly. "We live in a dreary world of ill women down here." Netta thought this hard on the American, on Mr. Cordier, and on the male Braunsweg twin, but none of them looked offended. "I've got no time for women," said Iris. She slapped down a glass of whiskey so that it splashed, and rapped on a table with her knuckles. "Shall I tell you why? Because women don't tick over. They just simply don't tick over." No one disputed this. Iris went on: Women were underinformed. One could have virile conversations only with men. Women were attached to the past through fear, whereas men had a fearless sense of history. "Men tick," she said, glaring at Jack.

"I am not attached to a past," said Netta, slowly. "The past holds no attractions." She was not used to general conversation. She thought that every word called for consideration and for an answer. "Nothing could be worse than the way we children were dressed. And our mothers—the hard waves of their hair, the white lips. I think of those pale profiles and I wonder if those women were ever young."

Poor Netta, who saw herself as profoundly English, spread consternation by being suddenly foreign and gassy. She talked the English of expatriate children, as if reading aloud. The twins looked shocked. But she had appealed to the American. He sat beside her on a scuffed velvet sofa. He was so large that she slid an inch or so in his direction when he sat down. He was Sandra Braunsweg's special friend: They had been in London together. He was trying to write.

"What do you mean?" said Netta. "Write what?"

"Well—a novel, to start," he said. His father had staked him to one year, then another. He mentioned all that Sandra had borne with, how she had actually kicked and punched him to keep him from being too American. He had embarrassed her to death in London by asking a waitress, "Miss, where's the toilet?"

Netta said, "Didn't you mind being corrected?"

"Oh, no. It was just friendly."

Jack meanwhile was listening to Sandra telling about her English forebears and her English education. "I had many years of undeniably excellent schooling," she said. "Mitten Todd."

"What's that?" said Jack.

"It's near Bristol. I met excellent girls from Italy, Spain. I took *him* there to visit," she said, generously including the American. "I said, 'Get a yellow necktie.' He went straight out and bought one. I wore a little Schiaparelli. Bought in Geneva but still a real ... A yellow jacket over a gray ... Well, we arrived at my excellent old school, and even though the day was drizzly I said, 'Put the top of the car back.' He did so at once, and then he understood. The interior of the car harmonized perfectly with the yellow and gray." The twins were orphaned. Iris was like a mother.

"When Mummy died we didn't know where to put all the Chippendale," said Sandra. "Iris took a lot of it."

Netta thought, She is so silly. How can he respond? The girl's dimples and freckles and soft little hands were nothing Netta could have ever described: She had never in her life thought a word like "pretty." People were beautiful or they were not. Her happiness had always been great enough to allow for despair. She knew that some people thought Jack was happy and she was not.

"And what made you marry your young cousin?" the old man boomed at Netta. Perhaps his background allowed him to ask impertinent questions; he must have been doing so nearly forever. He stroked his cat; he was confident. He was spokesman for a roomful of wondering people.

"Jack was a moody child and I promised his mother I would look after him," said Netta. In her hopelessly un-English way she believed she had said something funny.

At eleven o'clock the hotel car expected to fetch the Rosses was nowhere. They trudged home by moonlight. For the last hour of the evening Jack had been skewered on virile conversations, first with Iris, then with Sandra, to whom Netta had already given "Chippendale" as a private name. It proved that Iris was right about concentrating on men and their ticking—Jack even thought Sandra rather pretty.

"Prettier than me?" said Netta, without the faintest idea what she meant, but aware she had said something stupid.

"Not so attractive," said Jack. His slight limp returned straight out of childhood. *She* had caused his accident.

"But she's not always clear," said Netta. "Mitten Todd, for example."

"Who're you talking about?"

"Who are *you*?"

"Iris, of course."

As if they had suddenly quarreled they fell silent. In silence they entered their room and prepared for bed. Jack poured a whiskey, walked on the clothes he had dropped, carried his drink to the bathroom. Through the half-shut door he called suddenly, "Why did you say that asinine thing about promising to look after me?"

"It seemed so unlikely, I thought they'd laugh." She had a glimpse of herself in the mirrors picking up his shed clothes.

He said, "Well, is it true?"

She was quiet for such a long time that he came to see if she was still in the room. She said, "No, your mother never said that or anything like it."

"We shouldn't have gone to Roquebrune," said Jack. "I think those bloody people are going to be a nuisance. Iris wants her father to stay here, with the cat, while she goes to England for a month. How do we get out of that?"

"By saying no."

"I'm rotten at no."

"I told you not to be too pally with women," she said, as a joke again, but jokes were her way of having floods of tears.

Before this had a chance to heal, Iris's father moved in, bringing his cat in a basket. He looked at his room and said, "Medium large." He looked at his bed and said, "Reasonably long." He was, in short, daft about measurements. When he took books out of the reading room, he was apt to return them with "This volume contains about 70,000 words" written inside the back cover.

Netta had not wanted Iris's father, but Jack had said yes to it. She had not wanted the sick cat, but Jack had said yes to that too. The old man, who was lost without Iris, lived for his meals. He would appear at the shut doors of the dining room an hour too early, waiting for the menu to be typed and posted. In a voice that matched Iris's for carrying power, he read aloud, alone: "Consommé. Good Lord, again? Is there a choice between the fish and the cutlet? I can't possibly eat all of that. A bit of salad and a boiled egg. That's all I could possibly want." That was rubbish, because Mr. Cordier ate the menu and more, and if there were two puddings, or a pudding and ice cream, he ate both and asked for pastry, fruit, and cheese to follow. One day, after Dr. Blackley had attended him for faintness, Netta passed a message on to Iris, who had been back from England for a fortnight now but seemed in no hurry to take her father away.

"Keith Blackley thinks your father should go on a diet."

"He can't," said Iris. "Our other doctor says dieting causes cancer."

"You can't have heard that properly," Netta said.

"It is like those silly people who smoke to keep their figures," said Iris. "Dieting."

"Blackley hasn't said he should smoke, just that he should eat less of everything."

"My father has never smoked in his life," Iris cried. "As for his diet, I weighed his food out for years. He's not here forever. I'll take him back as soon as he's had enough of hotels."

He stayed for a long time, and the cat did too, and a nuisance they both were to the servants. When the cat was too ailing to walk, the old man carried it to a path behind the tennis courts and put it down on the gravel to die. Netta came out with the old man's tea on a tray (not done for everyone, but having him out of the way was a relief) and she saw the cat lying on its side, eyes wide, as if profoundly thinking. She saw unlicked dirt on its coat and ants exploring its paws. The old man sat in a garden chair, wearing a panama hat, his hands clasped on a stick. He called, "Oh, Netta, take her away. I am too old to watch anything die. I know what she'll do," he said, indifferently, his voice falling as she came near. "Oh, I know that. Turn on her back and give a shriek. I've heard it often."

Netta disburdened her tray onto a garden table and pulled the tray cloth under the cat. She was angered at the haste and indecency of the ants. "It would be polite to leave her," she said. "She doesn't want to be watched."

"I always sit here," said the old man.

Jack, making for the courts with Chippendale, looked as if the sight of the two conversing amused him. Then he understood and scooped up the cat and tray cloth and went away with the cat over his shoulder. He laid it in the shade of a Judas tree, and within an hour it was dead. Iris's father said, "I've got no one to talk to here. That's my trouble. That shroud was too small for my poor Polly. Ask my daughter to fetch me."

Jack's mother said that night, "I'm sure you wish that I had a devoted daughter to take me away too." Because of the attention given the cat she seemed to feel she had not been nuisance enough. She had taken to saying, "My leg is dying before I am," and imploring Jack to preserve her leg, should it be amputated, and make certain it was buried with her. She wanted Jack to be close by at nearly any hour now, so that she could lean on him. After sitting for hours at bridge she had trouble climbing two flights of stairs; nothing would induce her to use the lift.

"Nothing ever came of your music," she would say, leaning on him. "Of course, you have a wife to distract you now. I needed a daughter. Every woman does." Netta managed to trap her alone, and forced her to sit while she stood over her. Netta said, "Look, Aunt Vera, I forbid you, I absolutely forbid you, do you hear, to make a nurse of Jack, and I shall strangle you with my own hands if you go on saying nothing came of his music. You are not to say it in my hearing or out of it. Is that plain?"

Jack's mother got up to her room without assistance. About an hour later the gardener found her on a soft bed of wallflowers. "An inch to the left and she'd have landed on a rake," he said to Netta. She was still alive when Netta knelt down. In her fall she had crushed the plants, the yellow minted *giroflées de Nice*. Netta thought that she was now, at last, for the first time, inhaling one of the smells of death. Her aunt's arms and legs were turned and twisted; her skirt was pulled so that her swollen leg showed. It seemed that she had jumped carrying her walking stick—it lay across the path. She often slept in an armchair, afternoons, with one eye slightly open. She opened that eye now and, seeing she had Netta, said, "My son." Netta was thinking, I have never known her. And if I knew her, then it was Jack or myself I could not understand. Netta was afraid of giving orders, and of telling people not to touch her aunt before Dr. Blackley could be summoned, because she knew that she had always been mistaken. Now Jack was there, propping his mother up, brushing leaves and earth out of her hair. Her head dropped on his shoulder. Netta thought from the sudden heaviness that her aunt had died, but she sighed and opened that one eye again, saying this time, "Doctor?" Netta left everyone doing the wrong things to her dying—no, her murdered—aunt. She said quite calmly into a telephone, "I am afraid that my aunt must have jumped or fallen from the second floor."

Jack found a letter on his mother's night table that began, "Why blame Netta? I forgive." At dawn he and Netta sat at a card table with yesterday's cigarettes still not cleaned out of the ashtray, and he did not ask what Netta had said or done that called for forgiveness. They kept pushing the letter back and forth. He would read it and then Netta would. It seemed natural for them to be silent. Jack had sat beside his mother for much of the night. Each of them then went to sleep for an hour, apart, in one of the empty rooms, just as they had done in the old days when their parents were juggling beds and guests and double and single quarters. By the time the doctor returned for his second visit Jack was neatly dressed and seemed wide awake. He sat in the bar drinking black coffee and reading a travel book of Evelyn Waugh's called *Labels*. Netta, who looked far more untidy and underslept, wondered if Jack wished he might leave now, and sail from Monte Carlo on the *Stella Polaris*.

Dr. Blackley said, "Well, you are a dim pair. She is not in pu-hain, you know." Netta supposed this was the roundabout way doctors have of announcing death, very like "Her sufferings have ended." But Jack, looking hard at the doctor, had heard another meaning. "Jumped or fell," said Dr. Blackley. "She neither fell nor jumped. She is up there enjoying a damned good thu-hing."

Netta went out and through the lounge and up the marble steps. She sat down in the shaded room on the chair where Jack had spent most of the night. Her aunt did not look like anyone Netta knew, not even like Jack. She stared at the alien face and said, "Aunt Vera, Keith Blackley says there is nothing really the matter. You must have made a mistake. Perhaps you fainted on the path, overcome by the scent of wallflowers. What would you like me to tell Jack?"

Jack's mother turned on her side and slowly, tenderly, raised herself on an elbow. "Well, Netta," she said, "I daresay the fool is right. But as I've been given quite a lot of sleeping stuff, I'd as soon stay here for now."

Netta said, "Are you hungry?"

"I should very much like a ham sandwich on English bread, and about that much gin with a lump of ice."

She began coming down for meals a few days later. They knew she had crept down the stairs and flung her walking stick over the path and let herself fall hard on a bed of wallflowers—had even plucked her skirt up for a bit of accuracy; but she was also someone returned from beyond the limits, from the other side of the wall. Once she said, "It was like diving and suddenly realizing there was no water in the sea." Again, "It is not true that your life rushes before your eyes. You can see the flowers floating up to you. Even a short fall takes a long time."

Everyone was deeply changed by this incident. The effect on the victim herself was that she got religion hard.

"We are all hopeless nonbelievers!" shouted Iris, drinking in the bar one afternoon. "At least, I hope we are. But when I see you, Vera, I feel there might be something in religion. You look positively temperate."

"I am allowed to love God, I hope," said Jack's mother.

Jack never saw or heard his mother anymore. He leaned against the bar, reading. It was his favorite place. Even on the sunniest of afternoons he read by the red-shaded light. Netta was present only because she had supplies to check. Knowing she ought to keep out of this, she still said, "Religion is more than love. It is supposed to tell you why you exist and what you are expected to do about it."

"You have no religious feelings at all?" This was the only serious and almost the only friendly question Iris was ever to ask Netta.

"None," said Netta. "I'm running a business."

"I love God as Jack used to love music," said his mother. "At least he said he did when we were paying for lessons."

"Adam and Eve had God," said Netta. "They had nobody *but* God. A fat lot of good that did them." This was as far as their dialectic went. Jack had not moved once except to turn pages. He read steadily but cautiously now, as if every author had a design on him. That was one effect of his mother's incident. The other was that he gave up bridge and went back to playing the clarinet. Iris hammered out an accompaniment on the upright piano in the old music room, mostly used for listening to radio broadcasts. She was the only person Netta had ever heard who could make Mozart sound like an Irish jig. Presently Iris began to say that it was time Jack gave a concert. Before this could turn into a crisis Iris changed her mind and said what he wanted was a holiday. Netta thought he needed something: He seemed to be exhausted by love, friendship, by being a husband, someone's son, by trying to make a world out of reading and sense out of life. A visit to England to meet some stimulating people, said Iris. To help Iris with her tiresome father during the journey. To visit art galleries and bookshops and go to concerts. To meet people. To talk.

This was a hot, troubled season, and many persons were planning journeys—not to meet other people but for fear of a war. The hotel had emptied out by the end of March. Netta, whose father had known there would never be another catastrophe, had her workmen come in, as usual. She could hear the radiators being drained and got ready for painting as she packed Jack's clothes. They had never been separated before. They kept telling each other that it was only for a short holiday—for three or four weeks. She was surprised at how neat marriage was, at how many years and feelings could be folded and put under a lid. Once, she went to the window so that he would not see her tears and think she was trying to blackmail him. Looking out, she noticed the American, Chippendale's lover, idly knocking a tennis ball against the garage, as Jack had done in the early summers of their life; he had come round to the hotel looking for a partner, but that season there were none. She suddenly knew to a certainty that if Jack were to die she would search the crowd of mourners for a man she could live with. She would not return from the funeral alone.

Grief and memory, yes, she said to herself, but what about three o'clock in the morning?

By June nearly everyone Netta knew had vanished, or, like the Blackleys, had started to pack. Netta had new tablecloths made, and ordered new white awnings, and two dozen rosebushes from the nursery at Cap Ferrat. The American came over every day and followed her from room to room, talking. He had nothing better to do. The Swiss twins were in England. His father, who had been backing his writing career until now, had suddenly changed his mind about it—now, when he needed money to get out of Europe. He had projects for living on his own, but they required a dose of funds. He wanted to open a restaurant on the Riviera where nothing but chicken pie would be served. Or else a vast and expensive café where people would pay to make their own sandwiches. He said that he was seeing the food of the future, but all that Netta could see was customers asking for their money back. He trapped her behind the bar and said he loved her; Netta made other women look like stuffed dolls. He could still remember the shock of meeting her, the attraction, the brilliant answer she had made to Iris about attachments to the past.

Netta let him rave until he asked for a loan. She laughed and wondered if it was for the chicken-pie restaurant. No—he wanted to get on a boat sailing from Cannes. She said, quite cheerfully, "I can't be Venus and Barclays Bank. You have to choose."

He said, "Can't Venus ever turn up with a letter of credit?"

She shook her head. "Not a hope."

But when it was July and Jack hadn't come back, he cornered her again. Money wasn't in it now: His father had not only relented but had virtually ordered him home. He was about twenty-two, she guessed. He could still plead successfully for parental help and for indulgence from women. She said, no more than affectionately, "I'm going to show you a very pretty room."

A few days later Dr. Blackley came alone to say good-bye.

"Are you really staying?" he asked.

"I am responsible for the last eighty-one years of this lease," said Netta. "I'm going to be thirty. It's a long tenure. Besides, I've got Jack's mother and she won't leave. Jack has a chance now to visit America. It doesn't sound sensible to me, but she writes

encouraging him. She imagines him suddenly very rich and sending for her. I've discovered the limit of what you can feel about
people. I've discovered something else," she said abruptly. "It is
that sex and love have nothing in common. Only a coincidence,
sometimes. You think the coincidence will go on and so you get
married. I suppose that is what men are born knowing and
women learn by accident."

"I'm su-horry."

"For God's sake, don't be. It's a relief."

She had no feeling of guilt, only of amazement. Jack, as a memory, was in a restricted area—the tennis courts, the cardroom, the
bar. She saw him at bridge with Mrs. Blackley and pouring drinks
for temporary friends. He crossed the lounge jauntily with a cluster of little dark-haired girls wearing blue. In the mirrored bedroom there was only Netta. Her dreams were cleansed of him.
The looking glasses still held their blue-and-silver-water shadows, but they lost the habit of giving back the moods and gestures
of a Moslem wife.

About five years after this, Netta wrote to Jack. The war had
caught him in America, during the voyage his mother had so
wanted him to have. His limp had kept him out of the Army. As
his mother (now dead) might have put it, all that reading had finally got him somewhere: He had spent the last years putting out
a two-pager on aspects of European culture—part of a scrupulous
effort Britain was making for the West. That was nearly all Netta
knew. A Belgian Red Cross official had arrived, apparently in
Jack's name, to see if she was still alive. She sat in her father's
business room, wearing a coat and a shawl because there was no
way of heating any part of the hotel now, and she tried to get on
with the letter she had been writing in her head, on and off, for
many years.

"In June, 1940, we were evacuated," she started, for the tenth
or eleventh time. "I was back by October. Italians had taken over
the hotel. They used the mirror behind the bar for target practice.
Oddly enough it was not smashed. It is covered with spider-
webs, and the bullet hole is the spider. I had great trouble over

Aunt Vera, who disappeared and was found finally in one of the attic rooms.

"The Italians made a pet of her. Took her picture. She enjoyed that. Everyone who became thin had a desire to be photographed, as if knowing they would use this intimidating evidence against those loved ones who had missed being starved. Guilt for life. After an initial period of hardship, during which she often had her picture taken at her request, the Italians brought food and looked after her, more than anyone. She was their mama. We were annexed territory and in time we had the same food as the Italians. The thin pictures of your mother are here on my desk.

"She buried her British passport and would never say where. Perhaps under the Judas tree with Mr. Cordier's cat, Polly. She remained just as mad and just as spoiled, and that became dangerous when life stopped being ordinary. She complained about me to the Italians. At that time a complaint was a matter of prison and of death if it was made to the wrong person. Luckily for me, there was also the right person to take the message.

"A couple of years after that, the Germans and certain French took over and the Italians were shut up in another hotel without food or water, and some people risked their well-being to take water to them (for not everyone preferred the new situation, you can believe me). When she was dying I asked her if she had a message for one Italian officer who had made such a pet of her and she said, 'No, why?' She died without a word for anybody. She was buried as 'Rossini,' because the Italians had changed people's names. She had said she was French, a Frenchwoman named Ross, and so some peculiar civil status was created for us—the two Mrs. Rossinis.

"The records were topsy-turvy; it would have meant going to the Germans and explaining my dead aunt was British, and of course I thought I would not. The death certificate and permission to bury are for a Vera Rossini. I have them here on my desk for you with her pictures.

"You are probably wondering where I have found all this writing paper. The Germans left it behind. When we were being shelled I took what few books were left in the reading room down to what used to be the wine cellar and read by candlelight. You are probably wondering where the candles came from. A long story. I even have paint for the radiators, large buckets that have never been opened.

"I live in one room, my mother's old sitting room. The business room can be used but the files have gone. When the Italians were here your mother was their mother, but I was not their Moslem wife, although I still had respect for men. One yelled '*Luce*, *luce*,' because your mother was showing a light. She said, 'Bugger you, you little toad.' He said, 'Granny, I said "*luce*," not "*Duce*." '

"Not long ago we crept out of our shelled homes, looking like cave dwellers. When you see the hotel again, it will be functioning. I shall have painted the radiators. Long shoots of bramble come in through the cardroom windows. There are drifts of leaves in the old music room and I saw scorpions and heard their rustling like the rustle of death. Everything that could have been looted has gone. Sheets, bedding, mattresses. The neighbors did quite a lot of that. At the risk of their lives. When the Italians were here we had rice and oil. Your mother, who was crazy, used to put out grains to feed the mice.

"When the Germans came we had to live under Vichy law, which meant each region lived on what it could produce. As ours produces nothing, we got quite thin again. Aunt Vera died plump. Do you know what it means when I say she used to complain about me?

"Send me some books. As long as they are in English. I am quite sick of the three other languages in which I've heard so many threats, such boasting, such a lot of lying.

"For a time I thought people would like to know how the Italians left and the Germans came in. It was like this: They came in with the first car moving slowly, flying the French flag. The highest-ranking French official in the region. Not a German. No, just a chap getting his job back. The Belgian Red Cross people were completely uninterested and warned me that no one would ever want to hear.

"I suppose that you already have the fiction of all this. The fiction must be different, oh very different, from Italians sobbing with homesickness in the night. The Germans were not real, they were specially got up for the events of the time. Sat in the white dining room, eating with whatever plates and spoons were not broken or looted, ate soups that were mostly water, were forbidden to complain. Only in retreat did they develop faces and I noticed then that some were terrified and many were old. A radio broadcast from some untouched area advised the local population not to attack them as they retreated, it would make wild animals of them. But they were attacked by some young boys shooting out of a window and eight hostages were taken, including the son of the man who cut the maharaja's daughters' black hair, and they were shot and left along the wall of a café on the more or less Italian side of the border. And the man who owned the café was killed too, but later, by civilians—he had given names to the Gestapo once, or perhaps it was something else. He got on the wrong side of the right side at the wrong time, and he was thrown down the deep gorge between the two frontiers.

"Up in one of the hill villages Germans stayed till no one was alive. I was at that time in the former wine cellar, reading books by candlelight.

"The Belgian Red Cross team found the skeleton of a German deserter in a cave and took back the helmet and skull to Knokke-le-Zoute as souvenirs.

"My war has ended. Our family held together almost from the Napoleonic adventures. It is shattered now. Sentiment does not keep families whole—only mutual pride and mutual money."

This true story sounded so implausible that she decided never to send it. She wrote a sensible letter asking for sugar and rice and for new books; nothing must be older than 1940.

Jack answered at once: There were no new authors (he had been asking people). Sugar was unobtainable, and there were queues for rice. Shoes had been rationed. There were no women's stockings but lisle, and the famous American legs looked terrible. You could not find butter or meat or tinned pineapple. In restaurants, instead of butter you were given miniature golf balls of cream cheese. He supposed that all this must sound like small beer to Netta.

A notice arrived that a CARE package awaited her at the post office. It meant that Jack had added his name and his money to a mailing list. She refused to sign for it; then she changed her mind and discovered it was not from Jack but from the American she had once taken to such a pretty room. Jack did send rice and sugar and delicious coffee but he forgot about books. His letters followed; sometimes three arrived in a morning. She left them sealed for days. When she sat down to answer, all she could remember were implausible things.

Iris came back. She was the first. She had grown puffy in England—the result of drinking whatever alcohol she could get her hands on and grimly eating her sweets allowance: There would be that much less gin and chocolate for the Germans if ever they landed. She put her now wide bottom on a comfortable armchair—one of the few chairs the first wave of Italians had not burned with cigarettes or idly hacked at with daggers—and said Jack had been living with a woman in America and to spare the gossip had let her be known as his wife. Another Mrs. Ross? When Netta discovered it was dimpled Chippendale, she laughed aloud.

"I've seen them," said Iris. "I mean I saw them together. King Charles and a spaniel. Jack wiped his feet on her."

Netta's feelings were of lightness, relief. She would not have to tell Jack about the partisans hanging by the neck in the arches of the Place Masséna at Nice. When Iris had finished talking, Netta said, "What about his music?"

"I don't know."

"How can you not know something so important?"

"Jack had a good chance at things, but he made a mess of everything," said Iris. "My father is still living. Life really is too incredible for some of us."

A dark girl of about twenty turned up soon after. Her costume, a gray dress buttoned to the neck, gave her the appearance of being in uniform. She unzipped a military-looking bag and cried, in an unplaceable accent, "*Ha*llo, *ha*llo, Mrs. Ross? A few small gifts for you," and unpacked a bottle of Haig, four tins of corned beef, a jar of honey, and six pairs of American nylon stockings, which Netta had never seen before, and were as good to have under a mattress as gold. Netta looked up at the tall girl.

"Remember? I was the middle sister. With," she said gravely, "the typical middle-sister problems." She scarcely recalled Jack, her beloved. The memory of Netta had grown up with her. "I remember you laughing," she said, without loving that memory. She was a severe, tragic girl. "You were the first adult I ever heard laughing. At night in bed I could hear it from your balcony. You sat smoking with, I suppose, your handsome husband. I used to laugh just to hear you."

She had married an Iranian journalist. He had discovered that political prisoners in the United States were working under lamentable conditions in tin mines. President Truman had sent them there. People from all over the world planned to unite to get them out. The girl said she had been to Germany and to Austria, she had visited camps, they were all alike, and that was already the past, and the future was the prisoners in the tin mines.

Netta said, "In what part of the country are these mines?"

The middle sister looked at her sadly and said, "Is there more than one part?"

For the first time in years, Netta could see Jack clearly. They were silently sharing a joke; he had caught it too. She and the girl lunched in a corner of the battered dining room. The tables were scarred with initials. There were no tablecloths. One of the great-uncle's paintings still hung on a wall. It showed the Quai Laurenti, a country road alongside the sea. Netta, who had no use for the past, was discovering a past she could regret. Out of a dark, gentle silence—silence imposed by the impossibility of telling anything real—she counted the cracks in the walls. When silence failed she heard power saws ripping into olive trees and a lemon grove. With a sense of deliverance she understood that soon there would be nothing left to spoil. Her great-uncle's picture, which ought to have changed out of sympathetic magic, remained faithful. She regretted everything now, even the three anxious little girls in blue linen. Every calamitous season between then and now seemed to descend directly from Georgina Blackley's having said "white" just to keep three children in their place. Clad in buttoned-up gray, the middle sister now picked at corned beef and said she had hated her father, her mother, her sisters, and most of all the Dutch governess.

"Where is she now?" said Netta.

"Dead, I hope." This was from someone who had visited camps. Netta sat listening, her cheek on her hand. Death made death casual: she had always known. Neither the vanquished in their flight nor the victors returning to pick over rubble seemed half so vindictive as a tragic girl who had disliked her governess.

Dr. Blackley came back looking positively cheerful. In those days men still liked soldiering. It made them feel young, if they needed to feel it, and it got them away from home. War made the break few men could make on their own. The doctor looked years younger, too, and very fit. His wife was not with him. She had survived everything, and the hardships she had undergone had completely restored her to health—which had made it easy for her husband to leave her. Actually, he had never gone back, except to wind up the matter.

"There are things about Georgina I respect and admire," he said, as husbands will say from a distance. His war had been in Malta. He had come here, as soon as he could, to the shelled, gnawed, tarnished coast (as if he had not seen enough at Malta) to ask Netta to divorce Jack and to marry him, or live with him— anything she wanted, on any terms.

But she wanted nothing—at least, not from him.

"Well, one can't defeat a memory," he said. "I always thought it was mostly su-hex between the two of you."

"So it was," said Netta. "So far as I remember."

"Everyone noticed. You would vanish at odd hours. Dishuppear."

"Yes, we did."

"You can't live on memories," he objected. "Though I respect you for being faithful, of course."

"What you are talking about is something of which one has no specific memory," said Netta. "Only of seasons. Places. Rooms. It is as abstract to remember as to read about. That is why it is boring in talk except as a joke, and boring in books except for poetry."

"You never read poetry."

"I do now."

"I guessed that," he said.

"That lack of memory is why people are unfaithful, as it is so curiously called. When I see closed shutters I know there are lovers behind them. That is how the memory works. The rest is just convention and small talk."

"Why lovers? Why not someone sleeping off the wine he had for lunch?"

"No. Lovers."

"A middle-aged man cutting his toenails in the bathtub," he said with unexpected feeling. "Wearing bifocal lenses so that he can see his own feet."

"No, lovers. Always."

He said, "Have you missed him?"

"Missed who?"

"Who the bloody hell are we talking about?"

"The Italian commander billeted here. He was not a guest. He was here by force. I was not breaking a rule. Without him I'd have perished in every way. He may be home with his wife now. Or in that fortress near Turin where he sent other men. Or dead." She looked at the doctor and said, "Well, what would you like me to do? Sit here and cry?"

"I can't imagine you with a brute."

"I never said that."

"Do you miss him still?"

"The absence of Jack was like a cancer which I am sure has taken root, and of which I am bound to die," said Netta.

"You'll bu-hury us all," he said, as doctors tell the condemned.

"I haven't said I won't." She rose suddenly and straightened her skirt, as she used to do when hotel guests became pally. "Conversation over," it meant.

"Don't be too hard on Jack," he said.

"I am hard on myself," she replied.

After he had gone he sent her a parcel of books, printed on grayish paper, in warped wartime covers. All of the titles were, to Netta, unknown. There was *Fireman Flower* and *The Horse's Mouth* and *Four Quartets* and *The Stuff to Give the Troops* and *Better Than a Kick in the Pants* and *Put Out More Flags*. A note added that the next package would contain Henry Green and

Dylan Thomas. She guessed he would not want to be thanked, but she did so anyway. At the end of her letter was "Please remember, if you mind too much, that I said no to you once before." Leaning on the bar, exactly as Jack used to, with a glass of the middle sister's drink at hand, she opened *Better Than a Kick in the Pants* and read, ". . . two Fascists came in, one of them tall and thin and tough looking; the other smaller, with only one arm and an empty sleeve pinned up to his shoulder. Both of them were quite young and wore black shirts."

Oh, thought Netta, I am the only one who knows all this. No one will ever realize how much I know of the truth, the truth, the truth, and she put her head on her hands, her elbows on the scarred bar, and let the first tears of her after-war run down her wrists.

The last to return was the one who should have been first. Jack wrote that he was coming down from the north as far as Nice by bus. It was a common way of traveling and much cheaper than by train. Netta guessed that he was mildly hard up and that he had saved nothing from his war job. The bus came in at six, at the foot of the Place Masséna. There was a deep blue late-afternoon sky and pale sunlight. She could hear birds from the public gardens nearby. The Place was as she had always seen it, like an elegant drawing room with a blue ceiling. It was nearly empty. Jack looked out on this sunlighted, handsome space and said, "Well, I'll just leave my stuff at the bus office, for the moment"— perhaps noticing that Netta had not invited him anywhere. He placed his ticket on the counter, and she saw that he had not come from far away: he must have been moving south by stages. He carried an aura of London pub life; he had been in London for weeks.

A frowning man hurrying to wind things up so he could have his first drink of the evening said, "The office is closing and we don't keep baggage here."

"People used to be nice," Jack said.

"Bus people?"

"Just people."

She was hit by the sharp change in his accent. As for the way of speaking, which is something else again, he was like the heir to great estates back home after a Grand Tour. Perhaps the estates had run down in his absence. She slipped the frowning man a thousand francs, a new pastel-tinted bill, on which the face of a calm girl glowed like an opal. She said, "We shan't be long."

She set off over the Place, walking diagonally—Jack beside her, of course. He did not ask where they were headed, though he did make her smile by saying, "Did you bring a car?" expecting one of the hotel cars to be parked nearby, perhaps with a driver to open the door; perhaps with cold chicken and wine in a hamper, too. He said, "I'd forgotten about having to tip for every little thing." He did not question his destination, which was no farther than a café at the far end of the square. What she felt at that instant was intense revulsion. She thought, I don't want him, and pushed away some invisible flying thing—a bat or a blown paper. He looked at her with surprise. He must have been wondering if hardship had taught Netta to talk in her mind.

This is it, the freedom he was always offering me, she said to herself, smiling up at the beautiful sky.

They moved slowly along the nearly empty square, pausing only when some worn-out Peugeot or an old bicycle, finding no other target, made a swing in their direction. Safely on the pavement, they walked under the arches where partisans had been hanged. It seemed to Netta the bodies had been taken down only a day or so before. Jack, who knew about this way of dying from hearsay, chose a café table nearly under a poor lad's bound, dangling feet.

"I had a woman next to me on the bus who kept a hedgehog all winter in a basketful of shavings," he said. "He can drink milk out of a wineglass." He hesitated. "I'm sorry about the books you asked for. I was sick of books by then. I was sick of rhetoric and culture and patriotic crap."

"I suppose it is all very different over there," said Netta.

"God, yes."

He seemed to expect her to ask questions, so she said, "What kind of clothes do they wear?"

"They wear quite a lot of plaids and tartans. They eat at peculiar hours. You'll see them eating strawberries and cream just when you're thinking of having a drink."

She said, "Did you visit the tin mines, where Truman sends his political prisoners?"

"*Tin* mines?" said Jack. "No."

"Remember the three little girls from the maharaja trade?"

Neither could quite hear what the other had to say. They were partially deaf to each other.

Netta continued softly, "Now, as I understand it, she first brought an American to London, and then she took an Englishman to America."

He had too much the habit of women, he was playing too close a game, to waste points saying, "Who? What?"

"It was over as fast as it started," he said. "But then the war came and we were stuck. She became a friend," he said. "I'm quite fond of her"—which Netta translated as, "It is a subterranean river that may yet come to light." "You wouldn't know her," he said. "She's very different now. I talked so much about the south, down here, she finally found some land going dirt cheap at Bandol. The mayor arranged for her to have an orchard next to her property, so she won't have neighbors. It hardly cost her anything. He said to her, 'You're very pretty.'"

"No one ever had a bargain in property because of a pretty face," said Netta.

"Wasn't it lucky," said Jack. He could no longer hear himself, let alone Netta. "The war was unsettling, being in America. She minded not being active. Actually she was using the Swiss passport, which made it worse. Her brother was killed over Bremen. She needs security now. In a way it was sorcerer and apprentice between us, and she suddenly grew up. She'll be better off with a roof over her head. She writes a little now. Her poetry isn't bad," he said, as if Netta had challenged its quality.

"Is she at Bandol now, writing poetry?"

"Well, no." He laughed suddenly. "There isn't a roof yet. And, you know, people don't sit writing that way. They just think they're going to."

"Who has replaced you?" said Netta. "Another sorcerer?"

"Oh, *he* . . . he looks like George the Second in a strong light. Or like Queen Anne. Queen Anne and Lady Mary, somebody called them." Iris, that must have been. Queen Anne and Lady Mary

wasn't bad—better than King Charles and his spaniel. She was beginning to enjoy his story. He saw it, and said lightly, "I was too
preoccupied with you to manage another life. I couldn't see myself going on and on away from you. I didn't want to grow middle-
aged at odds with myself."

But he had lost her; she was enjoying a reverie about Jack
now, wearing one of those purple sunburns people acquire at golf.
She saw him driving an open car, with large soft freckles on his
purple skull. She saw his mistress's dog on the front seat and the
dog's ears flying like pennants. The revulsion she felt did not lend
distance but brought a dreamy reality closer still. He must be
thirty-four now, she said to herself. A terrible age for a man who
has never imagined thirty-four.

"Well, perhaps you have made a mess of it," she said, quoting Iris.

"What mess? I'm here. *He*—"

"Queen Anne?"

"Yes, well, actually Gerald is his name; he wears nothing but
brown. Brown suit, brown tie, brown shoes. I said, '*He* can't go to
Mitten Todd. He won't match.' "

"Harmonize," she said.

"That's it. Harmonize with the—"

"What about Gerald's wife? I'm sure he has one."

"Lucretia."

"No, really?"

"On my honor. When I last saw them they were all together,
talking."

Netta was remembering what the middle sister had said about
laughter on the balcony. She couldn't look at him. The merest
crossing of glances made her start laughing rather wildly into her
hands. The hysterical quality of her own laughter caught her in
midair. What were they talking about? He hitched his chair
nearer and dared to take her wrist.

"Tell me, now," he said, as if they were to be two old confidence men getting their stories straight. "What about you? Was
there ever..." The glaze of laughter had not left his face and
voice. She saw that he would make her his business, if she let
him. Pulling back, she felt another clasp, through a wall of fog.

She groped for this other, invisible hand, but it dissolved. It was a lost, indifferent hand; it no longer recognized her warmth. She understood: He is dead . . . Jack, closed to ghosts, deaf to their voices, was spared this. He would be spared everything, she saw. She envied him his imperviousness, his true unhysterical laughter.

Perhaps that's why I kicked him, she said. I was always jealous. Not of women. Of his short memory, his comfortable imagination. And I am going to be thirty-seven and I have a dark, an accurate, a deadly memory.

He still held her wrist and turned it another way, saying, "Look, there's paint on it."

"Oh, God, where is the waiter?" she cried, as if that were the one important thing. Jack looked his age, exactly. She looked like a burned-out child who had been told a ghost story. Desperately seeking the waiter, she turned to the café behind them and saw the last light of the long afternoon strike the mirror above the bar—a flash in a tunnel; hands juggling with fire. That unexpected play, at a remove, borne indoors, displayed to anyone who could stare without blinking, was a complete story. It was the brightness on the looking glass, the only part of a life, or a love, or a promise, that could never be concealed, changed, or corrupted.

Not a hope, she was trying to tell him. He could read her face now. She reminded herself, If I say it, I am free. I can finish painting the radiators in peace. I can read every book in the world. If I had relied on my memory for guidance, I would never have crept out of the wine cellar. Memory is what ought to prevent you from buying a dog after the first dog dies, but it never does. It should at least keep you from saying yes twice to the same person.

"I've always loved you," he chose to announce—it really was an announcement, in a new voice that stated nothing except facts.

The dark, the ghosts, the candlelight, her tears on the scarred bar—*they* were real. And still, whether she wanted to see it or not, the light of imagination danced all over the square. She did not dare to turn again to the mirror, lest she confuse the two and forget which light was real. A pure white awning on a cross street seemed to her to be of indestructible beauty. The window it sheltered was hollowed with sadness and shadow. She said with the same deep sadness, "I believe you." The wave of revulsion receded, sucked back under another wave—a powerful adolescent craving for something simple, such as true love.

Her face did not show this. It was set in adolescent stubbornness, and this was one of their old, secret meetings when, sullen and hurt, she had to be coaxed into life as Jack wanted it lived. It was the same voyage, at the same rate of speed. The Place seemed to her to be full of invisible traffic—first a whisper of tires, then a faint, high screeching, then a steady roar. If Jack heard anything, it could be only the blood in the veins and his loud, happy thought. To a practical romantic like Jack, dying to get Netta to bed right away, what she was hearing was only the uh-hebb and flo-ho of hormones, as Dr. Blackley said. She caught a look of amazement on his face: *Now* he knew what he had been deprived of. *Now* he remembered. It had been Netta, all along.

Their evening shadows accompanied them over the long square. "I still have a car," she remarked. "But no petrol. There's a train." She did keep on hearing a noise, as of heavy traffic rushing near and tearing away. Her own quiet voice carried across it, saying, "Not a hope." He must have heard that. Why, it was as loud as a shout. He held her arm lightly. He was as buoyant as morning. This *was* his morning—the first light on the mirror, the first cigarette. He pulled her into an archway where no one could see. What could I do, she asked her ghosts, but let my arm be held, my steps be guided?

Later, Jack said that the walk with Netta back across the Place Masséna was the happiest event of his life. Having no reliable counter-event to put in its place, she let the memory stand.

FROM THE FIFTEENTH DISTRICT

ALTHOUGH an epidemic of haunting, widely reported, spread through the Fifteenth District of our city last summer, only three acceptable complaints were lodged with the police.

Major Emery Travella, 31st Infantry, 1914-18, Order of the Leopard, Military Beech Leaf, Cross of St. Lambert First Class, killed while defusing a bomb in a civilian area 9 June, 1941, Medal of Danzig (posthumous), claims he is haunted by the entire congregation of St. Michael and All Angels on Bartholomew Street. Every year on the Sunday falling nearest the anniversary of his death, Major Travella attends Holy Communion service at St. Michael's, the church from which he was buried. He stands at the back, close to the doors, waiting until all the communicants have returned to their places, before he approaches the altar rail. His intention is to avoid a mixed queue of dead and living, the thought of which is disgusting to him. The congregation sits, hushed and expectant, straining to hear the Major's footsteps (he drags one foot a little). After receiving the Host, the Major leaves at once, without waiting for the Blessing. For the past several years, the Major has noticed that the congregation doubles in size as 9 June approaches. Some of these strangers bring cameras and tape recorders with them; others burn incense under the pews and wave amulets and trinkets in what they imagine to be his direction, muttering pagan gibberish all the while. References he is sure must be meant for him are worked into the sermons: "And he that was dead sat up, and began to speak" (Luke 7:15), or "So Job died, being old and full of days" (Job 42:17). The Major points out that he never speaks and never opens his mouth except to receive Holy Communion. He lived about sixteen thousand and sixty days, many of which he does not remember. On 23 September, 1914, as a young private, he was crucified to a cart wheel for five hours for having failed to salute an equally young lieutenant. One ankle was left permanently impaired.

The Major wishes the congregation to leave him in peace. The opacity of the living, their heaviness and dullness, the moisture of their skin, and the dustiness of their hair are repellent to a man of feeling. It was always his habit to avoid civilian crowds. He lived for six years on the fourth floor in Block E, Stoneflower Gardens, without saying a word to his neighbors or even attempting to learn their names. An affidavit can easily be obtained from the former porter at the Gardens, now residing at the Institute for Victims of Senile Trauma, Fifteenth District.

Mrs. Ibrahim, aged thirty-seven, mother of twelve children, complains about being haunted by Dr. L. Chalmeton of Regius Hospital, Seventh District, and by Miss Alicia Fohrenbach, social investigator from the Welfare Bureau, Fifteenth District. These two haunt Mrs. Ibrahim without respite, presenting for her ratification and approval conflicting and unpleasant versions of her own death.

According to Dr. Chalmeton's account, soon after Mrs. Ibrahim was discharged as incurable from Regius Hospital he paid his patient a professional call. He arrived at a quarter past four on the first Tuesday of April, expecting to find the social investigator, with whom he had a firm appointment. Mrs. Ibrahim was discovered alone, in a windowless room, the walls of which were coated with whitish fungus a quarter of an inch thick, which rose to a height of about forty inches from the floor. Dr. Chalmeton inquired, "Where is the social investigator?" Mrs. Ibrahim pointed to her throat, reminding him that she could not reply. Several dark-eyed children peeped into the room and ran away. "How many are yours?" the Doctor asked. Mrs. Ibrahim indicated six twice with her fingers. "Where do they sleep?" said the Doctor. Mrs. Ibrahim indicated the floor. Dr. Chalmeton said, "What does your husband do for a living?" Mrs. Ibrahim pointed to a workbench on which the Doctor saw several pieces of finely wrought jewelry; he thought it a waste that skilled work had been lavished on what seemed to be plastics and base metals. Dr. Chalmeton made the patient as comfortable as he could, explaining that he could not administer drugs for the relief of pain until the social investigator had signed a receipt for them. Miss Fohrenbach arrived at five o'clock. It had taken her forty minutes to find a suitable parking space: The street appeared to be poor, but everyone living on it owned one or two cars. Dr. Chalmeton, who was angry at having been kept waiting, declared he would not be responsible for the safety of his patient in a room filled with mold. Miss Fohrenbach retorted that the District could not resettle a family of fourteen persons who were foreign-born when there was a long list of native citizens waiting for accommodation. Mrs. Ibrahim had in any case relinquished her right to a domicile in the Fifteenth District the day she lost consciousness in the road and allowed an ambulance to transport her to a hospital in the Seventh. It was up to the hospital to look after her now. Dr. Chalmeton pointed out that housing of patients is not the business of hospitals. It was well known that the foreign poor preferred to crowd together in the Fifteenth, where they could sing and dance in the streets and attend one another's weddings. Miss Fohrenbach declared that Mrs. Ibrahim could easily have moved her bed into the kitchen, which was somewhat warmer and which boasted a window. When Mrs. Ibrahim died, the children would be placed in foster homes, eliminating the need for a larger apartment. Dr. Chalmeton remembers Miss Fohrenbach's then crying, "Oh, why do all these people come here, where nobody wants them?" While he was trying to think of an answer, Mrs. Ibrahim died.

In her testimony, Miss Fohrenbach recalls that she had to beg and plead with Dr. Chalmeton to visit Mrs. Ibrahim, who had been discharged from Regius Hospital without medicines or prescriptions or advice or instructions. Miss Fohrenbach had returned several times that April day to see if the Doctor had arrived. The first thing Dr. Chalmeton said on entering the room was "There is no way of helping these people. Even the simplest rules of hygiene are too complicated for them to follow. Wherever they settle, they spread disease and vermin. They have been responsible for outbreaks of aphthous stomatitis, hereditary hypoxia, coccidioidomycosis, gonorrheal arthritis, and scleroderma.

Their eating habits are filthy. They never wash their hands. The virus that attacks them breeds in dirt. We took in the patient against all rules, after the ambulance drivers left her lying in the courtyard and drove off without asking for a receipt. Regius Hospital was built and endowed for ailing Greek scholars. Now it is crammed with unteachable persons who cannot read or write." His cheeks and forehead were flushed, his speech incoherent and blurred. According to the social investigator, he was the epitome of the broken-down, irresponsible old rascals the Seventh District employs in its public services. Wondering at the effect this ranting of his might have on the patient, Miss Fohrenbach glanced at Mrs. Ibrahim and noticed she had died.

Mrs. Ibrahim's version of her death has the social investigator arriving first, bringing Mrs. Ibrahim a present of a wine-colored dressing gown made of soft, quilted silk. Miss Fohrenbach explained that the gown was part of a donation of garments to the needy. Large plastic bags, decorated with a moss rose, the emblem of the Fifteenth District, and bearing the words "Clean Clothes for the Foreign-Born," had been distributed by volunteer workers in the more prosperous streets of the District. A few citizens kept the bags as souvenirs, but most had turned them in to the Welfare Bureau filled with attractive clothing, washed, ironed, and mended, and with missing buttons replaced. Mrs. Ibrahim sat up and put on the dressing gown, and the social investigator helped her button it. Then Miss Fohrenbach changed the bed linen and pulled the bed away from the wall. She sat down and took Mrs. Ibrahim's hand in hers and spoke about a new, sunny flat containing five warm rooms which would soon be available. Miss Fohrenbach said that arrangements had been made to send the twelve Ibrahim children to the mountains for special winter classes. They would be taught history and languages and would learn to ski.

The Doctor arrived soon after. He stopped and spoke to Mr. Ibrahim, who was sitting at his workbench making an emerald patch box. The Doctor said to him, "If you give me your social-security papers, I can attend to the medical insurance. It will save you a great deal of trouble." Mr. Ibrahim answered, "What is social security?" The Doctor examined the patch box and asked

Mr. Ibrahim what he earned. Mr. Ibrahim told him, and the Doctor said, "But that is less than the minimum wage." Mr. Ibrahim said, "What is a minimum wage?" The Doctor turned to Miss Fohrenbach, saying, "We really must try and help them." Mrs. Ibrahim died. Mr. Ibrahim, when he understood that nothing could be done, lay facedown on the floor, weeping loudly. Then he remembered the rules of hospitality and got up and gave each of the guests a present—for Miss Fohrenbach a belt made of Syriac coins, a copy of which is in the Cairo Museum, and for the Doctor a bracelet of precious metal engraved with pomegranates, about sixteen pomegranates in all, that has lifesaving properties.

Mrs. Ibrahim asks that her account of the afternoon be registered with the police as the true version and that copies be sent to the Doctor and the social investigator, with a courteous request for peace and silence.

Mrs. Carlotte Essling, née Holmquist, complains of being haunted by her husband, Professor Augustus Essling, the philosopher and historian. When they were married, the former Miss Holmquist was seventeen. Professor Essling, a widower, had four small children. He explained to Miss Holmquist why he wanted to marry again. He said, "I must have one person, preferably female, on whom I can depend absolutely, who will never betray me even in her thoughts. A disloyal thought revealed, a betrayal even in fantasy, would be enough to destroy me. Knowing that I may rely upon some one person will leave me free to continue my work without anxiety or distraction." The work was the Professor's lifelong examination of the philosopher Nicholas de Malebranche, for whom he had named his eldest child. "If I cannot have the unfailing loyalty I have described, I would as soon not marry at all," the Professor added. He had just begun work on *Malebranche and Materialism*.

Mrs. Essling recalls that at seventeen this seemed entirely within her possibilities, and she replied something like "Yes, I see," or "I quite understand," or "You needn't mention it again."

Mrs. Essling brought up her husband's four children and had two more of her own, and died after thirty-six years of marriage at the age of fifty-three. Her husband haunts her with proof of her goodness. He tells people that Mrs. Essling was born an angel, lived like an angel, and is an angel in eternity. Mrs. Essling would like relief from this charge. "Angel" is a loose way of speaking. She is astonished that the Professor cannot be more precise. Angels are created, not born. Nowhere in any written testimony will you find a scrap of proof that angels are "good." Some are merely messengers; others have a paramilitary function. All are stupid.

After her death, Mrs. Essling remained in the Fifteenth District. She says she can go nowhere without being accosted by the Professor, who, having completed the last phase of his work *Malebranche and Mysticism*, roams the streets, looking in shop-windows, eating lunch twice, in two different restaurants, telling his life story to waiters and bus drivers. When he sees Mrs. Essling, he calls out, "There you are!" and "What have you been sent to tell me?" and "Is there a message?" In July, catching sight of her at the open-air fruit market on Dulac Street, the Professor jumped off a bus, upsetting barrows of plums and apricots, waving an umbrella as he ran. Mrs. Essling had to take refuge in the cold-storage room of the central market, where, years ago, after she had ordered twenty pounds of raspberries and currants for making jelly, she was invited by the wholesale fruit dealer, Mr. Lobrano, aged twenty-nine, to spend a holiday with him in a charming southern city whose Mediterranean Baroque churches he described with much delicacy of feeling. Mrs. Essling was too startled to reply. Mistaking her silence, Mr. Lobrano then mentioned a northern city containing a Gothic cathedral. Mrs. Essling said that such a holiday was impossible. Mr. Lobrano asked for one good reason. Mrs. Essling was at that moment four months pregnant with her second child. Three stepchildren waited for her out in the street. A fourth stepchild was at home looking after the baby. Professor Essling, working on his *Malebranche and Money*, was at home, too, expecting his lunch. Mrs. Essling realized she could not give Mr. Lobrano one good reason. She left the cold-storage room without another word and did not return to it in her lifetime.

Mrs. Essling would like to be relieved of the Professor's gratitude. Having lived an exemplary life is one thing; to have it thrown up at one is another. She would like the police to send for Professor Essling and tell him so. She suggests that the police find some method of keeping him off the streets. The police ought to threaten him; frighten him; put the fear of the Devil into him. Philosophy has made him afraid of dying. Remind him about how he avoided writing his *Malebranche and Mortality*. He is an old man. It should be easy.

SPECK'S IDEA

SANDOR SPECK'S first art gallery in Paris was on the Right Bank, near the Church of St. Elisabeth, on a street too narrow for cars. When his block was wiped off the map to make way for a five-story garage, Speck crossed the Seine to the shadow of Saint-Julien-le-Pauvre, where he set up shop in a picturesque slum protected by law from demolition. When this gallery was blown up by Basque separatists, who had mistaken it for a travel agency exploiting the beauty of their coast, he collected his insurance money and moved to the Faubourg Saint-Germain.

Here, at terrifying cost, he rented four excellent rooms—two on the loggia level, and a clean dry basement for framing and storage. The entrance, particularly handsome, was on the street side of an eighteenth-century *hôtel particulier* built around an elegant court now let out as a parking concession. The building had long before been cut up into dirty, decaying apartments, whose spiteful, quarrelsome, and avaricious tenants were forgiven every failing by Speck for the sake of being the Count of this and the Prince of that. Like the flaking shutters, the rotting window-sills, the slops and oil stains in the ruined court, they bore a Proustian seal of distinction, like a warranty, making up for his insanely expensive lease. Though he appreciated style, he craved stability even more. In the Faubourg, he seemed at last likely to find it: Not a stone could be removed without the approval of the toughest cultural authorities of the nation. Three Marxist embassies installed in former ducal mansions along the street required the presence of armed policemen the clock around. The only commercial establishments anywhere near Speck's—a restaurant and a bookstore—seemed unlikely targets for fire-bombs:

The first catered to lower-echelon civil servants, the second was painted royal blue, a conservative color he found reassuring. The bookstore's name, Amandine, suggested shelves of calm regional novels and accounts of travel to Imperial Russia signed "A Diplomat." Pasted inside the window, flat on the pane, was an engraving that depicted an old man, bearded and mitered, tearing a small demon limb from limb. The old man looked self-conscious, the imp resigned. He supposed that this image concealed a deep religious meaning, which he did not intend to plumb. If it was holy, it was respectable; as the owner of the gallery across the street, he needed to know nothing more.

Speck was now in the parish of St. Clotilde, near enough to the church for its bells to give him migraine headaches. Leaves from the church square blew as far as his door—melancholy reminders of autumn, a season bad for art. (Winter was bad, too, while the first chestnut leaves unfolding heralded the worst season of all. In summer the gallery closed.) In spite of his constant proximity to churches he had remained rational. Generations of highly intellectual Central European agnostics and freethinkers had left in his bones a mistrust of the bogs and quicksands that lie beyond reality perceived. Neither loss nor grief nor guilt nor fear had ever moved him to appeal to the unknown—any unknown, for there were several. Nevertheless, after signing his third lease in seven years, he decided to send Walter, his Swiss assistant, a lapsed Calvinist inching toward Rome, to light a candle at St. Clotilde's. Walter paid for a five-franc taper and set it before St. Joseph, the most reliable intermediary he could find: A wave of postconciliar puritanism seemed to have broken at St. Clotilde's, sweeping away most of the mute and obliging figures to whom desires and gratitude could be expressed. Walter was willing to start again in some livelier church—Notre Dame de Paris, for instance—but Speck thought enough was enough.

On a damp October evening about a year after this, there could be seen in Speck's window a drawing of a woman drying her feet (Speck permanent collection); a poster announcing the current exhibition, "Paris and Its Influence on the Tirana School, 1931–2";

five catalogues displayed attractively; and the original of the picture on the poster—a shameless copy of Foujita's *Mon Intérieur* reentitled *Balkan Alarm Clock*. In defiance of a government circular reminding Paris galleries about the energy crisis Speck had left the lights on. This was partly to give the lie to competitors who might be putting it about that he was having money troubles. He had set the burglar alarm, bolted the security door, and was now cranking down an openwork iron screen whose Art Nouveau loops and fronds allowed the works inside to be seen but nothing larger than a mouse to get in. The faint, floating sadness he always felt while locking up had to do with the time. In his experience, love affairs and marriages perished between seven and eight o'clock, the hour of rain and no taxis. All over Paris couples must be parting forever, leaving like debris along the curbs the shreds of canceled restaurant dates, useless ballet tickets, hopeless explanations, and scraps of pride; and toward each of these disasters a taxi was pulling in, the only taxi for miles, the light on its roof already dimmed in anticipation to the twin dots that in Paris mean "occupied." But occupied by whom?

"You take it."

"No, you. You're the one in a hurry."

The lover abandoned under a dripping plane tree would feel a damp victory of a kind, awarding himself a first-class trophy for selfless behavior. It would sustain him ten seconds, until the departing one rolled down the taxi window to hurl her last flint: "You Fascist!" Why was this always the final shot, the coup de grâce delivered by women? Speck's wife, Henriette, book critic on an uncompromising political weekly, had said it three times last spring—here, in the street, where Speck stood locking the iron screen into place. He had been uneasily conscious of his wellborn neighbors, hanging out their windows, not missing a thing. Henriette had then gone away in a cab to join her lover, leaving Speck, the gallery, her job—everything that mattered.

He mourned Henriette; he missed her steadying influence. Her mind was like a one-way thoroughfare, narrow and flat, maintained in repair. As he approached the age of forty he felt that his own intellect needed not just a direction but retaining walls. Unless his thoughts were nailed down by gallery business they tended to glide away to the swamps of imagination, behind which stretched the steamier marshland of metaphysics. Confessing this to Henriette was unlikely to bring her back. There had been something brisk and joyous about her going—her hailing of a taxi as though of a friend, her surprised smile as the third "Fascist!" dissolved in the April night like a double stroke from the belfry of St. Clotilde's. He supposed he would never see her again now, except by accident. Perhaps, long after he had forgotten Henriette, he would overhear someone saying in a restaurant, "Do you see that poor mad intellectual talking to herself in the corner? That is Henriette, Sandor Speck's second wife. Of course, she was very different then; Speck kept her in shape."

While awaiting this sop, which he could hardly call consolation, he had Walter and the gallery. Walter had been with him five years—longer than either of his marriages. They had been years of spiritual second-thinking for Walter and of strain and worry for Speck. Walter in search of the Eternal was like one of those solitary skippers who set out to cross an ocean only to capsize when barely out of port. Speck had been obliged to pluck his assistant out of Unitarian waters and set him on the firm shore of the Trinity. He had towed him to Transubstantiation and back; had charted the shoals and perils of careless prayer. His own aversion to superstitious belief made Speck particularly scrupulous; he would not commit himself on Free Will, for instance, uncertain if it was supposed to be an uphill trudge wearing tight boots or a downhill slide sitting on a tea tray. He would lie awake at night planning Walter's dismissal, only to develop a traumatic chest cold if his assistant seemed restless.

"What will the gallery do without you?" he would ask on the very morning he had been meaning to say, "Walter, sit down, please. I've got something to tell you." Walter would remind him about saints and holy men who had done without everything, while Speck would envision the pure hell of having to train someone new.

On a rainy night such as this, the street resembled a set in a French film designed for export, what with the policemen's white rain capes aesthetically gleaming and the lights of the bookstore, the restaurant, and the gallery reflected, quivering, in European-looking puddles. In reality, Speck thought, there was not even hope for a subplot. Henriette had gone forever. Walter's mission could not be photographed. The owner of the restaurant was in his eighties; the waiters were poised on the brink of retirement. As for the bookseller, M. Alfred Chassepoule, he seemed to spend most of his time wiping blood off the collected speeches of Mussolini, bandaging customers, and sweeping up glass. The fact was that Amandine's had turned out to have a fixed right-wing viewpoint, which made it subject to attack by commandos wielding iron bars. Speck, who had chosen the street for its upper-class hush, had grown used to the hoarse imprecation of the left and shriller keening of the right; he could tell the sob of an ambulance from the wail of a police van. The commerce of art is without bias: When insurance inspectors came round to ask what Speck might have seen, he invariably replied, "Seen where?" to which Walter, unsolicited, would add, "And I am Swiss."

Since Henriette's departure, Speck often ate his meals in the local restaurant, which catered to his frugal tastes, his vegetarian principles, and his desire to be left in peace. On the way, he would pause outside Amandine's, just enough to mark the halt as a comforting bachelor habit. He would glance over the secondhand books, the yellowing pamphlets, and the overpriced cartoons. The tone of the window display seemed old-fashioned rather than dangerous, though he knew that the slogan crowning the arrangement, "Europe for Europeans," echoed from a dark political valley. But even that valley had been full of strife and dissension and muddle, for hadn't the Ur-Fascists, the Italian ones, been in some way against an all-Europe? At least, some of their poets were. But who could take any of that seriously now? Nothing political had ever struck Speck as being above the level of a low-grade comic strip. On the cover of one volume, Uncle Sam shook hands with the Russian Bear over prostrate Europe, depicted as a maiden in a dead faint. A drawing of a spider on a field of banknotes (twelve hundred francs with frame, nine hundred without) jostled the image of a crablike hand clawing away at the map of France. Pasted against the pane, survivor of uncounted assaults, the old man continued to dismember his captive imp. Walter had told Speck he believed the old man to be St. Amand, Apostle of Flanders,

Bishop in 430. "Or perhaps," said Walter, after thinking it over, "435." The imp probably stood for Flemish paganism, which the Apostle had been hard put to it to overcome.

From the rainy street Speck could see four or five of Amandine's customers—all men; he had never noticed a woman in the place—standing, reading, books held close to their noses. They had the weak eyes, long chins, and sparse, sparrow-colored hair he associated with low governmental salaries. He imagined them living with grim widowed mothers whose company they avoided after work. He had seen them, or young men like them, staggering out of the store, cut by flying glass, kicked and beaten as they lay stunned on the pavement; his anxious imagination had set them on their feet, booted and belted, the right signal given at last, swarming across to the gallery, determined to make Speck pay for injuries inflicted on them by total strangers. He saw his only early Chagall (quite likely authentic) ripped from its frame; Walter, his poor little spectacles smeared with blood, lambasted with the complete Charles Maurras, fourteen volumes, full morocco; Speck himself, his ears offended by acute right-wing cries of "Down with foreign art!" attempting a quick counterstroke with *Significant Minor French Realists, Twentieth Century*, which was thick enough to stun an ox. Stepping back from the window, Speck saw his own smile reflected. It was pinched and tight, and he looked a good twenty years older than thirty-nine.

His restaurant, crammed with civil servants at noon, was now nearly empty. A smell of lunchtime pot roast hung in the air. He made for his own table, from which he could see the comforting lights of the gallery. The waiter, who had finally stopped asking how Henriette was liking Africa, brought his dinner at once, setting out like little votive offerings the raw-carrot salad, the pot-roast vegetables without the meat, the quarter ounce of low-fat cheese, and a small pear. It had long been established that Speck did not wish to be disturbed by the changing of plates. He extracted a yellow pad and three pencils from his briefcase and placed them within the half circle of dishes. Speck was preparing his May-June show.

The right show at the right time: It was trickier than getting married to the right person at any time. For about a year now,

Paris critics had been hinting at something missing from the world of art. These hints, poignant and patriotic on the right, neo-nationalist and pugnacious on the left, wistful but insistent dead center, were all in essence saying the same thing: "The time has come." The time had come; the hour had struck; the moment was ripe for a revival of reason, sanity, and taste. Surely there was more to art than this sickness, this transatlantic blight? Fresh winds were needed to sweep the museums and galleries. Two days ago there had been a disturbing article in *Le Monde* (front page, lower middle, turn to page 26) by a man who never took up his pen unless civilization was in danger. Its title—"Redemption Through Art—Last Hope for the West?"—had been followed by other disturbing questions: When would the merchants and dealers, compared rather unfairly to the money changers driven from the temple, face up to their share of responsibility as the tattered century declined? Must the flowering gardens of Western European culture wilt and die along with the decadent political systems, the exhausted parliaments, the shambling elections, the tired liberal impulses? What of the man in the street, too modest and confused to mention his cravings? Was he not gasping for one remedy and one only—artistic renovation? And where was this to come from? "In the words of Shakespr," the article concluded, supposedly in English, "That is the qustn."

As it happened, Speck had the answer: Say, a French painter, circa 1864–1949, forgotten now except by a handful of devoted connoisseurs. Populist yet refined, local but universal, he would send rays, beacons, into the thickening night of the West, just as Speck's gallery shone bravely into the dark street. Speck picked up a pencil and jotted rapidly: "Born in France, worked in Paris, went his own way, unmindful of fashion, knowing his hour would strike, his vision be vindicated. Catholical, as this retrospective so eloquently . . ." Just how does "catholical" come in, Speck wondered, forking up raw carrots. Because of ubiquity, the ubiquity of genius? No; not genius—leave that for the critics. His sense of harmony, then—his discretion.

Easy, Speck told himself. Easy on the discretion. This isn't interior decoration.

He could see the notices, knew which of the critics would

write "At last," and "It has taken Sandor Speck to remind us." Left, right, and center would unite on a single theme: how the taste of two full generations had been corrupted by foreign speculation, cosmopolitan decadence, and the cultural imperialism of the Anglo-Saxon hegemony.

"The calm agnostic face," Speck wrote happily, "the quiet Cartesian voice are replaced by the snarl of a nation betrayed (1914), as startling for the viewer as a child's glimpse of a beloved adult in a temper tantrum. The snarl, the grimace vanish (1919) as the serene observer of Universal Will (1929) and of Man's responsibility to himself return. But we are left shaken. We have stopped trusting our feelings. We have been shown not only the smile but the teeth."

Here Speck drew a wavy line and turned to the biography, which was giving him trouble. On a fresh yellow page he tried again:

1938—Travels to Nice. Sees Mediterranean.
1939—Abandons pacifist principle. Lies about age. Is mobilized.
1940—Demobilized.
1941—

It was here that Speck bogged down. Should he say, "Joins Resistance"? "Resistance" today meant either a heroic moment sadly undervalued by the young or a minor movement greatly inflated in order to absolve French guilt. Whatever it is, thought Speck, it is not chic. The youngest survivor must be something like seventy-three. They know nothing about art, and never subscribe to anything except monuments. Some people read "Resistance" in a chronology and feel quite frankly exasperated. On the other hand, what about museums, state-subsidized, Resistance-minded on that account? He chewed a boiled leek and suddenly wrote, "1941—Conversations with Albert Camus." I wonder where all this comes from, Speck said to himself. Inspiration was what he meant.

These notes, typed by Walter, would be turned over to the fashionable historian, the alarming critic, the sound political figure unlikely to be thrown out of office between now and spring, whom Speck would invite to write the catalogue introduction. "Just a few notes," Speck would say tactfully. "Knowing how busy you are." Nothing was as inspiriting to him as the thought of his own words in print on a creamy catalogue page, even over some-one else's name.

Speck took out of his briefcase the Directoire snuffbox Hen-riette had given him about a fortnight before suddenly calling him "Fascist." (Unexpected feminine generosity—first firm sign of adulterous love affair.) It contained three after-dinner tablets—one to keep him alert until bedtime, another to counter the stim-ulating effect of the first, and a third to neutralize the germ known as Warsaw flu now ravaging Paris, emptying schools and factories and creating delays in the postal service. He sat quietly, digesting, giving the pills a chance to work.

He could see the structure of the show, the sketchbooks and letters in glass cases. It might be worthwhile lacquering the walls black, concentrating strong spots on the correspondence, which straddled half a century, from Degas to Cocteau. The scrawl posted by Drieu la Rochelle just before his suicide would be par-ticularly effective on black. Céline was good; all that crowd was back in vogue now. He might use the early photo of Céline in reg-imental dress uniform with a splendid helmet. Of course, there would be word from the left, too, with postcards from Jean Jaurès, Léon Blum, and Paul Éluard, and a jaunty get-well message from Louis Aragon and Elsa. In the first room Speck would hang the stiff, youthful landscapes and the portraits of the family, the artist's first models—his brother wearing a sailor suit, the awkward but touching likeness of his sister (*Germaine-Isabelle at the Window*).

"Yes, yes," Speck would hear in the buzz of voices at the open-ing. "Even from the beginning you can tell there was *something*." The "something" became bolder, firmer in the second room. See his cities; watch how the streets turn into mazes, nets, prison corridors. Dark palette. Opaqueness, the whole canvas covered, immensities of indigo and black. "Look, 1929; he was doing it before What's-His-Name." Upstairs, form breaking out of shadow: bread, cheese, wine, wheat, ripe apples, grapes.

Hold it, Speck told himself. Hold the ripeness. This isn't so-cial realism.

He gathered up the pencils, the snuffbox, and the pad, and put them back in the briefcase. He placed seventy francs, tip included, in a saucer. Still he sat, his mind moving along to the second loggia room, the end room, the important one. Here on the neutral walls would be the final assurance, the serenity, the satire, the power, and the vision for which, at last, the time had come. For that was the one thing Speck was sure of: The bell had rung, the hour had struck, the moment was at hand.

Whose time? Which hour? Yes—whose, which, what? That was where he was stuck.

The street was now empty except for the policemen in their streaming capes. The bookstore had put up its shutter. Speck observed the walls of the three Marxist embassies. Shutters and curtains that once had shielded the particular privacy of the aristocracy—privacy open to servants but not to the street—now concealed the receptions and merry dinner parties of people's democracies. Sometimes at this hour gleaming motorcars rolled past the mysterious gates, delivering passengers Speck's fancy continued to see as the Duchesse de Guermantes and anyone she did not happen to despise. He knew that the chauffeurs were armed and that half the guests were spies; still, there was nothing to stop a foreign agent from having patrician tastes, or from admiring Speck's window as he drove by.

"This gallery will be an oasis of peace and culture," Walter had predicted as they were hanging the first show, "Little-Known Aspects of Post-Decorator Style." "An oasis of peace and culture in the international desert."

Speck breathed germ-laden night air. Boulevard theaters and music halls were deserted, their managers at home writing letters to the mayor of Paris deploring the decline of popular entertainment and suggesting remedies in the form of large cash subsidies. The sluggish river of autumn life congealed and stagnated around millions of television sets as Parisians swallowed aspirin and drank the boiling-hot Scotch believed to be a sovereign defense against Warsaw flu.

A few determined intellectuals slunk, wet, into the Métro on their way to cultural centers where, in vivid translations from the German, actors would address the occasional surly remark to the audience—that loyal, anxious, humorless audience in its costly fake working-class clothes. Another contingent, dressed in Burberry trench coats, had already fought its way into the Geographical Institute, where a lecture with colored slides, "Ramblings in Secret Greenland," would begin, after a delay owing to trouble with the projection machine, at about nine-twenty. The advantage of slides over films was that they were not forever jumping about and confusing one, and the voice describing them belonged to a real speaker. When the lights went up, one could see him, talk to him, challenge him over the thing he had said about shamanism on Disko Island. What had drawn the crowd was not Greenland but the word "secret." In no other capital city does the population wait more trustfully for the mystery to be solved, the conspiracy laid bare, the explanation of every sort of vexation to be supplied: why money slumps, why prices climb, why it rains in August, why children are ungrateful. The answers might easily come from a man with a box of slides.

In each of the city's twenty administrative districts, Communists, distinguished by the cleanliness of their no-iron shirts, the sobriety of their washable neckties, and the modesty of their bearing, moved serenely toward their local cell meetings. I must persuade Walter to take out membership sometime, Speck thought. It might be useful and interesting for the gallery and it would take his mind off salvation.

Walter was at this moment in the Church of St. Gervais, across the Seine, where an ecumenical gathering of prayer, music, and debate on Unity of Faith had been marred the week before by ugly scuffling between middle-aged latecomers and young persons in the lotus position, taking up too much room. Walter had turned to his neighbor, a stranger to him, and asked courteously, "Is it a string ensemble tonight, or just the organ?" Mistaken for a traditionalist demanding the Latin Mass, he had been punched in the face and had to be led to a side chapel to mop up his nosebleed. God knows what they might do to him tonight, Speck thought.

As for Speck himself, nine-thirty found him in good company, briskly tying the strings of his Masonic apron. No commitment stronger than prudence kept him from being at St. Gervais, listening for a voice in the night of the soul, or at a Communist Party cell meeting, hoping to acquire a more wholesome slant on art in a doomed society, but he had already decided that only the Infinite could be everywhere at once. The Masonic Grand Architect of the Universe laid down no rules, appointed no prophets, required neither victims nor devotion, and seemed content to exist as a mere possibility. At the lodge Speck rubbed shoulders with men others had to be content to glimpse on television. He stood now no more than three feet away from Kléber Schaumberger, of the Alsatian Protestant banking Schaumbergers; had been greeted by Olivier Ombrine, who designed all the Arabian princesses' wedding gowns; could see, without craning, the plume of white hair belonging to François-Xavier Blum-Bloch-Weiler—former ambassador, historian, member of the French Academy, author of a perennially best-selling book about Vietnam called *When France Was at the Helm*. Speck kept the ambassador's family tree filed in his head. The Blum-Bloch-Weilers, heavy art collectors, produced statesmen, magistrates, anthropologists, and generals, and were on no account to be confused with the Blum-Weiler-Blochs, their penniless and mystical cousins, who produced poets, librarians, and Benedictine monks.

Tonight Speck followed the proceedings mechanically; his mind was set on the yellow pad in his briefcase, now lying on the backseat of his car. Direct address and supplication to the unknown were frowned on here. Order reigned in a complex universe where the Grand Architect, insofar as he existed, was supposed to know what he was doing. However, having nowhere to turn, Speck decided for the first time in his life to brave whatever cosmic derangement might ensue and to unburden himself.

Whoever and whatever you are, said Speck silently, as many had said before him, remember in my favor that I have never bothered you. I never called your attention to the fake Laurencin, the stolen Magritte, the Bonnard the other gallery was supposed to have insured, the Maurice Denis notebook that slipped through my fingers, the Vallotton woodcut that got lost between Paris and Lausanne. All I want . . . But there was no point in his insisting. The Grand Architect, if he was any sort of omnipresence worth considering, knew exactly what Speck needed now: He needed the tiny, enduring wheel set deep in the clanking, churning machinery of the art trade—the artist himself.

Speck came out to the street refreshed and soothed, feeling that he had shed some of his troubles. The rain had stopped. A bright moon hung low. He heard someone saying, "...hats." On the glistening pavement a group of men stood listening while Senator Antoine Bellefeuille told a funny story. Facts from the Bellefeuille biography tumbled through Speck's mind: twenty years a deputy from a rich farming district, twice a cabinet minister, now senator; had married a sugar-beet fortune, which he inherited when his wife died; no children; his mother had left him majority shares in milk chocolate, which he had sold to invest in the first postwar plastics; owned a racing stable in Normandy, a château in Provence, one of the last fine houses of Paris; had taken first-class degrees in law and philosophy; had gone into politics almost as an afterthought.

What had kept the old man from becoming Prime Minister, even President of the Republic? He had the bearing, the brains, the fortune, and the connections. Too contented, Speck decided, observing his lodge brother by moonlight. But clever, too; he was supposed to have kept copies of files from the time he had been at Justice. He splashed around in the arts, knew the third-generation dealers, the elegant bachelor curators. He went to openings, was not afraid of new movements, but he never bought anything. Speck tried to remember why the wealthy Senator who liked art never bought pictures.

"She was stunning," the Senator said. "Any man of my generation will tell you that. She came down Boulevard Saint-Michel on her husband's arm. He barely reached her shoulder. She had a smile like a fox's. Straight little animal teeth. Thick red-gold hair. A black hat tilted over one eye. And what a throat. And what hands and arms. A waist no larger than this," said the Senator, making a circle with his hands. "As I said, in those days men wore hats. You tipped a bowler by the brim, the other sort you picked up by the crown. I was so dazzled by being near her, by having the famous Lydia Cruche smile at me, I forgot I was wearing a bowler and tried to pick it up by the crown. You can imagine what a fool I looked, and how she laughed."

And of course they laughed, and Speck laughed, too.

"Her husband," said the Senator. "Hubert Cruche. A face like a gargoyle. Premature senile dementia. He'd been kicked by Venus at some time or other"—the euphemism for syphilis. "In those days the cure was based on mercury—worse than the disease. He seemed to know me. There was light in his eyes. Oh, not the light of intelligence. It was too late for that, and he'd not had much to begin with. He recognized me for a simple reason. I had already begun to assemble my Cruche collection. I bought everything Hubert Cruche produced for sixteen years—the oils, the gouaches, the pastels, the watercolors, the etchings, the drawings, the woodcuts, the posters, the cartoons, the book illustrations. Everything."

That was it, Speck remembered. That was why the Senator who liked art never bought so much as a wash drawing. The house was full of Cruches; there wasn't an inch to spare on the walls.

With a monarch's gesture, the Senator dismissed his audience and stepped firmly toward the chauffeur, who stood holding the door of his Citroën. He said, perhaps to himself, perhaps to Speck, thin and attentive in the moonlight, "I suppose I ought to get rid of my Cruches. Who ever thinks about Cruche now?"

"No," said Speck, whom the Grand Architect of the Universe had just rapped over the head. The Senator paused—benevolent, stout. "Don't get rid of the Cruches," said Speck. He felt as if he were on a distant shore, calling across deep cultural waters. "Don't sell! Hang on! Cruche is coming back!"

Cruche, Cruche, Hubert Cruche, sang Speck's heart as he drove homeward. Cruche's hour had just struck, along with Sandor Speck's. At the core of the May-June retrospective would be his lodge brother's key collection: "Our thanks, in particular . . . who not only has loaned his unique and invaluable . . . but who also . . . and who . . ." Recalling the little he knew of Cruche's obscure career, Speck made a few changes in the imaginary catalogue, substituting with some disappointment *The Power Station at Gagny-sur-Orme* for *Misia Sert on Her Houseboat*, and *Peasant Woman*

Sorting Turnips for *Serge Lifar as Petrouchka*. He wondered if he could call Cruche heaven-sent. No; he would not put a foot beyond coincidence, just as he had not let Walter dash from saint to saint once he had settled for St. Joseph. And yet a small flickering marsh light danced upon the low-lying metaphysical ground he had done so much to avoid. Not only did Cruche overlap to an astonishing degree the painter in the yellow notebook but he was exactly the sort of painter that made the Speck gallery chug along. If Speck's personal collection consisted of minor works by celebrated artists, he considered them his collateral for a rainy, bank-loan day. Too canny to try to compete with international heavy-weights, unwilling to burden himself with insurance, he had developed as his specialty the flattest, palest, farthest ripples of the late-middle-traditional Paris school. This sensible decision had earned him the admiration given the devoted miniaturist who is no threat to anyone. "Go and see Sandor Speck," the great lions and tigers of the trade would tell clients they had no use for. "Speck's the expert."

Speck was expert on barges, bridges, cafés at twilight, nudes on striped counterpanes, the artist's mantelpiece with mirror, the artist's street, his staircase, his bed made and rumpled, his still life with half-peeled apple, his summer in Mexico, his wife reading a book, his girlfriend naked and dejected on a kitchen chair. He knew that the attraction of customer to picture was always accidental, like love; it was his business to make it overwhelming. Visitors came to the gallery looking for decoration and investment, left it believing Speck had put them on the road to a supreme event. But there was even more to Speck than this, and if he was respected for anything in the trade it was for his knack with artists' widows. Most dealers hated them. They were considered vain, greedy, unrealistic, and tougher than bulldogs. The worst were those whose husbands had somehow managed the rough crossing to recognition only to become washed up at the wrong end of the beach. There the widow waited, guarding the wreckage. Speck's skill in dealing with them came out of a certain sympathy. An artist's widow was bound to be suspicious and adamant. She had survived the discomfort and confusion of her marriage;

had lived through the artist's drinking, his avarice, his affairs, his obsession with constipation, his feuds and quarrels, his cowardice with dealers, his hypocrisy with critics, his depressions (which always fell at the most joyous seasons, blighting Christmas and spring); and then—oh, justice!—she had outlasted him.

Transfiguration arrived rapidly. Resurrected for Speck's approval was an ardent lover, a devoted husband who could not work unless his wife was around, preferably in the same room. If she had doubts about a painting, he at once scraped it down. Hers was the only opinion he had ever trusted. His last coherent words before dying had been of praise for his wife's autumnal beauty.

Like a swan in muddy waters, Speck's ancient Bentley cruised the suburbs where his painters had lived their last resentful seasons. He knew by heart the damp villa, the gravel path, the dangling bellpull, the shrubbery containing dead cats and plastic bottles. Indoors the widow sat, her walls plastered with portraits of herself when young. Here she continued the struggle begun in the Master's lifetime—the evicting of the upstairs tenant—her day made lively by the arrival of mail (dusty beige of anonymous threats, grim blue of legal documents), the coming and going of process servers, the outings to lawyers. Into this spongy territory Speck advanced, bringing his tactful presence, his subtle approximation of courtship, his gift for listening. Thin by choice, pale by nature, he suggested maternal need. Socks and cuff links suggested breeding. The drift of his talk suggested prosperity. He sent his widows flowers, wooed them with food. Although their taste in checks and banknotes ran to the dry and crisp, when it came to eating they craved the sweet, the sticky, the moist. From the finest pastry shops in Paris Speck brought soft macaroons, savarins soaked in rum, brioches stuffed with almond cream, mocha cake so tender it had to be eaten with a spoon. Sugar was poison to Speck. Henriette had once reviewed a book that described how refined sugar taken into one's system turned into a fog of hideous green. Her brief, cool warning, "A Marxist Considers Sweets," unreeled in Speck's mind if he was confronted with a cookie. He usually pretended to eat, reducing a mille-feuille to paste, concealing the wreck of an éclair under napkin and fork. He never lost track of his purpose—the prying of paintings out of a dusty studio on terms anesthetizing to the artist's widow and satisfactory to himself.

The Senator had mentioned a wife; where there had been wife there was relict. Speck obtained her telephone number by calling a rival gallery and pretending to be looking for someone else. "Cruche's widow can probably tell you," he finally heard. She lived in one of the gritty suburbs east of Paris, on the far side of the Bois de Vincennes—in Speck's view, the wrong direction. The pattern of his life seemed to come unfolded as he dialed. He saw himself stalled in industrial traffic, inhaling pollution, his Bentley pointed toward the seediest mark on the urban compass, with a vanilla cream cake melting beside him on the front seat.

She answered his first ring; his widows never strayed far from the telephone. He introduced himself. Silence. He gave the name of the gallery, mentioned his street, recited the names of painters he showed.

Presently he heard "D'you know any English?"

"Some," said Speck, who was fluent.

"Well, what do you want?"

"First of all," he said, "to meet you."

"What for?"

He cupped his hand round the telephone, as if spies from the embassies down the street were trying to overhear. "I am planning a major Cruche show. A retrospective. That's what I want to talk to you about."

"Not unless I know what you want."

It seemed to Speck that he had already told her. Her voice was languid and nasal and perfectly flat. An index to English dialects surfaced in his mind, yielding nothing useful.

"It will be a strong show," he went on. "The first big Cruche since the 1930s, I believe."

"What's that got to do with me?"

He wondered if the Senator had forgotten something essential—that Lydia Cruche had poisoned her husband, for instance. He said, "You probably own quite a lot of his work."

"None of it's for sale."

This, at last, was familiar; widows' negotiations always began with "No." "Actually, I am not proposing to buy anything," he said, wanting this to be clear at the start. "I am offering the hospitality of my gallery. It's a gamble I am willing to take because of my firm belief that the time—"

"What's the point of this show?"

"The point?" said Speck, his voice tightening as it did when Walter was being obtuse. "The point is getting Cruche back on the market. The time has come—the time to . . . to attack. To attack the museums with Hubert Cruche."

As he said this, Speck saw the great armor-plated walls of the Pompidou Art Center and the chink in the armor through which an 80 × 95 Cruche 1919 abstract might slip. He saw the provincial museums, cheeseparing, saving on lightbulbs, but, like the French bourgeoisie they stood for, so much richer than they seemed. At the name "Cruche" their curators would wake up from neurotic dreams of forced auction sales, remembering they had millions to get rid of before the end of the fiscal year. And France was the least of it; London, Zurich, Stockholm, and Amsterdam materialized as frescoes representing the neoclassical façades of four handsome banks. Overhead, on a Baroque ceiling, nymphs pointed their rosy feet to gods whose chariots were called "Tokyo" and "New York." Speck lowered his voice as if he had portentous news. Museums all over the world, although they did not yet know this, were starving for Cruche. In the pause that followed he seemed to feel Henriette's hand on his shoulder, warning him to brake before enthusiasm took him over the cliff.

"Although for the moment Cruche is just an idea of mine," he said, stopping cold at the edge. "Just an idea. We can develop the idea when we meet."

A week later, Speck parked his car between a ramshackle shopping center—survivor of the building boom of the sixties—and a municipal low-cost housing project that resembled a jail. In the space bounded by these structures crouched the late artist's villa, abiding proof in stucco that the taste of earlier generations had been as disastrous as today's. He recognized the shards of legal battle: Center and block had left the drawing board of some state-employed hack as a unit, only to be wedged apart by a widow's refusal to sell. Speck wondered how she had escaped expropriation. Either she knows someone powerful, he thought, or she can make such a pest of herself that they were thankful to give up.

A minute after having pushed the gate and tugged the rusted wire bellpull, he found himself alone in a bleak sitting room, from which his hostess had been called by a whistling kettle. He sat down on a faded sofa. The furniture was of popular local design, garnished with marble and ormolu. A television set encrusted with gilt acanthus leaves sat on a sideboard, like an objet d'art. A few rectangular shadings on the wallpaper showed where pictures had hung.

The melancholy tinged with foreboding Speck felt between seven and eight overtook him at this much earlier hour. The room was no more hideous than others he had visited in his professional quest for a bargain, but this time it seemed to daunt him, recalling sieges and pseudo courtships and expenditures of time, charm, and money that had come to nothing. He got up and examined a glass-fronted bookcase with nothing inside. His features, afloat on a dusty pane, were not quite as pinched as they had been the other night, but the image was still below par for a man considered handsome. The approach of a squeaking tea cart sent him scurrying back to the sofa, like a docile child invited somewhere for the first time.

"I was just admiring—" he began.

"I've run out of milk," she said. "I'm sure you won't mind your tea plain." With this governessy statement she handed him a cup of black Ceylon, a large slice of poisonous raisin cake, and a Mickey Mouse paper napkin.

Nothing about Cruche's widow tallied with the Senator's description. She was short and quite round, and reminded Speck of the fat little dogs one saw being reluctantly exercised in Paris streets. The abundant red-gold hair of the Senator's memory, or imagination, had gone ash-gray and was, in any case, pinned up. The striking fact of her person was simply the utter blankness of her expression. Usually widows' faces spoke to him. They said, "I am lonely," or "Can I trust you?" Lydia Cruche's did not suggest that she had so much as taken Speck in. She chose a chair at some distance from Speck, and proceeded to eat her cake without speaking. He thought of things to say, but none of them seemed appealing.

At last, she said, "Did you notice the supermarket next door?"

"I saw a shopping center."

"The market is part of it. You can get anything there now—bran, frozen pizzas, maple syrup. That's where I got the cake mix. I haven't been to Paris for three years."

Speck had been born in France. French education had left him the certainty that he was a logical, fair-minded person imbued with a culture from which every other Western nation was obliged to take its bearings. French was his first language; he did not really approve of any other. He said, rather coldly, "Have you been in this country long?"

"Around fifty years."

"Then you should know some French."

"I don't speak it if I don't have to. I never liked it."

He put down his cup, engulfed by a wave of second-generation distress. She was his first foreign widow. Most painters, whatever their origins, had sense enough to marry Frenchwomen—unrivaled with creditors, thrifty hoarders of bits of real estate, endowed with relations in country places where one could decamp in times of need and war.

"Perhaps, where you come from—"he began.

"Saskatchewan."

His tea had gone cold. Tannic scum had collected on its surface. She said, "This idea of yours, this show—what was it you called it? The hospitality of your gallery? I just want to say don't count on me. Don't count on me for anything. I don't mind showing you what I've got. But not today. The studio hasn't been dusted or heated for years, and even the light isn't working."

In Speck's experience, this was about average for a first attempt. Before making for civilization he stopped at a florist's in the shopping center and ordered two dozen roses to be delivered to Mme. Cruche. While these were lifted, dripping, from a plastic pail, he jotted down a warm message on his card, crossing out the engraved "Dr. Sandor Speck." His title, earned by a thesis on French neo-humanism and its ups and downs, created some confusion in Paris, where it was taken to mean that Speck could cure slipped disks and gastric ulcers. Still, he felt that it gave a grip to his name, and it was his only link with all the freethinking, agnostic Specks, who, though they had not been able to claim affinity by right of birth with Voltaire and Descartes, had probably been wise and intelligent and quite often known as "Dr."

As soon as he got back to the gallery, he had Walter look up Saskatchewan in an atlas. Its austere oblong shape turned his heart to ice. Walter said that it was one of the right-angled territories that so frequently contain oil. Oil seemed to Speck to improve the oblong. He saw a Chirico chessboard sliding off toward a horizon where the lights of derricks twinkled and blinked.

He let a week go by before calling Lydia Cruche.

"I won't be able to show you those roses of yours," she said. "They died right off."

He took the hint and arrived with a spray of pale green orchids imported from Brazil. Settled upon the faded sofa, which was apparently destined to be his place, he congratulated his hostess on the discovery of oil in her native plain.

"I haven't seen or heard of the place since Trotsky left the Soviet Union," she said. "If there is oil, I'd sooner not know about it. Oil is God's curse." The iron silence that followed this seemed to press on Speck's lungs. "That's a bad cough you've got there, Doctor," she said. "Men never look after those things. Who looks after you?"

"I look after myself," said Speck.

"Where's your wife? Where'd she run off to?"

Not even "Are you married?" He saw his hostess as a tough little pagan figure, with a goddess's gift for reading men's lives. He had a quick vision of himself clasping her knees and sobbing out the betrayal of his marriage, though he continued to sit upright, crumbling walnut cake so that he would not have to eat it.

"My wife," he said, "insofar as I can still be said to have one, has gone to live in a warm climate."

"She run off alone? Women don't often do that. They haven't got that kind of nerve."

Stepping carefully, for he did not wish to sound like a stage cuckold or a male fool, Speck described in the lightest possible manner how Henriette had followed her lover, a teacher of literature, to a depressed part of French-speaking Africa where the inhabitants were suffering from a shortage of Racine. Unable to halt once he had started, he tore on toward the edge: Henriette was a hopeless nymphomaniac (she had fallen in love) who lacked any sense of values (the man was broke); she was at the same time a grasping neurotic (having sunk her savings in the gallery, she wanted a return with 14 percent interest).

"You must be thankful you finally got rid of her," said Lydia Cruche. "You must be wondering why you married her in the first place."

"I felt sorry for Henriette," he said, momentarily forgetting any other reason. "She seemed so helpless." He told about Henriette living in her sixth-floor walk-up, working as slave labor on a shoddy magazine. A peasant from Alsace, she had never eaten anything but pickled cabbage until Speck drove his Bentley into her life. Under his tactful guidance she had tasted her first fresh truffle salad at Le Récamier; had worn her first mink-lined Dior raincoat; had published her first book-length critical essay, "A Woman Looks at Edgar Allan Poe." And then she had left him—just like that.

"You trained her," said Lydia Cruche. "Brought her up to your level. And now she's considered good enough to marry a teacher. You should feel proud. You shouldn't mind what happened. You should feel satisfied."

"I'm not satisfied," said Speck. "I do mind." He realized that something had been left out of his account. "I loved her." Lydia Cruche looked straight at him, for once, as though puzzled. "As you loved Hubert Cruche," he said.

There was no response except for the removal of crumbs from her lap. The goddess, displeased by his mortal impertinence, symbolically knocked his head off her knee.

"Hube liked my company," she finally said. "That's true enough. After he died I saw him sitting next to the television, by the radiator, where his mother usually crouched all winter looking like a sheep with an earache. I was just resting here, thinking of nothing in particular, when I looked up and noticed him. He said, 'You carry the seed of your death.' I said, 'If that's the case, I might as well put my head in the oven and be done with it.' '*Non*,' he said, '*ce n'est pas la peine*.' Now, his mother was up in her room, making lists of all the things she had to feel sorry about. I went up and said, 'Madame,' because you can bet your boots she never got a '*Maman*' out of me, 'Hube was in the parlor just now.' She answered, 'It was his mother he wanted. Any message was for me.' I said that if that was so, then all he needed to do was to materialize upstairs and save me the bother of climbing. She gave me some half-baked reason why he preferred not to, and then she *did* die. Aged a hundred and three. It was in *France-Soir*."

The French she had spoken rang to Speck like silver bells. Everything about her had changed—voice, posture, expression. If he still could not see the Lydia Cruche of the Senator's vision, at least he could believe in her.

"Do you talk to your husband often?" he said, trying to make it sound like a usual experience.

"How could I talk to Hube? He's dead and buried. I hope you don't go in for ghosts, Dr. Speck. I would find that very silly. That was just some kind of accident—a visitation. I never saw him again or ever expect to. As for his mother, there wasn't a peep out of her after she died. And here I am, alone in the Cruche house." It was hard to say if she sounded glad or sorry. "I gather you're on your own, too. God never meant men and women to live by themselves, convenient though it may seem to some of us. That's why he throws men and women together. Coincidence is God's plan."

So soon, thought Speck. It was only their second meeting. It seemed discourteous to draw attention to the full generation that lay between them; experience had taught him that acknowledging any fragment of this dangerous subject did more harm than good. When widows showed their cards, he tried to look like a man with no time for games. He thought of the young André Malraux, dark and tormented, the windblown lock on the worried brow, the stub of a Gauloise sending up a vagabond spiral of smoke. Unfortunately, Speck had been born forty years too late for the model; he belonged to a much reedier generation of European manhood. He thought of the Pope. White-clad, serene, he gazed out on St. Peter's Square, over the subdued heads of one hundred thousand artists' widows, not one of whom would dare.

"So this was the Cruche family home," he said, striking out, he hoped, in a safe direction.

"The furniture was his mother's," said Lydia Cruche. "I got rid of most of it, but there was stuff you couldn't pay them to cart away. *Sa petite Maman adorable*," she said softly. Again Speck heard the string of silver bells. "I thought she was going to hang around forever. They were a tough family—peasants from the west of France. She took good care of him. Cooked him sheep's heart, tripe and onions, big beefsteaks they used to eat half raw. He was good-looking, a big fellow, big for a Frenchman. At seventy you'd have taken him for forty. Never had a cold. Never had a headache. Never said he was tired. Drank a liter of Calvados every other day. One morning he just keeled over, and that was that. I'll show you a picture of him sometime."

"I'd also like to see *his* pictures," said Speck, thankful for the chance. "The pictures you said you had upstairs."

"You know how I met Hube? People often ask me that. I'm surprised you haven't. I came to him for lessons."

"I didn't know he taught," said Speck. His most reliable professional trait was his patience.

"He didn't. I admired him so much that I thought I'd try anyway. I was eighteen. I rang the bell. His mother let me in. I never left—he wouldn't let me go. His mother often said if she'd known the future she'd never have answered the door. I must have walked about four miles from a tram stop, carrying a big portfolio of my work to show him. There wasn't even a paved street then—just a patch of nettles out front and some vacant lots."

Her work. He knew he had to get it over with: "Would you like to show me some of your things, too?"

"I burned it all a long time ago."

Speck's heart lurched. "But not his work?"

"It wasn't mine to burn. I'm not a criminal." Mutely, he looked at the bare walls. "None of Hube's stuff ever hung in here," she said. "His mother couldn't stand it. We had everything *she* liked—Napoleon at Waterloo, lighthouses, coronations. I couldn't touch it when she was alive, but once she'd gone I didn't wait two minutes."

Speck's eighteenth-century premises were centrally heated. The system, which dated from the early 1960s, had been put in by Americans who had once owned most of the second floor. With the first dollar slide of the Nixon era they had wisely sold their holdings and gone home, without waiting for the calamity still to come. Their memorial was an expensive, casual gift nobody knew what to do with; it had raised everyone's property taxes, and it cost a fortune to run. Tenants, such as Speck, who paid a fat share of the operation, had no say as to when heat was turned on, or to what degree of temperature. Only owners and landlords had a vote. They voted overwhelmingly for the lowest possible fuel bills. By November there was scarcely a trace of warmth in Speck's elegant gallery, his cold was entrenched for the winter, and Walter was threatening to quit. Speck was showing a painter from Bruges, sponsored by a Belgian cultural-affairs committee. Cost-sharing was not a habit of his—it lowered the prestige of the gallery— but in a tight financial season he sometimes allowed himself a breather. The painter, who clearly expected Speck to put him under contract, talked of moving to Paris.

"You'd hate it here," said Speck.

Belgian television filmed the opening. The Belgian Royal Family, bidden by Walter, on his own initiative, sent regrets signed by aides-de-camp on paper so thick it would scarcely fold. These were pinned to the wall, and drew more attention than the show itself. Only one serious critic turned up. The rooms were so cold that guests could not write their names in the visitors' book— their hands were too numb. Walter, perhaps by mistake, had invited Blum-Weiler-Blochs instead of Blum-Bloch-Weilers. They came in a horde, leading an Afghan hound they tried to raffle off for charity.

The painter now sat in the gallery, day after day, smoking black cigarettes that smelled of mutton stew. He gave off a deep professional gloom, which affected Walter. Walter began to speak of the futility of genius—a sure sign of melancholia. Speck gave the painter money so that he could smoke in cafés. The bells of St. Clotilde's clanged and echoed, saying to Speck's memory,

"Fascist, Fascist, Fascist." Walter reminded Speck that November was bad for art. The painter returned from a café looking cheerful. Speck wondered if he was enjoying Paris and if he would decide to stay; he stopped giving him money and the gallery became once more infested with mutton stew and despair. Speck began a letter to Henriette imploring her to come back. Walter interrupted it with the remark that Rembrandt, Mozart, and Dante had lived in vain. Speck tore the letter up and started another one saying that a Guillaumin pastel was missing and suggesting that Henriette had taken it to Africa. Just as he was tearing this up, too, the telephone rang.

"I finally got Hube's stuff all straightened out," said Lydia Cruche. "You might as well come round and look at it this afternoon. By the way, you may call me Lydia, if you want to."

"Thank you," said Speck. "And you, of course, must call me—"

"I wouldn't dream of it. Once a doctor always a doctor. Come early. The light goes at four."

Speck took a pill to quiet the pounding of his heart.

In her summing-up of his moral nature, a compendium that had preceded her ringing "Fascist"s, Henriette had declared that Speck appraising an artist's work made her think of a real-estate loan officer examining Chartres Cathedral for leaks. It was true that his feeling for art stopped short of love; it had to. The great cocottes of history had shown similar prudence. Madame de Pompadour had eaten vanilla, believed to arouse the senses, but such recklessness was rare. Cool but efficient—that was the professional ticket. No vanilla for Speck; he knew better. For what if he were to allow passion for painting to set alight his common sense? How would he be able to live then, knowing that the ultimate fate of art was to die of anemia in safe-deposit vaults? Ablaze with love, he might try to organize raids and rescue parties, dragging pictures out of the dark, leaving sacks of onions instead. He might drop the art trade altogether, as Walter kept intending to do, and turn his talents to cornering the onion market. The same customers would ring at election time, saying, "Dr. Speck, what happens to my onion collection if the left gets in? Shouldn't we try to

unload part of it in New York now, just to be on the safe side?"
And Speck, unloading onions of his own in Tokyo, would answer,
"Don't worry. They can't possibly nationalize all the onions. Be-
sides, they aren't going to win."

Lydia seemed uninterested in Speck's reaction to Cruche. He
had expected her to hang about, watching his face, measuring his
interest, the better to nail her prices; but she simply showed him
a large, dim, dusty, north-facing room in which canvases were
thickly stacked against the walls and said, "I wasn't able to get
the light fixed. I've left a lamp. Don't knock it over. Tea will be
ready when you are." Presently he heard American country music
rising from the kitchen (Lydia must have been tuned to the BBC)
and he smelled a baking cake. Then, immersed in his ice-cold
Cruche encounter, he noticed nothing more.

About three hours later he came downstairs, slowly, wiping
dust from his hands with a handkerchief. His conception of the
show had been slightly altered, and for the better, by the total
Cruche. He began to rewrite the catalogue notes: "The time
has come for birth..." No—"for rebirth. In a world sated by
overstatement the moment is ripe for a calm..." How to avoid
"statement" and still say "statement"? The Grand Architect was
keeping Speck in mind. "For avouchment," said Speck, alone on
the stairs. It was for avouchment that the time had come. It was
also here for hard business. His face became set and distant, as
if a large desk were about to be shoved between Lydia Cruche
and himself.

He sat down and said, "This is going to be a strong show, a
powerful show, even stronger than I'd hoped. Does everything I've
looked at upstairs belong to you outright? Is there anything which
for any reason you are not allowed to lend, show, or sell?"

"Neither a borrower nor a lender be," said Lydia, cutting car-
amel cake.

"No. Well, I am talking about the show, of course."

"No show," she said. "I already told you that."

"What do you mean, no show?" said Speck.

"What I told you at the beginning. I told you not to count
on me. Don't drop boiled frosting on your trousers. I couldn't get
it to set."

"But you changed your mind," said Speck. "After saying 'Don't count on me,' you changed your mind."

"Not for a second."

"Why?" said Speck, as he had said to the departing Henriette. "Why?"

"God doesn't want it."

He waited for more. She folded her arms and stared at the blank television set. "How do you know that God doesn't want Hubert Cruche to have a retrospective?"

"Because He said so."

His first thought was that the Grand Architect had granted Lydia Cruche something so far withheld from Sandor Speck: a plain statement of intention. "Don't you know your Commandments?" she asked. "You've never heard of the graven image?"

He searched her face for the fun, the teasing, even the malice that might give shape to this conversation, allow him to take hold of it. He said, "I can't believe you mean this."

"You don't have to. I'm sure you have your own spiritual pathway. Whatever it is, I respect it. God reveals himself according to each person's mental capacity."

One of Speck's widows could prove she descended from Joan of Arc. Another had spent a summer measuring the walls of Toledo in support of a theory that Jericho had been in Spain. It was Speck's policy never to fight the current of eccentricity but to float with it. He said cautiously, "We are all held in a mysterious hand." Generations of Speck freethinkers howled from their graves; he affected not to hear them.

"I am a Japhethite, Dr. Speck. You remember who Noah was? And his sons, Ham, Shem, and Japheth? What does that mean to you?" Speck looked as if he possessed Old Testament lore too fragile to stand exposure. "Three," said Lydia. "The sacred number. The first, the true, the only source of Israel. That crowd Moses led into the desert were just Egyptian malcontents. The true Israelites were scattered all over the earth by then. The Bible hints at this for its whole length. Japheth's people settled in Scotland. Present-day Jews are impostors."

"Are you connected to this Japheth?"

"I do not make that claim. My Scottish ancestors came from

the border country. The Japhethites had been driven north long before by the Roman invasion. The British Israelite movement, which preceded ours, proved that the name 'Hebrides' was primitive Gaelic for 'Hebrew.' The British Israelites were distinguished pathfinders. It was good of you to have come all the way out here, Dr. Speck. I imagine you'll want to be getting back."

After backing twice into Lydia's fence, Speck drove straight to Galignani's bookshop, on Rue de Rivoli, where he purchased an English Bible. He intended to have Walter ransack it for contra-Japhethite pronouncements. The orange dust jacket surprised him; it seemed to Speck that Bibles were usually black. On the back flap the churches and organizations that had sponsored this English translation were listed, among them the National Bible Society of Scotland. He wondered if this had anything to do with Japheth.

As far as Speck could gather from passages Walter marked during the next few days, art had never really flourished, even before Moses decided to put a stop to it. Apart from a bronze snake cast at God's suggestion (Speck underscored this for Lydia in red), there was nothing specifically cultural, though Ezekiel's visions had a certain surrealistic splendor. As Speck read the words "the terrible crystal," its light flooded his mind, illuminating a simple question: Why not forget Hubert Cruche and find an easier solution for the cultural penury of the West? The crystal dimmed. Speck's impulsive words that October night, "Cruche is coming back," could not be reeled in. Senator Bellefeuille was entangled in a promise that had Speck at one end and Lydia at the other. Speck had asked if he might examine his lodge brother's collection and had been invited to lunch. Cruche *had* to come back.

Believing Speck's deliverance at hand, Walter assailed him with texts and encouragement. He left biblical messages on Speck's desk so that he had to see them first thing after lunch. Apparently the British Israelite movement had truly existed, enjoying a large and respectable following. Its premise that it was the British who were really God's elect had never been challenged, though membership had dwindled at mid-century; Walter could find no trace of Lydia's group, however. He urged Speck to drive to the north of Scotland, but Speck had already decided to abandon the religious approach to Cruche.

"No modern translation conveys the word of Japheth or of God," Lydia had said when Speck showed her Walter's finds. There had been something unusual about the orange dust jacket, after all. He did not consider this a defeat. Bible reading had raised his spirits. He understood now why Walter found it consoling, for much in it consisted of the assurance of downing one's enemies, dashing them against stones, seeing their children reduced to beggary and their wives to despair. Still, he was not drawn to deep belief: He remained rational, skeptical, anxious, and subject to colds, and he had not succeeded in moving Lydia Cruche an inch.

Lunch at Senator Bellefeuille's was balm. Nothing was served that Speck could not swallow. From the dining room he looked across at the dark November trees of the Bois de Boulogne. The Senator lived on the west side of Paris—the clients' side. A social allegory in the shape of a city separated Speck from Lydia Cruche. The Senator's collection was fully insured, free from dust, attractively framed or stored in racks built to order.

Speck began a new catalogue introduction as he ate lunch. "The Bellefeuille Cruches represent a unique aspect of Cruche's vision," he composed, heartily enjoying fresh crab soufflé. "Not nearly enough has been said about Cruche and the nude."

The Senator broke in, asking how much Cruche was likely to fetch after the retrospective. Speck gave figures to which his choice of socks and cuff links lent authority.

"Cruche-and-the-nude implies a definition of Woman," Speck continued, silently, sipping coffee from a gold-rimmed cup. "Lilith, Eve, temptress, saint, child, mother, nurse—Cruche delineated the feminine factor once and for all."

The Senator saw his guest to the door, took his briefcase from the hands of a manservant, and bestowed it on Speck like a diploma. He told Speck he would send him a personal invitation list for the Cruche opening next May. The list would include the estranged wife of a respected royal pretender, the publisher of an influential morning paper, the president of a nationalized bank, and the highest-ranking administrative official of a thickly populated area. Before driving away, Speck took a deep breath of west-end air. It was cool and dry, like Speck's new expression.

That evening, around closing time, he called Lydia Cruche.

He had to let her know that the show could go on without her. "I shall be showing the Bellefeuille Cruches," he said.

"The *what*?"

Speck changed the subject. "There is enormous American interest," he said, meaning that he had written half a dozen letters and received prudent answers or none at all. He was accustomed to the tense excitement "American interest" could arouse. He had known artists to enroll in crash courses at Berlitz, the better to understand prices quoted in English.

Lydia was silent; then she said, slowly, "Don't ever mention such a thing again. Hube was anti-American—especially during the war." As for Lydia, she had set foot in the United States once, when a marshmallow roast had taken her a few yards inside North Dakota, some sixty years before.

The time was between half past seven and eight. Walter had gone to early dinner and a lecture on lost Atlantis. The Belgian painter was back in Bruges, unsold and unsung. The cultural-affairs committee had turned Speck's bill for expenses over to a law firm in Brussels. Two Paris galleries had folded in the past month and a third was packing up for America, where Speck gave it less than a year. Painters set adrift by these frightening changes drifted to other galleries, shipwrecked victims trying to crawl on board waterlogged rafts. On all sides Speck heard that the economic decline was irreversible. He knew one thing—art had sunk low on the scale of consumer necessities. To mop up a few back bills, he was showing part of his own collection—his last-ditch old-age-security reserve. He clasped his hands behind his neck, staring at a Vlaminck India ink on his desk. It had been certified genuine by an expert now serving a jail sentence in Zurich. Speck was planning to flog it to one of the ambassadors down the street.

He got up and began turning out lights, leaving just a spot in the window. To have been anti-American during the Second

World War in France had a strict political meaning. Any hope of letters from Louis Aragon and Elsa withered and died: Hubert Cruche had been far right. Of course, there was right and right, thought Speck as he triple-locked the front door. Nowadays the Paris intelligentsia drew new lines across the past, separating coarse collaborators from fine-drawn intellectual Fascists. One could no longer lump together young hotheads whose passionate belief in Europe had led them straight to the Charlemagne Division of the Waffen-S.S. and the soft middle class that had stayed behind to make money on the black market. Speck could not quite remember why *pure* Fascism had been better for civilization than the other kind, but somewhere on the safe side of the barrier there was bound to be a slot for Cruche. From the street, he considered a page of Charles Despiau sketches—a woman's hand, her breast, her thigh. He thought of the Senator's description of that other, early Lydia and of the fragments of perfection Speck could now believe in, for he had seen the Bellefeuille nudes. The familiar evening sadness caught up with him and lodged in his heart. Posterity forgives, he repeated, turning away, crossing the road on his way to his dinner.

Speck's ritual pause brought him up to St. Amand and his demon just as M. Chassepoule leaned into his window to replace a two-volume work he had probably taken out to show a customer. The bookseller drew himself straight, stared confidently into the night, and caught sight of Speck. The two greeted each other through glass. M. Chassepoule seemed safe, at ease, tucked away in a warm setting of lights and friends and royal blue, and yet he made an odd little gesture of helplessness, as if to tell Speck, "Here I am, like you, over-taxed, hounded, running an honest business against dreadful odds." Speck made a wry face of sympathy, as if to answer that he knew, he knew. His neighbor seemed to belong to an old and desperate breed, its back to the wall, its birthright gnawed away by foreigners, by the heathen, by the blithe continuity of art, by Speck himself. He dropped his gaze, genuinely troubled, examining the wares M. Chassepoule had collected, dusted, sorted, and priced for a new and ardent generation. The work he had just put back in the window was *La France Juive*, by Édouard Drumont. A handwritten notice described it as a classic study, out of print, hard to find, and in good condition.

Speck thought, A few years ago, no one would have dared put it on display. It has been considered rubbish for fifty years. Édouard Drumont died poor, alone, cast off even by his old friends, completely discredited. Perhaps his work was always being sold, quietly, somewhere, and I didn't know. Had he been Walter and superstitious, he might have crossed his fingers; being Speck and rational, he merely shuddered.

Walter had a friend—Félicité Blum-Weiler-Bloch, the owner of the Afghan hound. When Walter complained to her about the temperature of the gallery, she gave him a scarf, a sweater, an old flannel bedsheet, and a Turkey carpet. Walter decided to make a present of the carpet to Speck.

"Get that thing out of my gallery," said Speck.

"It's really from Félicité."

"I don't want her here, either," said Speck. "Or the dog."

Walter proposed spreading the carpet on the floor in the basement. "I spend a lot of time there," he said. "My feet get cold."

"I want it out," said Speck.

Later that day Speck discovered Walter down in the framing room, holding a vacuum cleaner. The Turkey carpet was spread on the floor. A stripe of neutral color ran through the pattern of mottled reds and blues. Looking closer, Speck saw it was warp and weft. "Watch," said Walter. He switched on the vacuum; another strip of color vanished. "The wool lifts right out," said Walter.

"I told you to get rid of it," said Speck, trembling.

"Why? I can still use it."

"I won't have my gallery stuffed with filth."

"You'll never have to see it. You hardly ever come down here." He ran the vacuum, drowning Speck's reply. Over the noise Walter yelled, "It will look better when it's all one color."

Speck raised his voice to the right-wing pitch heard during street fights: "Get it out! Get it out of my gallery!"

Like a telephone breaking into a nightmare, delivering the sleeper, someone was calling, "Dr. Speck." There on the stairs stood Lydia Cruche, wearing an ankle-length fur coat and a brown velvet turban. "I thought I'd better have a look at the place," she said. "Just to see how much space you have, how much of Cruche you can hold."

Still trembling, Speck took her hand, which smelled as if she had been peeling oranges, and pressed it to his lips.

That evening, Speck called the Senator: Would he be interested in writing the catalogue introduction? No one was better fitted, said Speck, over senatorial modesty. The Senator had kept faith with Cruche. During his years of disappointment and eclipse Cruche had been heartened, knowing that guests at the Senator's table could lift their eyes from quail in aspic to feast on *Nude in the Afternoon.*

Perhaps his lodge brother exaggerated just a trifle, the Senator replied, though it was true that he had hung on to his Cruches even when their value had been wiped out of the market. The only trouble was that his recent prose had been about the capital-gains-tax project, the Common Market sugar-beet subsidy, and the uninformed ecological campaign against plastic containers. He wondered if he could write with the same persuasiveness about art.

"I have taken the liberty of drawing up an outline," said Speck. "Just a few notes. Knowing how busy you are."

Hanging up, he glanced at his desk calendar. Less than six weeks had gone by since the night when, by moonlight, Speck had heard the Senator saying ". . . hats."

A few days before Christmas Speck drove out to Lydia's with a briefcase filled with documents that were, at last, working papers: the list of exhibits from the Bellefeuille collection, the introduction, and the chronology in which there were gaps for Lydia to fill. He still had to draw up a financial arrangement. So far, she had said nothing about it, and it was not a matter Speck cared to rush.

He found another guest in the house—a man somewhat younger than he, slightly bald and as neat as a mouse.

"Here's the doctor I was telling you about," said Lydia, introducing Speck.

Signor Vigorelli of Milan was a fellow-Japhethite—so Speck gathered from their conversation, which took up, in English, as though he had never come in. Lydia poured Speck's tea in an offhand manner he found wounding. He felt he was being treated like the hanger-on in a Russian play. He smashed his lemon cupcake, scattering crumbs. The visitor's plate looked cleaner than his. After a minute of this, Speck took the catalogue material out of his briefcase and started to read. Nobody asked what he was reading. The Italian finally looked at his watch (expensive, of a make Speck recognized) and got to his feet, picking up car keys that had been lying next to his plate.

"That little man had an Alfa Romeo tag," said Speck when Lydia returned after seeing him out.

"I don't know why you people drive here when there is perfectly good bus service," she said.

"What does he do?"

"He is a devout, religious man."

For the first time, she sat down on the sofa, close to Speck. He showed her the introduction and the chronology. She made a number of sharp and useful suggestions. Then they went upstairs and looked at the pictures. The studio had been cleaned, the light repaired. Speck suddenly thought, I've done it—I've brought it off.

"We must discuss terms," he said.

"When you're ready," she replied. "Your cold seems a lot better."

Inching along in stagnant traffic, Speck tried one after the other the FM state-controlled stations on his car radio. He obtained a lecture about the cultural oppression of Cajuns in Louisiana, a warning that the road he was now driving on was saturated, and the disheartening squeaks and wails of a circumcision ceremony in Ethiopia. On the station called France-Culture someone said, "Henri Cruche."

"Not Henri, excuse me," said a polite foreigner. "His name was Hubert. Hubert Cruche."

"Strange that it should be an Italian to discover an artist so essentially French," said the interviewer.

Signor Vigorelli explained that his admiration for France was second only to his intense feelings about Europe. His career had been consecrated to enhancing Italian elegance with French refinement and then scattering the result abroad. He believed that the unjustly neglected Cruche would be a revelation and might even bring the whole of Western art to its senses.

Speck nodded, agreeing. The interview came to an end. Wild jungle drums broke forth, heralding the announcement that there was to be a reading of medieval Bulgarian poetry in an abandoned factory at Nanterre. It was then and then only that Speck took in the sense of what he had heard. He swung the car in a wild U-turn and, without killing himself or anyone else, ran into a tree. He sat quietly, for about a minute, until his breathing became steady again, then unlocked his safety belt and got out. For a long time he stood by the side of the road, holding his briefcase, feeling neither shock nor pain. Other drivers, noticing a man alone with a wrecked car, picked up speed. He began to walk in Lydia's direction. A cruising prostitute, on her way home to cook her husband's dinner, finally agreed to drop him off at a taxi stand. Speck gave her two hundred francs.

Lydia did not seem at all surprised to see him. "I'd invite you to supper," she said. "But all I've got is a tiny pizza and some of the leftover cake."

"The Italian," said Speck.

"Yes?"

"I've heard him. On the radio. He says he's got Cruche. That he discovered him. My car is piled up in the Bois. I tried to turn around and come back here. I've been walking for hours."

"Sit down," said Lydia. "There, on the sofa. Signor Vigorelli is having a big Cruche show in Milan next March."

"He can't," said Speck.

"Why can't he?"

"Because Cruche is mine. He was my idea. No one can have my idea. Not until after June."

"Then it goes to Trieste in April," said Lydia. "You could still have it by about the tenth of May. If you still want it."

If I want it, said Speck to himself. If I want it. With the best work sold and the insurance rates tripled and the commissions shared out like candy. And with everyone saying Speck jumped on the bandwagon, Speck made the last train.

"Lydia, listen to me," he said. "I invented Hubert Cruche. There would be no Hubert Cruche without Sandor Speck. This is an unspeakable betrayal. It is dishonorable. It is wrong." She listened, nodding her head. "What happens to me now?" he said. "Have you thought about that?" He knew better than to ask, "Why didn't you tell me about him?" Like all dissembling women, she would simply answer, "Tell you what?"

"It might be all the better," she said. "There'll be that much more interest in Hube."

"Interest?" said Speck. "The worst kind of interest. Third-rate, tawdry interest. Do you suppose I can get the Pompidou Center to look at a painter who has been trailing around in Trieste? It had to be a new idea. It had to be strong."

"You'll save on the catalogue," she said. "He will probably want to share."

"It's my catalogue," said Speck. "I'm not sharing. Senator Bellefeuille . . . my biography . . . never. The catalogue is mine. Besides, it would look as if he'd had the idea."

"He did."

"But after me," said Speck, falling back on the most useless of all lover's arguments. "*After* me. I was there first."

"So you were," she said tenderly, like any woman on her way out.

Speck said, "I thought you were happy with our arrangement."

"I was. But I hadn't met him yet. You see, he was so interested in the Japhethite movement. One day he opened the Bible and put his finger on something that seemed to make it all right about the graven image. In Ecclesiastes, I think."

Speck gave up. "I suppose it would be no use calling for a taxi?"

"Not around here, I'm afraid, though you might pick one up at the shopping center. Shouldn't you report the accident?"

"Which accident?"

"To the police," she said. "Get it on record fast. Make it a case. That squeezes the insurance people. The phone's in the hall."

"I don't care about the insurance," said Speck.

"You will care, once you're over the shock. Tell me exactly where it happened. Can you remember? Have you got your license? Registration? Insurance?"

Speck sank back and closed his eyes. He could hear Lydia dialing; then she began to speak. He listened, exactly as Cruche must have listened, while Lydia, her voice full of silver bells, dealt with creditors and dealers and Cruche's cast-off girlfriends and a Senator Bellefeuille more than forty years younger.

"I wish to report an accident," Lydia sang. "The victim is Dr. S. Speck. He is still alive—luckily. He was forced off the road in the Bois de Vincennes by a tank truck carrying high-octane fuel. It had an Italian plate. Dr. Speck was too shaken to get the number. Yes, I saw the accident, but I couldn't see the number. There was a van in the way. All I noticed was 'MI.' That must stand for Milan. I recognized the victim. Dr. Speck is well known in some circles . . . an intimate friend of Senator Antoine Bellefeuille, the former minister of . . . that's right." She talked a few minutes longer, then came back to Speck. "Get in touch with the insurance people first thing tomorrow," she said, flat Lydia again. "Get a medical certificate—you've had a serious emotional trauma. It can lead to jaundice. Tell your doctor to write that down. If he doesn't want to, I'll give you the name of a doctor who will. You're on the edge of nervous depression. By the way, the police will be towing your car to a garage. They know they've been very remiss, letting a foreign vehicle with a dangerous cargo race through the Bois. It might have hit a bus full of children. They must be looking for that tanker all over Paris. I've made a list of the numbers you're to call."

Speck produced his last card: "Senator Bellefeuille will never allow his Cruches to go to Milan. He'll never let them out of the country."

"Who—Antoine?" said Lydia. "Of course he will."

She cut a cupcake in half and gave him a piece. Broken, Speck crammed the whole thing in his mouth. She stood over him, humming. "Do you know that old hymn, Dr. Speck—'The day Thou gavest, Lord, is ended'?"

He searched her face, as he had often, looking for irony, or playfulness—a gleam of light. There floated between them the cold oblong on the map and the Chirico chessboard moving along to its Arctic destination. Trees dwindled to shrubs and shrubs to moss and moss to nothing. Speck had been defeated by a landscape.

Although Speck by no means considered himself a natural victim of hard luck, he had known disappointment. Shows had fallen flat. Galleries had been blown up and torn down. Artists he had nursed along had been lured away by siren dealers. Women had wandered off, bequeathing to Speck the warp and weft of a clear situation, so much less interesting than the ambiguous patterns of love. Disappointment had taught him rules: The first was that it takes next to no time to get used to bad news. Rain began to fall as he walked to the taxi stand. In his mind, Cruche was already being shown in Milan and he was making the best of it.

He gazed up and down the bleak road; of course there were no taxis. Inside a bus shelter huddled a few commuters. The thrust of their lives, their genetic destiny obliged them to wait for public transport—unlike Speck, thrown among them by random adventures. A plastic-covered timetable announced a bus to Paris every twenty-three minutes until five, every sixteen minutes from four to eight, and every thirty-one minutes thereafter. His watch had stopped late in the afternoon, probably at the time of the accident. He left the shelter and stood out in the wet, looking at windows of shops, one of which might contain a clock. He stood for a minute or two staring at a china tea set flanked by two notices, HAND PAINTED and CHRISTMAS IS COMING, both of which he found deeply sad. The tea set had been decorated with reproductions of the Pompidou Art Center, which was gradually replacing the Eiffel Tower as a constituent feature of French design. The day's shocks caught up with him: He stared at the milk jug, feeling surprise because it did not tell him the time. The arrival of a bus replaced this perplexity with one more pressing. He did not know what was needed on suburban buses—tickets or tokens or a monthly pass. He wondered whether the drivers accepted banknotes, and gave change, with civility.

"Dr. Speck, Dr. Speck!" Lydia Cruche, her raincoat open and

flying, waving a battered black umbrella, bore down on him out of the dark. "You were right," she said, gasping. "You were there first." Speck took his place at the end of the bus queue. "I mean it," she said, clutching his arm. "He can wait."

Speck's second rule of disappointment came into play: The deceitful one will always come back to you ten seconds too late. "What does it mean?" he said, wiping rain from the end of his nose. "Having it before him means what? Paying for the primary expenses and the catalogue and sweetening the Paris critics and letting him rake in the chips?"

"Wasn't that what you wanted?"

"Your chap from Milan thought he was first," said Speck. "He may not want to step aside for me—a humble Parisian expert on the entire Cruche context and period. You wouldn't want Cruche to miss a chance at Milan, either."

"Milan is ten times better for money than Paris," she said. "If that's what we're talking about. But of course we aren't."

Speck looked down at her from the step of the bus. "Very well," he said. "As we were."

"I'll come to the gallery," she called. "I'll be there tomorrow. We can work out new terms."

Speck paid his fare without trouble and moved to the far end of the bus. The dark shopping center with its windows shining for no one was a Magritte vision of fear. Lydia had already forgotten him. Having tampered with his pride, made a professional ass of him, gone off with his idea and returned it dented and chipped, she now stood gazing at the Pompidou Center tea set, perhaps wondering if the ban on graven images could possibly extend to this. Speck had often meant to ask her about the Mickey Mouse napkins. He thought of the hoops she had put him through—God, and politics, and finally the most dangerous one, which was jealousy. There seemed to be no way of rolling down the window, but a sliding panel at the top admitted half his face. Rising from his seat, he drew in a gulp of wet suburban air and threw it out as a shout: "Fascist! Fascist! Fascist!"

Not a soul in the bus turned to see. From the look of them, they had spent the best Sundays of their lives shuffling in demonstrations from Place de la République to Place de la Nation, tossing "Fascist"s around like confetti. Lydia turned slowly and looked at Speck. She raised her umbrella at arm's length, like a trophy. For the first time, Speck saw her smile. What was it the Senator had said? "She had a smile like a fox's." He could see, gleaming white, her straight little animal teeth.

The bus lurched away from the curb and lumbered toward Paris. Speck leaned back and shut his eyes. Now he understood about that parting shot. It was amazing how it cleared the mind, tearing out weeds and tree stumps, flattening the live stuff along with the dead. "Fascist" advanced like a regiment of tanks. Only the future remained—clean, raked, ready for new growth. New growth of what? Of Cruche, of course—Cruche, whose hour was at hand, whose time was here. Speck began to explore his altered prospects. "New terms," she had said. So far, there had been none at all. The sorcerer from Milan must have promised something dazzling, swinging it before her eyes as he had swung his Alfa Romeo key. It would be foolish to match the offer. By the time they had all done with bungling, there might not be enough left over to buy a new Turkey carpet for Walter.

I was no match for her, he thought. No match at all. But then, look at the help she had—that visitation from Cruche. "Only once," she said, but women always said that: "He asked if he could see me just once more. I couldn't very well refuse." Dead or alive, when it came to confusion and double-dealing, there was no such thing as "only once." And there had been not only the departed Cruche but the very living Senator Bellefeuille— "Antoine"; who had bought every picture of Lydia for sixteen years, the span of her early beauty. Nothing would ever be the same again between Speck and Lydia, of course. No man could give the same trust and confidence the second time around. All that remained to them was the patch of landscape they held in common—a domain reserved for the winning, collecting, and sharing out of profits, a territory where believer and skeptic, dupe and embezzler, the loving and the faithless could walk hand in hand. Lydia had a talent for money. He could sense it. She had never been given much chance to use it, and she had waited so much longer than Speck.

He opened his eyes and saw rain clouds over Paris glowing

with light—the urban aurora. It seemed to Speck that he was entering a better weather zone, leaving behind the gray, indefinite mist in which the souls of discarded lovers are said to wander. He welcomed this new and brassy radiation. He saw himself at the center of a shadeless drawing, hero of a sort of cartoon strip, subduing Lydia, taming Henriette. Fortunately, he was above petty grudges. Lydia and Henriette had been designed by a bachelor God who had let the creation get out of hand. In the cleared land of Speck's future, a yellow notebook fluttered and lay open at a new page. The show would be likely to go to Milan in the autumn now; it might be a good idea to slip a note between the Senator's piece and the biographical chronology. If Cruche had to travel, then let it be with Speck's authority as his passport.

The bus had reached its terminus, the city limit. Speck waited as the rest of the passengers crept inch by inch to the doors. He saw, with immense relief, a rank of taxis half a block long. He alighted and strode toward them, suddenly buoyant. He seemed to have passed a mysterious series of tests, and to have been admitted to some new society, the purpose of which he did not yet understand. He was a saner, stronger, wiser person than the Sandor Speck who had seen his own tight smile on M. Chassepoule's window only two months before. As he started to get into a taxi, a young man darted toward him and thrust a leaflet into his hand. Speck shut the door, gave his address, and glanced at the flier he was still holding. Crudely printed on cheap pink paper was this:

FRENCHMEN!
FOR THE SAKE OF EUROPE, FIGHT
THE GERMANO-AMERICANO-ISRAELO
HEGEMONY!
Germans in Germany!
Americans in America!
Jews in Israel!
For a True Europe, For One Europe,
Death to the Anti-European Hegemony!

Speck stared at this without comprehending it. Was it a Chasse-poule statement or an anti-Chassepoule plea? There was no way of knowing. He turned it over, looking for the name of an associa-tion, and immediately forgot what he was seeking. Holding the sheet of paper flat on his briefcase, he began to write, as well as the unsteady swaying of the cab would let him.

"It was with instinctive prescience that Hubert Cruche saw the need for a Europe united from the Atlantic to the ... That Cruche skirted the murky zone of partisan politics is a tribute to his ... even though his innocent zeal may have led him to the brink ... early meeting with the young idealist and future states-man A. Bellefeuille, whose penetrating essay ... close collabora-tion with the artist's wife and most trusted critic ... and now, posthumously ... from Paris, where the retrospective was planned and brought to fruition by the undersigned ... and on to Italy, to the very borders of ..."

Because this one I am keeping, Speck decided; this one will be signed: "By Sandor Speck." He smiled at the bright, wet streets of Paris as he and Cruche, together, triumphantly crossed the Alps.

BAUM, GABRIEL, 1935–(   )

At the start of the 1960s Gabriel Baum's only surviving relative, his Uncle August, turned up in Paris. There was nothing accidental about this; the International Red Cross, responding to an appeal for search made on Gabriel's behalf many years before, had finally found Gabriel in Montparnasse and his uncle in the Argentine. Gabriel thought of his uncle as "the other Baum," because there were just the two of them. Unlike Gabriel's father and mother, Uncle August had got out of Europe in plenty of time. He owned garages in Rosario and Santa Fe and commercial real estate in Buenos Aires. He was as different from Gabriel as a tree is from the drawing of one; nevertheless Gabriel saw in him something of the old bachelor he too might become.

Gabriel was now twenty-five; he had recently been discharged from the French Army after twenty months in Algeria. Notice of his uncle's arrival reached him at a theater seating two hundred persons where he had a part in a play about J. K. Huysmans. The play explained Huysmans's progress from sullen naturalism to mystical Christianity. Gabriel had to say, "But Joris Karl has written words of penetrating psychology," and four or five other things.

The two Baums dined at the Bristol, where Gabriel's uncle was staying. His uncle ordered for both, because Gabriel was taking too long to decide. Uncle August spoke German and Spanish and the pale scrupulous French and English that used to be heard at spas and in the public rooms of large, airy hotels. His clothes were old-fashioned British; watch and luggage were Swiss. His manners were German, prewar—pre-1914, that is. To Gabriel, his uncle seemed to conceal an obsolete social mystery; but a few

Central Europeans, still living, would have placed him easily as a tight, unyielding remainder of the European shipwreck.

The old man observed Gabriel closely, watching to see how his orphaned nephew had been brought up, whether he broke his bread or cut it, with what degree of confidence he approached his asparagus. He was certainly pleased to have discovered a younger Baum and may even have seen Gabriel as part of God's subtle design, bringing a surrogate son to lighten his old age, one to whom he could leave Baum garages; on the other hand it was clear that he did not want just any Baum calling him "Uncle."

"I have a name," he said to Gabriel. "I have a respected name to protect. I owe it to my late father." He meant his own name: August Ernest Baum, b. Potsdam 1899–.

After dinner they sat for a long time drinking brandy in the hushed dining room. His uncle was paying for everything.

He said, "But were your parents ever married, finally? Because we were never told he had actually *married* her."

Gabriel at that time seemed to himself enduringly healthy and calm. His hair, which was dark and abundant, fell in locks on a surprisingly serene forehead. He suffered from only two complaints, which he had never mentioned. The first had to do with his breathing, which did not proceed automatically, like other people's. Sometimes, feeling strange and ill, he would realize that heart and lungs were suspended on a stopped, held breath. Nothing disastrous had come of this. His second complaint was that he seemed to be haunted, or inhabited, by a child—a small, invisible version of himself, a Gabriel whose mauled pride he was called on to salve, whose claims against life he was forced to meet with whatever thin means time provided, whose scores he had rashly promised to settle before realizing that debt and payment never interlock. His uncle's amazing question and the remark that followed it awoke the wild child, who began to hammer on Gabriel's heart.

He fixed his attention on a bottle—one of the dark bottles whose labels bear facsimiles of gold medals earned at exhibitions no one has ever heard of, in cities whose names have been swept off the map: Breslau 1884, Dantzig 1897, St. Petersburg 1901.

"The only time I ever saw her, they certainly were not married," his uncle resumed. "It was during the very hot autumn of 1930. He had left the university announcing that he would earn his living writing satirical poetry. My father sent me to Berlin to see what was going on. *She* was going on. Her dress had short sleeves. She wore no stockings. She had a clockwork bear she kept winding up and sending round the table. She was hopelessly young. 'Have you thought about the consequences?' I asked him. 'No degree. Low-grade employment all your life. Your father's door forever closed to you. And what about *her*? Is she an heiress? Will her father adopt you?' She was said to be taking singing lessons," he added, as if there were something wrong with that.

"Shut him up," ordered the younger Gabriel, but Gabriel was struggling for breath.

"I have lost everything and everyone but I still have a name," said his uncle. "I have a name to protect and defend. There is always the trace of a marriage certificate somewhere. Even when the registry office was bombed. Even when the papers had to be left behind. How old were you the last time you saw them?"

"Eight," said Gabriel, now in control.

"Were they together?"

"Oh, yes."

"Did they have time to say good-bye?"

"They left me with a neighbor. The neighbor said they'd be back."

"Where was this?"

"Marseilles. We were supposed to be from Alsace, but their French sounded wrong. People noticed I wasn't going to school. Someone reported them."

"Sounded wrong!" said his uncle. "Everything must have sounded wrong from the minute he left the university. It is a terrible story," he said, after a moment. "No worse than most, but terrible all the same. Why, why did he wait until the last minute? And once he had got to Marseilles what prevented him from getting on a boat?"

"He was a man of action," said Gabriel.

If his uncle wanted another Baum, he did not want a frivolous one. He said, "He was much younger than I was. I never saw him after 1930. He went his own way. After the war I had the family traced. Everybody was dead—camps, suicide, old age. In his case, no one knew what had happened. He disappeared. Of course, it took place in a foreign country. Only the Germans kept accurate records. I wish you knew something about the marriage. I know that my late father would not have wanted a bastard in the family."

Uncle August visited Nice, Lugano, and Venice, which he found greatly changed, then he returned to South America. He sent long letters to Gabriel several times a year, undeterred by the fact that he seldom received an answer. He urged his nephew to take a strong, positive line with his life and above all to get out of Paris, which had never amounted to more than an émigré way station. Its moral climate invited apathy and rot.

Gabriel read his uncle's letters in La Méduse, a *bar-tabac* close to the old Montparnasse railway station. Actors and extras for television were often recruited there; no one remembered how or why this arrangement had come about. Gabriel usually sat with his back to the window, at a table to the right of the door facing the bar. He drank draft beer or coffee and looked at magazines other customers had left behind. Glancing up from one of his uncle's letters, he saw the misted window in the mirror behind the bar. In a polluted winter fog neon glowed warmly—the lights of home.

His uncle wrote that he had liquidated his holdings at a loss and was thinking of settling in South Africa. He must have changed his mind, for a subsequent letter described him retired and living near a golf course, looked after by the housekeeper he had often told Gabriel about—his first mention of any such person. A heart attack made it tiring for him to write. The housekeeper sent news. Gabriel, who did not know Spanish, tried to get the drift. She signed "Anna Meléndes," then "Anna Baum."

Gabriel was playing a Brecht season in a suburban cultural center when word came that his uncle had died. *The Caucasian Chalk Circle* and *Mother Courage* alternated for an audience of schoolchildren and factory workers brought in by the busload, apparently against their will. Gabriel thought of Uncle August, his obstinacy and his pride, and truly mourned him. His uncle had left him an envelope he did not bother to open, being fairly certain it did not contain a check.

No Baum memorial existed, and so he invented one. Upon its marble surface he inscribed:

Various Baums:	Gone
Father:	1909–1943 (probably)
Mother:	1912–1943 (probably)
Uncle:	1899–1977
Gabriel B.:	1935–( )

Beneath the last name he drew a line, meaning to say this was the end. He saw, however, that the line, far from ending the Baum question, created a new difficulty: It left the onlooker feeling that these dates and names were factors awaiting a solution. He needed to add the dead to the living, or subtract the living from the dead—to come to some conclusion.

He thought of writing a zero, but the various Baums plus four others did not add up to nothing. His uncle by dying had not diminished the total number of Baums but had somehow increased it. Gabriel, with his feet on the finish line and with uncounted Baums behind him, was a variable quantity: For some years he had been the last of the Baums, then there had been two of them. Now he was unique again.

Someone else would have to work it out, he decided—someone unknown to him, perhaps unborn. In the meantime he had the memorial in his head, where it could not be lost or stolen.

GABRIEL'S LISELOTTE

Soon after Gabriel's uncle's visit, a generation of extremely pretty German girls suddenly blossomed in Paris. There would be just that one flowering—that one bright growth. They came because their fathers were dead or exiled under unremarkable names. Some of them were attracted to Gabriel—Gabriel as he was, with the dark locks, the serene brow—and he was drawn in turn, as to a blurred reflection, a face half recalled.

Gabriel at that time still imagined that everyone's life must be about the same, something like a half-worked crossword puzzle. He was always on the lookout for definitions and new solutions. When he moved close to other people, however, he saw that their lives were not puzzles but problems set in code, no two of which ever matched.

The pretty girls went home, finally, whistled back by solemn young men with solemn jobs. They had two children apiece, were probably rinsing the gray out of their hair now. (Gabriel cut his own as short as possible as it grew scarce.) He remembered Freya, who had thrown herself in the Seine over a married man, but who could swim, and Barbara, whose abortion two or three of them had felt bound to pay for, and Marie, who had gone to Alsace and had nearly been crowned Miss Upper Rhine before they found out she was a foreigner. Gabriel's memory dodging behind one name after the other brought him face-to-face with his Liselotte. Daughter of a dead man and a whore of a mother (which seemed to be a standard biography then), embarked on the au-pair adventure, pursuing spiritual cleanness through culture, she could be seen afternoons in Parc Monceau reading books of verse whose close print and shoddy bindings seemed to assure a cultural warranty. There was something meek about the curve of her neck. She had heard once that if one were arrested and held without trial it was an aid to sanity to have an anthology of poems in one's head. Poor Liselotte, whose aid to sanity never got beyond *"Le ciel est, par-dessus le toit, Si bleu, si calme!"* held the book flat on her knees, following the words with her finger.

"Who would want to arrest you?" Gabriel asked.

"You never know."

Well, that was true. Thinking there might be a better career for her he gave her lines to try. She practiced, "Is it tonight that you *die*?" "Is it *tonight* that *you* die?" Gabriel counted six, seven, eight shades of green around the place in Parc Monceau, where she sat asking this. He used to take the No. 84 bus to see her—he who never went out of Montparnasse unless he had to, who had never bothered to learn about bus routes or the names of streets. For the sake of Liselotte he crossed the Seine with prim, gloved women, with old men wearing slivers of ribbon to mark this or that war. Liselotte, now seeking improvement by way of love, made him speak French to her. She heard, memorized, and recited back to him without flaw his life's story. He had promised the child-Gabriel he would never marry a German, but it was not that simple; in an odd way she did not seem German *enough*.

She had learned her lines for nothing. The director he introduced her to also thought she did not look German. She was one of the brown-eyed Catholic girls from around Speyer. She prayed for Gabriel, but his life after the prayers was the same as before. She had a catch in her voice, almost a stammer; she tried to ask Gabriel if he wanted to marry her, but the word caught. He said to himself that she might not enjoy being Liselotte Baum after having been Liselotte Pfligge. Her stepfather, Wilhelm Pfligge—of Swiss origin, she said—had tried to rape her; still, she had his name. Gabriel thought that if the custom of name-changing had been reversed and he had been required, through marriage, to become Gabriel Pfligge, he might have done so without cringing, or at least with tact. Perhaps he would have been expected to call Wilhelm Pfligge "Papa." He saw Papa Pfligge with a mustache, strangely mottled ears, sporty shoes, a springy walk, speaking with his lips to Gabriel's ear: "We both love Liselotte so much, eh?"

While Gabriel continued to develop this, giving Papa Pfligge increasingly preposterous things to say, Liselotte gave up on love and culture and the au-pair adventure and went home. He accompanied her to the Gare de l'Est and lifted her two cases to the overhead rack. Then he got down and stood on the gray platform and watched her being borne away. The train was blurred, as if he were looking at it through Liselotte's tears.

For a time her letters were like the trail of a child going ever deeper into the woods. He could not decide whether or not to follow; while he was still deciding, and not deciding, the trail stopped and the path became overgrown behind her.

THE INTERVIEW

Until he could no longer write letters, Gabriel's uncle nagged him with useless advice. Most of it was about money. Owing to

Gabriel's inability to produce his father's marriage certificate (in fact, he never tried), his uncle could not in all conscience leave him Baum possessions. It was up to Gabriel, therefore, to look after his own future. He begged Gabriel to find a job with some large, benevolent international firm. It would give him the assurance of money coming in, would encourage French social-security bureaucrats to take an interest in him, and would put him in the way of receiving an annuity at the age of sixty-five.

"Sixty-five is your next step," his uncle warned, for Gabriel's thirtieth birthday.

He counseled Gabriel to lay claim to those revenues known as "German money," but Gabriel's parents had vanished without trace; there was no way of proving they had not taken ship for Tahiti. And it would not have been in Gabriel's power to equate banknotes to a child's despair. His uncle fell back on the Algerian War. Surely Gabriel was entitled to a pension? No, he was not. War had never been declared. What Gabriel had engaged in was a long tactical exercise for which there was no compensation except experience.

The Algerian-pension affair rankled with Gabriel. He had to fill out employment forms that demanded assurance that he had "fulfilled his military obligations." Sometimes it was taken for granted he had been rejected out of hand. There was no rational basis for this; he supposed it must be because of "Profession: Actor." After his return he continued to take an interest in the war. He was like someone who has played twenty minutes of a match and has to know the outcome. As far as he could make out, it had ended in a draw. The excitement died down, and then no one knew what to put in the magazines and political weeklies anymore. Some journalists tried to interest Gabriel in Brittany, where there was an artichoke glut; others hinted that the new ecumenicity beginning to seep out of Rome was really an attack on French institutions. Gabriel doubted this. Looking for news about his pension, he learned about the Western European consumer society and the moral wounds that were being inflicted on France through full employment. Between jobs, he read articles about people who said they had been made unhappy by paper napkins and washing machines.

Most of the customers in La Méduse were waiting for a television call. The rest were refugees, poets' widows, and foreign
students looking for work to supplement their scholarships.
Up at the bar, where drinks were cheaper, were clustered the
second-generation émigré actors Gabriel thought of as bachelor
orphans. Unlike Gabriel, they had been everywhere—to Brazil,
where they could not understand the language, and to New York,
where they complained about the climate, and to Israel, where
they were disappointed with the food. Now they were in Paris,
where they disliked the police.

Sometimes Dieter Pohl shared Gabriel's table. He was a
Bavarian Gabriel's age—thirty—who played in films about the
Occupation. Dieter had begun as a private, had been promoted to
lieutenant, and expected to become a captain soon. He had two
good facial expressions, one for victory and one for defeat.
Advancing, he gazed keenly upward, as if following a hawk to the
vanishing point. Sometimes he pressed binoculars to his eyes.
Defeat found him staring at his boots. He could also be glimpsed
marching off into captivity with a bandage around his head. The
captivity scene took place in the last episode. Gabriel, enrolled
as a victim, had generally been disposed of in the first. His rapid
disappearance was supposed to establish the tone of the period
for audiences too young to recall it.

It was around this time, when French editorial alarm about the
morally destructive aspect of Western prosperity was at its most
feverish, that a man calling himself Briseglace wandered into the
bar and began asking all the aliens and strangers there if they were
glad to be poor. He said that he was a journalist, that his wife had
left him for a psychiatrist, and that his girlfriend took tickets in a
cinema farther along the street. He said that the Montparnasse
railway station was to be torn down and a dark tower built in its
place; no one believed him. He wore a tie made of some yellow
Oriental stuff. His clothes looked as if they had been stitched by
nuns on a convent sewing machine. Gabriel and his generation
had gone into black—black pullovers, black leather jackets, soft
black boots. Their haircuts still spoke of military service and colonial wars. Briseglace's straggling, grayish locks, his shapeless and
shabby and oddly feminine-looking overcoat, his stained fingers

and cheap cigarettes, his pessimism and his boldness and his belief in the moral advantages of penury all came straight from the Latin Quarter of the 1940s. He was the Occupation; he was the Liberation, too. The films that Dieter and Gabriel played in grew like common weeds from the heart of whatever young man he once had been. Gabriel's only feeling, seeing him, was disgust at what it meant to grow old.

The dark garments worn in La Méduse gave the place the appearance of a camp full of armed militia into which Briseglace, outdated civilian, had stumbled without cause. Actually, the leather jackets covered only perpetual worry. Some people thought Briseglace was with the CIA, others saw a KGB agent with terrifying credentials. The orphans were certain he was an inspector sent to see if their residence permits were forgeries. But his questions led only to one tame conclusion, which he begged them to ratify: It was that being poor they were free, and being free they were happy.

Released from immediate danger, a few of the aliens sat and stood straighter, looked nonchalant or offended, depending on how profound their first terrors had been. Dieter declared himself happy in a profession that had brought him moral satisfaction and material comfort, and that provided the general public with no- tions of history. Some of those at the bar identified themselves as tourists, briefly in Paris, staying at comfortable hotels. Someone mentioned the high prices that had to be paid for soccer stars. Another recalled that on the subject of personal riches Christ had been ambiguous yet reassuring. Briseglace wrote everything down. When he paid for his coffee he asked for the check, which he had to turn in for expenses. Gabriel, who had decided to have nothing to do with him, turned the pages of *Paris-Match*.

Six weeks later Gabriel emerged in the pages of a left-wing weekly as "Gabriel B., spokesman for the flotsam of Western Europe."

"His first language was German," Gabriel read. "Lacking the rudder of political motivation, his aimless wanderings have cast him up in Montparnasse, in the sad fragrance of coffee machines. Do you think he eats in the Jewish quarter, at Jo Goldenberg's, at La Rose d'Or? Never. You will find Gabriel B. gnawing veal cutlets at the Wienerwald, devouring potato dumplings at the Tannhaüser. For Gabriel B. this bizarre nourishment constitutes a primal memory, from infancy to age twelve." "Seven," Gabriel scrupulously corrected, but it was too late, the thing was in print. "This handsome Prince of Bohemia has reached the fatal age of thirty. What can he do? Where can he go? Conscience-money from the wealthy German republic keeps him in cigarettes. A holdover from bad times, he slips through the good times without seeing them. The Western European consumer society is not so much an economic condition as a state of mind."

Gabriel read the part about the Prince of Bohemia two or three times. He wondered where the Wienerwald was. In the picture accompanying the article was Dieter Pohl, with his eyes inked over so that he could not be identified and use the identification as an excuse for suing the magazine.

There was no explaining it; Dieter was sure he had not sat for a portrait; Gabriel was positive he had not opened his mouth. He thought of posting the article to Uncle August, but his uncle would take it to be a piece of downright nonsense, like the clockwork bear. Dieter bought half a dozen copies of the magazine for his relatives in Bavaria; it was the first time that a picture of him had ever been published anywhere.

Gabriel's escape from annihilation in two real wars (even though one had been called something else) had left him with reverence for unknown forces. Perhaps Briseglace had been sent to nudge him in some new direction. Perhaps the man would turn up again, confessing he had never been a journalist and had been feigning not in order to harm Gabriel but to ensure his ultimate safety.

Nothing of the kind ever happened, of course. Briseglace was never seen again in La Méduse. The only reaction to the interview came from a cousin of Dieter's called Helga. She did not read French easily and had understood some of it to mean that Dieter was not eating enough. She sent him a quantity of very good gingerbread in a tin box and begged him, not for the first time, to pack his things and come home and let a woman look after his life.

UNSETTLING RUMORS

As he grew older and balder, stouter, and more reflective, Gabriel found himself at odds with the few bachelors he still saw in Montparnasse. They tended to cast back to the 1960s as the springtime of life, though none of them had been all that young. Probably because they had outlived their parents and were without children, they had no way of measuring time. To Gabriel the decade now seemed to have been like a south wind making everyone fretful and jumpy. The colder their prospects, the steadier his friends had become. They slept well, cashed their unemployment checks without grumbling, strolled along the boulevards through a surf of fallen leaves, and discarded calls to revolution, stood in peaceful queues in front of those cinemas that still charged no more than eleven francs. Inside, the seats and carpets were moldering slowly. Half the line shuffling up to the ticket office was probably out of work. His friends preferred films in which women presented no obstacles and created no problems and were shown either naked or in evening dress.

Much of Gabriel's waking time was now spent like this, too—not idly, but immersed in the present moment.

Soon after the Yom Kippur War, a notice had been posted in La Méduse: OWING TO THE ECONOMIC SITUATION NO ONE MAY SIT FOR MORE THAN THIRTY MINUTES OVER A SINGLE ORDER. The management had no legal means of enforcing this; still the notice hung there, a symptom of a new harshness, the sourness engendered by the decline.

"That sign was the end of life as we knew it in the sixties," said Dieter Pohl. He was a colonel now, and as fussy as a monarch at a review about a badge misplaced or a button undone. Gabriel had no equivalent staircase to climb; who ever has heard of a victim's being promoted? Still, he had acquired a variety of victim experiences. Gabriel had been shot, stoned, drowned, suffocated, and marked off for hanging; had been insulted and betrayed; had been shoved aboard trains and dragged out of them; had been flung from the back of a truck with such accidental violence that he had broken his collarbone. His demise, seen by millions of people, some eating their dinner, was still needed in order to give a push to the old dishonorable plot—told ever more simply now, like a fable—while Dieter's fate was still part of its moral.

On this repeated game of death and consequences Dieter's seniority depended. He told Gabriel that the French would be bored with entertainment based on the Occupation by about 1982; by that time he would have been made a general at least once, and would have saved up enough money to buy a business of some kind in his native town.

He often spoke as if the parting were imminent, though he was still only a colonel: "Our biographies are not the same, and you are a real actor, who took lessons, and a real soldier, who fought in a real war. But look at the result—we ended up in the same place, doing the same work, sitting at the same table. Years and years without a disagreement. It is a male situation. Women would never be capable of such a thing."

Gabriel supposed Dieter to mean that women, inclined by nature to quick offense and unending grudges, were not gifted for loyal friendship. Perhaps it was true, but it seemed incomplete. Even the most solitary of the women he could observe—the poets' widows, for instance, with their crocheted berets, their mysterious shopping bags, their fat, waddling dogs—did not cluster together like anxious pigeons on the pretext of friendship. Each one came in alone and sat by herself, reading whatever fascinating stuff she could root out of the shopping bag, staring at strangers with ever-fresh interest, sometimes making comments about them aloud.

A woman can always get some practical use from a torn-up life, Gabriel decided. She likes mending and patching it, making sure the edges are straight. She spreads the last shred out and takes its measure: "What can I do with this remnant? How long does it need to last?" A man puts on his life ready-made. If it doesn't fit, he will try to exchange it for another. Only a fool of a man will try to adjust the sleeves or move the buttons; he doesn't know how.

Some of the older customers were now prey to unsettling rumors. La Méduse was said to have been sold by its owner, a dour Breton with very small eyes. It would soon be converted to a dry cleaner's establishment, as part of the smartening-up of Montparnasse. The chairs, the glasses, the thick, grayish cups and saucers, the zinc-covered bar, the neon tubes on the ceiling—sociological artifacts—had been purchased at roaring prices for a museum in Stockholm. It seemed far-fetched to Gabriel but not impossible; the Montparnasse station had been torn down, and a dark ugly tower had been put in its place. He remembered how Briseglace had predicted this.

Gabriel had noticed lately that he was not seeing Paris as it was but the way it had stayed in his mind; he still saw butchers and grocers and pastry shops, when in reality they had become garages and banks. There was a new smell in the air now, metallic and hot. He was changing too. Hunger was drawn to his attention by a feeling of sadness and loss. He breathed without effort. The child-Gabriel had grown still. Occupation films had fallen off a little, but Gabriel had more resources than Dieter. He wore a checked cap and sang the "Internationale"; he was one of a committee bringing bad news to Seneca. He had a summer season playing Flavius in *Julius Caesar*, and another playing Aston in *The Caretaker* and the zoo director in *The Bedbug*. These festivals were staged in working-class suburbs the inhabitants of which had left for the Côte d'Azur. During one of those summers La Méduse changed hands, shut for three months, and opened with rows of booths, automobile seats made of imitation leather, orange glass lampshades, and British First World War recruiting posters plastered on the walls. The notice about not sitting for more than thirty minutes had vanished, replaced by an announcement that ice cream and hamburgers could be obtained. Washrooms and telephones were one flight up instead of in the basement; there was someone on hand to receive tips and take messages. At each table was a bill of fare four pages long and a postcard advertising the café, which customers could send to their friends if they wanted to. The card showed a Medusa jellyfish with long eyelashes and a ribbon on its head, smiling out of a tiny screen. Beneath this one could read:

PUB LA MÉDUSE
THE OLDEST AND MOST CELEBRATED
MEETING-PLACE FOR TELEVISION
STARS IN PARIS

Gabriel tried a number of booths before finding one that suited him. Between the automobile seat and a radiator was a space where he could keep magazines. The draft beer was of somewhat lower quality than before. The main difference between the old place and the new one was its smell. For a time he could not identify it. It turned out to be the reek of a chicory drink, the color of boot polish, invented to fight inflation. The addition of sugar made it nauseating, and it was twice as expensive as coffee had ever been.

THE SURRENDER

Dieter heard that a thirteen-hour television project about the Occupation was to be launched in the spring; he had seen the outline.

He said, "For the moment they just need a few people to be deported and to jump off the train."

Some old-timers heard Dieter say, "They want to deport the Poles," and some heard, "They are rounding up the foreign-born Socialists," and others swore he had asked for twelve Jews to be run over by a locomotive.

Dieter wore a new civilian winter costume, a light brown fur-lined winter coat and a Russian cap. He ate roasted chestnuts, which he peeled with his fingernails. They were in a cornucopia made of half a page of *Le Quotidien de Paris*. In the old Méduse eating out of newspaper would have meant instant expulsion. Dieter spread the paper on Gabriel's table, sat down, and told him about the film. It would begin with a group of Resistance fighters who were being deported jumping out of a train. Their group would include a coal miner, an anti-Semitic aristocrat, a Communist militant, a peasant with a droll Provençal accent, a long-faced Protestant intellectual, and a priest in doubt about his vocation. Three Jews will be discovered to have jumped or fallen with them: one aged rabbi, one black-market operator, and one anything.

The one anything will be me, Gabriel decided, helping himself to chestnuts. He saw, without Dieter's needing to describe them, the glaring lights, the dogs straining at their leads, the guards running and blowing whistles, the stalled train, a rainstorm, perhaps.

The aristo will be against taking the extra three men along, Dieter said, but the priest will intercede for them. The miner, or perhaps the black-market man, will stay behind to act as decoy for the dogs while the others all get in a rowboat and make for the maquis. The peasant will turn out to be a British intelligence agent named Scott. The Protestant will fall out of the rowboat; the priest will drown trying to save him; the Communist—

"We know all that," Gabriel interrupted. "Who's there at the end?"

The aristo, said Dieter. The aristo and the aged rabbi will survive twelve episodes and make their way together back to Paris for the Liberation. There they will discover Dieter and his men holed up in the Palais du Luxembourg, standing fast against the local Resistance and a few policemen. The rabbi will die next to the Medici fountain, in the arms of the aristo.

Gabriel thought this did not bode well for the future, but Dieter reassured him: The aristo will now be a changed man. He will storm the Palais and be seen at the end writing MY FRIENDS REMEMBERED on the wall while Dieter and the others file by with their hands up.

"What about the one anything?" said Gabriel. "How long does he last?"

"Dear friend and old comrade," said Dieter, "don't take offense at this. Ten years ago you would have been the first man chosen. But now you are at the wrong age. Who cares what happens to a man of forty-three? You aren't old enough or young enough to make anyone cry. The fact is—forgive me for saying so—but you are the wrong age to play a Jew. A uniform has no age," he added, because he was also forty-three. "And no one is expected to cry at the end, but just to be thoughtful and satisfied."

While Gabriel sat mulling this over, Dieter told him about the helmets the Germans were going to wear. Some were heavy metal, museum pieces; they gave their wearers headaches and left red marks on the brow. A certain number of light plastic helmets would be distributed, but only to officers. The higher one's rank, the lighter the helmet. What Dieter was getting around to was this: He wondered if Gabriel might not care to bridge this stage of his Occupation career by becoming a surrendering officer, seen in the last episode instead of vanishing after the first. He would be a colonel in the Wehrmacht (humane, idealistic, opposed to extreme measures) while Dieter would have to be the S.S. one (not so good). He and Dieter would both have weightless helmets and comfortable, well-cut uniforms.

Gabriel supposed that Dieter was right, in a way. Certainly, he was at a bad age for dangerous antics. It was time for younger men to take their turn at jumping off moving vehicles, diving into ice-cold streams, and dodging blank shot; nor had he reached that time of life when he could die blessing and inspiring those the script had chosen to survive him. As an officer, doomed to defeat, he would at least be sure of his rank and his role and of being in one piece at the end.

Two weeks later Dieter announced to the old-timers that the whole first scene had been changed; there would now be a mass escape from a convoy of lorries, with dozens of men gunned down on the spot. The original cast was reduced, with the Protestant, the Communist, and the miner eliminated completely. This new position caused some argument and recrimination, in which Gabriel did not take part. All he had to wait for now was the right helmet and good weather.

The usual working delays occurred, so that it was not until May that the last of the Baums tried on his new uniform. Dieter adjusted the shoulders of the tunic and set the plastic helmet at a jaunty angle. Gabriel looked at himself. He removed the helmet and put it back on straight. Dieter spoke encouragingly; he seemed to think that Gabriel was troubled about seeming too stout, too bald, too old for his rank.

"There is nothing like a uniform for revealing a man's real age to him," said Dieter. "But from a distance everyone in uniform looks the same."

Gabriel in his new uniform seemed not just to be looking at himself in a glass but actually to be walking through it. He moved through a liquid mirror, back and forth. With each crossing his breath came a little shorter.

Dieter said generously, "A lot of soldiers went bald prematurely because the helmets rubbed their hair."

The surrender was again delayed, this time on account of bad weather. One sodden afternoon, after hanging about in the Luxembourg Gardens for hours, Dieter and Gabriel borrowed capes from a couple of actors who were playing policemen and, their uniforms concealed, went to a post office so that Dieter could make a phone call. His cousin, Helga, destined by both their families to be his bride, had waited a long time; just when it was beginning to look as if she had waited too long for anything, a widower proposed. She was being married the next day. Dieter had to call and explain why he could not be at the wedding; he was held up waiting for the surrender.

Helga talked to Dieter without drawing breath. He listened for a while, then handed the receiver to Gabriel. Helga continued telling Dieter, or Gabriel, that her husband-to-be had a grandchild who could play the accordion. The child was to perform at the wedding party. The accordion was almost as large as the little girl, and twice as heavy.

"You ought to see her fingers on the keyboard," Helga yelled. "They fly—fast, fast."

Gabriel gave the telephone to Dieter, who assumed a look of blank concentration. When he had heard enough he beckoned to Gabriel. Gabriel pressed the receiver to his ear and learned that Helga was worried. She had dreamed that she was married and that her husband would not make room for her in his apartment. When she wanted to try the washing machine, he was already washing his own clothes. "What do you think of the dream?" she said to Gabriel. "Can you hear me? I still love you." Gabriel placed the receiver softly on a shelf under the telephone and waved Dieter in so that he could say good-bye.

They came out of the post office to a drenching rain. Dieter wondered what shape their uniforms would be in by the time they surrendered. Gabriel argued that after the siege of the Palais du Luxembourg the original uniforms must have shown wear. Dieter answered that it was not up to him or Gabriel to decide such things.

Rain fell for another fortnight, but, at last, on a cool shining June day, they were able to surrender. During one of the long periods of inextricable confusion, Dieter and Gabriel walked as far as the Delacroix monument and sat on its rim. Dieter was disappointed in his men. There were no real Germans among them, but Yugoslavs, Turks, North Africans, Portuguese, and some unemployed French. The Resistance forces were not much better, he said. There had been complaints. Gabriel had to agree that they were a bedraggled-looking lot. Dieter recalled how in the sixties there used to be real Frenchmen, real Germans, authentic Jews. The Jews had played deportation the way they had seen it in films, and the Germans had surrendered according to film tradition, too, but there had been this difference: They had at least been doing something their parents had done before them. They had not only the folklore of movies to guide them but—in many cases—firsthand accounts. Now, even if one could assemble a true cast of players, they would be trying to imitate their grandfathers. They were at one remove too many. There was no assurance that a real German, a real Frenchman would be any more plausible now than a Turk.

Dieter sighed, and glanced up at the houses on the other side of the street edging the park. "It wouldn't be bad to live up there," he said. "At the top, with one of those long terraces. They grow real trees on them—poplars, birches."

"What would it cost?"

"Around a hundred and fifty million francs," said Dieter. "Without the furniture."

"Anyone can have a place like that with money," said Gabriel. "The interesting thing would be to live up there without it."

"How?"

Gabriel took off his helmet and looked deeply inside it. He said, "I don't know."

Dieter showed him the snapshots of his cousin's wedding. Helga and the groom wore rimless spectacles. In one picture they cut a cake together; in another they tried to drink out of the same champagne glass. Eyeglasses very like theirs, reduced in size, were worn by a plain little girl. On her head was a wreath of daisies. She was dressed in a long, stiff yellow gown. Gabriel could see just the hem of the dress and the small shoes, and her bashful anxious face and slightly crossed eyes. Her wrists were encircled by daisies, too. Most of her person was behind an accordion. The accordion seemed to be falling apart; she had all she could do to keep it together.

"My cousin's husband's granddaughter," said Dieter. He read Helga's letter: " 'She can play anything—fast, fast. Her fingers simply fly over the keyboard.' "

Gabriel examined every detail of the picture. The child was dazzled and alarmed, and the accordion was far too heavy. "What is her name?" he said.

Dieter read more of the letter and said, "Erna."

"Erna," Colonel Baum repeated. He looked again at the button of a face, the flower bracelets, the feet with the heels together— they must have told her to stand that way. He gave the snapshot back without saying anything.

A crowd had collected in the meantime, drawn by the lights and the equipment and the sight of the soldiers in German uniform. Some asked if they might be photographed with them; this often happened when a film of that kind was made in the streets.

An elderly couple edged up to the two officers. The woman said, in German, in a low voice, "What are you doing here?"

"Waiting to surrender," said Dieter.

"I can see that, but what are you *doing*?"

"I don't know," said Dieter. "I've been sitting on the edge of this monument for thirty-five years. I'm still waiting for orders."

The man tried to give them cigarettes, but neither colonel smoked. The couple took pictures of each other standing between Dieter and Gabriel, and went away.

Why is it, said Gabriel to himself, that when I was playing a wretched, desperate victim no one ever asked to have his picture taken with me? The question troubled him, seeming to proceed from the younger Gabriel, who had been absent for some time now. He hoped his unruly tenant was not on his way back, screaming for a child's version of justice, for an impossible world.

Some of the men put their helmets upside down on the ground and tried to make the visitors pay for taking their pictures. Dieter was disturbed by this. "Of course, you were a real soldier," he said to Gabriel unhappily. "All this must seem inferior." They sat without saying anything for a time and then Dieter began to talk about ecology. Because of ecology, there was a demand in Bavaria for fresh bread made of authentic flour, salt, water, and yeast. Because of unemployment, there were people willing to return to the old, forgotten trades, at which one earned practically nothing and had to work all night. The fact was that he had finally saved up enough money and had bought a bakery in his native town. He was through with the war, the Occupation, the Liberation, and captivity. He was going home.

This caused the most extraordinary change in Gabriel's view of the park. All the greens in it became one dull color, as if thunderous clouds had gathered low in the sky.

"You will always be welcome," said Dieter. "Your room will be ready, a bed made up, flowers in a vase. I intend to marry someone in the village—someone young."

Gabriel said, "If you have four or five children, how can you keep a spare room?"

Still, it was an attractive thought. The greens emerged again, fresh and bright. He saw the room that could be his. Imagine being wakened in a clean room by birds singing and the smell of freshly baked bread. Flowers in a vase—Gabriel hardly knew one from the other, only the caged flowers of parks. He saw, in a linen press, sheets strewn with lavender. His clothes hung up or folded. His breakfast on a white tablecloth, under a lime tree. A basket of warm bread, another of boiled eggs. Dieter's wife putting her hand on the white coffeepot to see if it was still hot enough for Gabriel. A jug of milk, another of cream. Dieter's obedient children drinking from mugs, their chins on the rim of the table. Yes, and the younger Gabriel, revived and outraged and jealous, thrashing around in his heart, saying, Think about empty rooms, letters left behind, cold railway stations washed down with disinfectant, dark glaciers of time. And, then, Gabriel knew nothing about the country. He could not see himself actually *in* it. He had never been to the country except to jump out of trains. It was only in films that he had seen mist lifting or paths lost in ferns.

They surrendered all the rest of the afternoon. The aristo wrote

"MY FRIENDS REMEMBERED" on the wall while Dieter and Gabriel led some Turks and Yugoslavs and some unemployed Frenchmen into captivity. The aristo did not even bother to turn around and look. Gabriel was breathing at a good rhythm—not too shallow, not too fast. An infinity of surrenders had preceded this one, in color and in black-and-white, with music and without. A long trail of application forms and employment questionnaires had led Gabriel here: "Baum, Gabriel, b. 1935, Germany, nat. French, mil. serv. obl. fulf." (Actually, for some years now his date of birth had rendered the assurance about military service unnecessary.) Country words ran meanwhile in Gabriel's head. He thought, Dense thickets, lizards and snakes, a thrush's egg, a bee, lichen, wild berries, dark thorny leaves, pale mushrooms. Each word carried its own fragrance.

At the end of the day Dieter's face was white and tired and perfectly blank. He might have been listening to Helga. The aristo came over, smoking a cigarette. About twenty-three years before this, he and Gabriel had performed before a jury in a one-act play of Jules Renard's. The aristo had received an honorable mention, Gabriel a first. The aristo hadn't recognized Gabriel until now because of the uniform. He said, "What's the matter with him?"

Dieter sat slumped in an iron chair belonging to the park administration, staring at his boots. He jerked his head up and looked around, crying, "Why? Where?" and something else Gabriel didn't catch.

Gabriel hoped Dieter was not going to snap now, with the bakery and the flowers and the children in sight. "Well, well, old friend!" said Dieter, clutching Gabriel and trying to get to his feet. "Save your strength! Don't take things to heart! You'll dance at my wedding!"

"Exhaustion," said the aristo.

Gabriel and Dieter slowly made their way to the street, where Volkswagen buses full of actors were waiting. The actors made signs meaning to tell them to hurry up; they were all tired and impatient and anxious to change into their own clothes and get home. Dieter leaned on his old friend. Every few steps he stopped to talk excitedly, as people put to a great strain will do, all in a rush, like the long babbling of dreams.

"You'll have to walk faster," said Gabriel, beginning to feel irritated. "The buses won't wait forever, and we can be arrested for wearing these uniforms without a reason."

"There's a very good reason," said Dieter, but he seemed all at once to recover.

That night at La Méduse Dieter drew the plan of the bakery and the large apartment above it, with an X marking Gabriel's room. He said that Gabriel would spend his summers and holidays there, and would teach Dieter's children to pronounce French correctly. The light shining out of the orange glass lampshade made the drawing seem attractive and warm. It turned out that Dieter hadn't actually bought the bakery but had made a down payment and was negotiating for a bank loan.

The proprietor of La Méduse now came over to their table, accompanied by a young couple—younger than Dieter and Gabriel, that is—to whom he had just sold the place. He introduced them, saying, "My oldest customers. You know their faces, of course. Television."

The new owners shook hands with Gabriel and Dieter, assuring them that they did not intend to tamper with the atmosphere of the old place; not for anything in the world would they touch the recruiting posters or the automobile seats.

After they had gone Dieter seemed to lose interest in his drawing; he folded it in half, then in half again, and finally put his glass down on it. "They are a pair of crooks, you know," he said. "They had to get out of Bastia because they had swindled so many people they were afraid of being murdered. Apparently they're going to turn La Méduse into a front for the Corsican Mafia." Having said this, Dieter gave a great sigh and fell silent. Seeing that he had given up talking about the bakery and Gabriel's room, Gabriel drew a magazine out from behind the radiator and began to read. Dieter let him go on reading for quite a while before he sighed again. Gabriel did not look up. Dieter unfolded the drawing and smoothed it flat. He examined it, made a change or two with a pencil, and said something indistinct.

Gabriel said, "What?" without raising his head. Dieter answered, "My father lived to be ninety."

THE REMISSION

WHEN IT became clear that Alec Webb was far more ill than anyone had cared to tell him, he tore up his English life and came down to die on the Riviera. The time was early in the reign of the new Elizabeth, and people were still doing this—migrating with no other purpose than the hope of a merciful sky. The alternative (Alec said to his only sister) meant queueing for death on the National Health Service, lying on a regulation mattress and rubber sheet, hearing the breath of other men dying.

Alec—as obituaries would have it later—was husband to Barbara, father to Will, Molly, and James. It did not occur to him or to anyone else that the removal from England was an act of unusual force that could rend and lacerate his children's lives as well as his own. The difference was that their lives were barely above ground and not yet in flower.

The five Webbs arrived at a property called Lou Mas in the course of a particularly hot September. Mysterious Lou Mas, until now a name on a deed of sale, materialized as a pink house wedged in the side of a hill between a motor road and the sea. Alec identified its style as Edwardian-Riviera. Barbara supposed he must mean the profusion of balconies and parapets, and the slender pillars in the garden holding up nothing. In the new southern light everything looked to her brilliant and moist, like color straight from a paintbox. One of Alec's first gestures was to raise his arm and shield his eyes against this brightness. The journey had exhausted him, she thought. She had received notice in dreams that their change of climates was irreversible; not just Alec but none of them could go back. She did not tell him so, though in better times it might have interested that part of his mind he kept fallow: Being entirely rational, he had a prudent respect for second sight.

The children had never been in a house this size. They chased each other and slid along the floors until Alec asked, politely, if they wouldn't mind playing outside, though one of the reasons he had wanted to come here was to be with them for the time remaining. Dispatched to a flagged patio in front of the house, the children looked down on terraces bearing olive trees, then a railway line, then the sea. Among the trees was a cottage standing empty which Barbara had forbidden them to explore. The children were ten, eleven, and twelve, with the girl in the middle. Since they had no school to attend, and did not know any of the people living around them, and as their mother was too busy to invent something interesting for them to do, they hung over a stone balustrade waving and calling to trains, hoping to see an answering wave and perhaps a decapitation. They had often been warned about foolish passengers and the worst that could happen. Their mother came out and put her arms around Will, the eldest. She kissed the top of his head. "Do look at that sea," she said. "Aren't we lucky?" They looked, but the vast, flat sea was a line any of them could have drawn on a sheet of paper. It was there, but no more than there; trains were better—so was the ruined cottage. Within a week James had cut his hand on glass breaking into it, but by then Barbara had forgotten her injunction.

The sun Alec had wanted turned out to be without compassion, and he spent most of the day indoors, moving from room to room, searching for some gray, dim English cave in which to take cover. Often he sat without reading, doing nothing, in a room whose one window, none too clean, looked straight into the blank hill behind the house. Seepage and a residue of winter rainstorms had traced calm yellowed patterns on its walls. He guessed it had once been assigned to someone's hapless, helpless paid companion, who would have marveled at the thought of its lending shelter to a dying man. In the late afternoon he would return to his bedroom, where, out on the balcony, an angular roof shadow slowly replaced the sun. Barbara unfolded his deck chair on the still burning tiles. He stretched out, opened a book, found the page he wanted, at once closed his eyes. Barbara knelt in a corner, in a triangle of light. She had taken her clothes off, all but a sun hat; bougainvillea grew so thick no one could see. She said, "Would you like me to read to you?" No; he did everything alone, or nearly. He was—always—bathed, shaved, combed, and dressed. His children would not remember him unkempt or disheveled, though it might not have mattered to them. He did not smell of sweat or sickness or medicine or fear.

When it began to rain, later in the autumn, the children played indoors. Barbara tried to keep them quiet. There was a French school up in the town, but neither Alec nor Barbara knew much about it; and, besides, there was no use settling them in. He heard the children asking for bicycles so they could ride along the motor road, and he heard Barbara saying no, the road was dangerous. She must have changed her mind, for he next heard them discussing the drawbacks and advantages of French bikes. One of the children—James, it was—asked some question about the cost.

"You're not to mention things like that," said Barbara. "You're not to speak of money."

Alec was leaving no money and three children—four, if you counted his wife. Barbara often said she had no use for money, no head for it. "Thank God I'm Irish," she said. "I haven't got rates of interest on the brain." She read Irishness into her nature as an explanation for it, the way some people attributed their gifts and failings to a sign of the zodiac. Anything natively Irish had dissolved long before, leaving only a family custom of Catholicism and another habit, fervent in Barbara's case, of anticlerical passion. Alec supposed she was getting her own back, for a mysterious reason, on ancestors she would not have recognized in Heaven. Her family, the Laceys, had been in Wales for generations. Her brothers considered themselves Welsh.

It was Barbara's three Welsh brothers who had put up the funds for Lou Mas. Houses like this were to be had nearly for the asking, then. They stood moldering at the unfashionable end of the coast, damaged sometimes by casual shellfire, difficult to heat, costly to renovate. What the brothers had seen as valuable in Lou Mas was not the villa, which they had no use for, but the undeveloped seafront around it, for which each of them had a different plan. The eldest brother was a partner in a firm of civil engineers;

another managed a resort hotel and had vague thoughts about building one of his own. The youngest, Mike, who was Barbara's favorite, had converted from the RAF to commercial flying. Like Alec, he had been a prisoner of war. The two men had that, but nothing else, in common. Mike was the best traveled of the three. He could see, in place of the pink house with its thick walls and high ceilings, one of the frail, domino-shaped blocks that were starting to rise around the Mediterranean basin, creating a vise of white plaster at the rim of the sea.

Because of United Kingdom income-tax laws, which made it awkward for the Laceys to have holdings abroad, Alec and Barbara had been registered as owners of Lou Mas, with Desmond, the engineer, given power of attorney. This was a manageable operation because Alec was entirely honorable, while Barbara did not know a legal document from the ace of diamonds. So that when the first scouts came round from the local British colony to find out what the Webbs were like and Barbara told them Lou Mas belonged to her family she was speaking the truth. Her visitors murmured that they had been very fond of the Vaughan-Thorpes and had been sorry to see them go—a reference to the previous owners, whose grandparents had built Lou Mas. Barbara did not suppose this to be a snub: She simply wondered why it was that a war out of which her brothers had emerged so splendidly should have left Alec, his sister, and the unknown Vaughan-Thorpes worse off than before.

The scouts reported that Mr. Webb was an invalid, that the children were not going to school, that Mrs. Webb must at one time have been pretty, and that she seemed to be spending a good deal of money, either her husband's or her own. When no improvements were seen in the house, the grounds, or the cottage, it began to be taken for granted that she had been squandering, on trifles, rather more than she had.

Her visitors were mistaken: Barbara never spent more than she had, but only the total of all she could see. What she saw now was a lump of money like a great block of marble, from which she could chip as much as she liked. It had come by way of Alec's sister. Alec's obstinate refusal to die on National Health had meant that his death had somehow to be paid for. Principle was a fine thing, one of Barbara's brothers remarked, but it came high. Alec's earning days were done for. He had come from a long line of medium-rank civil servants who had never owned anything except the cottages to which they had eventually retired, and which their heirs inevitably sold. Money earned, such as there was, disappeared in the sands of their male progeny's education. Girls were expected to get married. Alec's sister, now forty-four, had not done so, though she was no poorer or plainer than most. "I am better off like this," she had told Alec, perhaps once too often. She was untrained, unready, unfitted for any life save that of a woman civilian's in wartime; peace had no use for her, just as the postwar seemed too fast, too hard, and too crowded to allow for Alec. Her only asset was material: a modest, cautiously invested sum of money settled on her by a godparent, the income from which she tried to add to by sewing. Christening robes had been her special joy, but fewer babies were being baptized with pomp, while nylon was gradually replacing the silks and lawns she worked with such care. Nobody wanted the bother of ironing flounces and tucks in a world without servants.

Barbara called her sister-in-law "the mouse." She had small brown eyes; was vegetarian; prayed every night of her life for Alec and for the parents who had not much loved her. "If they would just listen to me," she was in the habit of saying—about Alec and Barbara, for instance. She never complained about her compressed existence, which seemed to her the only competent one at times; at least it was quiet. When Alec told her that he was about to die, and wanted to emigrate, and had been provided with a house but with nothing to run it on, she immediately offered him half her capital. He accepted in the same flat way he had talked about death—out of his driving need, she supposed, or because he still held the old belief that women never need much. She knew she had made an impulsive gesture, perhaps a disastrous one, but she loved Alec and did not want to add to her own grief. She was assured that anything left at the end would be returned enriched and amplified by some sort of nimble investment, but as Alec and his family intended to live on the capital she did not see how this could be done.

Alec knew that his sister had been sacrificed. It was merely another of the lights going out. Detachment had overtaken him even before the journey south. Mind and body floated on any current that chose to bear them.

For the first time in her life Barbara had enough money, and no one to plague her with useless instructions. While Alec slept, or seemed to, she knelt in the last triangle of sun on the balcony reading the spread-out pages of the *Continental Daily Mail*. It had been one thing to have no head for money when there was none to speak of; the present situation called for percipience and wit. Her reading informed her that dollars were still stronger than pounds. (Pounds were the decaying cottage, dollars the Edwardian house.) Alec's background and training made him find the word "dollars" not overnice, perhaps alarming, but Barbara had no class prejudice to hinder her. She had already bought dollars for pounds, at a giddy loss, feeling each time she had put it over on banks and nations, on snobs, on the financial correspondent of the *Mail*, on her own clever brothers. (One of the Webbs' neighbors, a retired Army officer, had confided to Alec that he was expecting the Russians to land in the bay below their villas at any time. He intended to die fighting on his doorstep; however, should anything happen to prevent his doing so, he had kept a clutch of dollars tucked in the pocket of an old dressing gown so that he and his mother could buy their way out.)

In Alec's darkened bedroom she combed her hair with his comb. Even if he survived he would have no foothold on the 1950s. She, Barbara, had been made for her time. This did not mean she wanted to live without him. Writing to one of her brothers, she advised him to open a hotel down here. Servants were cheap— twenty or thirty cents an hour, depending on whether you worked the official or the free-market rate. In this letter her brother heard Barbara's voice, which had stayed high and breathless though she must have been thirty-four. He wondered if this was the sort of prattle poor dying old Alec had to listen to there in the south.

"South" was to Alec a place of the mind. He had not deserted England, as his sad sister thought, but moved into one of its oldest literary legends, the Mediterranean. His part of this legend was called Rivabella. Actually, "Rivebelle" was written on maps and road signs, for the area belonged to France—at least, for the present. It had been tugged between France and Italy so often that it now had a diverse, undefinable character and seemed to be remote from any central authority unless there were elections or wars. At its heart was a town sprawled on the hill behind Lou Mas and above the motor road. Its inhabitants said "Rivabella"; they spoke, among themselves, a Ligurian dialect with some Spanish and Arabic expressions mixed in, though their children went to school and learned French and that they descended from a race with blue eyes. What had remained constant to Rivabella was its poverty, and the groves of ancient olive trees that only the strictest of laws kept the natives from cutting down, and the look and character of the people. Confined by his illness, Alec would never meet more of these than about a dozen; they bore out the expectation set alight by his reading, seeming to him classless and pagan, poetic and wise, imbued with an instinctive understanding of light, darkness, and immortality. Barbara expected them to be cunning and droll, which they were, and to steal from her, which they did, and to love her, which they seemed to. Only the children were made uneasy by these strange new adults, so squat and ill-favored, so quarrelsome and sly, so destructive of nature and pointlessly cruel to animals. But, then, the children had not read much, were unfamiliar with films, and had no legends to guide them.

Barbara climbed up to the town quite often during the first weeks, looking for a doctor for Alec, for a cook and maid, for someone to give lessons to the children. There was nothing much to see except a Baroque church from which everything removable had long been sold to antiquarians, and a crumbling palace along the very dull main street. In one of the palace rooms she was given leave to examine some patches of peach-colored smudge she was told were early Renaissance frescoes. Some guidebooks referred to these, with the result that a number of the new, hardworking breed of postwar traveler panted up a steep road not open to motor traffic only to find that the palace belonged to a cranky French countess who lived alone with her niece and would not let anyone in. (Barbara, interviewing the niece for the post of governess, had been admitted but was kept standing until the countess left the room.) Behind the palace she discovered a town hall with a post office and a school attached, a charming small hospital— where a doctor was obtained for Alec—and a walled graveyard. Only the graveyard was worth exploring; it contained Victorian English poets who had probably died of tuberculosis in the days when an enervating climate was thought to be good for phthisis, and Russian aristocrats who had owned some of the English houses, and Garibaldian adventurers who, like Alec, had never owned a thing. Most of these graves were overgrown and neglected, with the headstones all to one side, and wild grasses grown taller than roses. The more recent dead seemed to be commemorated by marble plaques on a high concrete wall; these she did not examine. What struck her about this place was its splendid view: She could see Lou Mas, and quite far into Italy, and of course over a vast stretch of the sea. How silly of all those rich foreigners to crowd down by the shore, with the crashing noise of the railway. I would have built up here in a minute, she thought.

Alec's new doctor was young and ugly and bit his nails. He spoke good English, and knew most of the British colony, to whose colds, allergies, and perpetually upset stomachs he ministered. British ailments were nursery ailments; what his patients really wanted was to be tucked up next to a nursery fire and fed warm bread-and-milk. He had taken her to be something like himself—an accomplice. "My husband is anything but childish," she said gently. She hesitated before trotting out her usual Irish claim, for she was not quite certain what he meant.

"Rivabella has only two points of cultural interest," he said. "One is the market on the church square. The other is the patron saint, St. Damian. He appears on the church roof, dressed in armor, holding a flaming sword in the air. He does this when someone in Rivabella seems to be in danger." She saw, in the way he looked at her, that she had begun her journey south a wife and mother whose looks were fading, and arrived at a place where her face seemed exotic. Until now she had thought only that a normal English family had taken the train, and the caricature of one had descended. It amounted to the same thing—the eye of the beholder.

From his balcony Alec saw the hill as a rough triangle, with a few straggling farms beneath the gray-and-umber town (all he could discern was its color) and the apex of graveyard. This, in its chalky whiteness, looked like an Andalusian or a North African village washed up on the wrong part of the coast. It was alien to the lush English gardens and the foreign villas, which tended to pinks, and beiges, and to a deep shade known as Egyptian red. Within those houses was a way of being he sensed and understood, for it was a smaller, paler version of colonial life, with chattering foreign servants who might have been budgerigars, and hot puddings consumed under brilliant sunlight. Rules of speech and regulations for conduct were probably observed, as in the last days of the dissolving Empire. Barbara had told him of one: it was bad form to say "Rivebelle" for "Rivabella," for it showed one hadn't known about the place in its rich old days, or even that Queen Victoria had mentioned *pretty* little Rivabella" to the Crown Princess of Prussia in one of her affectionate letters.

"All snobs," said Barbara. "Thank God I'm Irish," though there was something she did in a way mind: Saying "Rivebelle" had been one of her first mistakes. Another had been hiring a staff without taking advice. She was also suspected of paying twice the going rate, which was not so much an economic blunder as a social affront. "All snobs" was not much in the way of ammunition, but then, none of the other villas could claim a cook, a maid, a laundress, a gardener, and a governess marching down from Rivabella, all of them loyal, devoted, cheerful, hardworking, and kind.

She wrote to her pilot brother, the one she loved, telling him how self-reliant people seemed to be here, what pride they took in their jobs, how their philosophy was completely alien to the modern British idea of strife and grab. "I would love it if you would come and stay for a while. We have more rooms than we know what to do with. You and I could talk." But no one came. None of them wanted to have to watch poor old Alec dying.

The children would recall later on that their cook had worn a straw hat in the kitchen, so that steam condensing on the ceiling would not drop on her head, and that she wore the same hat to their father's funeral. Barbara would remind them about the food. She had been barely twenty at the beginning of the war, and there were meals for which she had never stopped feeling hungry. Three times a day, now, she sat down to cream and butter and fresh bread, new-laid eggs, jam you could stand a spoon in: breakfasts out of a storybook from before the war. As she preferred looking at food to eating it, it must have been the *idea* of her table spread that restored richness to her skin, luster to her hair. She had been all cream and gold, once, but war and marriage and Alec's illness and being hard up and some other indefinable disappointment had skimmed and darkened her. And yet she felt shot through with happiness sometimes, or at least by a piercing clue as to what bliss might be. This sensation, which she might have controlled more easily in another climate, became so natural, so insistent, that she feared sometimes that its source might be religious and that she would need to reject—out of principle—the felicity it promised. But no; she was, luckily, too earthbound for such nonsense. She could experience sudden felicity merely seeing her cook arrive with laden baskets, or the gardener crossing the terrace with a crate of flowering plants. (He would bed these out under the olive trees, where they perished rapidly.) Lou Mas at such times seemed to shrink to a toy house she might lift and carry; she would remember what it had been like when the children were babies still, and hers alone.

Carrying Alec's breakfast tray, she came in wearing the white dressing gown that had been his sister's parting gift to her. Her hair, which she now kept thick and loose, was shades lighter than it had been in England. He seemed barely to see her. But, then, everything dazzled him now. She buttered toast for him, and spread it with jam, saying, "Do try it, darling. You will never taste jam like this again." Of course, it thundered with prophecy. Her vision blurred—not because of tears, for she did not cry easily. It was as if a sheet of pure water had come down with an enormous crashing sound, cutting her off from Alec.

Now that winter was here, he moved with the sun instead of away from it. Shuffling to the balcony, he leaned on her shoulder. She covered him with blankets, gave him a book to read, combed his hair. He had all but stopped speaking, though he made an effort for strangers. She thought, What would it be like to be shot dead? Only the lingering question contained in a nightmare could account for this, but her visionary dreams had left her, probably because Alec's fate, and so to some measure her own, had been decided once and for all. Between house and sea the gardener crouched with a trowel in his hand. His work consisted of bedding-out, and his imagination stopped at salvia: The ground beneath the olive trees was dark red with them. She leaned against the warm parapet and thought of what he might see should he look up—herself, in white, with her hair blazing in the sun. But when he lifted his face it was only to wipe sweat from it with the shirt he had taken off. A dream of loss came back: She had been ordered to find new names for refugee children whose names had been forgotten. In real life, she had wanted her children to be called Giles, Nigel, and Samantha, but Alec had interfered. All three had been conceived on his wartime leaves, before he was taken prisoner. The children had her gray eyes, her skin that freckled, her small bones and delicate features (though Molly showed signs of belonging to a darker, sturdier race), but none of them had her richness, her shine. They seemed to her and perhaps to each other thin and dry, like Alec.

Everything Mademoiselle said was useless or repetitive. She explained, " 'Lou Mas' means 'the farm,' " which the children knew. When they looked out the dining-room window she remarked, "You can see Italy." She came early in order to share their breakfast; the aunt she lived with, the aunt with the frescoes, kept all the food in their palace locked up. "What do you take me for?" she sometimes asked them, tragically, of some small thing, such as their not paying intense attention. She was not teaching them much, only some French, and they were picking this up faster now than she could instruct. Her great-grandfather had been a French volunteer against Garibaldi (an Italian bandit, she explained); her grandfather was founder of a nationalist movement; her father had been murdered on the steps of his house at the end of the war. She was afraid of Freemasons, Socialists, Protestants, and Jews, but not of drowning or falling from a height or being attacked by a mad dog. When she discovered that the children had been christened (Alec having considered baptism a rational start to agnostic life), she undertook their religious education, which was not at all what Barbara was paying for.

After lunch, they went upstairs to visit Alec. He lay on his deck chair, tucked into blankets, as pale as clouds. James suddenly wailed out, believing he was singing, "We'll ring all the bells and kill all the Protestants." Silence, then James said, "Are there any left? Any Protestants?"

"I am left, for one," said his father.

"It's a good thing we came down here, then," said the child calmly. "They couldn't get at you."

Mademoiselle said, looking terrified, "It refers to old events in France."

"It wouldn't have mattered." His belief had gone to earth as soon as he had realized that the men he admired were in doubt. His conversation, like his reading, was increasingly simple. He was reading a book about gardening. He held it close to his face. Daylight tired him; it was like an intruder between memory and the eye. He read, "Nerine. Guernsey Lily. Ord. Amaryllidaceae. First introduced, 1680." Introduced into England, that meant. "Oleander, 1596. East Indian Rose Bay, 1770. Tamarind Tree, 1633. Chrysanthemum, 1764." So England had flowered, become bedecked, been bedded-out.

The book had been given him by a neighbor. The Webbs not only had people working for them, and delicious nursery food to eat, and a garden running down to the sea, but distinguished people living on either side—Mr. Edmund Cranefield of Villa Osiris to the right, and Mrs. Massie at Casa Scotia on the left. To reach their houses you had to climb thirty steps to the road, then descend more stairs on their land. Mr. Cranefield had a lift, which looked like a large crate stood on its side. Within it was a kitchen chair. He sat on the chair and was borne up to the road on an electric rail. No one had ever seen him doing this. When he went to Morocco during the worst of the winter, he had the lift disconnected and covered with rugs, the pond drained and the fish put in tanks, and his two peacocks, who screamed every dawn as if a fox were at them, boarded for a high fee with a private zoo. Casa Scotia belonged to Mrs. Massie, who was lame, wore a tweed cape, never went out without a hat, walked with a stick, and took a good twenty minutes to climb her steps.

Mr. Cranefield was a novelist, Mrs. Massie the author of a whole shelf of gardening books. Mr. Cranefield never spoke of his novels or offered to lend them; he did not even say what their titles were. "You must tell me every one!" Barbara cried, as if she were about to rush out and return with a wheelbarrow full of books by Mr. Cranefield.

He sat upstairs with Alec, and they talked about different things, quite often about the war. Just as Barbara was beginning to imagine Mr. Cranefield did not like her, he invited her to tea. She brought Molly along for protection, but soon saw he was not drawn to women—at least, not in the way she supposed men to be. She wondered then if she should keep Will and James away from him. He showed Barbara and Molly the loggia where he worked on windless mornings; a strong mistral had once blown one hundred and forty pages across three gardens—some were even found in a hedge at Casa Scotia. On a table were oval picture frames holding the likeness of a fair girl and a fair young man. Looking more closely, Barbara saw they were illustrations cut out of magazines. Mr. Cranefield said, "They are the pair I write about. I keep them there so that I never make a mistake."

"Don't they bore you?" said Barbara.

"Look at all they have given me." But the most dispossessed peasant, the filthiest housemaid, the seediest nail-biting doctor in Rivabella had what he was pointing out—the view, the sea. Of course, a wave of the hand cannot take in everything; he probably had more than this in reserve. He turned to Molly and said kindly, "When you are a little older you can do some typing for me," because it was his experience that girls liked doing that—typing for Mr. Cranefield while waiting for someone to marry. Girls were fond of him: He gave sound advice about love affairs, could read the future in handwriting. Molly knew nothing about him, then, but she would recall later on how Mr. Cranefield, who had invented women deep-sea divers, women test pilots, could not imagine—in his innocence, in his manhood—anything more thrilling to offer a girl when he met one than "You can type."

Barbara broke in, laughing: "She is only eleven."

This was true, but it seemed to Molly a terrible thing to say.

Mrs. Massie was not shy about bringing *her* books around. She gave several to Alec, among them *Flora's Gardening Encyclopaedia*, seventeenth edition, considered her masterpiece. All her books were signed "Flora," though it was not her name. She said about Mr. Cranefield, "Edmund is a great, pampered child. Spoiled by adoring women all his life. Not by me." She sat straight on the straightest chair, her hands clasped on her stick. "I do my own typing. My own gardening, too," though she did say to James and Will, "You can help in the garden for pocket money, if you like."

In the spring, the second Elizabeth was crowned. Barbara ordered a television set from a shop in Nice. It was the first the children had seen. Two men carried it with difficulty down the steps from the road, and soon became tired of lifting it from room to room while Barbara decided where she wanted it. She finally chose a room they kept shut usually; it had a raised platform at one end and until the war had been the site of amateur theatricals. The men set the box down on the stage and began fiddling with antennae and power points, while the children ran about arranging rows of chairs. One of the men said they might not have a perfect view of the Queen the next day, the day of the Coronation, because of Alps standing in the way. The children sat down and stared at the screen. Horizontal lightning streaked across its face. The men described implosion, which had killed any number of persons all over the world. They said that should the socket and plug begin to smoke, Barbara was to make a dash for the meter box and put out the appropriate fuse.

"The appropriate fuse?" said Barbara. The children minded sometime about the way she laughed at everything.

When the men had gone, they trooped upstairs to tell Alec about the Alps and implosion. He was resting in preparation for tomorrow's ceremony, which he would attend. It was clear to Molly that her father would not be able to get up and run if there was an accident. Kneeling on the warm tiles (this was in June) she pressed her face to his hand. Presently he slipped the hand away to turn a page. He was reading more of the book Mrs. Massie had pounded out on her 1929 Underwood—four carbons, single-spaced, no corrections, every page typed clean: "Brussels Sprouts— see Brassica." Brassica must be English, Alec thought. That was why he withdrew his hand—to see about Brassica. What use was his hand to Molly or her anxiety to him now? Why hold her? Why draw her into his pale world? She was a difficult, dull, clumsy child, something of a moper when her brothers teased her but sulky and tough when it came to Barbara. He had watched Barbara, goaded by Molly, lose control of herself and slap the girl's face, and he had heard Molly's pitiful credo: "You can't hurt me. My vaccination hurt worse than that." "Hurt more," Alec in silence had amended. "Hurt me *more* than that."

He found Brassica. It was Borecole, Broccoli, Cabbage, Cauliflower. His eyes slid over the rest of what it was until, "Native to Europe—BRITAIN," which Mrs. Massie had typed in capital letters during the war, with a rug around her legs in unheated Casa Scotia, waiting for the Italians or the Germans or the French to take her away to internment in a lorry. He was closer in temper to Mrs. Massie than to anyone else except his sister, though he had given up priorities. His blood was white (that was how he saw it), and his lungs and heart were bleached, too, and starting to disintegrate like snowflakes. He was a pale giant, a drained Gulliver, cast up on the beach, open territory for invaders. (Barbara and Will were sharing a paperback about flying saucers, whose occupants had built Stonehenge.) Alec's intrepid immigrants, his microscopic colonial settlers had taken over. He had been easy to subdue, being courteous by nature, diffident by choice. He had been a civil servant, then a soldier; had expected the best, relied on good behavior; had taken to prison camp thin books about Calabria and Greece; had been evasive, secretive, brave, unscrupulous only sometimes—had been English and middle class, in short.

That night Alec had what the doctor called "a crisis" and Alec termed "a bad patch." There was no question of his coming down for Coronation the next day. The children thought of taking the television set up to him, but it was too heavy, and Molly burst into tears thinking of implosion and accidents and Alec trapped. In the end the Queen was crowned in the little theater, as Barbara had planned, in the presence of Barbara and the children, Mr. Cranefield and Mrs. Massie, the doctor from Rivabella, a neighbor called Major Lamprey and his old mother, Mrs. Massie's housekeeper, Barbara's cook and two of her grandchildren, and Mademoiselle. One after the other these people turned their heads to look at Alec, gasping in the doorway, holding on to the frame. His hair was carefully combed and parted low on one side, like Mr. Cranefield's, and he had dressed completely, though he had a scarf around his neck instead of a tie. He was the last, the very last, of a kind. Not British but English. Not Christian so much as Anglican. Not Anglican but giving the benefit of the doubt. His children would never feel what he had felt, suffer what he had suffered, relinquish what he had done without so that this sacrament could take place. The new Queen's voice flowed easily over the Alps—thin, bored, ironed flat by the weight of what she had to remember—and came as far as Alec, to whom she owed her crown. He did not think that, precisely, but what had pulled him to his feet, made him stand panting for life in the doorway, would not occur to James or Will or Molly—not then, or ever.

He watched the rest of it from a chair. His breathing bothered the others: It made their own seem too quiet. He ought to have died that night. It would have made a reasonable ending. This was not a question of getting rid of Alec (no one wanted that) but of being able to say later, "He got up and dressed to see the Coronation." However, he went on living.

A nurse came every day, the doctor almost as often. He talked quietly to Barbara in the garden. A remission as long as this was unknown to him; it smacked of miracles. When Barbara would not hear of that, he said that Alec was holding on through willpower. But Alec was not holding on. His invaders had pushed him off the beach and into a boat. The stream was white and the shoreline, too. Everything was white, and he moved peacefully. He had glimpses of his destination—a room where the hems of thin curtains swept back and forth on a bare floor. His vision gave him green bronze doors sometimes; he supposed they were part of the same room.

He could see his children, but only barely. He had guessed what the boys might become—one a rebel, one turned inward. The girl was a question mark. She was stoic and sentimental, indifferent sometimes to pleasure and pain. Whatever she was or could be or might be, he had left her behind. The boys placed a row of bricks down the middle of the room they shared. In the large house they fought for space. They were restless and noisy, untutored and bored. "I'll always have a packet of love from my children," Barbara had said to a man once (not Alec).

At the start of their second winter one of the Laceys came down to investigate. This was Ron, the hotelkeeper. He had dark hair and was thin and pale and walked softly. When he understood that what Barbara had written about servants and dollars was true, he asked to see the accounts. There were none. He talked to Barbara without raising his voice; that day she let everyone working for her go with the exception of the cook, whom Ron had said she was to keep because of Alec. He seemed to feel he was in a position of trust, for he ordered her—there was no other word for it—to place the children at once in the Rivabella town school: Lou Mas was costing the Lacey brothers enough in local taxes— they might as well feel they were getting something back. He called his sister "Bab" and Alec "Al." The children's parents suddenly seemed to them strangers.

When Ron left, Barbara marched the children up to Rivabella and made them look at the church. They had seen it, but she made them look again. She held the mistaken belief that religion was taught in French state schools, and she wanted to arm them. The children knew by now that what their mother called "France" was not really France down here but a set of rules, a code for doing things, such as how to recite the multiplication table or label a wine. Instead of the northern saints she remembered, with their sorrowful preaching, there was a southern St. Damian holding up a blazing sword. Any number of persons had seen him; Mademoiselle had, more than once.

"I want you to understand what superstition is," said Barbara, in clear, carrying English. "Superstition is what is wrong with Uncle Ron. He believes what he can't see, and what he sees he can't believe in. Now, imagine intelligent people saying they've seen this—this apparition. This St. George, or whatever." The church had two pink towers, one bearing a cross and the other a weather vane. St. Damian usually hovered between them. "In armor," said Barbara.

To all three children occurred, "Why not?" Protect me, prayed the girl. Vanquish, said Will. Lead, ordered the youngest, seeing only himself in command. He looked around the square and said to his mother, "Could we go, soon, please? Because people are looking."

That winter Molly grew breasts; she thought them enormous, though each could have been contained easily in a small teacup. Her brothers teased her. She went about with her arms crossed. She was tall for her age, and up in the town there was always some man staring. Elderly neighbors pressed her close. Major Lamprey, calling on Alec, kissed her on the mouth. He smelled of gin and pipe smoke. She scrubbed her teeth for minutes afterward. When she began to menstruate, Barbara said, "Now, Molly, you are to keep away from men," as if she weren't trying to.

The boys took their bicycles and went anywhere they wanted. In the evening they wheeled round and round the church square. Above them were swallows, on the edge of the square men and boys. Both were starting to speak better French than English, and James spoke dialect better than French. Molly disliked going up to Rivabella, unless she had to. She helped Barbara make the beds and wash the dishes and she did her homework and then very often went over to talk to Mr. Cranefield. She discovered, by chance, that he had another name—E. C. Arden. As E. C. Arden he was the author of a series of thumbed, comfortable novels (it was Mrs. Massie who lent Molly these), one of which, called *Belinda at Sea*, was Molly's favorite book of any kind. It was about a girl who joined the crew of a submarine, disguised as a naval rating, and kept her identity a secret all the way to Hong Kong. In the end, she married the submarine commander, who apparently had loved her all along. Molly read *Belinda at Sea* three or four times without ever mentioning to Mr. Cranefield she knew he was E. C. Arden. She thought it was a matter of deep privacy and that it was up to him to speak of it first. She did, however, ask what he thought of the saint on the church roof, using the name Barbara had, which was St. George.

"What," said Mr. Cranefield. "That Ethiopian?"

The girl looked frightened—not of Ethiopians, certainly, but of confusion as to person, the adult world of muddle. Even Mr. Cranefield was *also* E. C. Arden, creator of Belinda.

Mr. Cranefield explained, kindly, that up at Rivabella they had made a patron saint out of a mixture of St. Damian, who was an intellectual, and St. Michael, who was not, and probably a local pagan deity as well. St. Michael accounted for the sword, the pagan for the fire. Reliable witnesses had seen the result, though none of these witnesses were British. "We aren't awfully good at seeing saints," he said. "Though we do have an eye for ghosts."

Another thing still troubled Molly, but it was not a matter she could mention: She did not know what to do about her bosom—whether to try to hold it up in some way or, on the contrary, bind it flat. She had been granted, by the mistake of a door's swinging wide, an upsetting glimpse of Mrs. Massie changing out of a bathing suit, and she had been worried about the future shape of her own body ever since. She pored over reproductions of statues and paintings in books belonging to Mr. Cranefield. The Eves and Venuses represented were not reassuring—they often seemed to be made of India rubber. There was no one she could ask. Barbara was too dangerous; the mention of a subject such as this always made her go too far and say things Molly found unpleasant.

She did remark to both Mrs. Massie and Mr. Cranefield that she hated the Rivabella school. She said, "I would give anything to be sent home to England, but I can't leave my father."

After a long conversation with Mrs. Massie, Mr. Cranefield agreed to speak to Alec. Interfering with other people was not his way, but Molly struck him as being pathetic. Something told him that Molly was not useful leverage with either parent and so he mentioned Will first: Will would soon be fourteen, too old for the school at Rivabella. Unless the Webb children were enrolled, and quickly, in good French establishments—say, in lycées at Nice—they would become unfit for anything save menial work in a foreign language they could not speak in an educated way. Of course, the ideal solution would be England, if Alec felt he could manage that.

Alec listened, sitting not quite straight in his chair, wearing a dressing gown, his back to a window. He found all light intolerable now. Several times he lifted his hand as if he were trying to see through it. No one knew why Alec made these odd gestures; some people thought he had gone slightly mad because death was too long in coming. He parted his lips and whispered, "French school . . . If you would look after it," and then, "I would be grateful."

Mr. Cranefield dropped his voice too, as if the gray of the room called for hush. He asked if Alec had thought of appointing a guardian for them. The hand Alec seemed to want transparent waved back and forth, stiffly, like a shut ivory fan.

All that Barbara said to Mr. Cranefield was "Good idea," once he had assured her French high schools were not priest-ridden.

"It might have occurred to *her* to have done something about it," said Mrs. Massie, when this was repeated.

"Things do occur to Barbara," said Mr. Cranefield. "But she doesn't herself get the drift of them."

The only disturbing part of the new arrangement was that the children had been assigned to separate establishments, whose schedules did not coincide; this meant they would not necessarily travel in the same bus. Molly had shot up as tall as Will now. Her hair was dark and curled all over her head. Her bones and her hands and feet were going to be larger, stronger, than her mother's and brothers'. She looked, already, considerably older than her age. She was obstinately innocent, turning her face away when Barbara, for her own good, tried to tell her something about men.

Barbara imagined her willful, ignorant daughter being enticed, trapped, molested, impregnated, and disgraced. *And* ending up wondering how it happened, Barbara thought. She saw Molly's seducer, brutish and dull. I'd get him by the throat, she said to herself. She imagined the man's strong neck and her own small hands, her brittle bird-bones. She said, "You are never, ever to speak to a stranger on the bus. You're not to get in a car with a man—not even if you know him."

"I don't know any man with a car."

"You could be waiting for a bus on a dark afternoon," said Barbara. "A car might pull up. Would you like a lift? No, you must answer. No and no and no. It is different for the boys. There are the two of them. They could put up a fight."

"Nobody bothers boys," said Molly.

Barbara drew breath but for once in her life said nothing.

Alec's remission was no longer just miraculous—it had become unreasonable. Barbara's oldest brother hinted that Alec might be better off in England, cared for on National Health: They were paying unholy taxes for just such a privilege. Barbara replied that Alec had no use for England, where the Labour government had sapped everyone's self-reliance. He believed in having exactly the amount of suffering you could pay for, no less and no more. She knew this theory did not hold water, because the Laceys and Alec's own sister had done the paying. It was too late now; they should have thought a bit sooner; and Alec was too ravaged to make a new move.

The car that, inevitably, pulled up to a bus stop in Nice was driven by a Mr. Wilkinson. He had just taken Major Lamprey and the Major's old mother to the airport. He rolled his window down and called to Molly, through pouring rain, "I say, aren't you from Lou Mas?"

If he sounded like a foreigner's Englishman, like a man in a British joke it was probably because he had said so many British-sounding lines in films set on the Riviera. Eric Wilkinson was the chap with the strong blue eyes and ginger mustache, never younger than thirty-four, never as much as forty, who flashed on for a second, just long enough to show there was an Englishman in the room. He could handle a uniform, a dinner jacket, tails, a monocle, a cigarette holder, a swagger stick, a polo mallet, could open a cigarette case without looking like a gigolo, could say without being an ass about it, "Bless my soul, wasn't that the little Maharani?" or even, "Come along, old boy—fair play with Monica, now!" Foreigners meeting him often said, "That is what the British used to be like, when they were still all right, when the Riviera was still fit to live in." But the British who knew him were apt to glaze over: "You mean Wilkinson?" Mrs. Massie and Mr. Cranefield said, "Well, Wilkinson, what are you up to now?" There was no harm to him: His one-line roles did not support him, but he could do anything, even cook. He used his car as a private taxi, driving people to airports, meeting them when they came off cruise ships. He was not a chauffeur, never said "sir," and at the same time kept a certain distance, was not shy about money changing hands—no fake pride, no petit bourgeois demand for a slipped envelope. Good-natured. Navy blazer. Summer whites in August. Wore a tie that carried a message. What did it stand for? A third-rate school? A disgraced, disbanded regiment? A club raided by the police? No one knew. Perhaps it was the symbol of something new altogether. "Still playing in those films of yours, Wilkinson?" He would flash on and off—British gent at roulette, British Army officer, British diplomat, British political agent, British anything. Spoke his line, fitted his monocle, pressed the catch on his cigarette case. His ease with other people was genuine, his financial predicament unfeigned. He had never been married, and had no children that he knew of.

"By Jove, it's nippy," said Wilkinson, when Molly had settled beside him, her books on her lap.

What made her do this—accept a lift from a murderer of schoolgirls? First, she had seen him somewhere safe once—at Mr. Cranefield's. Also, she was wet through, and chilled to the heart. Barbara kept refusing or neglecting or forgetting to buy her the things she needed: a lined raincoat, a jersey the right size. (The boys were wearing hand-me-down clothes from England now, but no one Barbara knew of seemed to have a daughter.) The sleeves of her old jacket were so short that she put her hands in her pockets, so that Mr. Wilkinson would not despise her. He talked to Molly as he did to everyone, as if they were of an age, informing her that Major Lamprey and his mother were flying to Malta to look at a house. A number of people were getting ready to leave the south of France now; it had become so seedy and expensive, and all the wrong people were starting to move in.

"What kind of wrong people?" She sat tense beside him until he said, "Why, like Eric Wilkinson, I should think," and she laughed when his own laugh said she was meant to. He was nice to her; even later, when she thought she had reason to hate him, she would remember that Wilkinson had been nice. He drove beyond his destination—a block of flats that he waved at in passing and that Molly in a confused way supposed he owned. They stopped in the road behind Lou Mas; she thanked him fervently, and then, struck with something, sat staring at him: "Mr. Wilkinson," she said. "Please—I am not allowed to be in cars with men alone. In case someone happened to see us, would you mind just coming and meeting my mother? Just so she can see who you are?"

"God bless my soul," said Wilkinson, sincerely.

Once, Alec had believed that Barbara was not frightened by anything, and that this absence of fear was her principal weakness. It was true that she had begun drifting out of her old life now, as calmly as Alec drifted away from life altogether. Her mock phrase for each additional Lou Mas catastrophe had become "the usual daily developments." The usual developments over seven rainy days had been the departure of the cook, who took with her all she could lay her hands on, and a French social-security fine that had come down hard on the remains of her marble block of money, reducing it to pebbles and dust. She had never filled out employer's forms for the people she had hired, because she had not known she was supposed to and none of them had suggested it; for a number of reasons having to do with government offices and tax files, none of them had wanted even this modest income to be registered anywhere. As it turned out, the gardener had also been receiving unemployment benefits, which, unfairly, had increased the amount of the fine Barbara had to pay. Rivabella turned out to be just as grim and bossy as England— worse, even, for it kept up a camouflage of wine and sunshine and olive trees and of amiable southern idiots who, if sacked, thought nothing of informing on one.

She sat at the dining-room table, wearing around her shoulders a red cardigan Molly had outgrown. On the table were the Sunday papers Alec's sister continued to send faithfully from England, and Alec's lunch tray, exactly as she had taken it up to him except that everything on it was now cold. She glanced up and saw the two of them enter—one stricken and guilty-looking, the other male, confident, smiling. The recognition that leaped between Barbara and Wilkinson was the last thing that Wilkinson in his right mind should have wanted, and absolutely everything Barbara now desired and craved. Neither of them heard Molly saying, "Mummy, this is Mr. Wilkinson. Mr. Wilkinson wants to tell you how he came to drive me home."

It happened at last that Alec had to be taken to the Rivabella hospital, where the local poor went when it was not feasible to let them die at home. Eric Wilkinson, new family friend, drove his car as far as it could go along a winding track, after which they placed Alec on a stretcher; and Wilkinson, Mr. Cranefield, Will, and the doctor carried him the rest of the way. A soft April rain was falling, from which they protected Alec as they could. In the rain the doctor wept unnoticed. The others were silent and absorbed. The hospital stood near the graveyard—shamefully near, Wilkinson finally remarked, to Mr. Cranefield. Will could see the cemetery from his father's new window, though to do so he had to lean out, as he'd imagined passengers doing and having their heads cut off in the train game long ago. A concession was made to Alec's status as owner of a large villa, and he was given a private room. It was not a real sickroom but the place where the staff went to eat and drink when they took time off. They cleared away the plates and empty wine bottles and swept up most of the crumbs and wheeled a bed in.

The building was small for a hospital, large for a house. It had been the winter home of a Moscow family, none of whom had come back after 1917. Alec lay flat and still. Under a drift of soot on the ceiling he could make out a wreath of nasturtiums and a bluebird with a ribbon in its beak.

At the window, Will said to Mr. Cranefield, "We can see Lou Mas from here, and even your peacocks."

Mr. Cranefield fretted, "They shouldn't be in the rain."

Alec's neighbors came to visit. Mrs. Massie, not caring who heard her (one of the children did), said to someone she met on the hospital staircase, "Alec is a gentleman and always will be, but Barbara . . . Barbara." She took a rise of the curved marble stairs at a time. "If the boys were girls they'd be sluts. As it is, they are ruffians. Their old cook saw one of them stoning a cat to death. And now there is Wilkinson. Wilkinson." She moved on alone, repeating his name.

Everyone was saying "Wilkinson" now. Along with "Wilkinson" they said "Barbara." You would think that having been married to one man who was leaving her with nothing, leaving her dependent on family charity, she would have looked around, been more careful, picked a reliable kind of person. "A foreigner, say," said Major Lamprey's mother, who had not cared for Malta. Italians love children, even other people's. She might have chosen—you know—one of the cheerful sort, with a clean shirt and a clean white handkerchief, proprietor of a linen shop. The shop would have kept Barbara out of mischief.

No one could blame Wilkinson, who had his reasons. Also, he had said all those British-sounding lines in films, which in a way made him all right. Barbara had probably said she was Irish once too often. "What can you expect?" said Mrs. Massie. "Think how they were in the war. They keep order when there is someone to bully them. Otherwise . . ." The worst she had to say about Wilkinson was that he was preparing to flash on as the colonel of a regiment in a film about desert warfare; it had been made in the hilly country up behind Monte Carlo.

"Not a grain of sand up there," said Major Lamprey. He said he wondered what foreigners thought they meant by "desert."

"A colonel!" said Mrs. Massie.

"Why not?" said Mr. Cranefield.

"They must think he looks it," said Major Lamprey. "Gets a fiver a day, I'm told, and an extra fiver when he speaks his line. He says, 'Don't underestimate Rommel.' For a fiver I'd say it," though he would rather have died.

The conversation veered to Wilkinson's favor. Wilkinson was merry; told irresistible stories about directors, unmalicious ones about film stars; repeated comic anecdotes concerning underlings who addressed him as "Guv." "I wonder who they can be?" said Mrs. Massie. "It takes a Wilkinson to find them." Mr. Cranefield was more indulgent; he had to be. A sardonic turn of mind would have been resented by E. C. Arden's readers. The blond-headed pair on his desk stood for a world of triumphant love, with which his readers felt easy kinship. The fair couple, though competent in any domain, whether restoring a toppling kingdom or taming a tiger, lived on the same plane as all human creatures except England's enemies. They raised the level of existence—raised it, and flattened it.

Mr. Cranefield—as is often and incorrectly said of children—lived in a world of his own, too, in which he kept everyone's identity clear. He did not confuse St. Damian with an Ethiopian, or Wilkinson with Raffles, or Barbara with a slut. This was partly out of the habit of neatness and partly because he could not make up his mind to live openly in the world he wanted, which was a homosexual one. He said about Wilkinson and Barbara and the blazing scandal at Lou Mas, "I am sure there is no harm in it. Barbara has too much to manage alone, and it is probably better for the children to have a man about the place."

When Wilkinson was not traveling, he stayed at Lou Mas. Until now his base had been a flat he'd shared with a friend who was a lawyer and who was also frequently away. Wilkinson left most of his luggage behind; there was barely enough of his presence to fill a room. For a reason no one understood Barbara had changed everyone's room around: She and Molly slept where Alec had been, the boys moved to Barbara's room, and Wilkinson was given Molly's bed. It seemed a small bed for so tall a man.

Molly had always slept alone, until now. Some nights, when Wilkinson was sleeping in her old room, she would waken just before dawn and find that her mother had disappeared. Her feeling at the sight of the empty bed was one of panic. She would get up, too, and go in to Will and shake him, saying, "She's disappeared."

"No, she hasn't. She's with Wilkinson." Nevertheless, he would rise and stumble, still nearly sleeping, down the passage—Alec's son, descendant of civil servants, off on a mission.

Barbara slept with her back against Wilkinson's chest. Outside, Mr. Cranefield's peacocks greeted first light by screaming murder. Years from now, Will would hear the first stirrings of dawn and dream of assassinations. Wilkinson never moved. Had he shown he was awake, he might have felt obliged to say a suitable one-liner—something like "I say, old chap, you are a bit of a trial, you know."

Will's mother picked up the nightgown and robe that lay white on the floor, pulled them on, flung her warm hair back, tied her sash—all without haste. In the passage, the door shut on the quiet Wilkinson, she said tenderly, "Were you worried?"

"Molly was."

Casual with her sons, she was modest before her daughter. Changing to a clean nightdress, she said, "Turn the other way."

Turning, Molly saw her mother, white and gold, in the depths of Alec's mirror. Barbara had her arms raised, revealing the profile of a breast with at its tip the palest wash of rose, paler than the palest pink flower. (Like a Fragonard, Barbara had been told, like a Boucher—not by Alec.) What Molly felt now was immense relief. It was not the fate of every girl to turn into India rubber. But in no other way did she wish to resemble her mother.

Like the residue left by winter rains, awareness of Barbara and Wilkinson seeped through the house. There was a damp chill about it that crept to the bone. One of the children, Will, perceived it as torment. Because of the mother defiled, the source of all such knowledge became polluted, probably forever. The boys withdrew from Barbara, who had let the weather in. James imagined ways of killing Wilkinson, though he drew the line at killing Barbara. He did not want her dead, but different. The mother he wanted did not stand in public squares pointing crazily up to invisible saints, or begin sleeping in one bed and end up in another.

Barbara felt that they were leaving her; she put the blame on Molly, who had the makings of a prude, and who, at worst, might turn out to be something like Alec's sister. Barbara said to Molly, "I had three children before I was twenty-three, and I was alone, and there were all the air raids. The life I've tried to give you and the boys has been so different, so happy, so free." Molly folded her arms, looked down at her shoes. Her height, her grave expression, her new figure gave her a bogus air of maturity: She was only thirteen, and she felt like a pony flicked by a crop. Barbara tried to draw near: "My closest friend is my own daughter," she wanted to be able to say. "I never do a thing without talking it over with Molly." So she would have said, laughing, her bright head against Molly's darker hair, if only Molly had given half an inch.

"What a cold creature you are," Barbara said, sadly. "You live in an ice palace. There is so little happiness in life unless you let it come near. I always at least had an *idea* about being happy." The girl's face stayed shut and locked. All that could cross it now was disappointment.

One night when Molly woke Will, he said, "I don't care where she is." Molly went back to bed. Fetching Barbara had become a habit. She was better off in her room alone.

When they stopped coming to claim her, Barbara perceived it as mortification. She gave up on Molly, for the moment, and turned to the boys, sat curled on the foot of their bed, sipping wine, telling stories, offering to share her cigarette, though James was still twelve. James said, "He told us it was dangerous to smoke in bed. People have died that way." "He" meant Alec. Was this all James would remember? That he had warned about smoking in bed?

James, who was embarrassed by this attempt of hers at making them equals, thought she had an odd smell, like a cat. To Will, at another kind of remove, she stank of folly. They stared at her, as if measuring everything she still had to mean in their lives. This expression she read as she could. Love for Wilkinson had blotted out the last of her dreams and erased her gift of second sight. She said unhappily to Wilkinson, "My children are prigs. But, then, they are only half mine."

Mademoiselle, whom the children now called by her name—Geneviève—still came to Lou Mas. Nobody paid her, but she corrected the children's French, which no longer needed correcting, and tried to help with their homework, which amounted to interference. They had always in some way spared her; only James, her favorite, sometimes said, "No, I'd rather work alone." She knew now that the Webbs were poor, which increased her affection: Their descent to low water equaled her own. Sometimes she brought a packet of biscuits for their tea, which was a dull affair now the cook had gone. They ate the biscuits straight from the paper wrapping: Nobody wanted to wash an extra plate. Wilkinson, playing at British something, asked about her aunt. He said "Madame la Comtesse." When he had gone, she cautioned the children not to say that but simply "your aunt." But as Geneviève's aunt did not receive foreigners, save for a few such as Mrs. Massie, they had no reason to ask how she was. When Geneviève realized from something said that Wilkinson more or less lived at Lou Mas, she stopped coming to see them. The Webbs had no further connection with Rivabella then except for their link with the hospital, where Alec still lay quietly, still alive.

Barbara went up every day. She asked the doctor, "Shouldn't he be having blood transfusions—something of that kind?" She had never been in a hospital except to be born and to have her children. She was remembering films she had seen: bottles dripping liquids, needles taped to the crook of an arm, nursing sisters wheeling oxygen tanks down white halls.

The doctor reminded her that this was Rivabella—a small town where half the population lived without employment. He had been so sympathetic at first, so slow to present a bill. She could not understand what had changed him; but she was hopeless at reading faces now. She could scarcely read her children's.

She bent down to Alec, so near that her eyes would have seemed enormous had he been paying attention. She told him the name of the scent she was wearing; it reminded her and perhaps Alec, too, of jasmine. Eric had brought it back from a dinner at Monte Carlo, given to promote this very perfume. He was often invited to these things, where he represented the best sort of Britishness. "Eric is being the greatest help," she said to Alec, who might have been listening. She added, for it had to be said sometime, "Eric has very kindly offered to stay at Lou Mas."

Mr. Cranefield and Mrs. Massie continued to plod up the hill, she with increasing difficulty. They brought Alec what they thought he needed. But he had no addictions, no cravings, no use for anything now but his destination. The children were sent up evenings. They never knew what to say or what he could hear. They talked as if they were still eleven or twelve, when Alec had stopped seeing them grow.

To Mr. Cranefield they looked like imitations of English children—loud, humorless, dutiful, clear. "James couldn't come with us tonight," said Molly. "He was quite ill, for some reason. He brought his dinner up." All three spoke the high, thin English of expatriate children who, unknowingly, mimic their mothers. The lightbulb hanging crooked left Alec's face in shadow. When the children had kissed Alec and departed, Mr. Cranefield could hear them taking the hospital stairs headlong, at a gallop. The children were young and alive, and Alec was forty-something and nearly always sleeping. Unequal chances, Mr. Cranefield thought. They can't really beat their breasts about it. When Mrs. Massie was present, she never failed to say, "Your father is tired," though nobody knew if Alec was tired or not.

The neighbors pitied the children. Meaning only kindness, Mr.

Cranefield reminded Molly that one day she would type, Mrs. Massie said something more about helping in the garden. That was how everyone saw them now—grubbing, digging, lending a hand. They had become Wilkinson's secondhand kin but without his panache, his ease in adversity. They were Alec's offspring: stiff. Humiliated, they overheard and garnered for memory: "We've asked Wilkinson to come over and cook up a curry. He's hours in the kitchen, but I must say it's worth every penny." "We might get Wilkinson to drive us to Rome. He doesn't charge all that much, and he's such good company." Always Wilkinson, never Eric, though that was what Barbara had called him from their first meeting. To the children he was, and remained, "Mr. Wilkinson," friend of both parents, occasional guest in the house.

The rains of their third southern spring were still driving hard against the villa when Barbara's engineer brother wrote to say they were letting Lou Mas. Everything dripped wet as she stood near a window, with bougainvillea soaked and wild-looking on one side of the pane and steam forming on the other, to read this letter. The new tenants were a family of planters who had been forced to leave Malaya; it had a connection with political events, but Barbara's life was so full now that she never looked at the papers. They would be coming there in June, which gave Barbara plenty of time to find another home. He—her brother—had thought of giving her the Lou Mas cottage, but he wondered if it would suit her, inasmuch as it lacked electric light, running water, an indoor lavatory, most of its windows, and part of its roof. This was not to say it could not be fixed up for the Webbs in the future, when Lou Mas had started paying for itself. Half the rent obtained would be turned over to Barbara. She would have to look hard, he said, before finding brothers who were so considerate of a married sister. She and the children were not likely to suffer from the change, which might even turn out to their moral advantage. Barbara supposed this meant that Desmond— the richest, the best-educated, the most easily flabbergasted of her brothers—was still mulling over the description of Lou Mas Ron must have taken back.

With Wilkinson helping, the Webbs moved to the far side of the hospital, on a north-facing slope, away from the sea. Here the houses were tall and thin with narrow windows, set in gardens of raked gravel. Their neighbors included the mayor, the more prosperous shopkeepers, and the coach of the local football team. Barbara was enchanted to find industrial activity she had not suspected—a thriving ceramics factory that produced figurines of monks whose heads were mustard pots, dogs holding thermometers in their paws, and the patron saint of Rivabella wearing armor of pink, orange, mauve, or white. These were purchased by tourists who had trudged up to the town in the hope of seeing early Renaissance frescoes.

Barbara had never missed a day with Alec, not even the day of the move. She held his limp hand and told him stories. When he was not stunned by drugs, or too far lost in his past, he seemed to be listening. Sometimes he pressed her fingers. He seldom spoke more than a word at a time. Barbara described to him the pleasures of moving, and how pretty the houses were on the north side, with their gardens growing gnomes and shells and tinted bottles. Why make fun of such people, she asked his still face. They probably knew, by instinct, how to get the best out of life. She meant every word, for she was profoundly in love and knew that Wilkinson would never leave her except for a greater claim. She combed Alec's hair and bathed him; Wilkinson came whenever he could to shave Alec and cut his nails and help Barbara change the bedsheets; for it was not the custom of the hospital staff to do any of this.

Sometimes Alec whispered, "Diana," who might have been either his sister or Mrs. Massie. Barbara tried to remember her old prophetic dreams, from that time when, as compensation for absence of passion, she had been granted second sight. In none had she ever seen herself bending over a dying man, listening to him call her by another woman's name.

They lived, now, in four dark rooms stuffed with furniture, some of it useful. Upstairs resided the widow of the founder of the ceramics factory. She had been bought out at a loss at the end of the war, and disapproved of the new line of production, especially the monks. She never interfered, never asked questions—simply came down once a month to collect her rent which was required in cash. She did tell the children that she had never seen the inside of an English villa, but did not seem to think her exclusion was a slight; she took her bearings from a very small span of the French middle-class compass.

Barbara and Wilkinson made jokes about the French widow-lady, but the children did not. To replace their lopped English roots they had grown the sensitive antennae essential to wanderers. They could have drawn the social staircase of Rivabella on a blackboard, and knew how low a step, now, had been assigned to them. Barbara would not have cared. Wherever she stood now seemed to suit her. On her way home from the hospital she saw two men, foreigners, stop and stare and exchange remarks about her. She could not understand the language they spoke, but she saw they had been struck by her beauty. One of them seemed to be asking the other, "Who can she be?" In their new home she took the only bedroom—an imposing matrimonial chamber. When Wilkinson was in residence he shared it as a matter of course. The boys slept on a pullout sofa in the dining room, and Molly had a couch in a glassed-in verandah. The verandah contained their landlady's rubber plants, which Molly scrupulously tended. The boys had stopped quarreling. They would never argue or ever say much to each other again. Alec's children seemed to have been collected under one roof by chance, like strays, or refugees. Their narrow faces, their gray eyes, their thinness and dryness, were similar, but not alike; a stranger would not necessarily have known they were of the same father and mother. The boys still wore secondhand clothes sent from England; this was their only connection with English life.

On market days Molly often saw their old housemaid or the laundress. They asked for news of Alec, which made Molly feel cold and shy. She was dressed very like them now, in a cotton frock and rope-soled shoes from a market stall. "Style is all you need to bring it off," Barbara had assured her, but she had none, at least not that kind. It was Molly who chose what the family would eat, who looked at prices and kept accounts and counted her change. Barbara was entirely busy with Alec at the hospital, and with Wilkinson at home. With love, she had lost her craving for nursery breakfasts. She sat at table smoking, watching Wilkinson telling stories. When Wilkinson was there, he did much of the cooking. Molly was grateful for that.

The new people at Lou Mas had everyone's favor. If there had been times when the neighbors had wondered how Barbara and Alec could possibly have met, the Malayan planter and his jolly wife were an old novel known by heart. They told about jungle terrorists, and what the British ought to be doing, and they described the owner of Lou Mas—a Welshman who was planning to go into politics. Knowing Barbara to be Irish, no one could place the Welshman. The story started up that Barbara's family were bankrupt and had sold Lou Mas to a Welsh war profiteer.

Mrs. Massie presented the new people with *Flora's Gardening Encyclopaedia*. "It is by way of being a classic," she said. "Seventeen editions. I do all my typing myself."

"Ah, well, poor Barbara," everyone said now. What could you expect? Luckily for her, she had Wilkinson. Wilkinson's star was rising. "Don't underestimate Rommel" had been said to some effect—there was a mention in the *Sunday Telegraph*. "Wilkinson goes everywhere. He's invited to everything at Monte Carlo. He must positively live on lobster salad." "Good for old Wilkinson. Why shouldn't he?" Wilkinson had had a bad war, had been a prisoner somewhere.

Who imagined that story, Mr. Cranefield wondered. Some were mixing up Wilkinson with the dying Alec, others seemed to think Alec was already dead. By August it had become established that Wilkinson had been tortured by the Japanese and had spent the years since trying to leave the memory behind. He never mentioned what he'd been through, which was to his credit. Barbara and three kids must have been the last thing he wanted, but that was how it was with Wilkinson—too kind for his own good, all too ready to lend a hand, to solve a problem. Perhaps, rising, he would pull the Webbs with him. Have you seen that girl hanging about in the market? You can't tell her from the butcher's child.

From Alec's bedside Barbara wrote a long letter to her favorite brother, the pilot, Mike. She told about Alec, "sleeping so peacefully as I write," and described the bunch of daisies Molly had put in a jug on the windowsill, and how well Will had done in his finals ("He will be the family intellectual, a second Alec"), and finally she came round to the matter of Wilkinson: "You probably saw the rave notice in the *Telegraph*, but you had no way of knowing of course it was someone I knew. Well, here is the whole story. Please, Mike, do keep it to yourself for the moment, you know how Ron takes things sometimes." Meeting Eric had confirmed her belief there was something in the universe more reasonable than God—at any rate more logical. Eric had taken a good look at the Lou Mas cottage and thought something might be done with it after all. "You will adore Eric," she promised. "He is marvelous with the children and so kind to Alec," which was true.

"Are you awake, love?" She moistened a piece of cotton with mineral water from a bottle that stood on the floor (Alec had no table) and wet his lips with it, then took his hand, so light it seemed hollow, and held it in her own, telling him quietly about the Lou Mas cottage, where he would occupy a pleasant room overlooking the sea. He flexed his fingers; she bent close: "Yes, dear; what is it, dear?" For the first time since she'd known him he said, "Mother." She waited; but no, that was all. She saw herself on his balcony at Lou Mas in her white dressing gown, her hair in the sun, saw what the gardener would have been struck by if only he had looked up. She said to herself, I gave Alec three beautiful children. That is what he is thanking me for now.

Her favorite brother had been away from England when her letter came, so that it was late in September when he answered to call her a bitch, a trollop, a crook, and a fool. He was taking up the question of her gigolo boyfriend with the others. They had been supporting Alec's family for three years. If she thought they intended to take on her lover (this written above a word scratched out); and here the letter ended. She went white, as her children did, easily. She said to Wilkinson, "Come and talk in the car, where we can be quiet," for they were seldom alone.

She let him finish reading, then said, in a voice that he had never heard before but that did not seem to surprise him—"I grew up blacking my brothers' boots. Alec was the first man who ever held a door open for me."

He said, "Your brothers all did well," without irony, meaning there was that much to admire.

"Oh," she said, "if you are comparing their chances with Alec's, if that's what you mean—the start Alec had. Well, poor Alec. Yes, a better start. I often thought, Well, there it is with him, that's the very trouble—a start too good."

This exchange, this double row of cards faceup, seemed all they intended to reveal. They instantly sat differently, she straighter, he more relaxed.

Wilkinson said, "Which one of them actually owns Lou Mas?"

"Equal shares, I think. Though Desmond has power of attorney and makes all the decisions. Alec and I *own* Lou Mas, but only legally. They put it in our name because we were emigrating. It made it easier for them, with all the taxes. We had three years, and not a penny in rent."

Wilkinson said, in a kind of anguish, "Oh, God bless my soul."

It was Wilkinson's English lawyer friend in Monte Carlo who drew up the papers with which Alec signed his share of Lou Mas over to Barbara and Alec and Barbara revoked her brother's power of attorney. Alec, his obedient hand around a pen and the hand firmly held in Barbara's, may have known what he was doing but not why. The documents were then put in the lawyer's safe to await Alec's death, which occurred not long after.

The doctor, who had sat all night at the bedside, turning Alec's head so that he would not strangle vomiting (for that was not the way he wished him to die), heard him breathing deeply and ever more deeply and then no longer. Alec's eyes were closed, but the doctor pressed the lids with his fingers. Believing in his own and perhaps Alec's damnation, he stood for a long time at the window while the roof and towers of the church became clear and flushed with rose; then the red rim of the sun emerged, and turned yellow, and it was as good as day.

There was only one nurse in the hospital, and a midwife on another floor. Summoning both, he told them to spread a rubber sheet under Alec, and wash him, and put clean linen on the bed.

At that time, in that part of France, scarcely anyone had a telephone. The doctor walked down the slope on the far side of Rivabella and presented himself unshaven to Barbara in her nightdress to say that Alec was dead. She dressed and came at once; there was no one yet in the streets to see her and to ask who she was. Eric followed, bringing the clothes in which Alec would be buried. All he could recall of his prayers, though he would not have said them around Barbara, were the first words of the Collect: "Almighty God, unto whom all hearts be open, all desires known, and from whom no secrets are hid."

Barbara had a new friend—her French widowed landlady. It was she who arranged to have part of Barbara's wardrobe dyed black within twenty-four hours, who lent her a black hat and gloves and a long crêpe veil. Barbara let the veil down over her face. Her friend, whose veil was tied around her hat and floated behind her, took Barbara by the arm, and they walked to the cemetery and stood side by side. The Webbs' former servants were there, and the doctor, and the local British colony. Some of the British thought the other woman in black must be Barbara's Irish mother:

Only the Irish poor or the Royal Family ever wore mourning of that kind.

The graveyard was so cramped and small, so crowded with dead from the time of Garibaldi and before, that no one else could be buried. The coffins of the recent dead were stored in cells in a thick concrete wall. The cells were then sealed, and a marble plaque affixed in lieu of a tombstone. Alec had to be lifted to shoulder level, which took the strength of several persons—the doctor, Mr. Cranefield, Barbara's brothers, and Alec's young sons. (Wilkinson would have helped, but he had already wrenched his shoulder quite badly carrying the coffin down the hospital steps.) Molly thrust her way into this crowd of male mourners. She said to her mother, "Not you—you never loved him."

God knows who might have heard that, Barbara thought.

Actually, no one had, except for Mrs. Massie. Believing it to be true, she dismissed it from memory. She was composing her own obituary: "Two generations of gardeners owed their..." "Two generations of readers owed their gardens..."

"Our Father," Alec's sister said, hoping no one would notice and mistake her for a fraud. Nor did she wish to have a scrap of consideration removed from Barbara, whose hour this was. Her own loss was beyond remedy, and so not worth a mention. There was no service—nothing but whispering and silence. To his sister, it was as if Alec had been left, stranded and alone, in a train stalled between stations. She had not seen him since the day he left England, and had refused to look at him dead. Barbara was aware of Diana, the mouse, praying like a sewing machine somewhere behind her. She clutched the arm of the older widow and thought, I know, I know, but she can get a job, can't she? I was working when I met Alec, wasn't I? But what Diana Webb meant by "work" was the fine stitching her own mother had done to fill time, not for a living. In Diana's hotel room was a box containing the most exquisite and impractical child's bonnet and coat made from some of the white silk Alec had sent her from India, before the war. Perhaps a luxury shop in Monte Carlo or one of Barbara's wealthy neighbors would be interested. Perhaps there was an Anglican clergyman with a prosperous parish. She opened her eyes and saw that absolutely no one in the cemetery looked like Alec—not even his sons.

The two boys seemed strange, even to each other, in their dark, new suits. The word "father" had slipped out of their grasp just now. A marble plaque on which their father's name was misspelled stood propped against the wall. The boys looked at it helplessly.

Is that all, people began wondering. What happens now?

Barbara turned away from the wall and, still holding the arm of her friend, led the mourners out past the gates.

It was I who knew what he wanted, the doctor believed. He had told me long before. Asked me to promise, though I refused. I heard his last words. The doctor kept telling himself this. I heard his last words—though Alec had not said anything, had merely breathed, then stopped.

"Her father was a late Victorian poet of some distinction," Mrs. Massie's obituary went on.

Will, who was fifteen, was no longer a child, did not look like Alec, spoke up in that high-pitched English of his: "Death is empty without God." Now where did that come from? Had he heard it? Read it? Was he performing? No one knew. Later, he would swear that at that moment a vocation had come to light, though it must have been born with him—bud within the bud, mind within the mind. I will buy back your death, he would become convinced he had said to Alec. Shall enrich it; shall refuse the southern glare, the southern void. I shall pay for your solitude, your humiliation. Shall demand for myself a stronger life, a firmer death. He thought, later, that he had said all this, but he had said and thought only five words.

As they shuffled out, all made very uncomfortable by Will, Mrs. Massie leaned half on her stick and half on James, observing, "You were such a little boy when I saw you for the first time at Lou Mas." Because his response was silence, she supposed he was waiting to hear more. "You three must stick together now. The Three Musketeers." But they were already apart.

Major Lamprey found himself walking beside the youngest of the Laceys. He told Mike what he told everyone now—why he had not moved to Malta. It was because he did not trust the Maltese. "Not that one can trust anyone here," he said. "Even the mayor belongs to an anarchist movement, I've been told. Whatever happens, I intend to die fighting on my own doorstep."

The party was filing down a steep incline. "You will want to be with your family," Mrs. Massie said, releasing James and leaning half her weight on Mr. Cranefield instead. They picked up with no trouble a conversation dropped the day before. It was about how Mr. Cranefield—rather, his other self, E. C. Arden—was likely to fare in the second half of the 1950s: "It is a question of your not being too modern and yet not slipping back," Mrs. Massie said. "I never have to worry. Gardens don't change."

"I am not worried about new ideas," he said. "Because there are none. But words, now. 'Permissive.'"

"What's that?"

"It was in the *Observer* last Sunday. I suppose it means something. Still. One mustn't. One can't. There are limits."

Barbara met the mayor coming the other way, too late, carrying a wreath with a purple ribbon on which was written, in gold, "From the Municipality—Sincere Respects." Waiting for delivery of the wreath had made him tardy. "For a man who never went out, Alec made quite an impression," Mrs. Massie remarked.

"His funeral was an attraction," said Mr. Cranefield.

"Can one call that a funeral?" She was still thinking about her own.

Mike Lacey caught up to his sister. They had once been very close. As soon as she saw him she stood motionless, bringing the line behind her to a halt. He said he knew this was not the time or place, but he had to let her know she was not to worry. She would always have a roof over her head. They felt responsible for Alec's children. There were vague plans for fixing up the cottage. They would talk about it later on.

"Ah, Mike," she said. "That is so kind of you." Using both hands she lifted the veil so that he could see her clear gray eyes.

The procession wound past the hospital and came to the church square. Mr. Cranefield had arranged a small after-funeral party, as a favor to Barbara, who had no real home. Some were coming and some were not; the latter now began to say good-bye. Geneviève, whose face was like a pink sponge because she had been crying so hard, flung herself at James, who let her embrace him. Over his governess's dark shoulder he saw the faces of people who had given him secondhand clothes, thus (he believed) laying waste to his life. He smashed their faces to particles, left the particles dancing in the air like midges until they dissolved without a sound. Wait, he was thinking. Wait, wait.

Mr. Cranefield wondered if Molly was going to become her mother's hostage, her moral bail—if Barbara would hang on to her to show that Alec's progeny approved of her. He remembered Molly's small, anxious face, and how worried she had been about St. George. "You will grow up, you know," he said, which was an odd thing to say, since she was quite tall. They walked down the path Wilkinson had not been able to climb in his car. She stared at him. "I mean, when you grow up you will be free." She shook her head. She knew better than that now, at fourteen: There was no freedom except to cease to love. She would love her brothers when they had stopped thinking much about her: women's fidelity. This would not keep her from fighting them, inch by inch, over money, property, remnants of the past: women's insecurity. She would hound them and pester them about Alec's grave, and Barbara's old age, and where they were all to be buried: women's sense of order. They would by then be another James, an alien Will, a different Molly.

Mr. Cranefield's attention slipped from Molly to Alec to the funeral, to the extinction of one sort of Englishman and the emergence of another. Most people looked on Wilkinson as a prewar survival, what with his "I say's" and "By Jove's," but he was really an English mutation, a new man, wearing the old protective coloring. Alec would have understood his language, probably, but not the person behind it. A landscape containing two male figures came into high relief in Mr. Cranefield's private image of the world, as if he had been lent trick spectacles. He allowed the vision to fade. Better to stick to the blond pair on his desk; so far they had never let him down. I am not impulsive, or arrogant, he explained to himself. No one would believe the truth about Wilkinson even if he were to describe it. I shall not insist, he decided, or try to have the last word. I am not that kind of fool. He breathed slowly, as one does when mortal danger has been averted.

The mourners attending Mr. Cranefield's party reached the motor road and began to straggle across: It was a point of honor for members of the British colony to pay absolutely no attention to cars. The two widows had fallen back, either so that Barbara could make an entrance, or because the older woman believed it would not be dignified for her to exhibit haste. A strong west wind flattened the black dresses against their breasts and lifted their thick veils.

How will he hear me, Molly wondered. You could speak to someone in a normal grave, for earth is porous and seems to be life, of a kind. But how to speak across marble? Even if she were to place her hands flat on the marble slab, it would not absorb a fraction of human warmth. She had to tell him what she had done—how it was she, Molly, who had led the intruder home, let him in, causing Alec, always courteous, to remove himself first to the hospital, then farther on. Disaster, the usual daily development, had to have a beginning. She would go back to the cemetery, alone, and say it, whether or not he could hear. The disaster began with two sentences: "Mummy, this is Mr. Wilkinson. Mr. Wilkinson wants to tell you how he came to drive me home."

Barbara descended the steps to Mr. Cranefield's arm in arm

with her new friend, who was for the first time about to see the inside of an English house. "Look at that," said the older widow. One of the peacocks had taken shelter from the wind in Mr. Cranefield's electric lift. A minute earlier Alec's sister had noticed, too, and had thought something that seemed irrefutable: No power on earth would ever induce her to eat a peacock.

Who is to say I never loved Alec, said Barbara, who loved Wilkinson. He was high-handed, yes, laying down the law as long as he was able, but he was always polite. Of course I loved him. I still do. He will have to be buried properly, where we can plant something—white roses. The mayor told me that every once in a while they turn one of the Russians out, to make room. There must be a waiting list. We could put Alec's name on it. Alec gave me three children. Eric gave me Lou Mas.

Entering Mr. Cranefield's, she removed her dark veil and hat and revealed her lovely head, like the sun rising. Because the wind had started blowing leaves and sand, Mr. Cranefield's party had to be moved indoors from the loggia. This change occasioned some confusion, in which Barbara did not take part; neither did Wilkinson, whose wrenched shoulder was making him feel ill. She noticed her children helping, carrying plates of small sandwiches and silver buckets of ice. She approved of this; they were obviously well brought up. The funeral had left Mr. Cranefield's guests feeling hungry and thirsty and rather lonely, anxious to hold on to a glass and to talk to someone. Presently their voices rose, overlapped, and created something like a thick woven fabric of blurred design, which Alec's sister (who was not used to large social gatherings) likened to a flying carpet. It was now, with Molly covertly watching her, that Barbara began in the most natural way in the world to live happily ever after. There was nothing willful about this: She was simply borne in a single direction, though she did keep seeing for a time her black glove on her widowed friend's black sleeve.

Escorting lame Mrs. Massie to a sofa, Mr. Cranefield said they might as well look on the bright side. (He was still speaking about the second half of the 1950s.) Wilkinson, sitting down because he felt sick, and thinking the remark was intended for him, assured Mr. Cranefield, truthfully, that he had never looked anywhere else. It then happened that every person in the room, at the same moment, spoke and thought of something other than Alec. This lapse, this inattention, lasting no longer than was needed to say "No, thank you" or "Oh, really?" or "Yes, I see," was enough to create the dark gap marking the end of Alec's span. He ceased to be, and it made absolutely no difference after that whether or not he was forgotten.

GRIPPES AND POCHE

At an early hour for the French man of letters Henri
Grippes—it was a quarter to nine, on an April morning—he sat
in a windowless, brown-painted cubicle, facing a slight, mop-
headed young man with horn-rimmed glasses and dimples. The
man wore a dark tie with a narrow knot and a buttoned-up blazer.
His signature was "O. Poche"; his title, on the grubby, pulpy
summons Grippes had read, sweating, was "Controller." He must
be freshly out of his civil-service training school, Grippes guessed.
Even his aspect, of a priest hearing a confession a few yards from
the guillotine, seemed newly acquired. Before him lay open a dun-
colored folder with not much in it—a letter from Grippes, full of
delaying tactics, and copies of his correspondence with a bank in
California. It was not true that American banks protected a de-
positor's secrets; anyway, this one hadn't. Another reason Grippes
thought O. Poche must be recent was the way he kept blushing.
He was not nearly as pale or as case-hardened as Grippes.

At this time, President de Gaulle had been in power five years,
two of which Grippes had spent in blithe writer-in-residenceship
in California. Returning to Paris, he had left a bank account behind. It was forbidden, under the Fifth Republic, for a French citizen to have a foreign account. The government might not have
cared so much about drachmas or zlotys, but dollars were supposed to be scraped in, converted to francs at bottom rate, and, of
course, counted as personal income. Grippes's unwise and furtive
moves with trifling sums, his somewhat paranoid disagreements
with California over exchange, had finally caught the eye of the
Bank of France, as a glistening minnow might attract a dozing
whale. The whale swallowed Grippes, found him too small to

matter, and spat him out, straight into the path of a water ox called Public Treasury, Direct Taxation, Personal Income. That was Poche.

What Poche had to discuss—a translation of Grippes's novel, the one about the French teacher at the American university and his doomed love affair with his student Karen-Sue—seemed to embarrass him. Observing Poche with some curiosity, Grippes saw, unreeling, scenes from the younger man's inhibited boyhood. He sensed, then discerned, the Catholic boarding school in bleakest Brittany: the unheated forty-bed dormitory, a nightly torment of unchaste dreams with astonishing partners, a daytime terror of real Hell with real fire.

"Human waywardness is hardly new," said Grippes, feeling more secure now that he had tested Poche and found him provincial. "It no longer shocks anyone."

It was not the moral content of the book he wished to talk over, said Poche, flaming. In any case, he was not qualified to do so: He had flubbed Philosophy and never taken Modern French Thought. (He must be new, Grippes decided. He was babbling.) Frankly, even though he had the figures in front of him, Poche found it hard to believe the American translation had earned its author so little. There must be another considerable sum, placed in some other bank. Perhaps M. Grippes could try to remember.

The figures were true. The translation had done poorly. Failure played to Grippes's advantage, reducing the hint of deliberate tax evasion to a simple oversight. Still, it hurt to have things put so plainly. He felt bound to tell Poche that American readers were no longer interested in the teacher-student imbroglio, though there had been some slight curiosity as to what a foreigner might wring out of the old sponge.

Poche gazed at Grippes. His eyes seemed to Grippes as helpless and eager as those of a gun dog waiting for a command in the right language. Encouraged, Grippes said more: In writing his novel, he had overlooked the essential development—the erring professor was supposed to come home at the end. He could be half dead, limping, on crutches, toothless, jobless, broke, impotent—it didn't matter. He had to be judged and shriven. As further modification, his wife during his foolish affair would have gone on to be a world-class cellist, under her maiden name. "Wife" had not entered Grippes's cast of characters, probably because, like Poche, he did not have one. (He had noticed Poche did not wear a wedding ring.) Grippes had just left his professor driving off to an airport in blessed weather, whistling a jaunty air.

Poche shook his head. Obviously, it was not the language he was after. He began to write on a clean page of the file, taking no more notice of Grippes.

What a mistake it had been, Grippes reflected, still feeling pain beneath the scar, to have repeated the male teacher–female student pattern. He should have turned it around, identified himself with a brilliant and cynical woman teacher. Unfortunately, unlike Flaubert (his academic stalking-horse), he could not put himself in a woman's place, probably because he thought it an absolutely terrible place to be. The novel had not done well in France, either. (Poche had still to get round to that.) The critics had found Karen-Sue's sociological context obscure. She seemed at a remove from events of her time, unaware of improved literacy figures in North Korea, never once mentioned, or that since the advent of Gaullism it cost twenty-five centimes to mail a letter. The Pill was still unheard-of in much of Europe; readers could not understand what it was Karen-Sue kept forgetting to take, or why Grippes had devoted a contemplative no-action chapter to the abstract essence of risk. The professor had not given Karen-Sue the cultural and political enlightenment one might expect from the graduate of a pre-eminent Paris school. It was a banal story, really, about a pair of complacently bourgeois lovers. The real victim was Grippes, seduced and abandoned by the American middle class.

It was Grippes's first outstanding debacle and, for that reason, the only one of his works he ever reread. He could still hear Karen-Sue—the true, the original—making of every avowal a poignant question: "I'm Cairn-Sioux? I know you're busy? It's just that I don't understand what you said about Flaubert and his own niece?" He recalled her with tolerance—the same tolerance that had probably weakened the book.

Grippes was wise enough to realize that the California-bank affair had been an act of folly, a con man's aberration. He had thought he would get away with it, knowing all the while he could not. There existed a deeper treasure for Poche to uncover, well below Public Treasury sights. Computers had not yet come into government use; even typewriters were rare—Poche had summoned Grippes in a cramped, almost secretive hand. It took time to strike an error, still longer to write a letter about it. In his youth, Grippes had received from an American patroness of the arts three rent-bearing apartments in Paris, which he still owned. (The patroness had been the last of a generous species, Grippes one of the last young men to benefit from her kind.) He collected the rents by devious and untraceable means, stowing the cash obtained in safe deposit. His visible way of life was stoic and plain; not even the most vigilant Controller could fault his underfurnished apartment in Montparnasse, shared with some cats he had already tried to claim as dependents. He showed none of the signs of prosperity Public Treasury seemed to like, such as membership in a golf club.

After a few minutes of speculative anguish in the airless cubicle, Grippes saw that Poche had no inkling whatever about the flats. He was chasing something different—the inexistent royalties from the Karen-Sue novel. By a sort of divine evenhandedness, Grippes was going to have to pay for imaginary earnings. He put the safe deposit out of his mind, so that it would not show on his face, and said, "What will be left for me, when you've finished adding and subtracting?"

To his surprise, Poche replied in a bold tone, pitched for reciting quotations: " 'What is left? What is left? Only what remains at low tide, when small islands are revealed, emerging...' " He stopped quoting and flushed. Obviously, he had committed the worst sort of blunder, had been intimate, had let his own personality show. He had crossed over to his opponent's ground.

"It sounds familiar," said Grippes, enticing him further. "Although, to tell the truth, I don't remember writing it."

"It is a translation," said Poche. "The Anglo-Saxon British author, Victor Prism." He pronounced it "Prissom."

"You've read Prism?" said Grippes, pronouncing correctly the name of an old acquaintance.

"I had to. Prissom was on the preparatory program. Anglo-Saxon Commercial English."

"They stuffed you with foreign writers?" said Grippes. "With so many of us having to go to foreign lands for a living?"

That was perilous: He had just challenged Poche's training, the very foundation of his right to sit there reading Grippes's private mail. But he had suddenly recalled his dismay when as a young man he had looked at a shelf in his room and realized he had to compete with the dead—Proust, Flaubert, Balzac, Stendhal, and on into the dark. The rivalry was infinite, a Milky Way of dead stars still daring to shine. He had invented a law, a moratorium on publication that would eliminate the dead, leaving the skies clear for the living. (All the living? Grippes still couldn't decide.) Foreign writers would be deported to a remote solar system, where they could circle one another.

For Prism, there was no system sufficiently remote. Not so long ago, interviewed in *The Listener*, Prism had dragged in Grippes, saying that he used to cross the Channel to consult a seer in Half Moon Street, hurrying home to set down the prose revealed from a spirit universe. "Sometimes I actually envied him," Prism was quoted as saying. He sounded as though Grippes were dead. "I used to wish ghost voices would speak to me, too," suggesting ribbons of pure Prism running like ticker tape round the equator of a crystal ball. "Unfortunately, I had to depend on my own creative intelligence, modest though I am sure it was."

Poche did not know about this recent libel in Anglo-Saxon Commercial English. He had been trying to be nice. Grippes made a try of his own, jocular: "I only meant, you could have been reading *me*." The trouble was that he meant it, ferociously.

Poche must have heard the repressed shout. He shut the file and said, "This dossier is too complex for my level. I shall have to send it up to the Inspector." Grippes made a vow that he would never let natural pique get the better of him again.

"What will be left for me?" Grippes asked the Inspector. "When you have finished adding and subtracting?"

Mme. de Pelle did not bother to look up. She said, "Somebody should have taken this file in hand a long time ago. Let us start at the beginning. How long, in all, were you out of the country?"

When Poche said "send up," he'd meant it literally. Grippes looked out on a church where Delacroix had worked and the slow summer rain. At the far end of the square, a few dark shops displayed joyfully trashy religious goods, like the cross set with tiny seashells Mme. de Pelle wore round her neck. Grippes had been raised in an anticlerical household, in a small town where opposing factions were grouped behind the schoolmaster—Grippes's father—and the parish priest. Women, lapsed agnostics, sometimes crossed enemy lines and started going to church. One glimpsed them, all in gray, creeping along a gray-walled street.

"You are free to lodge a protest against the fine," said Mme. de Pelle. "But if you lose the contestation, your fine will be tripled. That is the law."

Grippes decided to transform Mme. de Pelle into the manager of a brothel catering to the Foreign Legion, slovenly in her habits and addicted to chloroform, but he found the idea unpromising. In due course he paid a monstrous penalty, which he did not contest, for fear of drawing attention to the apartments. (It was still believed that he had stashed away million from the Karen-Sue book, probably in Switzerland.) A summons addresseed in O. Poche's shrunken hand, the following spring, showed Grippes he had been tossed back downstairs. After that he forgot about Mme. de Pelle, except now and then.

It was at about this time that a series of novels offered themselves to Grippes—shadowy outlines behind a frosted-glass pane. He knew he must not let them crowd in all together, or keep them waiting too long. His foot against the door, he admitted, one by one, a number of shadows that turned into young men, each bringing his own name and address, his native region of France portrayed on color postcards, and an index of information about his tastes in clothes, love, food, and philosophers, his bent of character, his tics of speech, his attitudes toward God and money, his political bias, and the intimation of a crisis about to explode underfoot. "Antoine" provided a Jesuit confessor, a homosexual affinity, and loss of faith. Spiritual shilly-shallying tends to run long; Antoine's covered more than six hundred pages, making it the thickest work in the Grippes canon. Then came "Thomas," with his Spartan mother on a Provençal fruit farm, rejected in favor of a civil-service career. "Bertrand" followed, adrift in frivolous Paris, tempted by neo-Fascism in the form of a woman wearing a bed jacket trimmed with marabou. "René" cycled round France, reading Chateaubriand when he stopped to rest. One morning he set fire to the barn he had been sleeping in, leaving his books to burn. This was the shortest of the novels, and the most popular with the young. One critic scolded Grippes for using crude symbolism. Another begged him to stop hiding behind "Antoine" and "René" and to take the metaphysical risk of revealing "Henri." But Grippes had tried that once with Karen-Sue, then with a roman à clef mercifully destroyed in the confusion of May 1968. He took these contretemps for a sign that he was to leave the subjective Grippes alone. The fact that each novel appeared even to Grippes to be a slice of French writing about life as it had been carved up and served a generation before made it seem quietly insurrectional. Nobody was doing this now; no one but Grippes. Grippes, for a time uneasy, decided to go on letting the shadows in.

The announcement of a new publication would bring a summons from Poche. When Poche leaned over the file, now, Grippes saw amid the mop of curls a coin-size tonsure. His diffident, steely questions tried to elicit from Grippes how many copies were likely to be sold and where Grippes had already put the money. Grippes would give him a copy of the book, inscribed. Poche would turn back the cover and glance at the signature, probably to make certain Grippes had not written something compromising and friendly. He kept the novels in a metal locker, fastened together with government-issue webbing tape and a military-looking buckle. It troubled Grippes to think of his work all in a bundle, in the dark. He thought of old-fashioned milestones, half hidden by weeds, along disused roads. The volumes marked time for Poche, too. He was still a Controller. Perhaps he had to wait for the woman upstairs to retire, so he could take over her title and office. The cubicle needed paint. There was a hole in the brown linoleum, just inside the door. Poche now wore a wedding ring. Grippes wondered if he should congratulate him, but decided to let Poche mention the matter first. He tried to imagine Mme. Poche.

Grippes could swear that in his string of novels nothing had been chipped out of his own past. Antoine, Thomas, Bertrand, and René (and, by now, Clément, Didier, Laurent, Hugues, and Yves) had arrived as strangers, almost like historical figures. At the same time, it seemed to Grippes that their wavering, ruffled reflection should deliver something he alone might recognize. What did he see, bending over the pond of his achievement? He saw a character closemouthed, cautious, unimaginative, ill at ease, obsessed with particulars. Worse, he was closed against progress, afraid of reform, shut into a literary, reactionary France. How could this be? Grippes had always and sincerely voted left. He had proved he could be reckless, open-minded, indulgent. He was like a father gazing round the breakfast table and suddenly realizing that none of the children are his. His children, if he could call them that, did not even look like him. From Antoine to Yves, his reflected character was small and slight, with a mop of curly hair, horn-rimmed glasses, and dimples.

Grippes believed in the importance of errors. No political system, no love affair, no native inclination, no life itself would be tolerable without a wide mesh for mistakes to slip through. It pleased him that Public Treasury had never caught up with the three apartments—not just for the sake of the cash piling up in safe deposit but for the black hole of error revealed. He and Poche had been together for some years—another blunder. Usually the Controller and taxpayer were torn apart after a meeting or two, so that revenue service would not start taking into consideration the client's aged indigent aunt, his bill for dental surgery, his alimony payments, his perennial mortgage. But possibly no one except Poche could be bothered with Grippes, always making some time-wasting claim for minute professional expenses, backed by a messy-looking certified receipt. Sometimes Grippes dared believe Poche admired him, that he hung on to the dossier out of devotion to his books. (This conceit was intensified when Poche began calling him "Maître.") Once, Grippes won some City of Paris award and was shown in *France-Soir* shaking hands with the mayor and simultaneously receiving a long, check-filled envelope.

Immediately summoned by Poche, expecting a discreet compliment, Grippes found him interested only in the caption under the photo, which made much of the size of the check. Grippes later thought of sending a sneering letter—"Thank you for your warm congratulations"—but he decided in time it was wiser not to fool with Poche. Poche had recently given him a 33 percent personal exemption, 3 percent more than the outer limit for Grippes's category of unsalaried earners—according to Poche, a group that included, as well as authors, door-to-door salesmen and prostitutes.

The dun-colored Gaullist-era jacket on Grippes's file had worn out long ago and been replaced, in 1969, by a cover in cool banker's green. Green presently made way for a shiny black-and-white marbled effect, reflecting the mood of opulence of the early seventies. Called in for his annual springtime confession, Grippes remarked about the folder: "Culture seems to have taken a decisive turn."

Poche did not ask what culture. He continued bravely, "Food for the cats, Maître. We *can't.*"

"They depend on me," said Grippes. But they had already settled the cats-as-dependents question once and for all. Poche drooped over Grippes's smudged and unreadable figures. Grippes tried to count the number of times he had examined the top of Poche's head. He still knew nothing about Poche, except for the wedding ring. Somewhere along the way, Poche had tied himself to a need for retirement pay and rich exemptions of his own. In the language of his generation, Poche was a fully structured individual. His vocabulary was sparse and to the point, centered on a single topic. His state training school, the machine that ground out Pelles and Poches all sounding alike, was in Clermont-Ferrand. Grippes was born in the same region.

That might have given them something else to talk about, except that Grippes had never been back. Structured Poche probably attended class reunions, was godfather to classmates' children, jotted their birthdays in a leather-covered notebook he never mislaid. Unstructured Grippes could not even remember his own age.

Poche turned over a sheet of paper, read something Grippes could not see, and said, automatically, "We *can't.*"

"Nothing is ever as it was," said Grippes, still going on about the marbled-effect folder. It was a remark that usually shut people up, leaving them nowhere to go but a change of subject. Besides, it was true. Nothing can be as it was. Poche and Grippes had just lost a terrifying number of brain cells. They were an instant closer to death. Death was of no interest to Poche. If he ever thought he might cease to exist, he would stop concentrating on other people's business and get down to reading Grippes while there was still time. Grippes wanted to ask, "Do you ever imagine your own funeral?" but it might have been taken as a threatening, gangster-ish hint from taxpayer to Controller—worse, far worse, than an attempted bribe.

A folder of a pretty mottled-peach shade appeared. Poche's cubicle was painted soft beige, the torn linoleum repaired. Poche sat in a comfortable armchair resembling the wide leathery seats in smart furniture stores at the upper end of Boulevard Saint-Germain. Grippes had a new, straight metallic chair that shot him bolt upright and hurt his spine. It was the heyday of the Giscard-ian period, when it seemed more important to keep the buttons polished than to watch where the regiment was heading. Grippes and Poche had not advanced one inch toward each other. Except for the paint and the chairs and "Maître," it could have been 1963. No matter how many works were added to the bundle in the locker, no matter how often Grippes had his picture taken, no matter how many Grippes paperbacks blossomed on airport book-stalls, Grippes to Poche remained a button.

The mottled-peach jacket began to darken and fray. Poche said to Grippes, "I asked you to come here, Maître, because I find we have overlooked something concerning your income." Grippes's heart gave a lurch. "The other day I came across an old ruling about royalties. How much of your income do you kick back?"

"Excuse me?"

"To publishers, to bookstores," said Poche. "How much?"

"Kick back?"

"What percentage?" said Poche. "Publishers. Printers."

"You mean," said Grippes, after a time, "how much do I pay editors to edit, publishers to publish, printers to print, and book-sellers to sell?" He supposed that to Poche such a scheme might sound plausible. It would fit his long view over Grippes's untidy life. Grippes knew most of the literary gossip that went round about himself; the circle was so small that it had to come back. In most stories there was a virus of possibility, but he had never heard anything as absurd as this, or as base.

Poche opened the file, concealing the moldering cover, apparently waiting for Grippes to mention a figure. The nausea Grippes felt he put down to his having come here without breakfast. One does not insult a Controller. He had shouted silently at Poche, years before, and had been sent upstairs to do penance with Mme. de Pelle. It is not good to kick over a chair and stalk out. "I have never been so insulted!" might have no meaning from Grippes, keelhauled month after month in one lumpy review or another. As his works increased from bundle to heap, so they drew intellectual abuse. He welcomed partisan ill-treatment, as warming to him as popular praise. Don't forget me, Grippes silently prayed, standing at the periodicals table in La Hune, the Left Bank bookstore, looking for his own name in those quarterlies no one ever takes home. Don't praise me. Praise is weak stuff. Praise me after I'm dead.

But even the most sour and despairing and close-printed essays were starting to mutter acclaim. The shoreline of the eighties, barely in sight, was ready to welcome Grippes, who had reestablished the male as hero, whose left-wing heartbeat could be heard, loyally thumping, behind the armor of his right-wing traditional prose. His reestablished hero had curly hair, soft eyes, horn-rimmed glasses, dimples, and a fully structured life. He was pleasing to both sexes and to every type of reader, except for a few thick-ribbed louts. Grippes looked back at Poche, who did not know how closely they were bound. What if he were to say, "This is a preposterous insinuation, a blot on a noble profession and on my reputation in particular," only to have Poche answer, "Too bad, Maître—I was trying to help"? He said, as one good-natured fellow to another, "Well, what if I own up to this crime?"

"It's no crime," said Poche. "I simply add the amount to your professional expenses."

"To my rebate?" said Grippes. "To my exemption?"

"It depends on how much."

"A third of my income?" said Grippes, insanely. "Half?"

"A reasonable figure might be twelve and a half percent."

All this for Grippes. Poche wanted nothing. Grippes considered with awe the only uncorruptible element in a porous society. No secret message had passed between them. He could not even invite Poche to lunch. He wondered if this arrangement had ever actually existed—if there could possibly be a good dodge that he, Grippes, had never heard of. He thought of contemporary authors for whose success there could be no other explanation: It had to be celestial playfulness or 12.5 percent. The structure, as Grippes was already calling it, might also just be Poche's innocent, indecent idea about writers.

Poche was reading the file again, though he must have known everything in it by heart. He was as absorbed, as contented, and somehow as pure as a child with a box of paints. At any moment he would raise his tender, bewildered eyes and murmur, "Four dozen typewriter ribbons in a third of the fiscal year, Maître? We *can't*."

Grippes tried to compose a face for Poche to encounter, a face above reproach. But writers considered above reproach always looked moody and haggard, about to scream. Be careful, he was telling himself. Don't let Poche think he's doing you a favor. These people set traps. Was Poche angling for something? Was this bait? "Attempting to bribe a public servant" the accusation was called. "Bribe" wasn't the word: It was "corruption" the law mentioned—"an attempt to corrupt." All Grippes had ever offered Poche was his books, formally inscribed, as though Poche were an anonymous reader standing in line in a bookstore where Grippes, wedged behind a shaky table, sat signing away. "Your name?" "Whose name?" "How do you spell your name?" "Oh, the book isn't for me. It's for a friend of mine." His look changed to one of severity and impatience, until he remembered that Poche had never asked him to sign anything. He had never concealed his purpose, to pluck from Grippes's plumage every bright feather he could find.

Careful, Grippes repeated. Careful. Remember what happened to Prism.

Victor Prism, keeping pale under a parasol on the beach at Torremolinos, had made the acquaintance of a fellow Englishman—pleasant, not well educated but eager to learn, blistered shoulders, shirt draped over his head, pages of the *Sunday Express* round his red thighs. Prism lent him something to read—his sunburn was keeping him awake. It was a creative essay on three émigré authors of the 1930s, in a review so obscure and ill-paying that Prism had not bothered to include the fee on his income-tax return. (Prism had got it wrong, of course, having Thomas Mann—whose plain name Prism could not spell—go to East Germany and with his wife start a theater that presented his own plays, sending Stefan Zweig to be photographed with movie stars in California, and putting Bertolt Brecht to die a bitter man in self-imposed exile in Brazil. As it turned out, none of Prism's readers knew the difference. Chided by Grippes, Prism had been defensive, cold, said that no letters had come in. "One, surely?" said Grippes. "Yes, I thought that must be you," Prism said.)

Prism might have got off with the whole thing if his new friend had not fallen sound asleep after the first lines. Waking, refreshed, he had said to himself, I must find out what they get paid for this stuff, a natural reflex—he was of the Inland Revenue. He'd found no trace, no record; for Inland Revenue purposes "Death and Exile" did not exist. The subsequent fine was so heavy and Prism's disgrace so acute that he fled England to spend a few days with Grippes and the cats in Montparnasse. He sat on a kitchen chair while Grippes, nose and mouth protected by a checked scarf, sprayed terror to cockroaches. Prism, weeping in the fumes and wiping his eyes, said, "I'm through with Queen and Country"—something like that—"and I'm taking out French citizenship tomorrow."

"You would have to marry a Frenchwoman and have at least five male children," said Grippes, through the scarf. He was feeling the patriotic hatred of a driver on a crowded road seeing foreign license plates in the way.

"Oh, well, then," said Prism, as if to say, "I won't bother."

"Oh, well, then," said Grippes, softly, not quite to Poche. Poche added one last thing to the file and closed it, as if something definite had taken place. He clasped his hands and placed them on the dossier; it seemed shut for all time now, like a grave. He said, "Maître, one never stays long in the same fiscal theater. I have been in this one for an unusual length of time. We may not meet again. I want you to know I have enjoyed our conversations."

"So have I," said Grippes, with caution.

"Much of your autobiographical creation could apply to other lives of our time, believe me."

"So you have read them," said Grippes, an eye on the locker.

"I read those I bought," said Poche.

"But they are the same books."

"No. The books I bought belong to me. The others were gifts. I would never open a gift. I have no right to." His voice rose, and he spoke more slowly. "In one of them, when What's-His-Name struggles to prepare his civil-service tests, '. . . the desire for individual glory seemed so inapposite, suddenly, in a nature given to renunciation.' "

"I suppose it *is* a remarkable observation," said Grippes. "I was not referring to myself." He had no idea what that could be from, and he was certain he had not written it.

Poche did not send for Grippes again. Grippes became a commonplace taxpayer, filling out his forms without help. The frosted-glass door was reverting to dull white; there were fewer shadows for Grippes to let in. A fashion for having well-behaved Nazi officers shore up Western culture gave Grippes a chance to turn Poche into a tubercular poet, trapped in Paris by poverty and the Occupation. Grippes threw out the first draft, in which Poche joined a Christian-minded Resistance network and performed a few simple miracles, unaware of his own powers. He had the instinctive feeling that a new generation would not know what he was talking about. Instead, he placed Poche, sniffling and wheezing, in a squalid hotel room, cough pastilles spilled on the table, a stained blanket pinned round his shoulders. Up the fetid staircase came a handsome colonel, a Curt Jurgens type, smelling of shaving lotion, bent on saving liberal values, bringing Poche butter, cognac, and a thousand sheets of writing paper.

After that, Grippes no longer felt sure where to go. His earlier books, government tape and buckle binding them into an œuvre, had accompanied Poche to his new fiscal theater. Perhaps, finding his career blocked by the woman upstairs, he had asked for early retirement. Poche was in a gangster-ridden Mediterranean city, occupying a shoddy boom-period apartment he'd spent twenty years paying for. He was working at black-market jobs, tax adviser to the local mayor, a small innocent cog in the regional Mafia. After lunch, Poche would sit on one of those southern balconies that hold just a deck chair, rereading in chronological order all Grippes's books. In the late afternoon, blinds drawn, Poche totted up Mafia accounts by a chink of light. Grippes was here, in Montparnasse, facing a flat-white glass door.

He continued to hand himself a 45.5 percent personal exemption—the astonishing 33 plus the unheard-of 12.5. No one seemed to mind. No shabby envelope holding an order for execution came in the mail. Sometimes in Grippes's mind a flicker of common sense flamed like revealecd truth: The exemption was an error. Public Treasury was now tiptoeing toward computers. The computer brain was bound to wince at Grippes and stop functioning until the Grippes exemption was settled. Grippes rehearsed: "I was seriously misinformed."

He had to go farther and farther abroad to find offal for the cats. One tripe dealer had been turned into a driving school, another sold secondhand clothes. Returning on a winter evening after a long walk, carrying a parcel of sheep's lung wrapped in newspaper, he crossed Boulevard du Montparnasse just as the lights went on— the urban moonrise. The street was a dream street, faces flat white in the winter mist. It seemed to Grippes that he had crossed over to the 1980s, had only just noticed the new decade. In a recess between two glassed-in sidewalk cafés, four plainclothes cops were beating up a pair of pickpockets. Nobody had to explain the scene to Grippes; he knew what it was about. One prisoner already wore handcuffs. Customers on the far side of the glass gave no more than a glance. When they had got handcuffs on the second man, the cops pushed the two into the entrance of Grippes's apartment building to wait for the police van. Grippes shuffled into a café. He put his parcel of lights on the zinc-topped bar and started to read an article on the wrapping. Someone unknown to him, a new name, pursued an old grievance: Why don't they write about real life anymore?

Because to depict life is to attract its ill-fortune, Grippes replied.

He stood sipping coffee, staring at nothing. Four gun-bearing young men in jeans and leather jackets were not final authority; final authority was something written, the printed word, even when the word was mistaken. The simplest final authority in Grippes's life had been O. Poche and a book of rules. What must have happened was this: Poche, wishing to do honor to a category that included writers, prostitutes, and door-to-door salesmen, had read and misunderstood a note about royalties. It had been in italics, at the foot of the page. He had transformed his mistake into a regulation and had never looked at the page again.

Grippes in imagination climbed three flights of dirty wooden stairs to Mme. de Pelle's office. He observed the seashell crucifix and a brooch he had not noticed the first time, a silver fawn curled up as nature had never planned—a boneless fawn. Squinting, Mme. de Pelle peered at the old dun-colored Gaullist-era file. She put her hand over a page, as though Grippes were trying to read upside down. "It has all got to be paid back," she said.

"I was seriously misinformed," Grippes intended to answer, willing to see Poche disgraced, ruined, jailed. "I followed instructions. I am innocent."

But Poche had vanished, leaving Grippes with a lunatic exemption, three black-market income-bearing apartments he had recently, unsuccessfully, tried to sell, and a heavy reputation for male-oriented, left-feeling, right-thinking books. This reputation Grippes thought he could no longer sustain. A Socialist government was at last in place (hence his hurry about unloading the flats and his difficulty in finding takers). He wondered about the new file cover. Pink? Too fragile—look what had happened with the mottled peach. Strong denim blue, the shade standing for *giovinezza* and workers' overalls? It was no time for a joke, not even a private one. No one could guess what would be wanted, now, in the way of literary entertainment. The fitfulness of voters is such that, having got the government they wanted, they were now reading nothing but the right-wing press. Perhaps a steady right-wing heartbeat ought to set the cadence for a left-wing outlook, with a complex, bravely conservative heroine contained within the slippery but unyielding walls of left-wing style. He would have to come to terms with the rightist way of considering female characters. There seemed to be two methods, neither of which suited Grippes's temperament: Treat her disgustingly, then cry all over the page, or admire and respect her—she is the equal at least of a horse. The only woman his imagination offered, with some insistence, was no use to him. She moved quietly on a winter evening to Saint-Nicolas-du-Chardonnet, the rebel church at the lower end of Boulevard Saint-Germain, where services were still conducted in Latin. She wore a hat ornamented with an ivory arrow, and a plain gray coat, tubular in shape, with a narrow fur collar. Kid gloves were tucked under the handle of her sturdy leather purse. She had never heard of video games, push-button telephones, dishwashers, frozen filleted sole, computer horoscopes. She entered the church and knelt down and brought out her rosary, oval pearls strung on thin gold. Nobody saw rosaries anymore. They were not even in the windows of their traditional venues, across the square from the tax bureau. Believers went in for different articles now: cherub candles, quick prayers on plastic cards. Her iron meekness resisted change. She prayed constantly into the past. Grippes knew that one's view of the past is just as misleading as speculation about the future. It was one of the few beliefs he would have gone to the stake for. She was praying to a mist, to mist-shrouded figures she persisted in seeing clear.

He could see the woman, but he could not approach her. Perhaps he could get away with dealing with her from a distance. All that was really needed for a sturdy right-wing novel was its pessimistic rhythm: and then, and then, and then, and death. Grippes had that rhythm. It was in his footsteps, coming up the stairs after the departure of the police van, turning the key in his triple-bolted front door. And then, and then, the cats padding and mewing, not giving Grippes time to take off his coat as they made for their empty dishes on the kitchen floor. Behind the gas stove, a beleaguered garrison of cockroaches got ready for the evening sortie. Grippes would be waiting, his face half veiled with a checked scarf.

In Saint-Nicolas-du-Chardonnet the woman shut her missal,

got up off her knees, scorning to brush her coat; she went out to the street, proud of the dust marks, letting the world know she still prayed the old way. She escaped him. He had no idea what she had on, besides the hat and coat. Nobody else wore a hat with an ivory arrow or a tubular coat or a scarf that looked like a weasel biting its tail. He could not see what happened when she took the hat and coat off, what her hair was like, if she hung the coat in a hall closet that also contained umbrellas, a carpet-sweeper, and a pile of old magazines, if she put the hat in a round box on a shelf. She moved off in a gray blur. There was a streaming window between them Grippes could not wipe clean. Probably she entered a dark dining room—fake Henri IV buffet, bottles of pills next to the oil and vinegar cruets, lace tablecloth folded over the back of a chair, just oilcloth spread for the family meal. What could he do with such a woman? He could not tell who was waiting for her or what she would eat for supper. He could not even guess at her name. She revealed nothing; would never help.

Grippes expelled the cats, shut the kitchen window, and dealt with the advance guard from behind the stove. What he needed now was despair and excitement, a new cat-and-mouse chase. What good was a computer that never caught anyone out?

After airing the kitchen and clearing it of poison, Grippes let the cats in. He swept up the bodies of his victims and sent them down the ancient cast-iron chute. He began to talk to himself, as he often did now. First he said a few sensible things, then he heard his voice with a new elderly quaver to it, virtuous and mean: "After all, it doesn't take much to keep me happy."

Now, that was untrue, and he had no reason to say it. Is that what I am going to be like, now, he wondered. Is this the new-era Grippes, pinch-mouthed? It was exactly the sort of thing that the woman in the dark dining room might say. The best thing that could happen to him would be shock, a siege of terror, a knock at the door and a registered letter with fearful news. It would sharpen his humor, strengthen his own, private, eccentric heart. It would keep him from making remarks in his solitude that were meaningless and false. He could perhaps write an anonymous letter saying that the famous author Henri Grippes was guilty of evasion of a most repulsive kind. He was, moreover, a callous landlord who had never been known to replace a doorknob. Fortunately, he saw, he was not yet that mad, nor did he really need to be scared and obsessed. He had got the woman from church to dining room, and he would keep her there, trapped, cornered, threatened, watched, until she yielded to Grippes and told her name—as, in his several incarnations, good Poche had always done.

FORAIN

ABOUT an hour before the funeral service for Adam Tremski, snow mixed with rain began to fall, and by the time the first of the mourners arrived the stone steps of the church were dangerously wet. Blaise Forain, Tremski's French publisher, now his literary executor, was not surprised when, later, an elderly woman slipped and fell and had to be carried by ambulance to the Hôtel-Dieu hospital. Forain, in an attempt to promote Cartesian order over Slavic frenzy, sent for the ambulance, then found himself obliged to accompany the patient to the emergency section and fork over a deposit. The old lady had no social security.

Taken together, façade and steps formed an escarpment—looming, abrupt, above all unfamiliar. The friends of Tremski's last years had been Polish, Jewish, a few French. Of the French, only Forain was used to a variety of last rites. He was expected to attend the funerals not only of his authors but of their wives. He knew all the Polish churches of Paris, the Hungarian mission, the synagogues on the Rue Copernic and the Rue de la Victoire, and the mock chapel of the crematorium at Père Lachaise cemetery. For nonbelievers a few words at the graveside sufficed. Their friends said, by way of a greeting, "Another one gone." However, no one they knew ever had been buried from this particular church. The parish was said to be the oldest in the city, yet the edifice built on the ancient site looked forbidding and cold. Tremski for some forty years had occupied the same walk-up flat on the fringe of Montparnasse. What was he doing over here, on the wrong side of the Seine?

Four months before this, Forain had been present for the last blessing of Barbara, Tremski's wife, at the Polish church on the

Rue Saint-Honoré. The church, a chapel really, was round in shape, with no fixed pews—just rows of chairs pushed together. The dome was a mistake—too imposing for the squat structure—but it had stood for centuries, and only the very nervous could consider it a threat. Here, Forain had noticed, tears came easily, not only for the lost friend but for all the broken ties and old, unwilling journeys. The tears of strangers around him, that is; grief, when it reached him, was pale and dry. He was thirty-eight, divorced, had a daughter of twelve who lived in Nice with her mother and the mother's lover. Only one or two of Forain's friends had ever met the girl. Most people, when told, found it hard to believe he had ever been married. The service for Tremski's wife had been disrupted by the late entrance of *her* daughter—child of her first husband—who had made a show of arriving late, kneeling alone in the aisle, kissing the velvet pall over the coffin, and noisily marching out. Halina was her name. She had straight, graying hair and a cross face with small features. Forain knew that some of the older mourners could remember her as a pretty, unsmiling, not too clever child. A few perhaps thought Tremski was her father and wondered if he had been unkind to his wife. Tremski, sitting with his head bowed, may not have noticed. At any rate, he had never mentioned anything.

Tremski was Jewish. His wife had been born a Catholic, though no one was certain what had come next. To be blunt, was she in or out? The fact was that she had lived in adultery—if one wanted to be specific—with Tremski until her husband had obliged the pair by dying. There had been no question of a divorce; probably she had never asked for one. For his wedding to Barbara, Tremski had bought a dark blue suit at a good place, Creed or Lanvin Hommes, which he had on at her funeral, and in which he would be buried. He had never owned another, had shambled around Paris looking as though he slept under restaurant tables, on a bed of cigarette ashes and crumbs. It would have taken a team of devoted women, not just one wife, to keep him spruce.

Forain knew only from hearsay about the wedding ceremony in one of the town halls of Paris (Tremski was still untranslated then, had a job in a bookstore near the Jardin des Plantes, had paid back the advance for the dark blue suit over eleven months)—the names signed in a register, the daughter's refusal to attend, the wine drunk with friends in a café on the Avenue du Maine. It was a cheerless place, but Tremski knew the owner. He had talked of throwing a party but never got round to it; his flat was too small. Any day now he would move to larger quarters and invite two hundred and fifty intimate friends to a banquet. In the meantime, he stuck to his rented flat, a standard émigré dwelling of the 1950s, almost a period piece now: two rooms on a court, windowless kitchen, splintered floors, unheatable bathroom, no elevator, intimidating landlord—a figure central to his comic anecdotes and private worries. What did his wife think? Nobody knew, though if he had sent two hundred and fifty invitations she would undoubtedly have started to borrow two hundred and fifty glasses and plates. Even after Tremski could afford to move, he remained anchored to his seedy rooms: There were all those books, and the boxes filled with unanswered mail, and the important documents he would not let anyone file. Snapshots and group portraits of novelists and poets, wearing the clothes and haircuts of the fifties and sixties, took up much of a wall. A new desire to sort out the past, put its artifacts in order, had occupied Tremski's conversation on his wedding day. His friends had soon grown bored, although his wife seemed to be listening. Tremski, married at last, was off on an oblique course, preaching the need for discipline and a thought-out future. It didn't last.

At Forain's first meeting with Barbara, they drank harsh tea from mismatched cups and appraised each other in the gray light that filtered in from the court. She asked him, gently, about his fitness to translate and publish Tremski—then still at the bookstore, selling wartime memoirs and paperbacks and addressing parcels. Did Forain have close ties with the Nobel Prize committee? How many of his authors had received important awards, gone on to international fame? She was warm and friendly and made him think of a large buttercup. He was about the age of her daughter, Halina; so Barbara said. He felt paternal, wise, rid of mistaken ideals. He would become Tremski's guide and father. He thought, This is the sort of woman I should have married— although most probably he should never have married anyone.

Only a few of the mourners mounting the treacherous steps can have had a thought to spare for Tremski's private affairs. His wife's flight from a brave and decent husband, dragging by the hand a child of three, belonged to the folklore, not the history, of mid-century emigration. The chronicle of two generations, displaced and dispossessed, had come to a stop. The evaluation could begin; had already started. Scholars who looked dismayingly youthful, speaking the same language, but with a new, jarring vocabulary, were trekking to Western capitals—taping reminiscences, copying old letters. History turned out to be a plodding science. What most émigrés settled for now was the haphazard accuracy of a memory like Tremski's. In the end it was always a poem that ran through the mind—not a string of dates.

Some may have wondered why Tremski was entitled to a Christian service; or, to apply another kind of reasoning, why it had been thrust upon him. Given his shifting views on eternity and the afterlife, a simple get-together might have done, with remarks from admirers, a poem or two read aloud, a priest wearing a turtleneck sweater, or a young rabbi with a literary bent. Or one of each, offering prayers and tributes in turn. Tremski had nothing against prayers. He had spent half his life inventing them.

As it turned out, the steep church was not as severe as it looked from the street. It was in the hands of a small charismatic order, perhaps full of high spirits but by no means schismatic. No one had bothered to ask if Tremski was a true convert or just a writer who sometimes sounded like one. His sole relative was his stepdaughter. She had made an arrangement that suited her: She lived nearby, in a street until recently classed as a slum, now renovated and highly prized. Between her seventeenth-century flat and the venerable site was a large, comfortable, cluttered department store, where, over the years, Tremski's friends had bought their pots of paint and rollers, their sturdy plates and cups, their burglarproof door locks, their long-lasting cardigan sweaters. The store was more familiar than the church. The stepdaughter was a stranger.

She was also Tremski's heir and she did not understand

Forain's role, taking executor to mean an honorary function, godfather to the dead. She had told Forain that Tremski had destroyed her father and blighted her childhood. He had enslaved her mother, spoken loud Polish in restaurants, had tried to keep Halina from achieving a French social identity. Made responsible, by his astonishing will, for organizing a suitable funeral, she had chosen a French send-off, to be followed by burial in a Polish cemetery outside Paris. Because of the weather and because there was a shortage of cars, friends were excused from attending the burial. Most of them were thankful: More than one fatal cold had been brought on by standing in the icy mud of a graveyard. When she had complained she was doing her best, that Tremski had never said what he wanted, she was probably speaking the truth. He could claim one thing and its opposite in the same sentence. Only God could keep track. If today's rite was a cosmic error, Forain decided, it was up to Him to erase Tremski's name from the ledger and enter it in the proper column. If He cared.

The mourners climbed the church steps slowly. Some were helped by younger relatives, who had taken time off from work. A few had migrated to high-rise apartments in the outer suburbs, to deeper loneliness but cheaper rents. They had set out early, as if they still believed no day could start without them, and after a long journey underground and a difficult change of direction had emerged from the Hôtel de Ville Métro station. They held their umbrellas at a slant, as if countering some force of nature arriving head-on. Actually, there was not the least stir in the air, although strong winds and sleet were forecast. The snow and rain came down in thin soft strings, clung to fur or woolen hats, and became a meager amount of slush underfoot.

Forain was just inside the doors, accepting murmured sympathy and handshakes. He was not usurping a family role but trying to make up for the absence of Halina. Perhaps she would stride in late, as at her mother's funeral, driving home some private grudge. He had on a long cashmere overcoat, the only black garment he owned. A friend had left it to him. More exactly, the friend, aware that he was to die very soon, had told Forain to collect it at the tailor's. It had been fitted, finished, paid for, never worn. Forain knew there was a mean joke abroad about his wearing dead men's clothes. It also applied to his professional life: He was supposed to have said he preferred the backlist of any dead writer to the stress and tension of trying to deal with a live one.

His hair and shoes felt damp. The hand he gave to be shaken must have chilled all those it touched. He was squarely in the path of one of those church drafts that become gales anywhere close to a door. He wondered if Halina had been put off coming because of some firm remarks of his, the day before (he had defended Tremski against the charge of shouting in restaurants), or even had decided it was undignified to pretend she cared for a second how Tremski was dispatched; but at the last minute she turned up, with her French husband—a reporter of French political affairs on a weekly—and a daughter of fourteen in jacket and jeans. These two had not been able to read a word of Tremski's until Forain had published a novel in translation about six years before. Tremski believed they had never looked at it—to be fair, the girl was only eight at the time—or any of the books that had followed; although the girl clipped and saved reviews. It was remarkable, Tremski had said, the way literate people, reasonably well traveled and educated, comfortably off, could live adequate lives without wanting to know what had gone before or happened elsewhere. Even the husband, the political journalist, was like that: A few names, a date looked up, a notion of geography satisfied him.

Forain could tell Tremski minded. He had wanted Halina to think well of him at least on one count, his life's work. She was the daughter of a former Army officer who had died—like Barbara, like Tremski—in a foreign city. She considered herself, no less than her father, the victim of a selfish adventure. She also believed she was made of better stuff than Tremski, by descent and status, and that was harder to take. In Tremski's own view, comparisons were not up for debate.

For the moment, the three were behaving well. It was as much as Forain expected from anybody. He had given up measuring social conduct, except where it ran its course in fiction. His firm made a specialty of translating and publishing work from Eastern and Central Europe; it kept him at a remove. Halina seemed tamed now, even thanked him for standing in and welcoming all those strangers. She had a story to explain why she was late, but it was far-fetched, and Forain forgot it immediately. The delay most likely had been caused by a knockdown argument over the jacket and jeans. Halina was a cold skirmisher, narrow in scope but heavily principled. She wore a fur-and-leather coat, a pale gray hat with a brim, and a scarf—authentic Hermès? Taiwan fake? Forain could have told by rubbing the silk between his fingers, but it was a wild idea, and he kept his distance.

The girl had about her a look of Barbara: For that reason, no other, Forain found her appealing. Blaise ought to sit with the family, she said—using his first name, the way young people did now. A front pew had been kept just for the three of them. There was plenty of room. Forain thought that Halina might begin to wrangle, in whispers, within earshot (so to speak) of the dead. He said yes, which was easier than to refuse, and decided no. He left them at the door, greeting stragglers, and found a place at the end of a pew halfway down the aisle. If Halina mentioned anything, later, he would say he had been afraid he might have to leave before the end. She walked by without noticing and, once settled, did not look around.

The pale hat had belonged to Halina's mother. Forain was sure he remembered it. When his wife died, Tremski had let Halina and her husband ransack the flat. Halina made several trips while the husband waited downstairs. He had come up only to help carry a crate of papers belonging to Tremski. It contained, among other documents, some of them rubbish, a number of manuscripts not quite complete. Since Barbara's funeral Tremski had not bothered to shave or even put his teeth in. He sat in the room she had used, wearing a dressing gown torn at the elbows. Her wardrobe stood empty, the door wide, just a few hangers inside. He clutched Forain by the sleeve and said that Halina had taken some things of his away. As soon as she realized her error she would bring them back.

Forain would have preferred to cross the Seine on horseback, lashing at anyone who resembled Halina or her husband, but he had driven to her street by taxi, past the old, reassuring, unchanging department store. No warning, no telephone call: He walked up a curving stone staircase, newly sandblasted and scrubbed, and pressed the doorbell on a continued note until someone came running.

She let him in, just so far. "Adam can't be trusted to look after his own affairs," she said. "He was always careless and dirty, but now the place smells of dirt. Did you look at the kitchen table? He must keep eating from the same plate. As for my mother's letters, if that's what you're after, he had already started to tear them up."

"Did you save any?"

"They belong to me."

How like a ferret she looked, just then; and she was the child of such handsome parents. A studio portrait of her father, the Polish officer, taken in London, in civilian clothes, smoking a long cigarette, stood on a table in the entrance hall. (Forain was admitted no farther.) Forain took in the likeness of the man who had fought a war for nothing. Barbara had deserted that composed, distinguished, somewhat careful face for Tremski. She must have forced Tremski's hand, arrived on his doorstep, bag, baggage, and child. He had never come to a resolution about anything in his life.

Forain had retrieved every scrap of paper, of course—all but the letters. Fired by a mixture of duty and self-interest, he was unbeatable. Halina had nothing on her side but a desire to reclaim her mother, remove the Tremski influence, return her—if only her shoes and blouses and skirts—to the patient and defeated man with his frozen cigarette. Her entitlement seemed to include a portion of Tremski, too; but she had resented him, which weakened her grasp. Replaying every move, Forain saw how strong her case might have been if she had acknowledged Tremski as her mother's choice. Denying it, she became—almost became; Forain stopped her in time—the defendant in a cheap sort of litigation

Tremski's friends sat with their shoes in puddles. They kept their gloves on and pulled their knitted scarves tight. Some had spent all these years in France without social security or health insurance, either for want of means or because they had never found their feet in the right sort of employment. Possibly they believed that a long life was in itself full payment for a safe old age. Should the end turn out to be costly and prolonged, then, please, allow us to dream and float in the thickest, deepest darkness, unaware of the inconvenience and clerical work we may cause. So, Forain guessed, ran their prayers.

Funerals came along in close ranks now, especially in bronchial winters. One of Forain's earliest recollections was the Mass in Latin, but he could not say he missed it: He associated Latin with early-morning hunger, and sitting still. The charismatic movement seemed to have replaced incomprehension and mystery with theatricals. He observed the five priests in full regalia sitting to the right of the altar. One had a bad cold and kept taking a handkerchief from his sleeve. Another more than once glanced at his watch. A choir, concealed or on tape, sang "Jesu, bleibet meine Freude," after which a smooth trained voice began to recite the Twenty-fifth Psalm. The voice seemed to emanate from Tremski's coffin but was too perfectly French to be his. In the middle of Verse 7, just after "Remember not the sins of my youth," the speaker wavered and broke off. A man seated in front of Forain got up and walked down the aisle, in a solemn and ponderous way. The coffin was on a trestle, draped in purple and white, heaped with roses, tulips, and chrysanthemums. He edged past it, picked up a black box lying on the ground, and pressed two clicking buttons. "Jesu" started up, from the beginning. Returning, the stranger gave Forain an angry stare, as if he had created the mishap.

Forain knew that some of Tremski's friends thought he was unreliable. He had a reputation for not paying authors their due. There were writers who complained they had never received the price of a postage stamp; they could not make sense of his elegant handwritten statements. Actually, Tremski had been the exception. Forain had arranged his foreign rights, when they began to occur, on a half-and-half basis. Tremski thought of money as a useful substance that covered rent and cigarettes. His wife didn't see it that way. Her forefinger at the end of a column of figures, her quiet, seductive voice saying, "Blaise, what's this?" called for a thought-out answer.

She had never bothered to visit Forain's office, but made him take her to tea at Angelina's, on the Rue de Rivoli. After her strawberry tart had been eaten and the plate removed, she would bring out of her handbag the folded, annotated account. Outdone, outclassed, slipping the tearoom check into his wallet to be dissolved in general expenses, he would look around and obtain at least one satisfaction: She was still the best-looking woman in sight, of any age. He had not been tripped up by someone of inferior appearance and quality. The more he felt harassed by larger issues, the more he made much of small compensations. He ran his business with a staff of loyal, worn-out women, connected to him by a belief in what he was doing, or some lapsed personal tie, or because it was too late and they had nowhere to go. At eight o'clock this morning, the day of the funeral, his staunch Lisette, at his side from the beginning of the venture, had called to tell him she had enough social-security points for retirement. He saw the points as splashes of ink on a clean page. All he could think to answer was that she would soon get bored, having no reason to get up each day. Lisette had replied, not disagreeably, that she planned to spend the next ten years in bed. He could not even coax her to stay by improving her salary: Except for the reserve of capital required by law, he had next to no money, had to scrape to pay the monthly settlement on his daughter, and was in continual debt to printers and banks.

He was often described in the trade as poor but selfless. He had performed an immeasurable service to world culture, bringing to the West voices that had been muffled for decades in the East. Well, of course, his thimble-size firm had not been able to attract the leviathan prophets, the booming novelists, the great mentors and tireless definers. Tremski had been at the very limit of Forain's financial reach—good Tremski, who had stuck to Forain even after he could have moved on. Common sense had kept Forain from approaching the next-best, second-level oracles, articulate and attractive, subsidized to the ears, chain-smoking and explaining, still wandering the universities and congresses of the West. Their travel requirements were beyond him: No grant could cover the unassuming but ruinous little hotel on the Left Bank, the long afternoons and evenings spent in bars with leather armchairs, where the visitors expected to meet clever and cultivated people in order to exchange ideas.

Forain's own little flock, by contrast, seemed to have entered the world with no expectations. Apart from the odd, rare, humble complaint, they were content to be put up on the top story of a hotel with a steep, neglected staircase, a wealth of literary associations, and one bath to a floor. For recreation, they went to the café across the street, made a pot of hot water and a tea bag last two and a half hours, and, as Forain encouraged them to keep in mind, could watch the Market Economy saunter by. Docile, holding only a modest estimation of their own gifts, they still provided a handicap: Their names, like those of their characters, all sounded alike to barbaric Western ears. It had been a triumph of perseverance on the part of Forain to get notice taken of their books. He wanted every work he published to survive in collective memory, even when the paper it was printed on had been pulped, burned in the city's vast incinerators or lay moldering at the bottom of the Seine.

Season after season, his stomach eaten up with anxiety, his heart pounding out hope, hope, hope, he produced a satirical novella set in Odessa; a dense, sober private journal, translated from the Rumanian, best understood by the author and his friends; or another wry glance at the harebrained makers of history. (There were few women. In that particular part of Europe they seemed to figure as brusque flirtatious mistresses or uncomplaining wives.) At least once a year he committed the near suicide of short stories and poetry. There were rewards, none financial. A few critics thought it a safe bet occasionally to mention a book he sent along for review: He was considered sound in an area no one knew much about, and too hard up to sponsor a pure disaster. Any day now some stumbling tender newborn calf of his could turn into a literary water ox. As a result, it was not unusual for one of his writers to receive a sheaf of tiny clippings, sometimes even illustrated by a miniature photograph, taken at the Place de la Bastille, with traffic whirling around. A clutch of large banknotes would have been good, too, but only Tremski's wife had held out for both.

Money! Forain's opinion was the same as that of any poet striving to be read in translation. He never said so. The name of the firm, Blaise Editions, rang with an honest chime in spheres where trade and literature are supposed to have no connection. When the minister of culture had decorated him, not long before, mentioning in encouraging terms Forain's addition to the House of Europe, Forain had tried to look diffident but essential. It seemed to him at that instant that his reputation for voluntary self-denial was a stone memorial pinning him to earth. He wanted to cry out for help—to the minister? It would look terrible. He felt honored but confused. Again, summoned to the refurbished embassy of a new democracy, welcomed by an ambassador and a cultural attaché recently arrived (the working staff was unchanged), Forain had dared say to himself, Why don't they just give me the check for whatever all this is costing?—the champagne, the exquisite catering, the medal in a velvet box—all the while hoping his thoughts would not show on his face.

The truth was that the destruction of the Wall—radiant paradigm—had all but demolished Forain. The difference was that Forain could not be hammered to still smaller pieces and sold all over the world. In much the same way Vatican II had reduced to bankruptcy more than one publisher of prayer books in Latin. A couple of them had tried to recoup by dumping the obsolete missals on congregations in Asia and Africa, but by the time the Third World began to ask for its money back the publishers had gone down with all hands. Briefly, Forain pondered the possibility of unloading on readers in Senegal and Cameroon the entire edition of a subtle and allusive study of corruption in Minsk, set in 1973. Could one still get away with it—better yet, charge it off to cultural cooperation? He answered himself: No. Not after November 1989. Gone were the stories in which Socialist incoherence was matched by Western irrelevance. Gone from Forain's intention to publish, that is: His flock continued to turn them in. He had instructed his underpaid, patient professional readers— teachers of foreign languages, for the most part—to look only at the first three and last two pages of any manuscript. If they promised another version of the East-West dilemma, disguised as a fresh look at the recent past, he did not want to see so much as a one-sentence summary.

By leaning into the aisle he could watch the last blessing. A line of mourners, Halina and her sobbing daughter at the head, shuffled around the coffin, each person ready to add an individual appeal for God's mercy. Forain stayed where he was. He neither pestered nor tried to influence imponderables; not since the death of the friend who had owned the cashmere coat. If the firm went into deeper decline, if it took the slide from shaky to foundering, he would turn to writing. Why not? At least he knew what he wanted to publish. It would get rid of any further need of dealing with living authors: their rent, their divorces, their abscessed teeth, not to speak of that new craze in the East—their psychiatrists. His first novel—what would he call it? He allowed a title to rise from his dormant unconscious imagination. It emerged, black and strong, on the cover of a book propped up in a store window: *The Cherry Orchard*. His mind accepted the challenge. What about a sly, quiet novel, teasingly based on the play? A former property owner, after forty-seven years of exile, returns to Karl-Marx-Stadt to reclaim the family home. It now houses sixteen hardworking couples and thirty-eight small children. He throws them out, and the novel winds down with a moody description of curses and fistfights as imported workers try to install a satellite dish in the garden, where the children's swings used to be. It would keep a foot in the old territory, Forain thought, but with a radical shift of focus. He had to move sidelong: He could not all of a sudden start to publish poems about North Sea pollution and the threat to the herring catch.

Here was a joke he could have shared with Tremski. The stepdaughter had disconnected the telephone while Tremski was still in hospital, waiting to die; not that Forain wanted to dial an extinct number and let it ring. Even in Tremski's mortal grief over Barbara, the thought of Forain as his own author would have made him smile. He had accepted Forain, would listen to nothing said against him—just as he could not be dislodged from his fusty apartment and had remained faithful to his wife—but he had considered Forain's best efforts to be a kind of amateur, Western fiddling, and all his bright ideas to be false dawns. Forain lived a publisher's dream life, Tremski believed—head of a platoon of self-effacing, flat-broke writers who asked only to be read, believing they had something to say that was crucial to the West, that might even goad it into action. What sort of action, Forain still wondered. The intelligent fellow whose remains had just been committed to eternity was no different. He knew Forain was poor but believed he was rich. He thought a great new war would leave Central Europe untouched. The liberating missiles would sail across without ruffling the topmost leaf of a poplar tree. As for the contenders, well, perhaps their time was up.

The congregation had risen. Instead of a last prayer, diffuse and anonymous, Forain chose to offer up a firmer reminder of Tremski: the final inventory of his flat. First, the entrance, where a faint light under a blue shade revealed layers of coats on pegs but not the boots and umbrellas over which visitors tripped. Barbara had never interfered, never scolded, never tried to clean things up. It was Tremski's place. Through an archway, the room Barbara had used. In a corner, the chair piled with newspapers and journals that Tremski still intended to read. Next, unpainted shelves containing files, some empty, some spilling foolscap not to be touched until Tremski had a chance to sort everything out. Another bookcase, this time with books. Above it, the spread of photographs of his old friends. A window, and the sort of view that prisoners see. In front of the window, a drop-leaf table that had to be cleared for meals. The narrow couch, still spread with a blanket, where Halina had slept until she ran away. (To the end, Barbara had expected her to return saying, "It was a mistake." Tremski would have made her welcome and even bought another sofa, at the flea market, for the child.) The dark red armchair in which Forain had sat during his first meeting with Barbara. Her own straight-backed chair and the small desk where she wrote business letters for Tremski. On the wall, a charcoal drawing of Tremski—by an amateur artist, probably—dated June 1945. It was a face that had come through; only just.

Mourners accustomed to the ceremonial turned to a neighbor to exchange the kiss of peace. Those who were not shrank slightly, as if the touch without warmth were a new form of aggression. Forain found unfocused, symbolized love positively terrifying. He refused the universal coming-together, rammed his hands in his pockets—like a rebellious child—and joined the untidy lines shuffling out into the rain.

Two hours later, the time between amply filled by the accident, the arrival and departure of the ambulance, the long admittance procedure, and the waiting-around natural to a service called Emergency, Forain left the hospital. The old lady was too stunned to have much to say for herself, but she could enunciate clearly, "No family, no insurance." He had left his address and, with even less inclination, a check he sincerely hoped was not a dud. The wind and sleet promised earlier in the day battered and drenched him. He skirted the building and, across a narrow street, caught sight of lines of immigrants standing along the north side of central police headquarters. Algerians stood in a separate queue.

There were no taxis. He was too hungry and wet to cross the bridge to the Place Saint-Michel—a three-minute walk. In a café on the Boulevard du Palais he hung his coat where he could keep an eye on it and ordered a toasted ham-and-cheese sandwich, a glass of Badoit mineral water, a small carafe of wine, and black coffee—all at once. The waiter forgot the wine. When he finally remembered, Forain was ready to leave. He wanted to argue about the bill but saw that the waiter looked frightened. He was young, with clumsy hands, feverish red streaks under his eyes, and coarse fair hair: foreign, probably working without papers, in the shadow of the most powerful police in France. All right, Forain said to himself, but no tip. He noticed how the waiter kept glancing toward someone or something at the far end of the room: His employer, Forain guessed. He felt, as he had felt much of the day, baited, badgered, and trapped. He dropped a tip of random coins on the tray and pulled on his coat. The waiter grinned but did not thank him, put the coins in his pocket, and carried the untouched wine back to the kitchen.

Shoulders hunched, collar turned up, Forain made his way to the taxi rank at the Place Saint-Michel. Six or seven people under streaming umbrellas waited along the curb. Around the corner a cab suddenly drew up and a woman got out. Forain took her place, as if it were the most natural thing in the world. He had stopped feeling hungry, but seemed to be wearing layers of damp towels. The driver, in a heavy accent, probably Portuguese, told Forain to quit the taxi. He was not allowed to pick up a passenger at that particular spot, close to a stand. Forain pointed out that the stand was empty. He snapped the lock shut—as if that made a difference—folded his arms, and sat shivering. He wished the driver the worst fate he could think of—to stand on the north side of police headquarters and wait for nothing.

"You're lucky to be working," he suddenly said. "You should see all those people without jobs, without papers, just over there, across the Seine."

"I've seen them," the driver said. "I could be out of a job just for picking you up. You should be waiting your turn next to that sign, around the corner."

They sat for some seconds without speaking. Forain studied the set of the man's neck and shoulders; it was rigid, tense. An afternoon quiz show on the radio seemed to take his attention, or perhaps he was pretending to listen and trying to decide if it was a good idea to appeal to a policeman. Such an encounter could rebound against the driver, should Forain turn out to be someone important—assistant to the office manager of a cabinet minister, say.

Forain knew he had won. It was a matter of seconds now. He heard, "What was the name of the Queen of Sheba?" "Which one?" "The one who paid a visit to King Solomon." "Can you give me a letter?" "B." "Brigitte?"

The driver moved his head back and forth. His shoulders dropped slightly. Using a low, pleasant voice, Forain gave the address of his office, offering the Saint Vincent de Paul convent as a landmark. He had thought of going straight home and changing his shoes, but catching pneumonia was nothing to the loss of the staunch Lisette; the sooner he could talk to her, the better. She should have come to the funeral. He could start with that. He realized that he had not given a thought to Tremski for almost three hours now. He continued the inventory, his substitute for a prayer. He was not sure where he had broken off—with the telephone on Barbara's desk? Tremski would not have a telephone in the room where he worked, but at the first ring he would call through the wall, "Who is it?" Then "What does he want? . . . He met me *where*? . . . When we were in high school? . . . Tell him I'm too busy. No—let me talk to him."

The driver turned the radio up, then down. "I could have lost my job," he said.

Every light in the city was ablaze in the dark rain. Seen through rivulets on a window, the least promising streets showed glitter and well-being. It seemed to Forain that in Tremski's dark entry there had been a Charlie Chaplin poster, relic of some Polish film festival. There had been crates and boxes, too, that had never been unpacked. Tremski would not move out, but in a sense he had never moved in. Suddenly, although he had not really forgotten them, Forain remembered the manuscripts he had snatched back from Halina. She had said none was actually finished, but what did she know? What if there were only a little, very little, left to be composed? The first thing to do was have them read by someone competent—not his usual painstaking and very slow professional readers but a bright young Polish critic, who could tell at a glance what was required. Filling gaps was a question of style and logic, and could just as well take place after translation.

When they reached the Rue du Bac the driver drew up as closely as he could to the entrance, even tried to wedge the cab between two parked cars, so that Forain would not have to step into a gutter filled with running water. Forain could not decide what to do about the tip, whether to give the man something extra (it was true that he could have refused to take him anywhere) or make him aware he had been aggressive. "You should be waiting your turn. . . ." still rankled. In the end, he made a Tremski-like gesture, waving aside change that must have amounted to 35 percent of the fare. He asked for a receipt. It was not until after the man had driven away that Forain saw he had not included the tip in the total sum. No Tremski flourish was ever likely to carry a reward. That was another lesson of the day.

More than a year later, Lisette—now working only part-time— mentioned that Halina had neglected to publish in *Le Monde* the anniversary notice of Tremski's death. Did Forain want one to appear, in the name of the firm? Yes, of course. It would be wrong to say he had forgotten the apartment and everything in it, but the inventory, the imaginary camera moving around the rooms, filled him with impatience and a sense of useless effort. His mind stopped at the narrow couch with the brown blanket, Halina's bed, and he said to himself, What a pair those two were. The girl was right to run away. As soon as he had finished the thought he placed his hand over his mouth, as if to prevent the words from emerging. He went one further—bowed his head, like Tremski at Barbara's funeral, promising himself he would keep in mind things as they once were, not as they seemed to him now. But the apartment was vacated, and Tremski had disappeared. He had been prayed over thoroughly by a great number of people, and the only enjoyment he might have had from the present scene was to watch Forain make a fool of himself to no purpose.

There were changes in the office, too. Lisette had agreed to stay for the time it would take to train a new hand: a thin, pretty girl, part of the recent, non-political emigration—wore a short leather skirt, said she did not care about money but loved literature and did not want to waste her life working at something dull. She got on with Halina and had even spared Forain the odd difficult meeting. As she began to get the hang of her new life, she lost no time spreading the story that Forain had been the lover of Barbara and would not let go a handsome and expensive coat that had belonged to Tremski. A posthumous novel-length manuscript of Tremski's was almost ready for the printer, with a last chapter knitted up from fragments he had left trailing. The new girl, gifted in languages, compared the two versions and said he would have approved; and when Forain showed a moment of doubt and hesitation she was able to remind him of how, in the long run, Tremski had never known what he wanted.

AUGUST

BONNIE MCCARTHY opened a drawer of her dressing table and removed the hat her sister-in-law had sent from New York. It was a summer hat of soft, silken material in a pretty shade of blue: the half-melon hat her sister-in-law had begun to wear at fifteen and had gone on wearing, in various colors and textures, until her hair was gray. This particular melon was designed for travel. It could be folded until it took no more place in a suitcase than a closed fan. Bonnie pushed her lips forward in a pout. She held the hat between thumb and forefinger, considering it. She pulled it on her head, tugging with both hands. The frown, the pout, the obstinate gestures, were those of a child. It was a deliberate performance, and new: after years of struggling to remain adult in a grown-up world, she had found it unrewarding, and, in her private moments, allowed herself the blissful luxury of being someone else.

The hat was a failure. Framed by the chaste blue brim, she seemed slightly demented, a college girl aged overnight. After a long look in the triple mirror, Bonnie said aloud, "This just isn't a normal hat." She dropped it on the table, among the framed pictures and the pots of cream. None of the clothes from America seemed normal to her now, because they no longer came from a known place. She had left her country between the end of the war and the onslaught of the New Look (this is how history was fixed in her memory) and, although she had been back for visits, the American scene of her mind's eye was populated with girls in short skirts and broad-shouldered coats—the war silhouette, 1-85, or whatever it was called. Her recollection of such details was faultless, but she could not have said under which President peace had been signed. The nation at war was not a permanent landscape: Bonnie's New York, the real New York, was a distant, gleaming city in a lost decade. A lost Bonnie existed there, pretty and pert, outrageously admired. This was the Bonnie she sought to duplicate every time she looked in the glass—Bonnie tender-eyed, blurry with the sun of a perished afternoon; Bonnie in her wedding dress, authentically innocent, with a wreath of miniature roses straight across her brow. With time—she was at this moment fifty-two—a second, super-Bonnie had emerged. Super-Bonnie was a classic, middle-aged charmer. She might have been out of Kipling—a kind of American Mrs. Hauksbee, witty and thin, with those great rolling violet blue eyes. When she was feeling liverish or had had a bad night, she knew this was off the mark, and that she had left off being tender Bonnie without achieving the safety of Mrs. Hauksbee. Then she would think of the woman she could have been, if her life hadn't been destroyed: and if she went on thinking about it too much, she gave up and consoled herself by playing at being a little girl.

When Bonnie was still under forty, her husband had caught her out in a surpassingly silly affair—she had not in the least loved the lover—and had divorced her, so that her conception of herself was fragmented, unreconciled. There was Bonnie, sweet-faced, with miniature roses; wicked Mrs. Hauksbee, the stormy petrel of a regimental outpost; and, something near the truth, a lost, sallow, frightened Bonnie wandering from city to city in Europe, clutching her daughter by the hand. The dressing table was littered with these Bonnies, and with pictures of Florence, her daughter. There was Flor as a baby, holding a ball in starfish hands, and Flor on her pony, and Flor in Venice, squinting and bored. To one side, isolated, in curious juxtaposition, were two small likenesses. One was a tinted image of St. Teresa of the Infant Jesus. (Bonnie had no taste for obscure martyrs. The Little Flower, good enough for most Catholics, was good enough for her.) The Saint had little function in Bonnie's life, except to act as a timid anchor to Bonnie's ballooning notion of the infinite. The second picture was of Bob Harris, Bonnie's son-in-law. It had been taken on the beach at Cannes, two summers before. He wore tartan bathing trunks, and had on and about his person the equipment for underwater fishing—flippers, spear, goggles, breathing tube—and seemed to be a monster of a sort.

When she had done with the hat, Bonnie licked her forefingers and ran them along her eyebrows. She pulled her eyebrows apart and counted twenty times, but when she released the skin, the line between her eyes returned. "La première ride," she said sentimentally. She put on a wry, ironic look: Mrs. Hauksbee conceding the passage of time. When she left the dressing table and crossed the room she continued to wear the look, although she was already thinking about something else. She sat down at a writing table very like the dressing table she had just abandoned. Both were what her son-in-law called "important pieces." Both had green marble tops, bandy legs, drawers like bosoms, brass fittings, and were kin to the stranded objects, garnished with dying flowers in a vase, that fill the windows of antique shops on the left bank of the Seine.

Bonnie was easily wounded, but she had sharp, malicious instincts where other people were concerned. She seldom struck openly, fearing the direct return blow. The petty disorder of her dressing table, with its cheap clutter of bottles and pictures, was an oblique stab at Bob Harris, whose apartment this was, and who, as he had once confided to Bonnie, liked things nice.

She pulled toward her a sheet of white paper with her address in Paris printed across the top, and wrote the date, which was the fifteenth of July. She began: "My darling Polly and Stu—First about the hat. You sweethearts! I wore it today for the first time as it really hasn't been summer until now. I was so proud to say this is from my brother and his wife from New York. Well darlings I am sorry about George I must say I never did hear of anybody ever getting the whooping cough at his age but I can quite see you couldn't let him come over to Paris in that condition in June. Two years since we have seen that boy. Flor asks about him every day. You know those two were so crazy about each other when they were kids, it's a shame Flor was seven years older instead of the other way around. At least we would all be still the same family and would know who was marrying who. Well, nuff said."

So far this letter was nearly illegible. She joined the last letter of each word on to the start of the next. All the vowels, as well as the letters n, m, and w, resembled u's. There were strings of letters that might as well have been nununu. Now, her writing became elegant and clear, like the voice of someone trying on a new accent: "The thing with him coming over in August is this, that he would have to be alone with Florence. Bob Harris's father is coming over here this year, and Bob Harris is going with him to the Beaujolais country and the Champagne country and I don't know what all countries for their business, and they will be in these countries all of August. Now I have been invited to stay with a dear friend in Deauville for the entire month. Now as you know Flor is doing this business with a psychiatrist and she REFUSES to leave Paris. It wouldn't be any fun for Georgie because Flor never goes out and wouldn't know where to go even if she did. It seems to me Georgie should go to England first, because he wants to go there anyway, and he should come here around the end of August when I will be back, and Bob will be back, and we can take Georgie around. Just as you like, dears, but this does seem best."

Bonnie was in the habit of slipping little pieces of paper inside her letters to her sister-in-law. These scraps, about the size of a calling card, bore a minutely scrawled message which was what she really wanted to say, and why she was bothering to write a letter at all. She cut a small oblong out of a sheet of paper and wrote in tiny letters: "Polly, Flor is getting so queer, I don't know her any more. I'm afraid to leave her alone in August, but she pulls such tantrums if I say I'll stay that I'm giving in. Don't let Georgie come, he'd only be upset. She's at this doctor's place now, and *I don't even like the doctor*."

It was three o'clock in the afternoon. Florence was walking with cautious steps along the Boulevard des Capucines when the sidewalk came up before her. It was like an earthquake, except that she knew there were no earthquakes here. It was like being drunk, except that she never drank anymore. It was a soundless upheaval, and it had happened before. No one noticed the disturbance, or the fact that she had abruptly come to a halt. It was possible that she had become invisible. It would not have astonished

her at all. Indeed, a fear that this might come about had caused
her to buy, that summer, wide-skirted dresses in brilliant tones
that (Bonnie said) made her look like a fortuneteller in a restaurant. All very well for Bonnie, who could be sure that she existed
in black; who did not have to steal glimpses of herself in shop
windows, an existence asserted in coral and red.

At this hour, at this time of year, the crowd around the Café de
la Paix was American. It was a crowd as apart from Flor as if an
invasion of strangers speaking Siamese had entered the city. But
they were not Siamese: they were her own people, and they spoke
the language she knew best, with the words she had been taught
to use when, long ago, she had seen shapes and felt desires that
had to be given names.

". . . upon the beached verge of the salt flood . . ."

She did not say this. Her lips did not move; but she had the
ringing impression of a faultless echo, as if the words had come to
her in her own voice. They were words out of the old days, when
she could still read, and relate every sentence to the sentence it
followed. A vision, clear as a mirror, of a narrowing shore, an en-
croaching sea, was all that was left. It was all that remained of her
reading, the great warehouse of stored phrases, the plugged casks
filled with liquid words—a narrowing shore, a moving sea: that
was all. And yet how she had read! She had read in hotel rooms,
sprawled on the bed—drugged, drowned—while on the other side
of the dark window rain fell on foreign streets. She had read on
buses and on trains and in the waiting rooms of doctors and dress-
makers, waiting for Bonnie. She had read with her husband across
from her at the table and beside her in bed. (She had been reading
a book, in a café, alone, the first time he had ever spoken to her.
He had never forgotten it.) She had read through her girlhood and
even love hadn't replaced the reading: only at times.

If Bonnie had been able to give some form to her own untidy
life; if she had not uprooted Flor and brought her over here to
live—one majestically wrong decision among a hundred indeci-
sions—Flor would not, at this moment, have feared the movement of the pavement under her feet and watched herself in shop
windows to make sure she was still there. She would not have
imagined life as a brightly lighted stage with herself looking on.

She would have depended less on words; she would have belonged to life. She told an imagined Bonnie, "It was always your fault. I might have been a person, but you made me a foreigner. It was always the same, even back home. I was the only Catholic girl at Miss Downland's. That was being foreign."

"What about the Catholic girls from Mexico?" said Bonnie, from among the crowd before the newspaper kiosk where Flor had paused to consult, blankly, the front page of the *Times*.

Trust Bonnie to put in a red herring like the Mexican girls at school: it didn't merit a reply. Still, the discovery that it had always been the same was worth noting. It was another clearing in the thicket that was Dr. Linnetti's favorite image: another path cleared, another fence down, light let through. She groped in her purse for the green notebook in which she recorded these discoveries, and she sat down on a vacant chair outside the café.

The table at which she had put herself was drawn up to its neighbor so that a party of four tourists could have plenty of room for their drinks, parcels, and pots of tea. One of the four had even pulled over an extra chair for her aching feet. Florence put her notebook on the edge of the table, pushing an ashtray to one side. The *vertige* she had felt on the street was receding. In her private language she called it "the little animal going to sleep." What was the good of an expression like Dr. Linnetti's "vertigo experienced in the presence of sharp lines and related objects"? The effort of lines to change their form (the heaving pavement), the nausea created by the sight of a double row of houses meeting at the horizon point, the triumph of the little fox, had begun being a torment when she was twelve, and had come to live abroad. In those days, Bonnie had put it down to faulty eyesight, via a troubled liver, and had proscribed whipped cream. Now that it was too late, Florence remembered and recognized the initial siege, the weakening of her forces so that the invader could take possession.

Accepting this, she had stopped believing in Dr. Linnetti's trees, clearings, and pools of light. She was beset, held. Nothing could help her but sleep and the dreams experienced in the gray terrain between oblivion and life—the country of gray hills and houses from which she was suddenly lifted and borne away. Coming into this landscape was the most difficult of all, for they were opposed to her reaching it—the doctor, her mother, her husband. Circumstances were needed, and they were coming soon. In two weeks it would be August, and she would be left alone. Between now and August was a delay filled with perils; her mother hesitating and quibbling, her husband trying to speak. (He no longer attempted to make love. He seemed to have a tenacious faith that one day Dr. Linnetti was going to return to him a new Flor, strangely matured, and more exciting than ever.) This period traversed, she saw herself in the heavy silence of August. She saw her image in her own bed in the silence of an August afternoon. By the dimming of light in the chinks of the shutters she would know when it was night: and, already grateful for this boon, she would think, Now it is all right if I sleep.

"Some people just don't care."

"Ask her what she wants to drink."

"Maybe she's after you, Ed Broadfoot, ha ha."

These were three of the four people on whom Flor had intruded. They thought she was French—foreign, at any rate: not American. She looked away from the notebook in which she had not yet started to write and she said, "I understand every word." A waiter stood over her. "*Madame désire?*" he said insultingly. In terror she scrawled: "Mex. girls wouldn't take baths," before she got up and fled—wholly visible—into the dark café. Inside, she was careful to find a place alone. She was the picture of prudence, now, watching the movements of her hands, the direction of her feet. She sat on the plush banquette with such exaggerated care that she had a sudden, lucid image of how silly she must seem, and this made her want to laugh. She spread the notebook flat and began to write the letter to Dr. Linnetti, using a cheap ball-point pen bought expressly for this. The letter was long, and changed frequently in tone, now curt and businesslike, when she gave financial reasons for ending their interviews, now timid and cajoling, so that Dr. Linnetti wouldn't be cross. Sometimes the letter was almost affectionate, for there were moments when she forgot Dr. Linnetti was a woman and was ready to pardon her; but then she remembered that this cheat was from a known tribe, subjected to the same indignities, the same aches and pains, practicing the same essential deceits. And here was this impostor presuming to help!—Dr. Linnetti, charming as a hippopotamus, elegant as the wife of a Soviet civil servant, emotional as a snail, intelligent—ah, there she has us, thought Flor. We shall never know. There are no clues.

"What help can you give me?" she wrote. "I have often been disgusted by the smell of your dresses and your rotten teeth. If in six months you have not been able to take your dresses to be cleaned, or yourself to a dentist, how can you help me? Can you convince me that I'm not going to be hit by a car when I step off the curb? Can you convince me that the sidewalk is a safe place to be? Let me put it another way," wrote Flor haughtily. Her face wore a distinctly haughty look. "Is your life so perfect? Is your husband happy? Are your children fond of you and well behaved? Are you so happy . . ." She did not know how to finish and started again: "Are you anything to me? When you go home to your husband and children do you wonder about me? Are we friends? Then why bother about me at all?" She had come to the last page in the notebook. She tore the pages containing the letter out and posted the letter from the mail desk in the café. She dropped the instrument of separation—the lethal pen—on the floor and kicked it out of sight. It was still too early to go home. They would guess she had missed her interview. There was nothing to do but walk around the three sides of the familiar triangle—Boulevard des Capucines, rue Scribe, rue Auber, the home of the homeless—until it was time to summon a taxi and be taken away.

Florence's husband left his office early. The movement of Paris was running down. The avenues were white and dusty, full of blowing flags and papers and torn posters, and under traffic signals there were busily aimless people, sore-footed, dressed for heat, trying to decide whether or not to cross that particular street; wondering whether Paris would be better once the street was crossed. The city's minute hand had begun to lag: in August it would stop. Bob Harris loved Paris, but then he loved anywhere. He had never been homesick in his life. He carried his birthright with him. He pushed into the cool of the courtyard of the ancient apartment house in which he lived (the last house in the world where a child played Czerny exercises on a summer's afternoon), waved to the concierge in her aquarium parlor, ascended in the perilous elevator, which had swinging doors, like a saloon, and let himself into the flat. "Let himself into" is too mild. He entered as he had once broken into Flor's and Bonnie's life. He was—and proud of it—a New York boy, all in summer tans today: like a café Liégeois, Bonnie had said at breakfast, but out of his hearing, of course. She was no fool. The sprawled old-fashioned Parisian apartment, the polished bellpull (a ring in a lion's mouth), the heavy doors and creamy, lofty ceilings, appealed to his idea of what Europe ought to be. The child's faltering piano notes, which followed him until he closed the door on them, belonged to the décor. He experienced a transient feeling of past and present fused—a secondhand, threadbare inkling of a world haunted by the belief that the best was outside one's scope or still to come. These perceptions, which came only when he was alone, when creaking or mournful or ghostly sounds emerged from the stairs and the elevator shaft and formed a single substance with the walls, curtains, and gray light from the court, he knew were only the lingering vapors of adolescent nostalgia—that fruitless, formless yearning for God knows what. It was not an ambience of mind he pursued. His office, which was off the Champs-Élysées, in a cake-shaped building of the thirties, was dauntingly new, like the lounge of a dazzling Italian airport building reduced in scale. The people he met in the course of business were sharp with figures, though apt to assume a monkish air of dedication because they were dealing in wine instead of, say, paper bags. There was nothing monkish about Bob: he knew about wine (that is, he knew about markets for wine); and he knew about money too.

Nothing is more reassuring to a European than the national who fits his national character: the waspish Frenchman, the jolly Hollander, the blunted Swiss, the sly Romanian—each of these paper dolls can find a niche. Bob Harris corresponded, superficially, to the French pattern for an American male—"un grand gosse"—and so he got on famously. He was the last person in the world to pose a problem. He was chatty, and cheerful, and he didn't much care what people did or what they were like so long as they were good-natured too. He frequented the red-interiored bars of the Eighth Arrondissement with cheerful friends—more or less Americans trying to raise money so as to start a newspaper in the Canary Islands, and apple-bosomed starlets with pinky-silver hair. Everyone wanted something from him, and everyone liked him very much. Florence's family, the indefatigable nicknamers, had called him the Seal, and he did have a seal's sleek head and soft eyes, and a circus seal's air of jauntily seeking applause. The more he was liked, and the more he was exploited, the more he was himself. It was only when he entered his darkened bedroom that he had to improvise an artificial way of thinking and behaving.

His wife's new habit of lying with the curtains drawn on the brightest days was more than a vague worry: it seemed to him wicked. If ever he had given a thought to the nature of sin, it would have taken that form: the shutting-out of light. Flor had stopped being cheerful; that was the very least you could say. Her sleeping was a longer journey each time over a greater distance. He did not know how to bring her back, or even if he wanted to, now. He had loved her: an inherent taste for exaggeration led him to believe he had worshiped her. She might have evaded him along another route, in drinking, or a crank religion, or playing bridge: it would have been the same betrayal. He was the only person she had trusted. The only journey she could make, in whatever direction, was away from him. Feeling came to him in blocks, compact. When he held on to one emotion there was no place for another. He had loved Flor: she had left him behind. It had happened quickly. She hadn't cried warning. He accepted what they told him—that Flor was sick and would get over it—but he could not escape the feeling that her flight was deliberate and that she could stop and turn back if she tried.

He might have profited by her absence, now, to go through her drawers, searching for drugs or diaries or letters—something that would indicate the reasons for change. But he touched nothing in the silent room that was not his own. Nothing remained of the person he had once seen in the far table of the dark café in Cannes, elbows on table, reading a book. She had looked up and before becoming aware that a man was watching her let him see on her drowned face everything he was prepared to pursue—passion, discipline, darkness. The secrets had been given up to Dr. Linnetti—"A sow in a Mother Hubbard," said Bonnie, who had met the lady. He felt obscurely cheated; more, the secrets now involved him as well. He would never pardon the intimacy exposed. Even her physical self had been transformed. He had prized her beauty. It had made her an object as cherished as anything he might buy. In museums he had come upon paintings of women—the luminous women of the Impressionists—in which some detail reminded him of Flor, the thick hair, the skin, the glance slipping away, and this had increased his sense of possession and love. She had destroyed this beauty, joyfully, willfully, as if to force him to value her on other terms. The wreckage was futile, a vandalism without cause. He could never understand and he was not sure that he ought to try.

His mother-in-law was in the drawing room, poised for discovery. She must have heard him come in, and, while he was having a shower and changing his clothes, composed her personal tableau. The afternoon light diffused through the thin curtains was just so. Bonnie was combed, made up, corseted, prepared for a thousand eyes. Her dress fitted without a wrinkle. She was ready to project her presence and create a mood with one intelligent phrase. She had been practicing having colored voices, thinking blue, violet, green, depending on the occasion. Her hands were apart, hovering over a bowl of asters—a bit of stage business she had just thought up.

If Bonnie had not been the mother of Flor, and guilty of a hundred assaults on his generosity and pride, he might have liked her. She was ludicrous, touching, aware she was putting on an act. But a natural relationship between them was hopeless. Too much had been hinted and said. She had wounded him too deeply. He had probably wounded her. She greeted the young man as if his being in his own apartment were a source of gay surprise, and he responded with his usual unblinking reverence, as if he were Chinese and she a revered but long-perished ancestor; at the same time, he could not stop grinning all over his face.

The effect of discovery was ruined. Bonnie had dressed and smiled and spoken in vain. Even the perfect lighting was a lost effect: the sun might just as well set, now, as far as Bonnie was concerned. She was only trying to look attractive and create a civilized, attractive atmosphere for them all, but nobody helped. He saw that she was once more offended, and was sorry. He offered her a drink, which she refused, explaining in a hurt voice that she was waiting for tea.

"Where's Flor?"

"*You* know," said Bonnie. On the merits of Dr. Linnetti they were in complete accord.

He sat down and opened the newspaper he had brought home. Bonnie gave a final poke at the flowers and sat down too, not so far away that it looked foolish, but leaving a distance so that he need not imagine for one second Bonnie expected him to *talk*. He looked at his paper and Bonnie thought her thoughts and waited for tea. She was nearly contented: it was a climate of mutual acceptance that had about it a sort of coziness: they might have been putting up with each other for years. The room seemed full of inherited furniture no one knew how to get rid of; yet they had taken the apartment as it was. They were trailing baggage out of a fabricated past. The furnishings had probably responded to Bob's need for a kind of buttery comfort; and the colors and textures reflected Bonnie's slightly lady-taste that ran to shot silk, pearly porcelain, and peacock green. Afloat on polished tables were the objects she had picked up on her travels, bibelots in silver and glass. There was a television set prudishly hidden away in a lacquered cabinet, and on the walls the paintings Bob had purchased. It was not a perfect room, but, as Bonnie often told her sister-in-law in her letters, it could have been so much worse. There was nothing in it of Flor.

When Flor came in a few minutes after this there was someone with her: a tall, round-faced young woman with blond hair, whose dress, voice, speech, and manner were so of a piece that she remained long afterward in Bob's memory as "The American," as though being American were exceptional or unique. Flor hung back. The visitor advanced into the room and smiled at them: "I'm Doris Fischer. I live down below. It's marvelous to find other Americans here."

"We met on the stairs," said Flor seriously.

"Met on the stairs, Flor? Met on the stairs?" Bonnie sounded fussed and overcontained, as if she might scream. Flor never spoke to strangers and, since spring, had given up even her closest friends. The two young women seemed about to reveal something: for an instant Bonnie had the crazy idea that one of the two had been involved in a fatal accident and that the other was about to describe it. That was how you became, living with Flor. Impossible, illogical pictures leaped upward in the mind and remained fixed, shining with more brilliance and clarity than the obvious facts. Later she realized that this expectation of disaster was owing to a quality in the newcomer. Doris Fischer, so assertive, so cheerfully sane, often took on the moody gestures of an Irish actress about to disclose that her father was a drunkard, her brother an anarchist, her mother a saint, et cetera. It gave a false start to her presence: any portentousness was usually owing to absentmindedness or social unease, although that could be grave enough.

"We were both down there waiting for the elevator," said Doris, in her friendly, normal way. "It was stuck some place. You know how it never works in this building . . ." They had started to climb the stairs together, and she had spoken to Flor. That was all. It was quite ordinary, really.

In Flor's mind, this meeting was extraordinary in the full sense of the word. That any one should accost and speak to her assumed the proportions of fatality. She had been pinpointed, sought out, approached. In her amazement she grasped something that was not far wrong: she had been observed. Doris Fischer had been watching the comings and goings of these people for days, and had obtained from the concierge that they were American. Thoughts of simply presenting herself at their door had occurred and been rejected: wisely, too, for Bonnie would not have tolerated that. This spider role was contrary to Doris's nature. She was observing when she wanted to be involved, and keeping still when everything compelled her to cry, "Accept me!" She was a compatriot and lonely and the others might take her at that value, but Flor's perspective was not wholly askew. Doris was like a card suddenly turned out of the pack: "Beware of a fair-haired woman. She attaches herself like a limpet to the married rock." She would want them all, and all their secrets. She would fill the idleness of her days with their affairs. She would disgorge secrets of her own, and the net would be woven and tight and over their heads.

Everyone remained standing. The fairly mundane social occasion—the person who lived downstairs coming to call—was an event. Doris Fischer saw the husband and the mother as standing forms against the hot summer light. Her eyes were dazzled by the color in the room. The chandelier threw spectrums over peacock walls; blue silk curtains belled and collapsed. Doris thought the room itself perfectly terrible. Her own taste rotated on the blond-wood exports from sanitary Sweden; on wrought-iron in its several forms; on the creeping green plants that prosper in centrally heated rooms but die in the sun. Nothing in her background or her experience could make her respond to the cherished object or the depth of dark, polished wood. She saw there were modern paintings on the walls, and was relieved, for she disliked the past. Radiating confidence now, she stepped farther inside, pointed at the wall opposite, and accused something hanging there.

"It's very interesting," she said, in an agreeable but slightly aggressive voice. "What is it? I mean, who's it by?"

"It is by an Australian who is not yet recognized in his own country," said Bob. He often spoke in this formal manner, never slurring words, particularly when he was meeting someone new. He considered Doris's plain brown-and-white shoes, her plain shirtwaist dress of striped blue cotton, her short, fluffy hair. He was anything but aggressive. He smiled.

They all turned to the painting. Bonnie looked at a bright patch on the bright wall, and Doris at something a child of six might have done as well. Flor saw in the forms exploding with nothing to hold them together absolute proof that the universe was disintegrating and that it was vain and foolish to cry for help. Bob looked at a rising investment that, at the same time, gave him aesthetic pleasure; that was the way to wrap up life, to get the best of everything. Quite simply, he told the price he had paid for the painting last year, and the price it would fetch now that the artist was becoming known: not boasting, but showing that a taste for beauty paid—something like that.

Distress on the fringe of horror covered the faces of the three women, like a glaze, endowing them with a sudden, superficial resemblance. Florence's horror was habitual: it was almost her waking look. Bonnie suffered acutely at her son-in-law's trampling of taste. Doris, the most earnest, thought of how many children in vague, teeming, starving places could have been nourished with that sum of money. Doris stayed to tea; they kept her for dinner. She came from Pennsylvania but had lived in New York. She knew no one Bonnie knew, and Bob thought it typically wicked of his mother-in-law to have asked. They were all in a strange land and out of context. Divisions could be recognized; they needn't be stressed. Doris said that her husband was a cameraman. Sometimes she said "cameraman," sometimes "film technician," sometimes "special consultant." He was in Rome on a job, and would be there all summer. Doris had decided to stay in Paris and get to know the place; when Frank was working, she only got in his way. She was imprecise about the Roman job. A transferred thought hovered like an insect in the room: She's lying. Bonnie thought, He's gone off with a girl: Bob thought, They're broke. He's down there looking for work. Doris was clumsy and evasive, she was without charm or fantasy or style, but they insisted she stay. Flor could do with an American friend.

In honor of the meal, Doris went home and returned wearing some sort of finery. She looked like a social worker going to the movies with a girl friend, Bonnie thought. Unjust appraisal always made her kind: she all but took Doris in her arms. Doris was surprised at the meal, which was scanty and dull. She was accustomed to the food of her childhood, the hillocks of mashed potatoes, the gravy made with cream; she knew the diet of a later bohemia, spaghetti with wine and the bottles saved for candleholders. She could not decide if these well-to-do people were ascetic or plain stingy. Flor ate next to nothing. Doris looked at her over the table and saw a bodiless face between lighted candles—a thin face and thick, lusterless hair. They had lighted the candles without drawing the curtains, and, as the summer night had not yet descended, the room was neither dark nor light, which, for some reason, Doris found faintly disturbing. The dining room was Chinese: throughout the meal she was glared at by monsters. It was enough to put anybody off. Bonnie chattered and nervously rattled the little bell before her. Bob was all indifference and charm. He couldn't stop charming people: it was a reflex. But it didn't mean much, and Doris left him cold. She sensed this, and wished she could make him pay. She would have been distant and mysterious, but she had already talked too much about herself. She had given it all away first go. They had bantering jokes together, underneath which moved a river of recognition. Bonnie listened to them with a glued smile, and fell into a melancholy state of mind, wondering if she were to spend the rest of her life with moral, mental, social, and emotional inferiors. She thought these two were perfectly matched. Actually, they were alike, but not in a way that could draw them together. Neither Bob nor Doris had much feeling for the importance of time: either of them could have been persuaded that the world began the day he was born. It was not enough on which to base a friendship; in any case, Doris had decided she was chiefly interested in Flor. One day she would ask Flor if Bob really loved her, and if he had any intellectual interests other than painting, and what they talked about when they were alone, and if he was any good in bed. This was the relationship she was accustomed to and sorely missed: warm, womanly, with a rich exchange of marital secrets. She smiled at Flor, and Bonnie intercepted the smile and turned it toward herself.

"Florence is spending August in Paris," Bonnie said, with a curved, smiling, coral-colored voice. "True Parisians prefer the city then." Bob Harris looked at his mother-in-law and was visibly shaken by a private desire to laugh. His mother-in-law stopped being Mrs. Hauksbee and glared. It seemed to Doris good-humored enough, though exclusive. She wondered if Flor was pregnant, and if that was why Flor was so quiet.

That night, Bonnie got the invitation to Deauville out of the bottom tray of her jewelry case, where she kept letters, medical prescriptions, and the keys to lost and forgotten trunks. She scarcely knew the woman who had sent it. They had met at a party. The signature evoked a fugitive image: thin, dark, sardonic, French. She began saying to herself, I hardly know Gabrielle, but it was a case of affinity at first sight.

Gabrielle—the Frenchwoman—had rented a villa at Deauville. She was inviting a few people for the month of August, and she stated in her letter what Bonnie's share of costs would be. Bonnie was not offended. Possibly she had always wanted this. She sat at her dressing table, in her lace-and-satin slip, and read the letter. She wore horn-rimmed reading glasses, which gave her appearance an unexpected dimension. When she looked up the mirror reflected her three ways. Her nose was pointed; underneath her chin hung a slack, soft little pouch. She saw clearly what Gabrielle was and who the other guest would be and that she had been selected to pay. She saw that she was no longer a young woman, and that she depended for nearly everything material on a son-in-law she had opposed and despised. She closed her eyes and put the edge of the letter between her teeth. She emptied her mind, as if emptying a bottle, and waited for inspiration. Inspiration came, as warm as milk, and told her that she had been born a Fairlie, that her husband had ill-used her, that her daughter had made a *mésalliance*, and possessed a heart as impierceable as a nutmeg, whereas Bonnie's heart was a big, floppy cushion in which her loved ones were forever sticking needles and pins. This daughter now bore the virus of a kind of moral cholera that threatened everyone. Inspiration counseled Bonnie to fly, and told her that her dingy aspirations might save her. She opened her eyes but did not look at herself in the glass, for she no longer knew which Bonnie she expected to see. She said aloud, in an exceedingly silly voice, "Well, everybody deserves a little fun."

Later, she said to Flor: "I won't feel so badly about leaving you, now that you've got this nice friend." She made this sound as casual as she could.

Flor gave no sign. She was cunning as a murderer: "If I seem too pleased, she'll be hurt, she won't go away." She imagined the hall filled with suitcases and someone coming up the stairs to carry them away.

Flor had given as her reason for spending August in Paris that Dr. Linnetti had deemed it essential. Even if she went away, she would have to continue paying for the three weekly appointments. She related the story, now firmly ensconced in modern mythology, of Dr. Freud's patients, and how they all went skiing at the same time every year, and all broke their legs in the same way, without warning, and how, as a result of his winter difficulties, a tradition of payment while on holiday had become established. If she left Dr. Linnetti in the lurch, Dr. Linnetti might resent her, and then where would they all be? "Morally, it stinks," said Bob. He threatened to go and see the doctor, but Flor knew he wouldn't. He had insisted on treating the whole thing as nothing at all, hoping it would become nothing, and he would not have committed a positive act. Bonnie now began talking about Flor's August in Paris quite gaily, as a settled event, which left Bob without an ally. He was perplexed. His father was expected from New York any day now. He could not leave his wife alone in Paris, he could not really take her with him on a long business trip, and he did not want his father to see what Flor, or their marriage, had become. He had depended on Bonnie, whose influence had seldom failed. After a time he understood about Deauville. Bonnie knew that he understood. She remembered the philosophy of self-sacrifice she had preached, and that still moped in a corner of their lives like a poor, molting bird. She would have smothered if she could this old projection of herself; but it remained, indestructible as the animal witness in a fairy tale. Bob ignored her now. He seemed to have turned his back. He continued to offer holiday pictures to Flor with accelerated enthusiasm: Spain, Portugal, Portofino, Lausanne, Scotland, gaudy as posters, and as unsubstantial, were revealed and whisked away. "I have to stay here," she said. He obtained nothing more.

Because of Bob's nagging, Bonnie became possessed with the fear that Flor might decide not to stay alone after all, and oblige Bonnie to take her to Deauville. This was hardly feasible, seeing how queer Flor had become. She was likely to say and do anything. She had always been a moody girl, with an unpredictable temper, but that was the personality that went with red hair. Then, too, she had been pretty: a pretty girl can get away with a lot. But, since spring, she had floated out of Bonnie's grasp: she dressed oddly, and looked a wraith. If she did queer things in front of these people at Deauville, Bonnie felt she wouldn't know where to hide from shame. If Flor and Doris Fischer became good friends, Flor might remain more easily in Paris, doing all the sensible things, chatting away to Dr. Linnetti, visiting couturiers with Doris, eating light lunches of omelette and fruit, and so forth. Diet was of great importance in mental equilibrium: you are what you eat. Friendship mattered, said Bonnie, not losing sight of Doris: friendship, rest, good food, relaxing books. In the autumn, Flor would be a different girl.

Flor heard and thought, I used to believe she was God.

Five days remained. Bonnie was rushed off her feet and wore an expression of frank despair. She had left essential duties such as hair, nails, massage, until the end, and every moment was crowded. Nevertheless, because of the importance of the Flor-Doris friendship, she accepted Doris's suggestion one day that they all three go for a walk. Doris liked wandering around Paris, but when she walked alone, she imagined North Africans were following her. Being fair, she was a prize. She might be seized, drugged, shipped to Casablança, and obliged to work in a brothel. Even in New York, she had never taken a taxi without making certain the window could be lowered. This cherished fear apart, she was sensible enough.

The three women took a taxi to the Place de la Concorde one afternoon and walked to the Pont Neuf. They crossed to the Left Bank over the tip of the Île de la Cité. It was a hot, transparent day; slumbering summer Paris; a milky sky, a perspective of bridges and shaking trees. Flor had let her long hair free and wore sandals on her feet. She seemed wild, yet urban, falsely contrived, like a gypsy in a musical play. Bonnie walked between the two girls and was shorter than both. She was conscious only of being shorter than Flor. It was curious, being suddenly smaller than the person over whom you had once exercised complete control. Bonnie's step was light: she had been careful to keep a young figure. Doris, the big blond, thought she looked beaky and thin, like a bird. A mean little bird, she amended. There was something about Bonnie she didn't like. Doris wore the dress they had come to consider her day-duty uniform: the neat, standard shirtmaker. Bonnie's little blue hat would have suited her well. Bonnie thought of this, and wondered how to offer it. Doris expressed from time to time her sense of well-being on this lovely day. She said she could hardly believe she was really alive and in Paris. It was like that feeling after a good meal, she said, sincerely, for the gratification of her digestion compared favorably with any pleasure she had known until now. Although neither Flor nor Bonnie answered, Bonnie had an instant's awareness that their reaction to Doris was the same: they needn't share a look, or the pressure of hands. Later, this was one of her most anguished memories. She forgot the time and the year and who was with them, remembering only that on a lost day, with her lost, loved, girl, there had existed a moment of unity while crossing a bridge.

Flor was letting herself see in high, embossed relief, changing the focus of her eyes, even though she knew this was dangerous. Human cunning was keeping the ruin of Paris concealed. The ivy below Notre Dame had swelled through the city's painted crust: it was the tender covering of a ruin. The invasion of strangers resembled the busloads of tourists arriving at Pompeii. They were disoriented and out of place. Recording with their cameras, they tried not to live the day but to fix a day not their own. It had so little to do with the present that something she had suspected became clear: there was no present here, and the strangers were perfectly correct to record, to stare, to giggle, to display the unease a healthy visitor feels in a hospital—the vague fear that a buried illness might emerge, obliging one to remain. Her heart had left its prison and was beating under her skin. The smell of her own hands was nauseating. Nobody knew.

When they reached the opposite shore, Bonnie decided the walk had gone on long enough. She began looking for a taxi. But Flor suddenly said she wanted to continue. The others fell in step: three women strolling by the Seine on a summer's day.

"There is a window with a horse in it," Florence said seriously. "I want to see that."

Bonnie hoped Doris hadn't heard. There was nothing she could do now. Her daughter's eyes were wide and anguished. Her lips moved. Bonnie continued to walk between the two young women so that any conversation would, as it were, sift through her.

"Didn't we walk along here when I was little?" said Flor.

Flor never spoke of the past. To have her go into it now was unsettling. It was also a matter of time and place. It was four o'clock, and Bonnie had a fitting with her dressmaker at five. She said, "Oh, honey, we never came to Paris until you were a big girl. You know that."

"I thought we used to come along here and look at the horse."

This was so bizarre, and yet Bonnie could not help giving Doris an anxious, pathetic glance, as if to say, "We used to do things together—we used to be friends." They were still on the Quai de Montebello when Flor made them cross the street and led them to a large corner window. Well, there was a stuffed horse. Flor wasn't so crazy after all.

An American woman, dressed rather like Doris, stood before the window, holding a child by the hand. Crouched on the pavement, camera to his eyes, was the husband, trying to get all of them in the picture—wife, child, horse. The boy wore a printed shirt that matched his father's, and his horn-rimmed glasses were the same, but smaller. He looked like the father reduced. Doris's delighted eyes signaled that this was funny, but Bonnie was too bothered with Flor to mind: Flor looked at the child, then at the horse, with a fixed, terrified stare. Her skin had thickened and paled. There was a film of sweat on her cheeks.

The child said, "Why's the horse there?" and the mother replied in a flat bored voice, "*I* dunno. He's dead."

"That's wrong," said Flor harshly. "He's guarding the store. At night he goes out and gallops along the river and he wears a white and red harness. You can see him in the parks at night after the gates are locked."

Doris, joining in what she imagined the play of a whimsical mind, said, "Ah, but if the gates are locked, how do you get in to see him?"

"There's a question!" cried Bonnie gaily.

She was not listening to her own voice. Everything was concentrated on getting Flor away, or getting the three open-mouthed tourists away from her.

"We did come here when I was little," said Flor, weeping, clasping her hands. "I remember this horse. I'm sure I remember. Even when I was playing in the grass at home I remembered it here." She saw the leafy tunnels of the Tuileries on an autumn day, and the galloping horse: she could not convey this picture, an image of torment, nostalgia, and unbearable pain.

"Oh, love," said her mother, and she was crying now too. There was something in this scene of the old days, when they had been emotional and close. But their closeness had been a trap, and each could now think, If it hadn't been for you, my life would have been different. If only you had gone out of my life at the right time.

Doris thought: Spoiled. Fuss over nothing. She also thought, I'm like a sister, one of the family. They say anything in front of me.

Perhaps this was true, because it seemed natural that Doris find a taxi, take them home, and put Flor to bed. She even ordered a nice cup of coffee all around, putting on a harmless comedy of efficiency before the cook. By now, after a few days, she might have known them for years. She came into their lives dragging her existence like a wet raincoat, and no one made a move to keep her out. She called them by their Christian names and had heard Bonnie's troubles and hinted at plenty of her own. Bob referred to her as Moonface because she was all circles, round face, round brown eyes. The first impression of American crispness had collapsed. Her hair often looked as if mice had been at it. The shirt-maker dresses were held together with pins. Dipping hems had been stitched with thread the wrong color. She carried foolish straw baskets with artificial flowers wound around the handle, and seemed to have chosen her clothes with three aims in mind: they mustn't cost much, they must look as if anybody could wear them, and they must be suitable for a girl of sixteen. She did not belong in their lives or in the Paris summer. She belonged to an unknown cindery city full of used-car lots. She sat by Flor's bed, hunched forward, hands around her knees. "I know how you feel in a way," she said. "Sometimes I feel so depressed I honestly don't like going out on the street. I feel as if it's written all over me that something's wrong. I get the idea that the mob will turn on me and pull me apart because I'm unhappy and unhappiness is catching." She seemed genial and lively enough, saying this. She was fresh from a different world, where generalized misery was possibly taken for granted. Bob said that Moonface was stupid, and Flor, for want of any opinion, had agreed, but could Flor be superior? She would have given anything to be a victor, one of that trampling mob.

There wasn't much to be had from Flor, and Doris turned to

Bonnie instead. She would try every member of the family in turn, and only total failure would drive her away. Within the family, on whatever bankrupt terms, she was at least *somewhere*. She had been afraid of never knowing anyone in Paris: she spoke very little French, and had never wanted to come abroad. But it was not long before she understood that even though they had lived here for years, and used some French words in their private family language, they were not in touch with life in France. They had friends: Bob and Bonnie seemed to go about; but they were not in touch with life in the way Doris—so earnest, so sociologically minded—would have wanted. Still, she enjoyed the new intimacy with Bonnie. For the few days that remained, she had tea every day in Bonnie's bedroom. Bonnie was packing like a fury now. They would shut themselves up in the oyster-colored room, Bonnie dressed in a slip because a dress was a psychological obstacle when she had something to do, and gossip and pack. Doris sat on the floor: the chairs were laden with the dresses Bonnie was or was not going to take to Deauville. Bonnie was careful to avoid dropping the Deauville hostess's name, out of an inverted contempt for Doris, but Doris got the point very soon. She was not impressed. She suspected all forms of titled address, and thought Bonnie would have been a nicer and more sincere person if she had used her opportunities to cultivate college professors and their wives.

Bonnie didn't care what Doris thought. Everything was minimal compared with Flor's increasing queerness and her own headlong and cowardly flight. She talked about Flor, and how Flor was magnifying Bonnie's failings for Dr. Linnetti.

"All children hate their parents," said Doris, shrugging at this commonplace. She was sewing straps for Bonnie. She bit off a thread. There were subjects on which she permitted herself a superior tone. These people had means but were strictly uneducated. Only Bob had a degree. As far as Doris could make out, Flor had hardly even been to school. Doris was proud of her education—a bundle of notions she trundled before her like a pram containing twins. She could not have told you that the shortest distance between two points was a straight line, but she did know that "hostility" was the key word in human relations, and that a man with an abscessed tooth was only punishing himself.

"All I can say is I adored my mother," said Bonnie. "That's all I can say."

"You haven't faced it. Or else you don't remember."

Bonnie remembered other things: she remembered herself, Bonnie, at thirty-seven, her name dragged in the mud, vowing to Flor she would never look at a man again; swearing that Flor could count on her for the rest of her life. She had known in her heart it was a temporary promise and she had said, "I still have five good years." At forty-two, she thought, My life isn't finished. I still have five good years. And so it had been, the postponement of life five years at a time, until now Flor was married and in a dream, and Bonnie was fifty-two. She wanted Flor to hold off; to behave well; not to need help now, this very minute. She was pulled this way and that, now desperate for her own safety, now aghast with remorse and the stormy knowledge of failure. She left Doris sitting on the floor and went into her daughter's room. Flor was lying on the bed, wide-eyed, with a magazine. She kept a magazine at hand so that she could pretend to be reading in case someone came. None of them liked her habit of lying immobile in the semi-dark.

Bonnie sat down on the bed. She wanted to say, Flor, I've had a hell of a life. Your father was a Catholic. He made me be a Catholic and believe a lot of things and then he left off being one and divorced me. And that isn't everything, it's only a fragment. What she said was: "Darling, I'm not going to suggest you see a priest, because I know you wouldn't. But I do agree with Bob, I don't think Dr. Linnetti is any good. If you're going to stay here in August anyway you should see someone else. You know, I used to know a doctor . . ."

"I know," said Flor, loathing awakened.

But Bonnie hadn't meant that old, disastrous love affair. She had meant a perfectly serious professional man out in Neuilly. Flor's eyes alarmed her. She fingered the magazine between them and thought of the other doctor, the lover, and wondered how much Flor had seen in those days. Flor must have been eleven, twelve. She felt as though she had been staring in the sun, the room seemed so dark.

"You see," said Flor, "I'm perfectly all right and I don't need a priest. Mama. Listen. I'm all right. I'm slightly anemic. It makes me pale. Don't you remember, I was always a bit anemic?"

Flor had said what Bonnie wanted said.

"Oh, I know," said Flor's mother eagerly. "I remember! Oh, lambie, when you were small, the awful chopped raw liver mess you had to eat! You were anemic. Of course I remember now."

"It makes me tired," said Flor gently. "Then there's Doctor L., three times a week. That's tiring too. It just wears me out. And so, I lie down. August alone will be just wonderful. I'll lie down all the time. I'm *anemic*, Mama."

Bonnie's soft eager eyes were on her daughter. She would have cried at her, if she dared, Yes, tell me, make me believe this.

Now, that was the disarming thing about Flor. She could be so sensible, she could explain everything as though you were the nitwit. She could smile: "Don't *worry* about me," and you would think, Flor knows what she's doing. She's all right.

All the same, thought Bonnie, it was a pity that she was only twenty-six and had lost her looks.

Bob Harris had no division of purpose. He wanted Flor to go away from Paris for the next four weeks. Sometimes he said Cannes, because she liked the sea. He mentioned Deauville, but Bonnie pulled a long face. He knew there was more to it than getting through August, but that was all there was time for now. His father had arrived from New York. He was a mild old man, who had not wanted this marriage. He seemed to take up no space in the apartment, and he made everyone generous gifts. Bonnie tried to charm him, and failed. She tried to treat him like a joint parent, with foolish young people to consider, but that failed too. She gave up. She felt that disapproval of the match should be her own family's prerogative and that the Harrises were overstepping. The old man saw Flor, her silence, her absence, and believed she had a lover and that her pallor was owing to guilty thoughts. The young people had been married two years: it seemed to him a sad and wretched affair. There were no children and no talk of any. He thought, *I warned him*, but he held still: he did not want to cause the estrangement of his only son. His gentle sadness affected them all. He was thinly polite, and looked unwell. His skin had the bluish clarity of skimmed milk. Bonnie wanted to scream at him: I didn't want your son! She wondered why he felt he had to be so damned courtly. In her mind there was no social gap between a Jewish wine merchant and her ex-husband's old bootlegger of thirty years before.

Bonnie and her son-in-law were linked in one effort: keeping the old man from knowing the true state of affairs. Bonnie was always willing to unite when their common existence was threatened. She deplored the marriage and believed Flor might have made a better match, but most of the time she was grateful. She worshiped the Harris money: she would have washed all the Harris feet every day if that had been part of the deal. There had always been an unspoken, antagonistic agreement with Bob, which Flor had never understood. She never understood why Bob was nice to her mother. She guessed—that was at the start, when she was still curious and working things out—that it was Jewishness, respect for parents. But this was a subject from which he slid away. Evasion was seared into his personality. He had a characteristic sliding movement of head and body when conversation took a turn he didn't like. It was partly because of this that they had named him the Seal.

The façade they put up now was almost flawless: the old man may even have been deceived. In the effort, they were obliged to look at themselves, and these moments, near-horror, near-perfection, were unrehearsed. They dragged resisting Flor to parties, to restaurants, to the theater. At times Bob and Bonnie began to believe in the situation, and they would say, in amazement, "There, do you see how good life can be?" Flor seemed quite normal, except that she complained of being tired, but many women are like that. One day they made an excursion to Montparnasse: Bob bought pictures, and Bonnie had unearthed a young artist. She said he was Polish and full of genius. It was a bad outing: Bob was irritated because Bonnie had promised to help the young man without telling him first. The studio was like dozens more in Paris: there was a stove with last year's ashes, and the pictures he showed them were cold and stale. There was a flattering drawing of Bonnie tacked to the wall. The painter talked as if he owed his diction to an attentive study of old Charles Boyer films. He had a ripe-pear voice and a French accent.

"I don't like him," said Bob, when they were driving home. "He's nothing. He paints like a little girl. Anyway, he's a phony. What's that accent? He's just a New York boy."

"He has lived here for many years," said Bonnie, the bristling mother-bird.

"I may live here a lot longer but that won't change my voice," said Bob. "He's afraid. He's scared of being what he really is. If he talked naturally he wouldn't be Michel Colbert. Colbert. Colbert. What is that?"

"What is Harris?" said Bonnie, trembling.

Nothing was said, nothing was said about anything, and the silence beat about them like waves. The elevator in the building wasn't working again. Bonnie clutched at Flor as they climbed the stairs. "What have I gone and done?" she whispered heavily, pinching Flor's arm.

Flor had not been lying down a minute before her husband came in and slammed the door behind him. He stood over her and said, "Why the hell didn't you back me up?"

"I didn't listen," said Flor in terror. "I didn't speak."

"That's what I'm saying. What do you suppose my father thinks?"

He didn't go on with it. Too much had been taken away from him. He did not want to diminish what remained. Flor seemed frightened, looking up at him, curled on the bed like a child, and he was filled with pity for her and for them all. She had been dragged from her bed for the futile visit to the studio and now he had to drag her out again. She was a sick girl: he had to remember that. He sat on the bed with his back half turned and said gently, "We have to go out for dinner, you know?"

"Oh, no, no."

"It's my father and some of his friends," he said. "You know I have to be there. These people have invited us. Bonnie's coming." By this he meant that Bonnie understood the requirements of life.

"I'd rather not go."

He was so tired, yet he was someone who had never been tired.

He thought, You shouldn't have to plead with your wife over such simple things. "It'll do you good," he said.

"I went to the studio," she said plaintively.

"People go two places in one day," he said. "It's not late. It's summer. It's still light outside. If you'd open those shutters you'd see." He had a fixed idea that she feared the dark.

Light and dark were outside the scope of her fears. She moved her head, unable to speak. He would have taken her hand only he never touched her now. In the spring, she had begun pleading with him to let her sleep. She had behaved like a prisoner roused for questioning. Tomorrow, she had promised, or in the morning. Any moment but now. He woke her one dawn and was humiliated at what they had become, remembering Cannes, the summer they had met. He couldn't discuss it. He never touched her again. He couldn't look at her now. Her hair, loose on the pillow, was a parody of Cannes. So were the shuttered windows.

Flor felt his presence. She had closed her eyes but held his image under the lids. He was half turned away. His back and the shape of his head were against the faint summer light that came in between the slats of the shutters. One hand was flat on the bed, and there was the memory of their hands side by side on the warm sand. When he had moved his hand to cover hers, there remained the imprint of his palm, and, because they were both instinctively superstitious, they had brushed this mold away.

He said in such a miserable voice, "Are you really all that tired?" that she wanted to help him.

She said, "I've already told you. I'm afraid."

He had heard of her fear of cars but couldn't believe it. He had never been afraid: he was the circus seal. They had always clapped and approved. He tried to assemble some of the practical causes of fear. "Are you afraid of the next war? I mean, do you think about the bombs and all that?"

Flor moved her head on the pillow. "It's nothing like that. I don't think about the war. I'm used to the idea, like everyone else." She tried again. "Remember once when we were out walking, remember under the bridge, the boy kicking the man? The man was lying down."

"What's the good of thinking about that?" he said. "Somebody's kicking somebody else all the time. You can't make yourself responsible for everything."

"Why didn't the man at least get up? His eyes were open."

He had been afraid she would say, Why didn't we help him? The incident had seemed even when they were witnessing it far away and grotesque. When you live in a foreign country you learn to mind your own business. But all this reasoning was left in the air. He knew she was making a vertiginous effort to turn back on her journey out. He said something he hadn't thought of until now. It seemed irrefutable: "We don't know what the man had done to him first." Perhaps she accepted this; it caused a silence. "I'm glad you're talking to me," he said humbly, even though he felt she had put him in the wrong.

"I'm afraid of things like that," said Flor.

"Nobody's going to pull you under a bridge and kick you." He looked at her curiously, for she had used a false voice; not as Bonnie sometimes did, but as if someone were actually speaking for her.

"Sometimes when I want to speak," she said in the same way, "something comes between my thoughts and the words." She loathed herself at this moment. She believed she gave off a rank smell. She was the sick redhead; the dying, quivering fox. "It's only being anemic," she said wildly. "The blood doesn't reach the brain."

On an impulse stronger than pride he had already taken her hand. This hand was warm and dry and belonged to someone known. He had loved her: he tried to reconstruct their past, not sentimentally, but as a living structure of hair, skin, breath. This effort surpassed his imagination and was actually repugnant. It seemed unhealthy. Still, remembering, he said, "I do love you," but he was thinking of the hot, faded summer in Cannes, and the white walls of his shuttered room on a blazing afternoon, and coming in with Flor from the beach. He saw the imprint of his fingers on her brown shoulder; he thought he tasted salt. Suddenly he felt as if he might vomit. His mouth was flooded with saliva. He thought, I'll go crazy with this. He was appalled at the tenderness of the wound. He remembered what it was to be sick with love.

"You'd better come out," he said. "It'll do you good. You'll see there's nothing to be afraid of." With these words he caused them to resume their new roles: the tiresome wife, the patient husband.

He had never insisted so much before; but too much had been taken away in his wife's retreat and he had been, without knowing it, building on what was left: money, and his own charm. He could not stop charming people. The concierge was minutes recovering from his greeting every day. These elements—the importance of business, his own attractive powers—pulled away like the sea and left him stranded and without his wife.

Flor's crisis had passed. The sharp-muzzled animal who inhabited her breast had gone to sleep. She looked at her husband and saw that whatever protected him had left him at that moment; he seemed pitiable and without confidence. She might have said, Forgive me, or even, Help me, and it might have been different between them, if not better, but Bonnie came in. She knocked and must have thought she heard an answer. Neither Bob nor Flor heard clearly what she said. The present rushed in with a clatter, for Bonnie threw the shutters apart with an exclamation of annoyance, and past love, that delicate goblet, was shattered on the spot.

Bob stood beside Bonnie. Between them, joined enemies again, they got Flor up and out. "I shall never forgive you," said Flor; but she rose, bathed, put up her hair. Their joint feeling—her and Bob's—was one of relief: there was no need to suffer too deeply after all. No present horror equaled the potential suffering of the past. Reliving the past, with full knowledge of what was to come, was a test too strong for their powers. It would have been too strong for anyone; they were not magical, they were only human beings.

Two days after this, on the fourth of August, everyone except Flor went away. The cook and the maid had already departed for Brittany, each weighted with a full, shabby suitcase. Bob and his father left by car in the morning. Bob was hearty and rather vulgar and distrait, saying goodbye. He patted Flor on the buttocks and kissed her mouth. This took place on the street. She had come down to see them loading the car—just like any young woman seeing vacationers off. She stood with her arms around her body, as if the day were cold. The old man, now totally convinced that Flor had a lover in Paris, did not look at her directly. In the afternoon, Bonnie took off from the Gare St. Lazare and Flor went there too. The station was so crowded that they had to fight their way to the train. Bonnie kept behaving as though it were all slick and usual and out of a page entitled "Doings of the International Smart Set": young Mrs. Robert Harris seeing her mother off for Deauville. Bonnie was beautifully dressed. She wore a public smile and gave her daughter a woman's kiss, embracing the air.

Flor saw the train out. She went home and got out of her clothes and into a nightgown covered with a pattern of butterflies. She had left a message for the cleaning woman, telling her not to come. She went from room to room and closed the shutters. Then she got into bed.

She slept without stirring until the next morning, when there was a ring at the door. Doris Fischer was there. She looked glossy and sunburned, and said she had caught a throat virus from the swimming pool in the Seine. She was hard, sunny reality; the opponent of dreams. She sat by Flor's bed and talked in disconnected sentences about people back in the States Flor had never seen. At noon, she went into the kitchen and heated soup, which they drank from cups. Then she went away. Flor lay still. She thought of the names of streets she had lived in and of hotel rooms in which she had spent the night. She leaned on her elbow and got her notebook from the table nearby. This was an invalid's gesture: the pale hand fretfully clutching the magic object. There were no blank pages. She had used them all in the letter. She looked at a page on which she had written this:

Maids dancing in Aunt Dottie Fairlie's kitchen.

Father Doyle: If you look in the mirror too much you will see the devil.

Granny's gardener

B. H.: The only thing I like about Christ is when he raised the little girl from the dead and said she should be given something to eat.

She turned the pages. None of these fragments led back or

forward to anything and many called up no precise image at all. There was nothing to add, even if there had been space. The major discovery had been made that July afternoon before the Café de la Paix, and the words, "it was always this way," were the full solution. Even Dr. Linnetti would have conceded that.

She could not sleep unless her box of sleeping tablets was within sight. She placed the round box on the notebook and slept again. The next day, Doris returned. She sat by Flor's bed because Bonnie had gone and there was no one else. The traffic outside was muffled to a rustling of tissue paper, the room green-dark.

"What are those pill things for?" Doris said.

"Pains," said Flor. "My teeth ache. It's something that only happens in France and it's called *rage de dents*."

"I've got good big teeth and I've never had a filling," said Doris, showing them. "That's from the German side. I'm half Irish, half German. Florence, why don't you get up? If you lie there thinking you're sick you'll *get* sick."

"I know perfectly well I'm not sick," said Flor.

Doris thought she was on to something. "You know, of course," she said, fixing Flor sternly, "that this is a retreat from life."

For the first time since Doris had known her, Flor laughed. She laughed until Doris joined in too, good-natured, but slightly vexed, for she guessed she was being made fun of.

"Don't worry about me," said Flor, as lucidly as you pleased. "I'm a Victorian heroine."

"The trouble is," Doris said, "you've never had to face a concrete problem. Like mine. Like . . ." and she was away, divulging the affairs she had only hinted at until now. Her husband had left her, but only for the summer. He intended to return, and she knew she would take him back, and that should have been the end of it. That was the story, but Doris couldn't leave it alone. Behind the situation struggled memories and impulses she could neither relate nor control. Trying to bring order through speech, she sat by Flor's bed and told her about their life in New York, which had been so different. Names emerged: Beth and Howard, Peter and Jan, Bernie and Madge, Lina, who was brilliant, and Wolff and Louis, who always came to see them on Sundays, and lived in a stable or garage or something like that. They were prudently left-wing, and on speaking terms with a number of jazz musicians. They had among their friends Chinese, Javanese, Peruvians, and Syrians. They had a wonderful life. Then this year abroad things had happened and her husband, filming a documentary for television, had met a woman studying Egyptian at the École du Louvre. "Don't laugh," said Doris miserably to Flor, who was not laughing at all.

Why did these things happen? Why was Doris alone in Paris, who had never been alone in her life? Why weren't they still in college or still in New York? Why was she nearly thirty and in a foreign place and everything a mess? "You tell me," Doris demanded.

Flor had no replies. She lay on the bed, in a butterfly-covered nightgown, and her dreams were broken by Doris's ring at the door. Doris occupied the chair beside her bed as if she had a right to it. She came every day. She opened cans of soup in the kitchen and she never washed the saucepan or the cups. She took clean dishes from the cupboard each time, and it was like the Mad Tea Party; although even there, eventually, it must have become impossible to move along. The dishes here would finally reach an end too, and she would have to do something—go home, or follow her husband, whether he wanted her around or not, or stay here and wash cups. Flor was not making the division between days and nights clearly, but she knew that Doris came most frequently in the afternoon. She told Flor that she woke up fairly optimistically each day, but that the afternoon was a desert and she couldn't cross it alone.

Then a disaster occurred: Flor's sleeping tablets disappeared. She took the bed apart and rolled back the carpet. Doris helped, unexpectedly silent. It was a disaster because without the pills in the room she was unable to sleep. Her desire for sleep and dreams took the shape of a boat. Every day it pulled away from shore but was forced to return. She had left the doorkey under the mat so that Doris could come in when she wanted, after a warning ring. She got up early one day and took the key inside. She heard a ring and didn't answer. The ring was repeated, and Doris knocked as well, but Flor lay still, her eyes closed. Once the imperative ring surprised her in the kitchen, where she was distractedly looking

around for something to eat. There were empty cans everywhere, which Doris had opened for her, and dirty cups, and a
spilled box of crackers. She found cornflakes and some sour milk
in a jug and a sticky packet of dates. In a store cupboard there
were more tins. She opened a tin of mushrooms and ate them
with her fingers and went back to bed. This scene had the air of
a robbery. It was midday, but the light was on; the kitchen
was shuttered, like every other room. Flor's quest for food was
stealthy and uncertain, partly because the kitchen was not her
province and she seldom entered it. When Doris rang, she stood
frozen, in her nightgown, her head thrown back, her heart beating
in hard, painful, slow thumps. She had a transient fear that Doris
possessed a miraculous key and could come in whenever she
wanted to. She felt the warmth and weight of her thick hair. Her
neck was damp with fear.

The ringing stopped. That afternoon she slept and half
slept and had her first real dream, which was of floating, sailing,
going away. It was pleasant, brightly lit, and faintly erotic. There
emerged the face of a Russian she and her mother had once talked
to in a hotel. She remembered that in the presence of a whirlwind
you defied Satan and made the sign of the cross. She opened her
eyes with interest and wonder. She had followed someone exor-
cising a number of rooms. She was not in the least frightened, but
she was half out of bed.

The building was empty now. She heard the concierge cleaning
on the stairs. In the daytime there was light through the shutters.
She was happiest at night, but her plans were upset by the loss of
the pills. Once her husband telephoned and she replied and spoke
quite sensibly, although she could not remember afterward what
she had said. She turned her room upside down again, but the
pills were gone. Well, the pills might turn up. There were other
things to be done: cupboards to be shut, drawers tidied, stockings
put away. She knew she would be unable to lie in peace until
everything was settled, and August was wearing away. Every day
she did one useful thing. There were the gold sandals Bonnie
wanted repaired: she had left them on a chest in the hall so that
Flor would see them on her way out. These sandals did not belong
in the hall. The need to find a place for the broken sandals drove

her out of bed one afternoon. She carried the sandals all around the flat, from shuttered room to room. There was no sound from the street. In her mother's bedroom she forgot why she had come. She let the sandals fall on a chair; that was how Bonnie found them, one on the chair, one on the floor, with its severed strap like a snapped twig some inches away.

Once she had told Dr. Linnetti that her husband was her mother's lover. She had described in a composed voice the scene of discovery: he came home very late and instead of going into his own room went into Bonnie's. She knew it was he, for she knew his step, and the words this man used were his. She heard her mother whisper and her mother laugh. "Then," said Flor, "he tried to come to me, but I wouldn't have it. No, never again." A month later she said, "That wasn't true, about Bob and my mother." "I know," said Dr. Linnetti.

"How do you know?" said Flor, trembling, in Bonnie's room. "How do you know?"

She saw herself in a long glass, in the long loose butterfly-covered nightdress. She looked like a pale rose model in a fashion magazine, neat, sweet, a porcelain figure, intended to suggest that it suffices to be desirable—that the dream of love is preferable to love in life.

"You might cut your hair," said Bonnie.

"Yes," said Flor. "You'd love that, wouldn't you?"

Bonnie's windows were closed and the oyster-silk fringed curtains pulled together. But still light came into the room, the milky light of August, in which Flor, the dreamer, floated like a seed. Bonnie had not entirely removed herself to Deauville, for her scent clouded the room—the cat's-fur Spanish-servant-girl scent she bought for herself in expensive bottles. Flor moved out of the range of the looking glass and could no longer be witnessed. She opened a mothproof closet and looked at dresses without touching them. She looked at chocolates from Holland in a tin box. She looked desultorily for her pills. She forgot what she was doing here and returned to bed.

She knew that time was going by and the city was emptying, and still she hadn't achieved the dreams she desired. One day she opened the shutters of her bedroom and the summer afternoon fell on her white face and tangled hair. There was the feeling of summer ending; it had reached its peak and could only wane. Nostalgia came into the room—for the past, for the waning of a day, for a shadow through a blind, for the fear of autumn. It was a season not so much ending as already used up, like a love too long discussed or a desire deferred. An accumulation of shadows and seasons ending led back to some scene: maids dancing in Aunt Dottie's kitchen? She held the shutters out and apart with both hands, frozen, as if calling for aid. None came, and she drew in her thin arms and brought the shutters to.

She was interrupted by the concierge, who brought letters, and said, "Are you still not better?" She left unopened the letters from her husband because she knew he was not saying anything to her. She opened all the letters from Dr. Linnetti, those addressed to herself, and to her mother and her husband as well. She had long ago intercepted and destroyed the first letter to Bob: "Her hostility to me was expected . . ." (Oh, she had no pride!) "but she is in need of help." She gave the name of another doctor and said that this doctor was a man.

Flor had no time for doctors. She had to finish sewing a dress. She became brisk and busy and decided to make one dress of two, fastening the bodice of one to the skirt of the other. For two days she sewed this dress and in one took it apart. She unpicked it stitch by stitch and left the pieces on the floor. She was quite happy, humming, remembering the names of songs. She wandered into Bonnie's room. The mothproof closet was open, as she had left it. She took down a heavy brocaded cocktail dress and with Bonnie's nail scissors began picking the seams apart. There was a snowdrift of threads on the parquet. The carpet had been taken away. When she went back to bed, she could sleep, but she was sleeping fitfully. There were no dreams. It was days since she had looked into the notebook. The plants were dying without water and the kitchen light left burning night and day. For the first time in her memory she was frightened of the dark. When she awoke at night it was to a whirling world of darkness and she was frightened. Then she remembered that Bonnie had taken the prescription for the sleeping tablets and she found it easily in the jewel case, lower tray.

She dressed and went down the stairs, trembling like an invalid, holding the curving rail. The concierge put letters in her hand, saying something Flor could not hear. She went out into the empty city. The quarter was completely deserted and there was no one in the park. She saw from the fit of her dress that she had lost pounds. It was the last Sunday of August, and every pharmacy she came to was closed. The air was heavy and still. There was no variation in the color of the sky. It might have been nine in the morning or four in the afternoon. The city had perished and everyone in it died or gone away: she had perceived this on a July day, crossing the Pont Neuf. It was more than a fancy, it was true. The ruin was incomplete. The streets lacked the crevices in which would appear the hellebore, the lizards, the poppies, the ivy, the nesting birds. High up at one of the windows was a red geranium, the only color on the gray street. It flowered, abandoned, on its ledge, like the poppies and the cowslips whose seeds are carried by the wind and by birds to the highest point of a ruin.

There were no cars. She was able to cross every street. The only possible menace came from one of the letters the concierge had put in her hand. She came to a café filled with people, huddled together on the quiet avenue. She sat down and opened the letter. It was nearly impossible to read, but one sentence emerged with clarity: "I am writing to Dr. Linnetti and telling her I think it is *unprofessional* to say the least," and one page she read from the start to the end: "I want this man to see you. It is something entirely new. Everything we think of as mental comes from a different part of your body and it is only a matter of getting all these different parts under control. You have always been so strong-minded darling it should be easy for you. It is *not* that Swiss and *not* that Russian but someone quite new, and he had helped thousands. When he came into the room darling we all got to our feet, it was as if some unseen force was pulling us, and although he said very little every word counted. He is most attractive darling but of course above and outside all that. I asked him what I thought of The Box and he said it was all nonsense so you see darling he isn't a fake. When I explained about The Box and how you put a drop of blood on a bit of blotting paper and The Box makes a diagnosis he was absolutely horrified so you see love he isn't a fake at all. I remember how you were so scornful when The Box diagnosed my liver trouble (that all the doctors thought was heart) so it must be an assurance for you that he doesn't believe in it too. Darling he was so interested in hearing about you. I am going to ask Dr. Linnetti why you must pay even if away and why you must have sessions in August. He is coming to Paris and you must meet. He doesn't have fees or fixed hours, you come when you need him and you give what you can to his Foundation."

She became conscious of a sound, as a sound in the fabric of a dream. Florence looked away from Bonnie's letter and saw that this sound was real. At one of the café tables, a laughing couple were pretending to give a child away to a policeman. The policeman played his role well, swinging his cape, pretending to be fierce. "She is very naughty," said the mother, when she could stop laughing enough to speak, "and I think prison is the best solution." All the people in the café laughed, except Flor. They opened their mouths in the same way, eyes fixed on the policeman and the child. The child cried out that it would be good, now, but everyone was too excited to pay attention. The child gave one more promise and suddenly went white and stiff in the policeman's grasp. He gave her back to her parents, who sat her on a chair. "She'll be good now," the policeman said.

The closed face of Paris relaxed. This was Paris: this was France. Oh, it was not only France. Her mother's mother's gardener had broken the necks of goldfinches. "If you tell you saw, you'll get hit by lightning," he had said.

"It's because of things like that," said Florence earnestly, retracing her steps home, "I'm not afraid of bombs."

She unlocked the empty apartment and the element she recognized and needed but that had evaded her until now rushed forward to meet her, and she knew it was still August, that she was still alone, and there was still time. "I only need a long sleep," she said to the empty air. The unopened letters from Bob she put on the chest in the hall. Her advancing foot kicked something along and it was a trodden, folded letter that had been pushed under the door. It was dirty and had been walked on and was greasy with city dust. She carried this letter—three sheets folded one over the other—around the flat. She closed all the doors except the door of the kitchen and the door of her bedroom. The passage was a funnel. Her sleep had been a longer and longer journey away from shore. She lay down on the bed, having been careful to remove her shoes. The letter spoke to her in peaked handwriting. She had no idea who it was from.

"I have stupid ideas," said this pointed hand, "and you are right to have nothing to do with me. You are so beautiful and clever." It groveled on like this for lines. Who is the writer of this letter? Her husband loves her but has gone away with another woman. "The girl knows I know, and it doesn't work, we are all unhappy, he has his work, and I can't just make a life of my own as he suggests. I thought you would help me but why should you? You are right not to let anyone hang on your skirts. The important thing is that I have made a decision, because I understood when you locked me out that what is needed is not slow suffering or hanging on to someone else, but a solution. I went out on the street that day and wanted to die because you had locked me out and I realized that there was a solution for me and the solution was a decision and so now I am going home. I am not going *away* but going *home*. He can follow, or he can stay, or he can do what he likes, but I have made a decision and I have cabled my father and he is cabling the money and I am going home. I'm leaving on the sixteenth and I'll wait for you every evening, come down if you want to say goodbye. I won't bother you again. All I want to tell you is I hid your sleeping pills and now I know I had no right to do that, because every person's decision is his own. I know I was silly because you're young and pretty and have everything to live for and you wouldn't do what I was afraid you would. I can't even write the word. You may have been wanting those pills and I'm sorry. They're in the kitchen, inside the white tin box with 'Recipes' written on it. Don't be angry with my interference and please Florence come and say goodbye. Florence, another thing. Everybody makes someone else pay for something, I don't know why. If you are as awful to your mother as she says you are, you are making her pay, but then, Florence, your mother could turn around and say, 'Yes, but look at my parents,' and they could have done and said the same thing, so you see how pointless it is to fix any blame. I think my husband is making me pay, but I don't know what for or why. Everyone does it. We all pay and pay for someone else's troubles. All children eventually make their parents pay, and pay, and pay. That's the way I see it now, although I may come to change my mind when I have children of my own. Florence, come once and say goodbye."

She had no time and no desire to say, They have paid. At the edge of the sea, the Fox departed. She saw the animal head breaking the water and the fan-shaped ripples diminishing against the shore. She turned her back and left the sea behind. At last she was going in the right direction. She rode Chief, her pony, between an alley of trees. Chief was a devil: he daren't bolt, or rear, but he sometimes tried to catch her leg against a tree. Nearby somebody smiled. She held herself straight. She was perfect. Everyone smiled now. Everyone was pleased. She emerged in triumph from the little wood and came off Chief, her pony, and into her father's arms.

MLLE. DIAS DE CORTA

You MOVED into my apartment during the summer of the year before abortion became legal in France; that should fix it in past time for you, dear Mlle. Dias de Corta. You had just arrived in Paris from your native city, which you kept insisting was Marseilles, and were looking for work. You said you had studied television-performance techniques at some provincial school (we had never heard of the school, even though my son had one or two actor friends) and received a diploma with "special mention" for vocal expression. The diploma was not among the things we found in your suitcase, after you disappeared, but my son recalled that you carried it in your handbag, in case you had the good luck to sit next to a casting director on a bus.

The next morning we had our first cordial conversation. I described my husband's recent death and repeated his last words, which had to do with my financial future and were not overly optimistic. I felt his presence and still heard his voice in my mind. He seemed to be in the kitchen, wondering what you were doing there, summing you up: a thin, dark-eyed, noncommittal young woman, standing at the counter, bolting her breakfast. A bit sullen, perhaps; you refused the chair I had dragged in from the dining room. Careless, too. There were crumbs everywhere. You had spilled milk on the floor.

"Don't bother about the mess," I said. "I'm used to cleaning up after young people. I wait on my son, Robert, hand and foot." Actually, you had not made a move. I fetched the sponge mop from the broom closet, but when I asked you to step aside you started to choke on a crust. I waited quietly, then said, "My husband's illness was the result of eating too fast and never chewing his food." His silent voice told me I was wasting my time. True, but if I hadn't warned you I would have been guilty of withholding assistance from someone in danger. In our country, a refusal to help can be punished by law.

The only remark my son, Robert, made about you at the beginning was "She's too short for an actress." He was on the first step of his career climb in the public institution known then as Post, Telegrams, Telephones. Now it has been broken up and renamed with short, modern terms I can never keep in mind. (Not long ago I had the pleasure of visiting Robert in his new quarters. There is a screen or a machine of some kind everywhere you look. He shares a spacious office with two women. One was born in Martinique and can't pronounce her r's. The other looks Corsican.) He left home early every day and liked to spend his evenings with a set of new friends, none of whom seemed to have a mother. The misteachings of the seventies, which encouraged criticism of earlier generations, had warped his natural feelings. Once, as he was going out the door, I asked if he loved me. He said the answer was self-evident: We were closely related. His behavior changed entirely after his engagement and marriage to Anny Clarens, a young lady of mixed descent. (Two of her grandparents are Swiss.) She is employed in the accounting department of a large hospital and enjoys her work. She and Robert have three children: Bruno, Elodie, and Félicie.

It was for companionship rather than income that I had decided to open my home to a stranger. My notice in Le Figaro mentioned "young woman only," even though those concerned for my welfare, from coiffeur to concierge, had strongly counseled "young man." "Young man" was said to be neater, cleaner, quieter, and (except under special circumstances I need not go into) would not interfere in my relationship with my son. In fact, my son was seldom available for conversation and had never shown interest in exchanging ideas with a woman, not even one who had known him from birth.

You called from a telephone on a busy street. I could hear the coins jangling and traffic going by. Your voice was low-pitched and agreeable and, except for one or two vowel sounds, would have passed for educated French. I suppose no amount of coaching at a school in or near Marseilles could get the better of the southern o, long where it should be short and clipped when it ought to be broad. But, then, the language was already in decline, owing to lax teaching standards and uncontrolled immigration. I admire your achievement and respect your handicaps, and I know Robert would say the same if he knew you were in my thoughts.

Your suitcase weighed next to nothing. I wondered if you owned warm clothes and if you even knew there could be such a thing as a wet summer. You might have seemed more at home basking in a lush garden than tramping the chilly streets in search of employment. I showed you the room—mine—with its two corner windows and long view down Avenue de Choisy. (I was to take Robert's and he was to sleep in the living room, on a couch.) At the far end of the avenue, Asian colonization had begun: a few restaurants and stores selling rice bowls and embroidered slippers from Taiwan. (Since those days the community has spread into all the neighboring streets. Police keep out of the area, preferring to let the immigrants settle disputes in their own way. Apparently, they punish wrongdoers by throwing them off the Tolbiac Bridge. Robert has been told of a secret report, compiled by experts, which the mayor has had on his desk for eighteen months. According to this report, by the year 2025 Asians will have taken over a third of Paris, Arabs and Africans three-quarters, and unskilled European immigrants two-fifths. Thousands of foreign-sounding names are deliberately "lost" by the authorities and never show up in telephone books or computer directories, to prevent us from knowing the true extent of their progress.)

I gave you the inventory and asked you to read it. You said you did not care what was in the room. I had to explain that the inventory was for me. Your signature, "Alda Dias de Corta," with its long loops and closed a's, showed pride and secrecy. You promised not to damage or remove without permission a double bed, two pillows, and a bolster, a pair of blankets, a beige satin spread with hand-knotted silk fringe, a chaise longue of the same color, a wardrobe and a dozen hangers, a marble fireplace (ornamental), two sets of lined curtains and two of écru voile, a walnut bureau with four drawers, two framed etchings of cathedrals (Reims and Chartres), a bedside table, a small lamp with parchment shade, a Louis XVI-style writing desk, a folding card table and four chairs, a gilt-framed mirror, two wrought-iron wall fixtures fitted with electric candles and lightbulbs shaped like flames, two medium-sized "Persian" rugs, and an electric heater, which had given useful service for six years but which you aged before its time by leaving it turned on all night. Robert insisted I include breakfast. He did not want it told around the building that we were cheap. What a lot of coffee, milk, bread, apricot jam, butter, and sugar you managed to put away! Yet you remained as thin as a matchstick and that great thatch of curly hair made your face seem smaller than ever.

You agreed to pay a monthly rent of fifty thousand francs for the room, cleaning of same, use of bathroom, electricity, gas (for heating baths and morning coffee), fresh sheets and towels once a week, and free latchkey. You were to keep a list of your phone calls and to settle up once a week. I offered to take messages and say positive things about you to prospective employers. The figure on the agreement was not fifty thousand, of course, but five hundred. To this day, I count in old francs—the denominations we used before General de Gaulle decided to delete two zeros, creating confusion for generations to come. Robert has to make out my income tax; otherwise, I give myself earnings in millions. He says I've had more than thirty years now to learn how to move a decimal, but a figure like "ten thousand francs" sounds more solid to me than "one hundred." I remember when a hundred francs was just the price of a croissant.

You remarked that five hundred was a lot for only a room. You had heard of studios going for six. But you did not have six hundred francs or five or even three, and after a while I took back my room and put you in Robert's, while he continued to sleep on the couch. Then you had no francs at all, and you exchanged beds with Robert, and, as it turned out, occasionally shared one. The arrangement—having you in the living room—never worked: It was hard to get you up in the morning, and the room looked as though five people were using it, all the time. We borrowed a folding bed and set it up at the far end of the hall, behind a screen, but you found the area noisy. The neighbors who lived upstairs used to go away for the weekend, leaving their dog. The concierge took it out twice a day, but the rest of the time it whined and barked, and at night it would scratch the floor. Apparently, this went on right over your head. I loaned you the earplugs my husband had used when his nerves were so bad. You complained that with your ears stopped up you could hear your own pulse beating. Given a choice, you preferred the dog.

I remember saying, "I'm afraid you must think we French are cruel to animals, Mlle. Dias de Corta, but I assure you not everyone is the same." You protested that you were French, too. I asked if you had a French passport. You said you had never applied for one. "Not even to go and visit your family?" I asked. You replied that the whole family lived in Marseilles. "But where were they born?" I asked. "Where did they come from?" There wasn't so much talk about European citizenship then. One felt free to wonder.

The couple with the dog moved away sometime in the eighties. Now the apartment is occupied by a woman with long, streaky, brass-colored hair. She wears the same coat, made of fake ocelot, year after year. Some people think the man she lives with is her son. If so, she had him at the age of twelve.

What I want to tell you about has to do with the present and the great joy and astonishment we felt when we saw you in the oven-cleanser commercial last night. It came on just at the end of the eight o'clock news and before the debate on hepatitis. Robert and Anny were having dinner with me, without the children: Anny's mother had taken them to visit Euro Disney and was keeping them overnight. We had just started dessert—crème brûlée—when I recognized your voice. Robert stopped eating and said to Anny, "It's Alda. I'm sure it's Alda." Your face has changed in some indefinable manner that has nothing to do with time. Your smile seems whiter and wider; your hair is short and has a deep mahogany tint that mature actresses often favor. Mine is still ash blond, swept back, medium long. Alain—the stylist I sent you to, all those years ago—gave it shape and color, once and for all, and I have never tampered with his creation.

Alain often asked for news of you after you vanished, mentioning you affectionately as "the little Carmencita," searching TV guides and magazines for a sign of your career. He thought you must have changed your name, perhaps to something short and easy to remember. I recall the way you wept and stormed after he cut your hair, saying he had charged two weeks' rent and cropped it so drastically that there wasn't a part you could audition for now except Hamlet. Alain retired after selling his salon to a competent and charming woman named Marie-Laure. She is thirty-seven and trying hard to have a baby. Apparently, it is her fault, not the husband's. They have started her on hormones and I pray for her safety. It must seem strange to you to think of a woman bent on motherhood, but she has financial security with the salon (although she is still paying the bank). The husband is a car-insurance assessor.

The shot of your face at the oven door, seen as though the viewer were actually in the oven, seemed to me original and clever. (Anny said she had seen the same device in a commercial about refrigerators.) I wondered if the oven was a convenient height or if you were crouched on the floor. All we could see of you was your face, and the hand wielding the spray can. Your nails were beautifully lacquered holly red, not a crack or chip. You assured us that the product did not leave a bad smell or seep into food or damage the ozone layer. Just as we had finished taking this in, you were replaced by a picture of bacteria, dead or dying, and the next thing we knew some man was driving you away in a Jaguar, all your household tasks behind you. Every movement of your body seemed to express freedom from care. What I could make out of your forehead, partly obscured by the mahogany-tinted locks, seemed smooth and unlined. It is only justice, for I had a happy childhood and a wonderful husband and a fine son, and I recall some of the things you told Robert about your early years. He was just twenty-two and easily moved to pity.

Anny reminded us of the exact date when we last had seen you: April 24, 1983. It was in the television film about the two friends, "Virginie" and "Camilla," and how they meet two interesting but very different men and accompany them on a holiday in Cannes. One of the men is a celebrated singer whose wife (not shown) has left him for some egocentric reason (not explained). The other is an architect with political connections. The singer does not know the architect has been using bribery and blackmail to obtain government contracts. Right at the beginning you make a mistake and choose the architect, having rejected the singer because of his social manner, diffident and shy. "Virginie" settles for the singer. It turns out that she has never heard of him and does not know he has sold millions of records. She has been working among the deprived in a remote mountain region, where reception is poor.

Anny found that part of the story hard to believe. As she said, even the most forlorn Alpine villages are equipped for winter tourists, and skiers won't stay in places where they can't watch the programs. At any rate, the singer is captivated by "Virginie," and the two sit in the hotel bar, which is dimly lighted, comparing their views and principles. While this is taking place, you, "Camilla," are upstairs in a flower-filled suite, making mad love with the architect. Then you and he have a big quarrel, because of his basic indifference to the real world, and you take a bunch of red roses out of a vase and throw them in his face. (I recognized your quick temper.) He brushes a torn leaf from his bare chest and picks up the telephone and says, "Madame is leaving the hotel. Send someone up for her luggage." In the next scene you are on the edge of a highway trying to get a lift to the airport. The architect has given you your air ticket but nothing for taxis.

Anny and Robert had not been married long, but she knew about you and how much you figured in our memories. She sympathized with your plight and thought it was undeserved. You had shown yourself to be objective and caring and could have been won round (by the architect) with a kind word. She wondered if you were playing your own life and if the incident at Cannes was part of a pattern of behavior. We were unable to say, inasmuch as you had vanished from our lives in the seventies. To me, you seemed not quite right for the part. You looked too quick and intelligent to be standing around with no clothes on, throwing flowers at a naked man, when you could have been putting on a designer dress and going out for dinner. Robert, who had been perfectly silent, said, "Alda was always hard to cast." It was a remark that must have come out of old café conversations, when he was still seeing actors. I had warned Anny he would be hard to live with. She took him on trust.

My husband took some people on trust, too, and he died disappointed. I once showed you the place on Place d'Italie where our restaurant used to be. After we had to sell it, it became a pizza restaurant, then a health-food store. What it is now I don't know. When I go by I look the other way. Like you, he picked the wrong person. She was a regular lunchtime customer, as quiet as Anny; her husband did the talking. He seemed to be involved with the construction taking place around the Porte de Choisy and at that end of the avenue. The Chinese were moving into these places as fast as they were available; they kept their promises and paid their bills, and it seemed like a wise investment. Something went wrong. The woman disappeared, and the husband retired to that seaside town in Portugal where all the exiled kings and queens used to live. Portugal is a coincidence: I am not implying any connection with you or your relations or fellow citizens. If we are to create the Europe of the twenty-first century, we must show belief in one another and take our frustrated expectations as they come.

What I particularly admired, last night, was your pronunciation of "ozone." Where would you be if I hadn't kept after you about your o's? "Say '*Rhône*,'" I used to tell you. "Not '*run*.'" Watching you drive off in the Jaguar, I wondered if you had a thought to spare for Robert's old Renault. The day you went away together, after the only quarrel I ever had with my son, he threw your suitcase in the backseat. The suitcase was still there the next morning, when he came back alone. Later, he said he hadn't noticed it. The two of you had spent the night in the car, for you had no money and nowhere to go. There was barely room to sit. He drives a Citroën BX now.

I had been the first to spot your condition. You had an interview for a six-day modeling job—Rue des Rosiers, wholesale—and nothing to wear. I gave you one of my own dresses, which, of course, had to be taken in. You were thinner than ever and had lost your appetite for breakfast. You said you thought the apricot jam was making you sick. (I bought you some honey from Provence, but you threw that up, too.) I had finished basting the dress seams and was down on my knees, pinning the hem, when I suddenly put my hand flat on the front of the skirt and said,

"How far along are you?" You burst into tears and said something I won't repeat. I said, "You should have thought of all that sooner. I can't help you. I'm sorry. It's against the law and, besides, I wouldn't know where to send you."

After the night in the Renault you went to a café, so that Robert could shave in the washroom. He said, "Why don't you start a conversation with that woman at the next table? She looks as if she might know." Sure enough, when he came back a few minutes later, your attention was turned to the stranger. She wrote something on the back of an old Métro ticket (the solution, most probably) and you put it away in your purse, perhaps next to the diploma. You seemed to him eager and hopeful and excited, as if you could see a better prospect than the six-day modeling job or the solution to your immediate difficulty or even a new kind of life—better than any you could offer each other. He walked straight out to the street, without stopping to speak, and came home. He refused to say a word to me, changed his clothes, and left for the day. A day like any other, in a way.

When the commercial ended we sat in silence. Then Anny got up and began to clear away the dessert no one had finished. The debate on hepatitis was now deeply engaged. Six or seven men who seemed to be strangling in their collars and ties sat at a round table, all of them yelling. The program presenter had lost control of the proceedings. One man shouted above the others that there were people who sincerely wanted to be ill. No amount of money poured into the health services could cure their muddled impulses. Certain impulses were as bad as any disease. Anny, still standing, cut off the sound (her only impatient act), and we watched the debaters opening and shutting their mouths. Speaking quietly, she said that life was a long duty, not a gift. She often thought about her own and had come to the conclusion that only through reincarnation would she ever know what she might have been or what important projects she might have carried out. Her temperament is Swiss. When she speaks, her genes are speaking.

I always expected you to come back for the suitcase. It is still here, high up on a shelf in the hall closet. We looked inside—not to pry but in case you had packed something perishable, such as a sandwich. There was a jumble of cotton garments and a pair of worn sandals and some other dresses I had pinned and basted for you, which you never sewed. Or sewed with such big, loose stitches that the seams came apart. (I had also given you a warm jacket with an embroidered Tyrolian-style collar. I think you had it on when you left.) On that first day, when I made the remark that your suitcase weighed next to nothing, you took it for a slight and said, "I am small and I wear small sizes." You looked about fifteen and had poor teeth and terrible posture.

The money you owed came to a hundred and fifty thousand francs, counted the old way, or one thousand five hundred in new francs. If we include accumulated inflation, it should amount to a million five hundred thousand; or, as you would probably prefer to put it, fifteen thousand. Inflation ran for years at 12 percent, but I think that over decades it must even out to 10. I base this on the fact that in 1970 half a dozen eggs were worth one new franc, while today one has to pay nine or ten. As for interest, I'm afraid it would be impossible to work out after so much time. It would depend on the year and the whims of this or that bank. There have been more prime ministers and annual budgets and unpleasant announcements and changes in rates than I can count. Actually, I don't want interest. To tell the truth, I don't want anything but the pleasure of seeing you and hearing from your own lips what you are proud of and what you regret.

My only regret is that my husband never would let me help in the restaurant. He wanted me to stay home and create a pleasant refuge for him and look after Robert. His own parents had slaved in their bistro, trying to please greedy and difficult people who couldn't be satisfied. He did not wish to have his only child do his homework in some dim corner between the bar and the kitchen door. But I could have been behind the bar, with Robert doing homework where I could keep an eye on him (instead of in his room with the door locked). I might have learned to handle cash and checks and work out tips in new francs and I might have noticed trouble coming, and taken steps.

I sang a lot when I was alone. I wasn't able to read music, but I could imitate anything I heard on records that suited my voice, airs by Delibes or Massenet. My muses were Lily Pons and Ninon Vallin. Probably you have never heard of them. They were before your time and are traditionally French.

According to Anny and Marie-Laure, fashions of the seventies are on the way back. Anny never buys herself anything, but Marie-Laure has several new outfits with softly draped skirts and jackets with a peasant motif—not unlike the clothes I gave you. If you like, I could make over anything in the suitcase to meet your social and professional demands. We could take up life where it was broken off, when I was on my knees, pinning the hem. We could say simple things that take the sting out of life, the way Anny does. You can come and fetch the suitcase any day, at any time. I am up and dressed by half past seven, and by a quarter to nine my home is ready for unexpected guests. There is an elevator in the building now. You won't have the five flights to climb. At the entrance to the building you will find a digit-code lock. The number that lets you in is K630. Be careful not to admit anyone who looks suspicious or threatening. If some stranger tries to push past just as you open the door, ask him what he wants and the name of the tenant he wishes to see. Probably he won't even try to give you a credible answer and will be scared away.

The concierge you knew stayed on for another fifteen years, then retired to live with her married daughter in Normandy. We voted not to have her replaced. A team of cleaners comes in twice a month. They are never the same, so one never gets to know them. It does away with the need for a Christmas tip and you don't have the smell of cooking permeating the whole ground floor, but one misses the sense of security. You may remember that Mme. Julie was alert night and day, keeping track of everyone who came in and went out. There is no one now to bring mail to the door, ring the doorbell, make sure we are still alive. You will notice the row of mailboxes in the vestibule. Some of the older tenants won't put their full name on the box, just their initials. In their view, the name is no one's business. The postman knows who they are, but in summer, when a substitute makes the rounds, he just throws their letters on the floor. There are continual complaints. Not long ago, an intruder tore two or three boxes off the wall.

You will find no changes in the apartment. The inventory you once signed could still apply, if one erased the words "electric heater." Do not send a check—or, indeed, any communication. You need not call to make an appointment. I prefer to live in the expectation of hearing the elevator stop at my floor and then your ring, and of having you tell me you have come home.

IN PLAIN SIGHT

ON THE first Wednesday of every month, sharp at noon, an air-raid siren wails across Paris, startling pigeons and lending an edge to the midday news. Older Parisians say it has the tone and pitch of a newsreel sound track. They think, Before the war, and remember things in black-and-white. Some wonder how old Hitler would be today and if he really did escape to South America. Others say an order to test warning equipment was given in 1956, at the time of the Suez crisis, and never taken off the books. The author Henri Grippes believes the siren business has to do with high finance. (High finance, to Grippes, means somebody else's income.) The engineer who installed the alert, or his estate, picks up a dividend whenever it goes off.

At all events, it is punctual and reliable. It keeps Grippes's rare bursts of political optimism in perspective and starts the month off with a mixture of dread and unaccountable nostalgia: the best possible mixture for a writer's psyche. The truth is he seldom hears it, not consciously. When he was still young, Grippes got in the habit of going to bed at dawn and getting up at around three in the afternoon. He still lives that way—reading and writing after dark, listening to the radio, making repetitive little drawings on a pad of paper, watching an American rerun on a late channel, eating salted hard-boiled eggs, drinking Badoit or vodka or champagne (to wash the egg down) or black coffee so thickly sweetened that it can act as a sedative.

He is glad to have reached an age when no one is likely to barge in at all hours announcing that salt is lethal and sugar poison. (Vodka and champagne are considered aids to health.) Never again will he be asked to hand over the key to his apartment, as a safety measure, or receive an offer to sleep in the little room off the kitchen and never get in the way. In fact, offers to cherish him seem to be falling off. The last he remembers was put forward a few years ago, when his upstairs neighbor, Mme. Parfaire (Marthe), suggested her constant presence would add six years to his life. Since then, peace and silence. Put it a different way: Who cares if Grippes slips into the darkest pocket of the universe, still holding a bitten egg? Now when Mme. Parfaire (no longer "Marthe") meets Grippes in an aisle of the Inno supermarket, on Rue du Départ, she stares at his hairline. Grazing his shopping cart with her own, she addresses a cold apology to "Monsieur," never "Henri." Years of admiration, of fretting about his health and, who knows, of love of a kind have been scraped away; yet once she had been ready to give up her smaller but neater flat, her wider view over Boulevard du Montparnasse, the good opinion of her friends (proud widows, like herself), for the sake of moving downstairs and keeping an eye on his diet. She also had a strong desire to choose all his clothes, remembering and frequently bringing up his acquisition of a green plastic jacket many years before.

What went wrong? First, Grippes didn't want the six extra years. Then, she handed him a final statement of terms at the worst point of the day, five past three in the afternoon—a time for breakfast and gradual wakening. He was barely on his feet, had opened the front door to pick up mail and newspapers left on the mat (the concierge knows better than to ring), and came face-to-face with Marthe. She stood with her back to the stair rail, waiting—he supposed—for Allégra, her small white dog, to catch up. Allégra could be heard snuffling and clawing her way along the varnished steps. There was an elevator now, tucked inside the stairwell, the cost shared by all, but Mme. Parfaire continued to climb. She knew a story about a woman who had been trapped in a lift of the same make and had to be rescued by firemen.

Grippes made his first tactless remark of the day, which was "What do you want?" Not even a civilized, if inappropriate, "I see you're up early" or "It's going to be a fine day." He took in the contents of her nylon-net shopping bag: a carton of milk, six Golden Delicious E.C. standard-size Brussels-approved apples, six eggs, ditto, and a packet of Autumn Splendor tinted shampoo.

The tilt of her dark head, her expression—brooding and defiant—brought to mind the great Marie Bell and the way she used to stand here and there on the stage, in the days when "tragedienne" still had meaning. He thought of Racine, of Greek heroines; he hoped he would not be obliged to think about Corneille and the cruel dilemma of making a simple choice. His friend seemed to him elegantly turned out—skirt length unchanged for a decade or so, Chanel-style navy jacket, of the kind favored by wives of politicians in the last-but-one right-wing government. Only her shoes, chosen for comfort and stair climbing, maintained a comfortable, shambling Socialist appearance, like a form of dissent.

As for Grippes, he had on heavy socks, jogging pants, a T-shirt with tiger-head design (a gift), and a brown cardigan with bone buttons, knitted by Mme. Parfaire two Christmases before. She examined the tiger head, then asked Grippes if he had given any more thought to their common future. He knew what she was talking about, she said, a bit more sharply. They had been over it many times. (Grippes denies this.) The two-apartment system had not worked out. She and Grippes had not so much grown apart as failed to draw together. She knew he would not quit the junk and rubble of his own dwelling: His creative mind was rooted in layers of cast-off books, clothes, and chipped ashtrays. For that reason, she was willing to move downstairs and share his inadequate closets. (No mention this time of keeping to the little room off the kitchen, he noticed.) Whenever he wanted to be by himself, she would go out and sit on a bench at the Montparnasse-Stanislas bus stop. For company, she would bring along one of his early novels, the kind critics kept begging him to reread and learn from. At home, she would put him on a memory-preserving, mental-stimulation regime, with plenty of vegetable protein; she would get Dr. Planche to tell her the true state of Grippes's hearing (would he be stone deaf very soon?) and to report on the vital irrigation of Grippes's brain (clogged, sluggish, running dry?). Her shy Allégra would live in harmony with his cats—an example for world leaders. Finally, she would sort his mail, tear up the rubbish, answer the telephone and the doorbell, and treat with sensitivity but firmness the floating shreds of his past.

Grippes recalls that he took "floating shreds" to mean Mme.

Obier (Charlotte), and felt called on to maintain a small amount of exactitude. It was true that Mme. Obier—dressed in layers of fuzzy black, convinced that any day was the ninth of September, 1980, and that Grippes was expecting her for tea—could make something of a nuisance of herself on the fourth-floor landing. However, think of the sixties, when her flowing auburn hair and purple tights had drawn cheers in the Coupole. In those days, the Coupole was as dim as a night train and served terrible food. Through a haze rising from dozens of orders of fried whiting, the cheapest dish on the menu, out-of-town diners used to search for a glimpse of Sartre or Beckett and try to make out if the forks were clean. Now the renovated lighting, soft but revealing, showed every crease and stain on the faces and clothes of the old crowd. Sociable elderly ladies, such as Mme. Obier, no longer roamed the aisles looking for someone to stand them a drink but were stopped at the entrance by a charming person holding a clipboard and wanting to know if they were expected. There might be grounds for calling her a shred, Grippes concluded, but she was the fragment of a rich cultural past. If she seemed on in years, it was only by comparison with Grippes. Not only did Grippes look younger than his age but from early youth he had always preferred the company of somewhat older women, immovably married to someone else. (His reasons were so loaded with common sense that he did not bother to set them out.) Unfortunately, he had never foreseen the time when his friends, set loose because the husband had died or decamped to Tahiti, would start to scamper around Paris like demented ferrets. Having preceded Grippes in the field of life, they maintained an advance, beating him over the line to a final zone of muddle, mistakes, and confused expectations.

The only sound, once Grippes had stopped speaking to Mme. Parfaire, was the new elevator, squeaking and grinding as if it were very old. Allégra waddled into view and stood with her tongue hanging. Mme. Parfaire turned away and prepared to resume her climb. He thought he heard, "I am not likely to forget this insult." It occurred to him, later, that he ought to have carried her net bag the extra flight or invited her in for coffee; instead, he had stepped back and shut the door. Where she was concerned, perhaps he had shut it forever. What had she offered him, exactly? An unwelcome occupation of his time and space, true, but something else that he might have done well to consider: unpaid, unending, unflagging, serious-minded female service. Unfortunately, his bulwark against doing the sensible thing as seen through a woman's mind had always been to present a masculine case—which means to say densely hedged and full of dead-end trails—and get behind it. Anyone taking up residence in his routine seemed to have got there by mistake or been left behind by a previous tenant. The door to Grippes stood swinging on its hinges, but it led to a waiting room.

The difference between Mme. Parfaire and other applicants, he thinks now, was in her confident grasp on time. She never mislaid a day or a minute. On her deathbed she will recall that on the day when Grippes made it plain he had no use for her it became legal for French citizens to open a bank account abroad. The two events are knotted together in her version of late-twentieth-century history. She will see Grippes as he was, standing in the doorway, no shoes on his feet, unshaven, trying to steal a glance at the headlines while she tries to make him a present of her last good years. But then that dishonoring memory will be overtaken by the image of a long, cream-colored envelope bearing the address of a foreign, solvent bank. On that consoling vision she will close her eyes.

No one dies in Grippes's novels; not anymore. If Mme. Parfaire were to be carried down the winding staircase, every inch of her covered up (the elevator is too small to accommodate a stretcher), her presence would remain as a blur and a whisper. Like Grippes, she will be buried from the church of Notre Dame des Champs. Mme. Parfaire as a matter of course, Grippes because he has left instructions. One has to be buried from somewhere. He will attend her funeral, may even be asked to sit with the relatives. Her family was proud of that long literary friendship—that was how they saw it. (She had composed many optimistic poems in her day.) They used to save reviews of his books, ask him courteous questions about sales and inspiration. Leaving the church, narrowing his eyes against the bright street, he will remember other lives and other shadows of existence, some invented, some recalled. The other day he noticed that his father and grandfather had merged into a single strong-minded patriarch. It took a second of strict appraisal to pull them apart.

Grippes needs help with the past now. He wants a competent assistant who can live in his head and sort out the archives. A resident inspiring goddess, a muse of a kind, created by Grippes, used to keep offhand order, but her interest in him is slackening. She has no name, no face, no voice, no visible outline, yet he believes in her as some people do in mermaids or pieces of jade or a benevolent planet or simple luck. Denied substance, she cannot answer the door and stave off bores and meddlers. Mme. Parfaire would have dealt with them smartly, but Grippes made a choice between real and phantom attendance on that lamentable afternoon, when he talked such a lot before shutting the door. The talking was unlike him. He had sounded like any old fool in Montparnasse telling about the fifties and sixties. No wonder she has not encouraged him to speak ever since.

Before turning in at dawn he closes the shutters and heavy curtains. The gurgling of pigeons stirred by early light is a sound he finds disgusting. They roost on stone ledges under his windows, even on the sills, drawn by Mme. Parfaire's impulsive scattering of good things to eat. Instead of trying to look after Grippes, she now fosters urban wildlife—her term for this vexation. Some of the scraps of crumbled piecrust and bits of buttered bread she throws from her dining-room windows shower over the heads or umbrellas of people waiting in cinema queues directly below. The rest seem to be meant for Grippes. Actually, the custom of dropping small quantities of rubbish from a height is becoming endemic in his part of Paris. Not everyone has the nerve to splash paint or call a bus driver names or scribble all over a parking ticket before tearing it into strips, but to send flying a paper filter of wet coffee grounds and watch it burst on the roof of someone else's car is a way of saying something.

On the same floor as Mme. Parfaire lives a public prosecutor, lately retired. His windows face the courtyard at the back of the house. He began to show signs of unappeasable distress in the early eighties, when a Socialist government, newly elected, abolished the guillotine, making his profession less philosophical and more matter-of-fact. For years now he has been heaving into the courtyard anything he suddenly hates the sight of. He has thrown out a signed photograph of a late president of the Court of Appeal, a biography of Maria Callas and all her early records, an electric coffee grinder, a saucepan containing fish soup, and the lid of the saucepan. Grippes's kitchen window seems to be in the line of fire, depending upon whether the prosecutor makes a good strong pitch or merely lets things drop. Only this morning a great blob of puréed carrots struck the kitchen windowsill, spattering the panes and seriously polluting a pot of thyme.

Every so often Grippes types a protest and posts it downstairs in the lobby: "Residents are again reminded that it is against the law to feed pigeons and to throw foodstuff and household objects out of windows. Further incidents will be reported to the proper authorities. Current legislation allows for heavy fines." Occasionally, an anonymous neighbor will scrawl "Bravo!" but most seem resigned. Crank behavior is a large part of city life. Filling the courtyard with rubbish serves to moderate the prosecutor's fidgety nerves. (Yesterday, Mme. Parfaire dropped two stale croissants, smeared with plum jam, on the stone ledge, street-side. Grippes had to use a long-handled stiff broom to get them off.)

Sometimes a long ribbon of sound unwinds in his sleep. He can see strangers, whole families, hurrying along an unknown street. Everything is gray-on-gray—pavement, windows, doorways, faces, clothes—under an opaque white sky. A child turns toward the camera—toward Grippes, the unmoving witness. Then, from a level still deeper than the source of the scene rises an assurance that lets him go on sleeping: None of this is real. Today is the first Wednesday of a new month. It is sharp noon, the air-raid signal is calling, and he has wrapped up the call in a long dream.

Later, at breakfast, he will remember war movies he saw in his youth. Paris, about to be liberated, shone like polished glass. Nazi holdouts, their collars undone, gave themselves up to actors wearing white bandages and looking reliable. A silvery plane, propeller-driven, droned inland from the Channel. The wisecracking bomber crew was like an element of the dense postwar American mystery, never entirely solved. Films are the best historical evidence his waking mind can muster: He spent much of that indistinct war on his grandfather's farm, where his parents had sent him so he would get enough to eat and stay out of trouble. His father was a schoolmaster in a small town. He believed in General de Gaulle—a heretical faith, severely punished. The young Henri had been warned to keep his mouth shut, never to draw notice to his parents—to behave as if he had none, in fact.

As it happened, his grandfather enjoyed a life of stealth and danger, too. The components were not safe houses and messages from London but eggs, butter, meat, flour, cream, sugar, and cheese. One afternoon Henri left the farm for good, dragging a suitcase with a broken lock, and got on a slow, dirty train to Paris. It was near the end of events. Everyone connected to the recent government was under arrest or in flight, and everything in Germany was on fire. Only the police were the same. It seems to him now that he actually heard the air-raid siren in Paris for the first time a long while later. Nevertheless, it still belongs to black-and-white adventures—in a habitual dream, perhaps to peace of a kind.

Two days ago, the lift stalled between floors. No one was injured, but since then everyone has had to use the stairs, as repairmen settle in for a long stay: They play radios, eat ham sandwiches, drink red wine out of plastic bottles. Except for Mme. Parfaire, residents have lost the habit of climbing. Grippes and the public prosecutor, meeting by chance on the day of the mishap, took a long time and needed a rest on each landing. The prosecutor wanted to know what Grippes made of the repeated break-ins at Mme. Parfaire's apartment: three in less than two months, the most recent only last night. Two hooded men had entered easily, in spite of the triple-point safety lock and chain, and had departed without taking anything, daunted by the sight of Mme. Parfaire, draped in a bedsheet like a toga and speaking impressively.

Grippes thought it sounded like a dream but did not say so. His attention at the time of the intrusion had been fixed on a late-night documentary about army ants. He supposed the roar and rattle of ants waging war, amplified a hundred thousand times, must have overtaken the quieter sound of thieves hammering down a door. The prosecutor changed the subject, and mentioned a man who had pried open a CD player with a chisel and some scissors, letting out a laser beam that killed him instantly. "I believe it cut him in two," the prosecutor said. Between the third and fourth floors he brought up the nuclear threat. The nuclear threat lately had slipped Grippes's mind, which seemed to be set on pigeons. According to the prosecutor, luxurious shelters had been got ready for the nation's leaders. The shelters were stocked with frozen food of high quality and the very best wines. There were libraries, screening rooms, and gymnasiums, handsomely equipped. One could live down there for years and never miss a thing. A number of attractive rooms were set aside for valuable civil servants, even those in retirement. It was clear from the prosecutor's tone and manner that no place of safety existed for Grippes.

Since that conversation, Grippes had been taking stock of his means of escape and deliverance. The siren may start to wail on the wrong day, at an inconvenient time—signaling an emergency. A silvery plane, propeller-driven, follows its own clear-cut shadow over the heart of Paris. Perhaps they are shooting a film and want the panic in the streets to look authentic. Without waiting to find out, Grippes will crowd his cats into a basket and make for the nearest entrance to the Montparnasse-Bienvenüe Métro station, just after the newsstand and the couscous restaurant. He will buy newspapers to spread on the concrete platform so he can sit down, and a few magazines to provide a harmless fantasy life until the all-clear.

He can imagine the dull lights down there, the transistors barking news bulletins and cheap rock, the children walking on his outstretched legs and dropping cookie crumbs on the cats. He will have just a small amount of cash, enough to appease a mugger. "It's all I have in the world," he hears himself telling the lout holding the blunt side of a knife to his neck. (For the moment, the lout is only playing.) They take banknotes, gold jewelry, credit cards, leather garments: So Grippes has been told. It would be best to dress comfortably but not too well, though it would be worst of all to look down-and-out. Perhaps, then, in worn but quite decent trousers and the apple-green plastic jacket he acquired a whole generation ago. The jacket might seem too decorative for these leaden times—it is the remnant of a more frivolous decade, worth nothing now except to collectors of vintage plastic tailoring, but it is not shabby. Shabbiness arouses contempt in the world outlook of a goon. It brings on the sharp edge of the knife.

Late last night, Grippes hauled the jacket out of the relief-agency collection bag where it had been stored for years. (Every winter, he forgets to have the bag picked up, then spring comes, and the agency closes down.) He wiped it with a soapy sponge and hung it to dry at the kitchen window. The jacket looked fresh and verdant on its wire hanger. He wondered why he had ever wanted to give it away, except to alleviate the distress that the sight of it caused Mme. Parfaire. There must have been a moment of great haste, as well as generosity, at one time, for he had forgotten to search the pockets for stray coins and had almost parted with a newspaper clipping that looked important, a silver coffee spoon, and an unopened letter addressed to himself. On the back of the envelope, an earlier Grippes had written "Utopia Reconsidered," as well as a few scribbled sentences he could not make out. He found his spectacles, put them on but still needed a magnifying glass. I used to write much smaller, he decided.

The words seemed to be the start of a stern and rueful overview of the early eighties, the first years of a Socialist government trying hard to be Socialist. As far as Grippes could recall, he had never completed the piece. He slit the envelope, using the handle of the silver spoon, and discovered a leaflet of the sort circulated by some penniless and ephemeral committee, devoted to the rights of pedestrians or cyclists or rent-paying tenants or put-upon landlords. (Tenants, this time.) Along with the leaflet was a handwritten appeal to Henri Grippes, whose published works and frequent letters to newspapers had always taken the side of the helpless.

"Well, it was a long time ago," said Grippes aloud, as if the sender of the letter were sitting on the edge of a kitchen chair, looking pale and seedy, smoking nervously, displaying without shame (it was too late for shame) his broken nails and unwashed hair. He fixed on Grippes nearsighted gray eyes, waiting for Grippes to show him the way out of all his troubles. The truth is, Grippes announced to this phantom, that you have no rights. You have none as a tenant, none in your shaky, ill-paid job, none when it comes to applying to me.

Perhaps by now the man had come into a fortune, owned a string of those run-down but income-producing hotels crammed with illegal immigrants. Or had lost his employment and been forced into early and thread-bare retirement. Perhaps he was an old man, sitting down to meals taken in common in some beige-painted institutional dining room with soft-hued curtains at the windows. A woman said to be the oldest living person in France had frequently been shown in such a place, blowing out birthday candles. She smoked one cigarette a day, drank one glass of port, had known van Gogh and Mistral, and remembered both vividly. Perhaps the writer of the letter, in his frustration and despera-tion, had joined an extremist movement, right or left, and gone to live in exile. Wherever he was, whatever he had become, he had never received a kind or a decent or even a polite reply from Henri Grippes.

Grippes felt humbled suddenly. Political passion and early love had in common the promise of an unspoilt future, within walking distance of any true believer. Once, Grippes had watched Utopia rising out of calm waters, like Atlantis emerging, dripping wet and full of promise. He had admired the spires and gleaming windows, the marble pavements and year-round unchanging sun-rise; had wondered if there was room for him there and what he would do with his time after he moved in. The vision had oc-curred at eight in the evening on Sunday, the tenth of May, 1981, and had vanished immediately—lost, as one might have read at the time, in the doctrinal night. At the same moment, a com-puterized portrait of François Mitterrand, first Socialist president of the Fifth Republic, had unrolled on the television screen, in the manner of a window blind. Grippes had felt stunned and de-ceived. Only a few hours before, he had cast his vote for precisely such an outcome. Nevertheless, he had been expecting a win-dow blind bearing the leaner, more pensive features of the Con-servative incumbent. He had voted for a short list of principles, not their incarnation. In fact, he resented having to look at any face at all.

Utopia was a forsaken city now, bone-dry, the color of scorched newsprint. Desiccated, relinquished, it announced a plaintive message. Grippes placed the newspaper clipping, the coffee spoon, and the envelope side by side on the kitchen table, like exhibits in a long and inconclusive trial. He turned the spoon over and read the entwined initials of his ex-friend upstairs. Short of calling Mme. Parfaire to ask if she had ever, in any year, slipped a spoon into his pocket, he had no means of ever finding out how it had got there. Had he taken it by mistake? Only the other day, buying a newspaper, he had left it on the counter and started to walk off with another man's change. The vendor had called after him. Grippes had heard him telling the stranger, "It's Henri Grippes." Respect for authors, still a factor of Paris life, meant that the other man looked chastened as he accepted his due, as if he were unworthy of contemporary literature. Apologizing, Grippes had said it was the first time he had ever done an absentminded thing. Now he wondered if he ought to turn out the kitchen drawers and see how much in them really belonged to other people.

The spoon recalled to Grippes abundant, well-cooked meals, the dining room upstairs with the rose velvet portières, the Japanese screen, the brass urn filled with silk chrysanthemums, the Sèvres coffee service on the buffet. It was a room that contained at all hours a rich and comforting smell of leek-and-potato soup. Often, as Grippes sopped up the last of the sauce of a blanquette or daube, his hostess would describe enthusiastic reviews she had just read of books by other people, citing phrases he might appreciate or even want to use, such as "Cyclopean vision" (a compliment, apparently) or "the superstructure of essential insincerity," another sort of flattery. Later, she might even coax him into watching a literary talk show. Grippes, digesting, would stare hard at false witnesses, plagiarists, ciphers, and mountebanks, while Mme. Parfaire praised their frank and open delivery and the way they wore their hair. When, occasionally, there was a woman on hand, prepared to be interviewed and to announce in the same straightforward manner, "Well, you see, in *my* book . . . ," Mme. Parfaire would make the comment that the women all looked the same, had terrible legs, and lacked the restraint and distinction of men. Whatever misleading reply Grippes might give when she asked what he was writing—"writing *about*" was the actual phrase—she responded with unflagging loyalty: "At least you always know what you are trying to say."

The night of Utopia had alarmed her, and Grippes had been no help. He remembered now that the tenth of May, 1981, had begun blue and bright and ended under a black cloudburst. It was possible that God, too, had expected a different face on the window blind. Rain had soaked through the hair and shoes of revelers in the Place de la Bastille. Older voters, for whom the victory was the first in a lifetime, wept in the downpour. Their children responded to the presence of television cameras by dancing in puddles. The public prosecutor called Mme. Parfaire to say that Soviet tanks would be rumbling under her windows before next Tuesday. She arrived at Grippes's door, asking for reassurance and an atlas: She thought she might emigrate. Unfortunately, all the foreign maps were unwelcoming and un-French. Grippes offered champagne, so they could toast the death of the middle classes. The suggestion struck her as heartless and she went away.

Left to himself, he had turned his back on the damp, bewildering celebration and stood at the window, imagining tanks, champagne in his hand and disquiet in his mind. He had helped create the intemperate joy at the Place de la Bastille, but why? Out of a melancholy habit of political failure, he supposed. He had never for a moment expected his side to win. By temperament, by choice, by the nature of most of his friendships, by the cross-grained character of his profession he belonged in perpetual opposition. Now a devastating election result had made him a shareholder in power, morally responsible for cultural subsidies to rock concerts and nuclear testing in the Pacific. Unfolding a copy of the left-wing daily *Libération* on the No. 82 bus, which runs through diehard territory, no longer would signify a minority rebellion but majority complacency. Grippes was nearing the deep end of middle age. For the first time he had said to himself, "I'm getting old for all this."

Down in the street, as if the tenth of May were a Sunday like any other, cinema lines straggled across the sidewalk to the curb. It seemed to Grippes that it was not the usual collection of office workers and students and pickpockets and off-duty waiters but well-to-do dentists from the western regions of the city and their wives. The dentists must have known the entrepreneurial game was up and had decided to spend their last loose cash on an action movie set in Hong Kong. Grippes pictured them sorted into ranks, surging along the boulevard, the lights of pizza restaurants flashing off their glasses in red and green. Their women kept pace, swinging gold-link necklaces like bicycle chains. There were no shouts, no threats, no demands but just the steady trampling that haunts the nights of aging radicals. Wistfully, as if it were now lost forever, Grippes had recalled the warm syncopation of a leftist demo: "Step! Shuffle! Slogan! Stop!/Slogan! Step! Shuffle!" How often had he drummed that rhythm of progress on the windowsill before he was forced by the sting of tear gas to pull his head in!

Having set his dentists on the march, Grippes no longer knew what to do with them. Perhaps they could just disband. Those to whom the temptation of power had given an appetite could stroll into Chez Hansi, at the corner of Rue de Rennes, and enjoy one last capitalist-size lobster, chosen from the water tank. What about Grippes? What was he supposed to be doing on the night of change? Reminded of the steadfast role of the writer in a restless universe, he had poured himself another glass and settled down to compose a position piece, keeping it as cloudy and imprecise as his native talent could make it. Visions of perfection emerge and fade but the written word remains to trip the author who runs too fast for his time or lopes alongside at not quite the required pace. He wrote well into the night, first by hand, then after removing a new version of "Residents are again reminded . . ." made about fifteen typed revisions of the final text.

The next day (as Grippes recalls the affair), he deposited his article at the editorial offices of the most distinguished newspaper in France. The paper had printed it, finally; not on page 1, with nationwide debate to follow, but on 2, the repository for unsolicited opinions too long-winded to pass as letters to the editor. Under a provocative query of some kind—say, "What Tomorrow for Social Anthropology?"—page 2 allowed the escape of academic steam and measured the slightly steadier breathing of neomonetarists, experts on regional history, and converts to Islam. A footnote in italics described the correspondent's sphere of activity. Grippes's label, "man of letters," confirmed his status and showed he was no amateur thinker.

His entry looked a bit crowded, wedged next to that of a dealer in rare stamps calling for parasocialist reform of his profession, but Grippes was pleased with the two-column heading: "UTOPIA OUR WAY." "Now that the profit motive has been lopped from every branch of French cultural life," his piece began, "or so it would seem," it continued, thus letting Grippes off some future charge of having tried to impoverish the intelligentsia, "surely." After "surely" came a blank: Page 2 had let the sentence die. In the old days (Grippes's prose had suddenly resumed), when he went to the cinema there was room for his legs. He could place a folded jacket under the seat without having it stuck with gum. Ice cream, sold by a motherly vendor, tasted of real vanilla. Audiences at musical comedies had applauded every dance number: Think of "Singin' in the Rain." In spite of a flat cloud of tobacco smoke just overhead one seemed to breathe the purest of air. Now the capacious theater under Grippes's windows had been cut into eight small places, each the size of a cabin in a medium-haul jet. Whenever he ventured inside, he expected to be told to fasten his seat belt and handed a plastic tray. Subtitles of foreign films dissolved in a white blur, while spoken dialogue could not be heard at all— at least not by Grippes. He knew that twenty-three years of right-wing government had produced a sullen and mumbling generation, but he felt sure that a drastic change, risen from the very depths of an ancient culture, would soon restore intelligible speech.

This was the clipping Grippes had found in the jacket pocket, along with the spoon. He had to admit it was not perfect. Nothing had ever been done about the cinemas. The part about rising from the depths made the 1981 Socialist plan of intentions sound like wet seaweed. Still, he had staked a claim in the serene confusion of the era and had launched an idea no one could fault, except owners of theater chains. And "man of letters" had remained on the surface of the waters, a sturdy and recognizable form of literary plant life, still floating.

Last June, it rained every night. Wet clouds soaked up the lights of Montparnasse and gave them back as a reddish glow. At about three o'clock one morning, mild, moist air entered the room where Grippes sat at his writing desk. A radio lying flat on the table played soft jazz from a studio in Milan. A cat slept under the desk lamp. Moths beat about inside the red shade. Grippes got up, pulled a book from the shelf, blew the dust off, found the entry he wanted: "19th June—Half past one. Death of my father. One can say of him, 'It is only a man, mayor of a poor, small village,' and still speak of his death as being like that of Socrates. I do not reproach myself for not having loved him enough. I reproach myself for not having understood him."

It so happened that Grippes had just written the last two sentences: same words, same order. Almost instantly, the cartoon drawing of a red-bearded man wearing a bowler hat had come to mind—not his father, of course. It was Jules Renard, dead for some eighty-odd years. Renard's journals had been admired and quoted often by Grippes's father, dead now for more than forty. A gust of night wind pushed the window wide and brought it to with a bang. The cat made a shuddering movement but continued to sleep. Lifted on a current, a moth escaped and flew straight back.

Grippes wondered how much of the impressive clutter in his imagination could still be called his own. "At least you always know what you are trying to say" referred to unexamined evidence. Like his father, like Jules Renard, he had been carried along the slow, steady swindle of history and experience. Pictures taken along the way, the untidy record, needed to be rearranged by category or discarded for good. Thousands of similar views had been described in hundreds of thousands of manuscripts and books, some in languages Grippes had never heard of. His inspiring goddess had found nothing better to dish up in the middle of the night than another man's journal, and even had the insolence to pass it off as original.

A few notches away from Milan, the BBC was proposing a breakdown in human relations. (Cressida to Quentin: "My cab is waiting, Quentin. I think everything has been said." Quentin to Cressida: "Am I allowed to say good-bye?" Door slams. High heels on pavement. Taxi loud, then fading. Quentin to no one: "Good-bye. I shan't be denied the last word."} The departure of Cressida was stirring dejection or inducing sleep across Europe and the Middle East, down the length of Africa, in India, in Singapore, in Western Samoa. Men and women who had their own cats, moths, lamps, wet weather, and incompetent goddesses were pondering Quentin's solitude and wondering if it served him right. Grippes pulled a large pad of writing paper from under the sleeping cat and drew a picture of a London taxi. He drew a Citroën of the 1960s and a Peugeot with an elegant dashboard, out of some fifties film, set on the Riviera, then a tall Renault, all right angles, built in the thirties, still driven in the early forties by black-market operators and the police. He shaded it black and put inside three plainclothes inspectors.

The Renault, as it approached his grandfather's house, could be heard from a distance; it was a quiet afternoon, close to the end of things. The car turned into the courtyard. Two of the men got out. They had on city suits, felt hats, and creaky, towny shoes. Young Henri's grandfather stood in the kitchen with his arms folded, saying nothing. The two men looked in the usual places, turned up loose tiles and floorboards, slashed all the pillows and bolsters with a knife. As a rule, these sudden descents ended with everyone around the kitchen table. His grandmother had already wiped the faded red-and-blue oilcloth and had begun to set out the thick glasses and plates.

From the window of his wrecked bedroom (the gashed pillows lay on the floor) Henri watched the strangers digging aimlessly outside. They were clumsy, did not know how to use a spade, how to lift the clods they turned up. He saw them the way his grandfather did, cheap and citified. But to hold the law cheap one needed to have powerful allies. His grandfather had physical strength and a native ability to hoard and hang on. The men threw the spades down and came back to the house. Their shoes left mud prints across the kitchen floor and up the scrubbed stairs.

In his room, which had been his father's, down and feathers rose and hovered with every approaching step. One of the visitors took a book down from a shelf over the washstand. He made the remark that he had never seen books in a bedroom before. Henri started to answer that these were his father's old schoolbooks but remembered he was not to mention him. The man gave the book a shake, releasing a shower of handwritten verse: Henri's father's adolescent attempts to reconcile the poetry of sexual craving, as explained in literature, with barnyard evidence. The second stranger offered Henri an American cigarette. It was too precious to waste in smoke. He placed it carefully behind an ear and waited for the question. It was, "Where would you put a lot of contraband money, if you had any?"

Henri answered, truthfully, "In the dark and in plain sight."

They went down to the cellar, pushing Henri, and ran beams of yellow light along racks of wine and shelves of preserved fruit in earthenware crocks. About every fourth crock was stuffed with gold coins and bank-notes. The men asked for a crate. Henri, promoted to honest member of the clan, checked the count. He droned, ". . . four, five, six . . ." while his grandmother wept. A few minutes later, he and his grandmother watched his grandfather being handcuffed and hustled into the Renault. He could have brained all three men with his locked hands but held still.

"Forgive me," said Henri. "I didn't know it was down there."

"You had better be a long way from here before he gets back," his grandmother said.

"Won't they keep him, this time?"

"They'll work something out," she said, and dried her eyes.

Today Grippes was wakened abruptly at about eleven-thirty. Two policemen were at the door, wanting to know if he had heard anything suspicious during the night. There had been another incident concerning Mme. Parfaire. This time, the intruders had broken a Sèvres sugar bowl and threatened the dog. All Grippes could say was that the dog was nineteen years old and deaf and had certainly not taken the threat to heart. After they went away, he shuffled along the passage to the kitchen. The cats—a tabby and a young stray—ran ahead. (He swears they are the last.) The first things he saw were the jacket on its wire hanger and the soiled windowpanes. At a window across the court a woman, another early riser according to Grippes time, parted her curtains. She had nothing on except a man's shirt, unbuttoned. Standing between the flowery folds, she contemplated the sunless enclosure. (The cobblestones below are never dry, owing to a stopped drain. For years now tenants on the lower floors have been petitioning to have the drain repaired. Their plight gets not much sympathy from occupants of upper stories, who suffer less inconvenience or accept the miasma of mosquitoes and flies in summer as the triumph of nature over urban sterility.)

Having observed that nothing had changed during the night, the woman closed the curtains with a snap and (Grippes supposes) went back to bed. He had seen her before, but never at that hour. The entrance to her building must be somewhere around the corner. He cannot place it on a map of Montparnasse, which is half imagined anyway. For a time he supposed she might be a hostess in a club along the boulevard, a remnant of the Jazz Age, haunted by the ghost of Josephine Baker. The other day, he noticed that the club had become an ordinary restaurant, with a fixed-price menu posted outside. Inquiring, he was told the change had come about in the seventies.

He put some food down for the cats, plugged in the coffeemaker, and started to clean the window and stone sill. The jacket got in the way, so he removed it from its wire hanger and put it on. The movement of opinion in the building concerning Mme. Parfaire and pigeons has turned against Grippes. She seems to be suffering from a wasting and undiagnosed fatigue of the nerves—so such ailments of the soul are called. Some think the two men who keep breaking in are nephews impatient to come into their inheritance. They hope to scare her to death. Others believe they are professional thugs hired by the nephews. The purpose is to induce her to sell her apartment and move into a residence for the elderly and distribute the money before she dies. Greedy families, the avoidance of death duties are among the basic certainties of existence. No one can quite believe Grippes does not know what is taking place upstairs. Perhaps he is in on the plot. Perhaps he is lazy or just a coward or slumps dead drunk with his head on the typewriter. Perhaps he doesn't care.

Whispered echoes, mean gossip, ignorant assurances reach his ears. Mme. Parfaire when she descends the curving staircase clutches the banister, halts every few steps, wears a set expression. Strands of hair hang about her face. Even in her wan and precarious condition, popular sentiment now runs, she finds enough strength to open her windows and sustain the life of pigeons. Garbage-throwing, once seen as a tiresome and dirty habit, has become a demonstration of selflessness. Once a week she totters across the Seine to the Quai de la Mégisserie and buys bird food laced with vitamin E, to ensure the pigeons a fulfilled and fertile span. "Residents are again reminded..." is viewed with a collective resentment. Not long ago an anonymous hand wrote "Sadist!"—meaning Grippes.

Yesterday he happened to see her in the lobby, talking in a low voice to a neighbor holding a child by the hand. She fell silent as Grippes went by. The women watched him out of sight; he was sure of it, could feel the pressure of their staring. He heard the child laugh. It was clear to him that Mme. Parfaire was doped to the eyes on tranquilizers, handed out in Paris like salted peanuts, but he could not very well put up a notice saying so. People would shrug and say it was none of their business. Would they be interested in a revelation such as "Mme. Parfaire wants to spend her last years living in sin, or quasi-sin, or just in worshipful devotion, with the selfish and disagreeable and eminently unmarriageable Henri Grippes"? True, but it might seem unlikely. As an inventor of a great number of imaginary events Grippes knows that the reflection of reality is no more than just that; it is as flat and mute as a mirror. Better to sound plausible than merely in touch with facts.

He had just finished cleaning the window when the siren began to wail. He looked at the electric clock on top of the refrigerator: twelve sharp. Today was a Wednesday, the first one of the month. He could hear two distinct tones and saw them as lines across the sky: a shrill humming—a straight, thin path— and a lower note that rose and dipped and finally descended in a slow spiral, like a plane shot down. Five minutes later, as he sat drinking coffee, the warning started again. This time, the somewhat deeper note fell away quite soon; the other, more piercing cry streamed on and on, and gradually vanished in the bright day.

Stirring his coffee, using his old friend's spoon, Grippes thought of how he might put a stop to the pigeon business, her nighttime fantasies, and any further possibility of being wakened at an unacceptable hour. He could write a note inviting himself to lunch, take it upstairs, and slide it under her door. He would go as he was now, with the plastic jacket on top of a bathrobe. Serving lunch would provide point and purpose to her day. It would stop the downward spiral of her dreams. Composing the note (it would require tact and skill) might serve to dislodge "Residents are again reminded . . ." from his typewriter and his mind.

He pictured, with no effort, a plate of fresh mixed seafood with mayonnaise or just a bit of lemon and olive oil, saw an omelette folded on a warmed plate, marinated herring and potato salad, a light ragout of lamb kidneys in wine. He could see himself proceeding along the passage and sitting down on the chair where, as a rule, he spent much of every night and writing the note. From the window, if he leaned a bit to the right, he would see the shadow of the Montparnasse tower, and the office building that had replaced the old railway station with its sagging wooden floor. Only yesterday, he started to tell himself—but no. A generation of Parisians had never known anything else.

An empty space, as blank and infinite as the rectangle of sky above the court, occurred in his mind, somewhere between the sliding of the invitation—if one could call it that—under her door and the materialization of the omelette. The question was, How to fill the space? He was like someone reading his own passport, the same information over and over. "My dearest Marthe," he began (going back to the first thing). "Don't you think the time has come . . ." But *he* did not think it. "Remember that woman who said she had known van Gogh?" She had no connection to their dilemma. It was just something he liked to consider. "You should not be living alone. Solitude is making you . . ." No; above all, not that. "Perhaps if one of those nephews of yours came to live with you . . ." They were all married, some with grown children. "I think it only fair to point out that I never once made a firm . . ." The whine of the dissembler. "The occasional meal taken together..." The thin edge. "You know very well that it is against the law to feed pigeons and that increasingly heavy fines..."

How good it would be to lie down on the kitchen floor and let his inspiring goddess kneel beside him, anxiously watching for the flutter of an eyelid, as he deftly lifts her wallet. As it turns out, there is nothing in it except "Residents are again reminded..." Like Grippes, like the prosecutor, like poor Marthe, in a way, his goddess is a victim of the times, hard up for currency and short of ideas, ideas of divine origin in particular. She scarcely knows how to eke out the century. Meanwhile, she hangs on to "Residents are again...," hoping (just as Grippes does) that it amounts to the equivalent of the folding money every careful city dweller keeps on hand for muggers.

SCARVES, BEADS, SANDALS

AFTER three years, Mathilde and Theo Schurz were divorced, without a mean thought, and even Theo says she is better off now, married to Alain Poix. (Or "Poids." Or "Poisse." Theo may be speaking the truth when he says he can't keep in mind every facet of the essential Alain.) Mathilde moved in with Alain six months before the wedding, in order to become acquainted with domestic tedium and annoying habits, should they occur, and so avoid making the same mistake (marriage piled onto infatuation) twice. They rented, and are now gradually buying, a two-bedroom place on Rue Saint-Didier, in the Sixteenth Arrondissement. In every conceivable way it is distant from the dispiriting south fringe of Montparnasse, where Theo continues to reside, close to several of the city's grimmest hospitals, and always under some threat or other—eviction, plagues of mice, demolition of the whole cul-de-sac of sagging one-story studios. If Theo had been attracted by her "physical aspect"—Mathilde's new, severe term for beauty—Alain accepts her as a concerned and contributing partner, intellectually and spiritually. This is not her conclusion. It is her verdict.

Theo wonders about "spiritually." It sounds to him like a moist west wind, ready to veer at any minute, with soft alternations of sun and rain. Whatever Mathilde means, or wants to mean, even the idea of the partnership should keep her fully occupied. Nevertheless, she finds time to drive across Paris, nearly every Saturday afternoon, to see how Theo is getting along without her. (Where is Alain? In close liaison with a computer, she says.) She brings Theo flowering shrubs from the market on Île de la Cité, still hoping to enliven the blighted yard next to the studio, and food in covered dishes—whole, delicious meals, not Poix leftovers—and fresh news about Alain.

Recently, Alain was moved to a new office—a room divided in two, really, but on the same floor as the minister and with part of an eighteenth-century fresco overhead. If Alain looks straight up, perhaps to ease a cramp in his neck, he can take in Apollo—just Apollo's head—watching Daphne turn into a laurel tree. Owing to the perspective of the work, Alain has the entire Daphne—roots, bark, and branches, and her small pink Enlightenment face peering through leaves. (The person next door has inherited Apollo's torso, dressed in Roman armor, with a short white skirt, and his legs and feet.) To Theo, from whom women manage to drift away, the situation might seem another connubial bad dream, but Alain interprets it as an allegory of free feminine choice. If he weren't so pressed with other work, he might write something along that line: an essay of about a hundred and fifty pages, published between soft white covers and containing almost as many colored illustrations as there are pages of print; something a reader can absorb during a weekend and still attend to the perennial border on Sunday afternoon.

He envisions (so does Mathilde) a display on the "recent non-fiction" table in a Saint-Germain-des-Prés bookshop, between stacks of something new about waste disposal and something new about Jung. Instead of writing the essay, Alain applies his trained mind and exacting higher education to shoring up French values against the Anglo-Saxon mud slide. On this particular Saturday, he is trying to batter into proper French one more untranslatable expression: "air bag." It was on television again the other day, this time spoken by a woman showing black-and-white industrial drawings. Alain would rather take the field against terms that have greater resonance, are more blatantly English, such as "shallow" and "bully" and "wishful thinking," but no one, so far, has ever tried to use them in a commercial.

So Mathilde explains to Theo as she sorts his laundry, starts the machine, puts clean sheets on the bed. She admires Theo, as an artist—it is what drew her to him in the first place—but since becoming Mme. Poix she has tended to see him as unemployable. At an age when Theo was still carrying a portfolio of drawings up and down and around Rue de Seine, looking for a small but adventurous gallery to take him in, Alain has established a position in the cultural apparat. It may even survive the next elections: He is too valuable an asset to be swept out and told to find a job in the private sector. Actually, the private sector could ask nothing better. Everyone wants Alain. Publishers want him. Foreign universities want him. Even America is waiting, in spite of the uncompromising things he has said about the hegemony and how it encourages well-bred Europeans to eat pizza slices in the street.

Theo has never heard of anybody with symbolic imagery, or even half an image, on his office ceiling outlasting a change of government. The queue for space of that kind consists of one ravenous human resource after the other, pushing hard. As for the private sector, its cultural subdivisions are hard up for breathing room, in the dark, stalled between floors. Alain requires the clean horizons and rich oxygen flow of the governing class. Theo says none of this. He removes foil from bowls and dishes, to see what Mathilde wants him to have for dinner. What can a Theo understand about an Alain? Theo never votes. He has never registered, he forgets the right date. All at once the campaign is over. The next day familiar faces, foxy or benign, return to the news, described as untested but eager to learn. Elections are held in spring, perhaps to make one believe in growth, renewal. One rainy morning in May, sooner or later, Alain will have to stack his personal files, give up Apollo and Daphne, cross a ministry courtyard on the first lap of a march into the private sector. Theo sees him stepping along cautiously, avoiding the worst of the puddles. Alain can always teach, Theo tells himself. It is what people say about aides and assistants they happen to know, as the astonishing results unfold on the screen.

Alain knows Theo, of course. Among his mixed feelings, Alain has no trouble finding the esteem due to a cultural bulwark: Theo and his work have entered the enclosed space known as "time-honored." Alain even knows about the Poids and Poisse business, but does not hold it against Theo; according to Mathilde, one no longer can be sure when he is trying to show he has a sense of humor or when he is losing brain cells. He was at the wedding, correctly dressed, suit, collar, and tie, looking distinguished—something like Braque at the age of fifty, Alain said, but thinner, taller, blue-eyed, lighter hair, finer profile. By then they were at the reception, drinking champagne under a white marquee, wishing they could sit down. It was costing Mathilde's father the earth—the venue was a restaurant in the Bois de Boulogne—but he was so thankful to be rid of Theo as a son-in-law that he would have hired Versailles, if one could.

The slow, winding currents of the gathering had brought Theo, Alain, and Mathilde together. Theo with one finger pushed back a strayed lock of her hair; it was reddish gold, the shade of a persimmon. Perhaps he was measuring his loss and might even, at last, say something embarrassing and true. Actually, he was saying that Alain's description—blue-eyed, etc.—sounded more like Max Ernst. Alain backtracked, said it was Balthus he'd had in mind. Mathilde, though not Alain, was still troubled by Theo's wedding gift, a botched painting he had been tinkering with for years. She had been Mme. Poix for a few hours, but still felt responsible for Theo's gaffes and imperfections. When he did not reply at once, she said she hoped he did not object to being told he was like Balthus. Balthus was the best-looking artist of the past hundred years, with the exception of Picasso.

Alain wondered what Picasso had to do with the conversation. Theo looked nothing like him: He came from Alsace. He, Alain, had never understood the way women preferred male genius incarnated as short, dark, and square-shaped. "Like Celtic gnomes," said Theo, just to fill in. Mathilde saw the roses in the restaurant garden through a blur which was not the mist of happiness. Alain had belittled her, on their wedding day, in the presence of her first husband. Her first husband had implied she was attracted to gnomes. She let her head droop. Her hair slid over her cheeks, but Theo, this time, left it alone. Both men looked elsewhere—Alain because tears were something new, Theo out of habit. The minister stood close by, showing admirable elegance of manner—not haughty, not familiar, careful, kind, like the Archbishop of Paris at a humble sort of funeral, Theo said, thinking to cheer up Mathilde. Luckily, no one overheard. Her mood was beginning to draw attention. Many years before, around the time of the Algerian War, a relative of Alain's mother had married an aunt of the minister. The outer rims of the family circles had quite definitely overlapped. It was the reason the minister had come to the reception and why he had stayed, so far, more than half an hour.

Mathilde was right; Theo must be losing brain cells at a brisk rate now. First Celtic gnomes, then the Archbishop of Paris; and, of course, the tactless, stingy, offensive gift. Alain decided to smile, extending greetings to everyone. He was attempting to say, "I am entirely happy on this significant June day." He was happy, but not entirely. Perhaps Mathilde was recalling her three years with Theo and telling herself nothing lasts. He wished Theo would do something considerate, such as disappear. A cluster of transparent molecules, the physical remainder of the artist T. Schurz, would dance in the sun, above the roses. Theo need not be dead—just gone.

"Do you remember, Theo, the day we got married," said Mathilde, looking up at the wrong man, by accident intercepting the smile Alain was using to reassure the minister and the others. "Everybody kept saying we had made a mistake. We decided to find out how big a mistake it was, so in the evening we went to Montmartre and had our palms read. Theo was told he could have been an artist but was probably a merchant seaman. His left hand was full of little shipwrecks." She may have been waiting for Alain to ask, "What about you? What did your hand say?" In fact, he was thinking just about his own. In both palms he had lines that might be neat little roads, straight or curved, and a couple of spidery stars.

At first, Theo had said he would give them a painting. Waiting, they kept a whole wall bare. Alain supposed it would be one of the great recent works; Mathilde thought she knew better. Either Alain had forgotten about having carried off the artist's wife or he had decided it didn't matter to Theo. That aside, Theo and Theo's dealer were tight as straitjackets about his work. Mathilde owned nothing, not even a crumpled sketch saved from a dustbin. The dealer had taken much of the earlier work off the market, which did not mean Theo was allowed to give any away. He burned most of his discards and kept just a few unsalable things in a shed. Speaking of his wedding gift, Theo said the word "painting" just once and never again: He mentioned some engravings— falling rain or falling snow—or else a plain white tile he could dedicate and sign. Mathilde made a reference to the empty wall. A larger work, even unfinished, even slightly below Theo's dealer's exacting standards, would remind Mathilde of Theo for the rest of her life.

Five days later, the concierge at Rue Saint-Didier took possession of a large oil study of a nude with red hair—poppy red, not like Mathilde's—prone on a bed, her face concealed in pillows. Mathilde recognized the studio, as it had been before she moved in and cleaned it up. She remembered the two reproductions, torn out of books or catalogues, askew on the wall. One showed a pair of Etruscan figures, dancing face-to-face, the other a hermit in a landscape. When the bed became half Mathilde's, she took them down. She had wondered if Theo would mind, but he never noticed—at any rate, never opened an inquiry.

"Are you sure this thing is a Schurz?" said Alain. Nothing else bothered him. He wondered, at first, if Theo had found the picture at a junk sale and had signed it as a joke. The true gift, the one they were to cherish and display, would come along later, all the more to be admired because of the scare. But Theo never invented jokes; he blundered into them.

"I am not that woman," Mathilde said. Of course not. Alain had never supposed she was. There was the crude red of the hair, the large backside, the dirty feet, and then the date—"1979"— firm and black and in the usual place, to the right of "T. Schurz." At that time, Mathilde was still reading translations of Soviet poetry, in love with a teacher of Russian at her lycée, and had never heard of "T. Schurz." In saying this, Alain showed he remembered the story of her life. If she'd had a reason to forgive him, about anything, she would have absolved him on the spot; then he spoiled the moment by declaring that it made no difference. The model was not meant to be anyone in particular.

Mathilde thought of Emma, Theo's first long-term companion (twelve years), but by '79 Emma must have been back in Alsace, writing cookery books with a woman friend. Julita (six years) fit the date but had worn a thick yellow braid down her back. She was famous for having tried to strangle Theo, but her hands were too small—she could not get a grip. After the throttling incident, which had taken place in a restaurant, Julita had packed a few things, most of them Theo's, and moved to the north end of Paris, where she would not run into him. Emma left Theo a microwave oven, Julita a cast-iron cat, standing on its hind legs, holding a tray. She had stolen it from a stand at the flea market, Theo told Mathilde, but the story sounded unlikely: The cat was heavy to lift, let alone be fetched across a distance. Two people would have been needed; perhaps one had been Theo. Sometimes, even now, some old friend from the Julita era tells Theo that Julita is ill or hard up and that he ought to help her out. Theo will say he doesn't know where she is or else, yes, he will do it tomorrow. She is like art taken off the market now, neither here nor there. The cat is still in the yard, rising out of broken flowerpots, empty bottles. Julita had told Theo it was the one cat that would never run away. She hung its neck with some amber beads Emma had overlooked in her flight, then pocketed the amber and left him the naked cat.

When Mathilde was in love with Theo and jealous of women she had never met, she used to go to an Indian shop, in Montparnasse, where first Emma, then Julita had bought their flat sandals and white embroidered shifts and long gauzy skirts, black and pink and indigo. She imagined what it must have been like to live, dress, go to parties, quarrel, and make up with Theo in the seventies. Emma brushed her brown hair upside down, to create a great drifting mane. A woman in the Indian store did Julita's braid, just because she liked Julita. Mathilde bought a few things, skirts and sandals, but never wore them. They made her look alien, bedraggled, like the Romanian gypsy women begging for coins along Rue de Rennes. She did not want to steal from a market or fight with Theo in bistros. She belonged to a generation of women who showed a lot of leg and kept life smooth, tight-fitting, close-woven. Theo was right: She was better off with Alain.

Still, she had the right to know something about the woman she had been offered as a gift. It was no good asking directly; Theo might say it was a journalist who came to tape his memoirs or the wife of a Lutheran dignitary or one of his nieces from Alsace. Instead, she asked him to speak to Alain; out of aesthetic curiosity, she said, Alain acquired the facts of art. Theo often did whatever a woman asked, unless it was important. Clearly, this was not. Alain took the call in his office; at that time, he still had a cubicle with a bricked-up window. Nobody recalled who had ordered the bricks or how long ago. He worked by the light of a neon fixture that flickered continually and made his eyes water. Summoned by an aide to the minister, on propitious afternoons by the minister himself (such summonses were more and more frequent), he descended two flights, using the staircase in order to avoid a giddy change from neon tube to the steadier glow of a chandelier. He brought with him only a modest amount of paperwork. He was expected to store everything in his head.

Theo told Alain straight out that he had used Julita for the pose. She slept much of the day and for that reason made an excellent model: was never tired, never hungry, never restless, never had to break off for a cigarette. The picture had not worked out and he had set it aside. Recently he had looked at it again and decided to alter Julita from the neck up. Alain thought he had just been told something of consequence; he wanted to exchange revelations, let Theo know he had not enticed Mathilde away but had merely opened the net into which she could jump. She had grabbed Theo in her flight, perhaps to break the fall. But Alain held still; it would be unseemly to discuss Mathilde. Theo was simply there, like an older relative who has to be considered and mollified, though no one knows why. There was something flattering about having been offered an unwanted and unnecessary explanation; few artists would have bothered to make one. It was as though Theo had decided to take Alain seriously. Alain thanked him.

Unfortunately, the clarification had made the painting even less interesting than it looked. Until then, it had been a dud Schurz but an honest vision. The subject, a woman, entirely womanly, had been transfigured by Schurz's reactionary visual fallacy (though honest, if one accepted the way his mind worked) into a hefty platitude; still, it was art. Now, endowed with a name and, why not, an address, a telephone number, a social-security number, and a personal history, Theo's universal statement dwindled to a footnote about Julita—second long-term companion of T. Schurz, first husband of Mathilde, future first wife of Alain Poix. A white tile with a date and a signature would have shown more tact and common sense.

All this Alain said to Mathilde that night, as they ate their dinner next to the empty wall. Mathilde said she was certain Theo had gone to considerable trouble to choose something he believed they would understand and appreciate and that would enhance their marriage. It was one of her first lies to Alain: Theo had gone out to the shed where he kept his shortfalls and made a final decision about a dead loss. Perhaps he guessed they would never hang it and so damage his reputation, although as a rule he never imagined future behavior more than a few minutes away. Years ago, in a bistro on Rue Stanislas, he had drawn a portrait of Julita on the paper tablecloth, signed and dated it, torn it off, even made the edges neat. It was actually in her hands when he snatched it back, ripped it to shreds, and set the shreds on fire in an ashtray. It was then that Julita had tried to get him by the throat.

Yesterday, Friday, an April day, Theo was awakened by a hard beam of light trained on his face. There was a fainter light at the open door, where the stranger had entered easily. The time must have been around five o'clock. Theo could make out an outline, drawn in gray chalk: leather jacket, close-cropped head. (Foreign Legion deserter? Escaped prisoner? Neo-Nazi? Drugs?) He spoke a coarse, neutral, urban French—the old Paris accent was dying out—and told Theo that if he tried to move or call he, the intruder, might hurt him. He did not say how. They all watch the same programs, Theo told himself. He is young and he repeats what he has seen and heard. Theo had no intention of moving and there was no one to call. His thoughts were directed to the privy, in the yard. He hoped the young man would not take too long to discover there was nothing to steal, except a small amount of cash. He would have told him where to find it, but that might be classed as calling out. His checkbook was in a drawer of Emma's old desk, his bank card behind the snapshot of Mathilde, propped on the shelf above the sink. The checkbook was no good to the stranger, unless he forced Theo to sign all the checks. Theo heard him scuffing about, heard a drawer being pulled. He shut his eyes, opened them to see the face bent over him, the intent and watchful expression, like a lover's, and the raised arm and the flashlight (probably) wrapped in one of Mathilde's blue-and-white tea towels.

He came to in full daylight. His nose had bled all over the pillows, and the mattress was sodden. He got up and walked quite steadily, barefoot, over the stones and gravel of the yard; returning to the studio, he found some of yesterday's coffee still in the pot. He heated it up in a saucepan, poured in milk, drank, and kept it down. Only when that was done did he look in a mirror. He could hide his blackened eyes behind sunglasses but not the raw bruise on his forehead or his swollen nose. He dragged the mattress outside and spread it in the cold April sunlight. By four o'clock, Mathilde's announced arrival time—for it seemed to him today could be Saturday—the place was pretty well cleaned up, mattress back on the bed, soiled bedclothes rolled up, pushed in a corner. He found a banquet-size tablecloth, probably something of Emma's, and drew it over the mattress. Only his cash had vanished; the checkbook and bank card lay on the floor. He had been attacked, for no reason, by a man he had never seen before and would be unable to recognize: His face had been neutral, like his voice. Theo turned on the radio and, from something said, discovered this was still Friday, the day before Mathilde's habitual visiting day. He had expected her to make the mattress dry in some magical and efficient, Mathilde-like way. He kept in the shed a couple of sleeping bags, for rare nights when the temperature fell below freezing. He got one of them out, gave it a shake, and spread it on top of the tablecloth. It would have to do for that night.

Today, Saturday, Mathilde brought a meal packed in a black-and-white bag from Fauchon: cooked asparagus, with the lemon-and-oil sauce in a jar, cold roast lamb, and a gratin of courgettes and tomatoes—all he has to do is turn on Emma's microwave—a Camembert, a round loaf of that moist and slightly sour bread, from the place on Rue du Cherche-Midi, which reminds Schurz of the bread of his childhood, a carton of thick cream, and a bowl of strawberries, washed and hulled. It is too early for French strawberries. These are from Spain, picked green, shipped palely pink, almost as hard as radishes, but they remind one that it is spring. Schurz barely notices seasons. He works indoors. If rain happens to drench the yard when he goes outside to the lavatory, he puts on the Alpine beret that was part of his uniform when he was eighteen and doing his military service.

Mathilde, moving out to live with Alain, took with her a picture of Theo from that period, wearing the beret and the thick laced-up boots and carrying the heavy skis that were standard issue. He skied and shot a rifle for eighteen months, even thought he might have made it a permanent career, if that was all there was to the Army. No one had yet fallen in love with him, except perhaps his mother. His life was simple then, has grown simpler now. The seasons mean nothing, except that green strawberries are followed by red. Weather means crossing the yard bareheaded or covered up.

Mathilde has noticed she is starting to think of him as "Schurz." It is what his old friends call Theo. This afternoon, she had found him looking particularly Schurz-like, sitting on a chair he had dragged outside, drinking tea out of a mug, with the string of the tea bag trailing. He had on an overcoat and the regimental beret. He did not turn to the gate when she opened it or get up to greet her or say a word. Mathilde had to walk all round him to see his face.

"My God, Schurz, what happened?"

"I tripped and fell in the dark and struck my head on the cat."

"I wish you'd get rid of it," she said.

She took the mug from his hands and went inside, to unpack his dinner and make fresh tea. The beret, having concealed none of the damage, was useless now. He removed it and hung it rakishly on the cat, on one ear. Mathilde returned with, first, a small folding garden table (her legacy), then with a tray and teacups and a teapot and a plate of sliced gingerbread, which she had brought him the week before. She poured his tea, put sugar in, stirred it, and handed him the cup.

She said, "Theo, how long do you think you can go on living here, alone?" (It was so pathetic, she rehearsed, for Alain. Theo was like a child; he had made the most absurd attempt at covering up the damage, and instead of putting the mattress out to dry he had turned the wet side down and slept on top of it, in a sleeping bag. Who was that famous writer who first showed signs of senility and incontinence on a bridge in Rome? I kept thinking of him. Schurz just sat there, like a guilty little boy. He caught syphilis when he was young and gave it to Emma; he said it was from a prostitute, in Montmartre, but I believe it was a married woman, the wife of the first collector to start buying his work. He can't stay there alone now. He simply can't. His checkbook and bank card were lying next to the trash bin. He must have been trying to throw them away.)

Her picture had been on the floor, too, the one taken the day she married Theo. Mathilde has a small cloud of red-gold hair and wears a short white dress and a jacket of the eighties, with shoulders so wide that her head seems unnaturally small, like a little ball of reddish fluff. Theo is next to her, not too close. He could be a relative or a family friend or even some old crony who heard the noise of the party and decided to drop in. The photograph is posed here, in the yard. One can see a table laden with bottles, and a cement-and-stucco structure—the privy, with the door shut, for a change—and a cold-water tap and a bucket lying on its side. You had to fill the bucket and take it in with you.

Schurz never tried to improve the place or make it more comfortable. His reason was, still is, that he might be evicted at any time. Any month, any day, the police and the bailiffs will arrive. He will be rushed off the premises, with just the cast-iron cat as a relic of his old life.

"I'll tell you what happened," he said, showing her his mess of a face. "Yesterday morning, while I was still asleep, a man broke in, stole some money, and hit me with something wrapped in a towel. It must have been his flashlight."

(Oh, if you had heard him! she continued to prepare for Alain. A comic-strip story. The truth is he is starting to miss his footing and to do himself damage, and he pees in his sleep, like a baby. What kind of doctor do we need for him? What sort of specialist? A geriatrician? He's not really old, but there's been the syphilis, and he has always done confused and crazy things, like giving us that picture, when we really wanted a plain, pure tile.)

Schurz at this moment is thinking of food. He would like to be handed a plate of pork ragout with noodles, swimming in gravy; but nobody makes that now. Or stewed eels in red wine, with the onions cooked soft. Or a cutlet of venison, browned in butter on both sides, with a purée of chestnuts. What he does not want is clear broth with a poached egg in it, or any sort of a salad. When he first came to Paris the cheapest meals were the heartiest. His mother had said, "Send me a Paris hat," not meaning it; though perhaps she did. His money, when he had any, went to supplies for his work or rent or things to eat.

Only old women wore hats now. There were hats in store windows, dusty windows, in narrow streets—black hats, for funerals and widows. But no widow under the age of sixty ever bought one. Young women wore hats at the end of summer, tilted straw things, that they tried on just for fun. When they took the hats off, their hair would spring loose. The face, freed of shadow, took on a different shape, seemed fuller, unmysterious, as bland as the moon. There was a vogue for bright scarves, around the straw hats, around the hair, wound around the neck along with strings of bright beads, loosely coiled—sand-colored or coral or a hard kind of blue. The beads cast colored reflections on the skin of a throat or on a scarf of a different shade, like a bead diluted in water. Schurz and his friends ate cheap meals in flaking courtyards and on terraces where the tables were enclosed in a hedge of brittle, unwatered shrubs. Late at night, the girls and young women would suddenly find that everything they had on was too tight. It was the effect of the warm end-of-summer night and the food and the red wine and the slow movement of the conversation. It slid without wavering from gossip to mean gossip to art to life-in-art to living without boundaries. A scarf would come uncoiled and hang on the back of a chair or a twig of the parched hedge; as it would hang, later, over the foot of someone's bed. Not often Schurz's (not often enough), because he lived in a hotel near the Café Mabillon, long before all those places were renovated and had elevators put in and were given a star in some of the guidebooks. A stiff fine had to be paid by any client caught with a late-night visitor. The police used to patrol small hotels and knock on doors just before morning, looking for French people in trouble with the law and for foreigners with fake passports and no residence permits. When they found an extra guest in the room, usually a frantic young woman trying to pull the sheet over her face, the hotelkeeper was fined, too, and the tenant thrown out a few hours later. It was not a question of sexual morality but just of rules.

When dinner was almost finished, the women would take off their glass beads and let them drop in a heap among the ashtrays and coffee cups and on top of the wine stains and scribbled drawings. Their high-heeled sandals were narrow and so tight that they had to keep their toes crossed; and at last they would slip them off, unobserved, using first one foot, then the other. Scarfless, shoeless, unbound, delivered, they waited for the last wine bottle to be emptied and the last of the coffee to be drunk or spilled before they decided what they specifically wanted or exactly refused. This was not like a memory to Theo but like part of the present time, something that unfolded gradually, revealing mysteries and satisfactions.

In the studio, behind him, Mathilde was making telephone calls. He heard her voice but not her words. On a late Saturday afternoon, she would be recording her messages on other people's machines: He supposed there must be one or two to doctors, and one for the service that sends vans and men to take cumbersome objects away, such as a soiled mattress. Several brief inquiries must have been needed before she could find Theo a hotel room, free tonight, at a price he would accept and on a street he would tolerate. The long unbroken monologue must have been for Alain, explaining that she would be much later than expected, and why. On Monday she would take Theo to the Bon Marché department store and make him buy a mattress, perhaps a whole new bed. Now here was a memory, a brief, plain stretch of the past: Love apart, she had married him because she wanted to be Mme. T. Schurz. She would not go on attending parties and gallery openings as Schurz's young friend. Nobody knew whether she was actually living with him or writing something on his work or tagging along for the evening. She did not have the look of a woman who would choose to settle for a studio that resembled a garage or, really, for Schurz. It turned out she could hardly wait to move in, scrape and wax whatever he had in the way of furniture, whitewash the walls. She trained climbing plants over the wire fence outside, even tried to grow lemon trees in terra-cotta tubs. The tubs are still there.

She came toward him now, carrying the bag she had packed so that he would have everything he needed at the hotel. "Don't touch the bruise," she said, gently, removing the hand full of small shipwrecks. The other thing she said today, which he is bound to recall later on, was "You ought to start getting used to the idea of leaving this place. You know that it is going to be torn down."

Well, it is true. At the entrance to the doomed and decaying little colony there is a poster, damaged by weather and vandals, on which one can still see a depiction of the structure that will cover the ruin, once it has finally been brought down: a handsome biscuit-colored multipurpose urban complex comprising a library, a crèche, a couple of municipal offices, a screening room for projecting films about Bedouins or whales, a lounge where elderly people may spend the whole day playing board games, a theater for amateur and professional performances, and four low-rent work units for painters, sculptors, poets, musicians, and photographers. (A waiting list of two thousand names was closed some years ago.) It seems to Theo that Julita was still around at the time when the poster was put up. The project keeps running into snags—aesthetic, political, mainly economic. One day the poster will have been his view of the future for more than a third of his life.

Mathilde backed out of the cul-de-sac, taking care (he does not like being driven), and she said, "Theo, we are near all these hospitals. If you think you should have an X ray at once, we can go to an emergency service. I can't decide, because I really don't know how you got hurt."

"Not now." He wanted today to wind down. Mathilde, in her mind, seemed to have gone beyond dropping him at his hotel. He had agreed to something on Rue Delambre, behind the Coupole and the Dôme. She was on the far side of Paris, with Alain. As she drove on, she asked Theo if he could suggest suitable French for a few English expressions: "divided attention" and "hard-driven" and "matchless perfection," the latter in one word.

"I hope no one steals my Alpine beret," he said. "I left it hanging on the cat."

Those were the last words they exchanged today. It is how they said good-bye.

AFTERWORD

ABOUT THE STORIES

SAMUEL BECKETT, answering a hopeless question from a Paris newspaper—"Why do you write?"—said it was all he was good for: "*Bon qu'a ça.*" Georges Bernanos said that writing was like rowing a boat out to sea: The shoreline disappears, it is too late to turn back, and the rower becomes a galley slave. When Colette was seventy-five and crippled with arthritis she said that now, at last, she could write anything she wanted without having to count on what it would bring in. Marguerite Yourcenar said that if she had inherited the estate left by her mother and then gambled away by her father, she might never have written another word. Jean-Paul Sartre said that writing is an end in itself. (I was twenty-two and working on a newspaper in Montreal when I interviewed him. I had not asked him the *why* of the matter but the *what*.) The Polish poet Aleksander Wat told me that it was like the story of the camel and the Bedouin; in the end, the camel takes over. So that was the writing life: an insistent camel.

I have been writing or just thinking about things to write since I was a child. I invented rhymes and stories when I could not get to sleep and in the morning when I was told it was too early to get up, and I uttered dialogue for a large colony of paper dolls. Once, I was astonished to hear my mother say, "Oh, she talks to herself all the time." I had not realized that that kind of speech could be overheard, and, of course, I was not talking but supplying a voice. If I pin it down as an adult calling, I have lived in writing, like a spoonful of water in a river, for more than forty-five years. (If I add the six years I spent on a weekly newspaper—*The Standard*, dead and buried now—it comes to more than fifty. At that time, at home, I was steadily filling an old picnic hamper with notebooks and manuscripts. The distinction between journalism and fiction is the difference between without and within. Journalism recounts as exactly and economically as possible the weather in the street; fiction takes no notice of that particular weather but brings to life a distillation of all weathers, a climate of the mind. Which is not to say it need not be exact and economical: It is precision of a different order.)

I still do not know what impels anyone sound of mind to leave dry land and spend a lifetime describing people who do not exist. If it is child's play, an extension of make-believe—something one is frequently assured by persons who write about writing—how to account for the overriding wish to do that, just that, only that, and consider it as rational an occupation as riding a racing bike over the Alps? Perhaps the cultural attaché at a Canadian embassy who said to me "Yes, but what do you really do?" was expressing an adult opinion. Perhaps a writer is, in fact, a child in disguise, with a child's lucid view of grown-ups, accurate as to atmosphere, improvising when it tries to make sense of adult behavior. Peter Quennell, imagining Shakespeare, which means imagining the inexplicable, says that Shakespeare heard the secret summons and was sent along his proper path. The secret summons, the proper path, are what saints and geniuses hold in common. So do great writers, the semi-great, the good, the lesser, the dogged, the trudgers, and the merely anxious. All will discover that Paradise (everybody's future) is crisscrossed with hedges. Looking across a hedge to the green place where genius is consigned, we shall see them assembled, waiting to receive a collective reward if only they will agree on the source of the summons and the start of the proper path. The choir of voices floating back above the hedge probably will be singing, "*Bon qu'a ça,*" for want of knowing.

Janet Flanner, a great journalist of the age, the *New Yorker* correspondent in Paris for half a century, when on the brink of her eighties said she would rather have been a writer of fiction. The need to make a living, the common lot, had kept her from leaving something she did brilliantly and setting off for, perhaps, nowhere. She had published fiction, but not much and not satisfactorily. Now she believed her desire to write had been greater than her talent. Something was missing. My father, who was younger than Janet Flanner and who died in his early thirties, never thought of himself as anything but a painter. It may have been just as well—for him—that he did not go on to discover that he could never have been more than a dedicated amateur. He did not try and fail: In a sense, he never started out, except along the path of some firm ideal concerning life and art. The ideality required displacement; he went from England to Canada. His friends would recall him as levelheaded. No one ever heard him say that he had hoped for this or regretted that. His persona as an artist was so matter-of-fact, so taken for granted, so fully accepted by other people, that it was years until I understood what should have been obvious: He also had worked and gone to an office, before he became too ill to work at anything.

"What did you imagine you lived on?" said the family friend who had just let me know that my father was, after all, like most other people. He was with a firm that imported massive office furnishings of heavy wood and employed Englishmen.

Not every business wanted Englishmen. They had a reputation for criticizing Canada and failing to pull their weight. Quite often they just filled posts where they could do no real harm or they held generic job titles. It created a small inflation of inspectors, controllers, estimators, managers, assistants, counselors, and vice-presidents. Some hung on to a military rank from the First World War and went about as captains and majors. This minor imperial sham survived into the 1930s, when the Depression caved in on jobs and pseudo-jobs alike.

At eighteen I went to look at the office building, which was a gray stone house on Beaver Hall Hill. I remembered having been taken there, wearing my convent school uniform of black serge with a clerical collar, and being introduced to a man with an English accent. My father was inclined to show me off, and I was used to it. What I had retained of the visit (or so it came back) was a glowing lampshade made of green glass and a polished desk of some dark wood and a shadowy room, a winter room. It was on Beaver Hall Hill, around the same time, that another stranger stopped me in the street because I looked so startlingly like my late father. The possibility of a grown daughter cannot have been uppermost: I had vanished from Montreal at ten and come back on my own. The legal age for making such decisions was twenty-one: I had made it at eighteen and hoped no one would notice. A few people in Montreal believed I had died. It was a rumor, a floating story with no setting or plot, and it had ceased to affect anyone, by now, except for a family of French Canadians who had been offering prayers every year on my birthday.

Years later, in a town called Châteauguay, I would hear a trailing echo of the report. We had spent summers there and, once, two whole winters. The paralyzing winter wind blowing from the Châteauguay River was supposed to be restorative for the frail. My mother, who never had a cold, breathed it in and said, sincerely, "Isn't it glorious!" I came back to Châteauguay fifty years after taking the Montreal train for the last time, across the bridge, over the river. I came with a television crew from Toronto. We were looking at places where I had been as a child. At one address in Montreal we had found a bank. My first school had become a vacant lot. The small building where I had rented my first independent apartment, installed my own furniture, filled shelves with books and political pamphlets (as many as possible of them banned in Quebec), hung pictures, bought inch by inch from Montreal painters, then a flourishing school, was now a students' residence, run-down, sagging, neglected. I would never have returned alone to Châteauguay. It was the last place where we had lived as a family. When my father died, I was told he had gone to England and would be back before long, and I had believed it. A television unit is composed of strangers, largely indifferent, intent on getting the assignment over and a flight home. Their indifference was what I needed: a thick glass wall against the effects of memory.

I drew a map of the place—town, river, bridge, railway station, Catholic church, Anglican church, Protestant school, houses along a road facing the river, even candy store—and gave it to the producer. Everything was exact, except perhaps the Protestant school, which we forgot to look for. I saw the remembered house, still standing, though greatly altered. The candy store had been turned into a ramshackle coffee shop with a couple of pool tables, the Duranseau farm replaced by a sign, RUE DURANSEAU, indicating not much of a street. I recognized Dundee Cottage, now called something else, and Villa Crépina, where the Crépin boys had lived. They threw stones at other people's dogs, especially English dogs. Their low evergreen hedge along the sidewalk still put out red berries. I had once been warned not to touch the leaves or berries, said to be poisonous. I ate only small quantities of leaves, and nothing happened. They tasted like strong tea, also forbidden, and desirable on that account. There was a fairy-tale look of danger about the berries. One could easily imagine long fairy-tale sleep.

At the café I spoke to some men sitting huddled at a counter. The place had gone silent when we came in speaking English. I asked if anyone had ever heard of families I remembered—the Duranseaus, whose children I had played with, or the tenants of Dundee Cottage, whose name suddenly returned and has again dissolved, or another elderly neighbor—elderly in recollection, perhaps not even forty—who complained to my mother when I said "bugger" and complained again when I addressed him, quite cheerfully, as "old cock." I had no idea what any of it meant. None of the men at the counter looked my way. Their hunched backs spoke the language of small-town distrust. Finally, a younger man said he was a relation of the Crépins. He must have been born a whole generation after the time when I picked a poisoned leaf whenever I went by his great-uncle's hedge. He knew about our house, so radically modified now, because of some child, a girl, who had lived there a long time before and been drowned in the river. He gave me his great-aunt's telephone number, saying she knew about every house and stone and tree and vanished person. I never called. There was nothing to ask. Another English Canadian family with just one child had lived on the same side of the river. They had a much larger house, with a stone wall around it, and the drowned child was a boy. The Protestant school was named after him.

The fear that I had inherited a flawed legacy, a vocation without the competence to sustain it, haunted me from early youth. It was the reason why I tore up more than I saved, why I was slow to show my work except to one or two friends—and then not often. When I was twenty-one, someone to whom I had given two stories, just to read, handed them to a local literary review, and I was able to see what a story looked like surrounded by poetry and other fiction. I sent another story to a radio station. They paid me something and read it over the air, and I discovered what my own work could sound like in a different voice. After that I went on writing, without attempting to have anything published or asking for an opinion, for another six years. By then I was twenty-seven and becoming exactly what I did not want to be: a journalist who wrote fiction along some margin of spare time. I thought the question of writing or stopping altogether had to be decided before thirty. The only solution seemed to be a clean break and a try: I would give it two years. What I was to live on during the two years does not seem to have troubled me. Looking back, I think my entire concentration was fixed on setting off. No city in the world drew me as strongly as Paris. (When I am asked why, I am unable to say.) It was a place where I had no friends, no connections, no possibility of finding employment should it be necessary—although, as I reasoned things, if I was to go there with a job and salary in mind, I might as well stay where I was—and where I might run out of money. That I might not survive at all, that I might have to be rescued from deep water and ignominiously shipped home, never entered my head. I believed that if I was to call myself a writer, I should live on writing. If I could not live on it, even simply, I should destroy every scrap, every trace, every notebook, and live some other way. Whatever happened, I would not enter my thirties as a journalist—or an anything else—with stories piling up in a picnic hamper. I decided to send three of my stories to The New Yorker, one after the other. One acceptance would be good enough. If all three were refused, I would take it as decisive. But then I did something that seems contradictory and odd: A few days before I put the first story in the mail (I was having all the trouble in the world measuring if it was all right or rubbish), I told the newspaper's managing editor I intended to quit. I think I was afraid of having a failure of nerve. Not long before, the newspaper had started a pension plan, and I had asked if I could keep out of it. I had worked in an office where I had watched people shuffle along to retirement time, and the sight had scared me. The managing editor thought I was dissatisfied about something. He sent me to someone else, who was supposed to find out what it was. In the second office, I was told I was out of my mind; it was no use training women, they always leave; one day I would come creeping back, begging for my old job; all reporters think they can write; I had the audacity to call myself a writer when I was like an architect who had never designed a house. I went back to my desk, typed a formal resignation, signed it, and turned it in.

The first story came back from *The New Yorker* with a friendly letter that said, "Do you have anything else you could show us?" The second story was taken. The third I didn't like anymore. I tore it up and sent the last of the three from Paris.

Newspaper work was my apprenticeship. I never saw it as a drag or a bind or a waste of time. I had no experience and would never have been taken on if there had been a man available. It was still very much a man's profession. I overheard an editor say, "If it hadn't been for the goddamned war, we wouldn't have hired even one of the goddamned women." The appalling labor laws of Quebec made it easy for newspapers to ban unions. I received half the salary paid to men and I had to hear, frequently and not only from men, that I had "a good job, for a girl." Apparently, by holding on to it I was standing in the way of any number of qualified men, each with a wife and three children to support. That was the accepted view of any young female journalist, unless she was writing about hemlines or three-fruit jam.

My method of getting something on paper was the same as for the fiction I wrote at home: I could not move on to the second sentence until the first sounded true. True to what? Some arrangement in my head, I suppose. I wrote by hand, in pencil, made multitudinous changes, erased, filled in, typed a clean page, corrected, typed. An advantage to early practice of journalism is said to be that it teaches one how to write fast. Whatever I acquired did not include a measure of speed. I was always on the edge of a deadline, and even on the wrong side. Thinking back on my outrageous slowness, I don't know why I wasn't fired a dozen times. Or, rather, perhaps I do: I could write intelligible English, I was cheaper by half than a man, and I seemed to have an unending supply of ideas for feature stories and interviews, or picture stories to work on with a photographer. It was the era of photo features. I liked inventing them. They were something like miniature scripts; I always saw the pictures as stills from a film. I knew Quebec to the core, and not just the English-speaking enclaves of Montreal. I could interview French Canadians without dragging them into English, a terrain of wariness and ill will. I suggested stories on subjects I wanted to know more about and places I wanted to see and people I was curious to meet. Only a few were turned down, usually because they scraped against political power or the sensibilities of advertisers. I wrote feature stories from the beginning; was an occasional critic, until I gave a film an impertinent review and a string of theatres canceled a number of ads; wrote a weekly column, until the head of an agency protested about a short item that poked fun at a radio commercial, at which point the column was dropped. All this is a minor part of the social history of an era, in a region of North America at a political standstill.

I managed to carve out an astonishing amount of autonomy, saved myself from writing on the sappy subjects usually reserved for women, and was not sacked—not even when someone wrote to protest about "that Marxist enfant terrible." (It was not a safe time or place for such accusations.) My salary was modest, but whole families were living on less. I had amassed an enormous mental catalog of places and people, information that still seeps into my stories. Journalism was a life I liked, but not the one I wanted. An American friend has told me that when we were fifteen I said I intended to write and live in Paris. I have no recollection of the conversation, but she is not one to invent anecdotes based on hindsight. It is about all I have in the way of a blueprint. The rest is memory and undisputed evidence.

The impulse to write and the stubbornness needed to keep going are supposed to come out of some drastic shaking up, early in life.

There is even a term for it: the shock of change. Probably, it means a jolt that unbolts the door between perception and imagination and leaves it ajar for life, or that fuses memory and language and waking dreams. Some writers may just simply come into the world with overlapping vision of things seen and things as they might be seen. All have a gift for holding their breath while going on breathing: It is the basic requirement. If shock and change account for the rest of it, millions of men and women, hit hard and steadily, would do nothing but write; in fact, most of them don't. No childhood is immunized against disturbance. A tremor occurs underfoot when a trusted adult says one thing and means another. It brings on the universal and unanswerable wail "It's not fair!"—to which the shabby rejoinder that life isn't does nothing to restore order.

I took it for granted that life was tough for children and that adults had a good time. My parents enjoyed themselves, or seemed to. If I want to bring back a Saturday night in full summer, couples dancing on the front gallery (Quebec English for veranda), a wind-up gramophone and a stack of brittle records, all I need to hear is the beginning of "West End Blues." The dancers are down from Montreal or up from the States, where there is Prohibition. Prohibition would be out of the question in Quebec, although the rest of Canada enjoys being rather dry. I mention it just to say that there is no such thing as a Canadian childhood. One's beginnings are regional. Mine are wholly Quebec, English and Protestant, yes, but with a strong current of French and Catholic. My young parents sent me off on that current by placing me in a French convent school, for reasons never made plain. I remember my grandmother's saying, "Well, I give up." It was a singular thing to do and in those days unheard of. It left me with two systems of behavior, divided by syntax and tradition; two environments to consider, one becalmed in a long twilight of nineteenth-century religiosity; two codes of social behavior; much practical experience of the difference between a rule and a moral point.

Somewhere in this duality may be the exact point of the beginning of writing. All I am certain of is that the fragile root, the tentative yes or no, was made safe by reading. I cannot recall a time when I couldn't read; I do remember being read to and wanting to take the book and decipher it for myself. A friend of my parents recalled seeing my father trying to teach me the alphabet as I sat in a high chair. He held the book flat on a tray—any book, perhaps a novel, pulled off a shelf—and pointed out the capital letters. At a young age, apparently, I could translate at sight, English to French, reading aloud without stumbling. I was in no other way precocious: For years I would trail far behind other children in grasping simple sums or telling the time (I read the needles in reverse, five o'clock for seven) or separating left from right. I thought the eldest child in a family had been born last. At seven, I wondered why no one ever married some amiable dog. When my mother explained, I remained unenlightened. (The question possibly arose from my devoted reading of an English comic strip for children, *Pip and Squeak*, in which a dog and a penguin seem to be the parents of a rabbit named Wilfred.) I did not know there was a particular bodily difference between boys and girls until I was eight; I had thought it a matter of clothes, haircuts, and general temperament. At nine, I still looked for mermaids in the Châteauguay River. My father had painted for me a screen that showed mermaids, with long red hair, rising out of green waves. I had not yet seen an ocean, just lakes and rivers. The river across the road froze white in winter and thawed to a shade of clear golden brown. Apart from the error as to color, it seemed unlikely he would paint something untrue.

Four weeks after my fourth birthday, when I was enrolled as a boarder in my first school, run by a semi-cloistered order of teaching and missionary nuns, I brought, along with my new, strange, stiff, uncomfortable and un-English uniform and severely buttoned underclothes, some English storybooks from home. (I owned a few books in French, the gift of a doctor, a French Canadian specialist, who had attended me for a mastoid infection after scarlet fever and become a close friend of my parents. I was far too young to understand them. They were moral tales for older children, and even years later I would find them heavy going.) It was a good thing—to have books in English, that is—because I would hear and speak next to no English now, except in the summer holidays and at Christmas and Easter and on the odd weekend when I was fetched home. I always went back to school with new books, which had to be vetted; but no one knew any English and the nun who taught it could not speak it at all, and so the illustrations were scanned for decency and the books handed back, to be stored in the small night-table next to my bed.

I owe it to children's books—picture books, storybooks, then English and American classics—that I absorbed once and for all the rhythm of English prose, the order of words in an English sentence and how they are spelled. I was eight before I was taught to write and spell English in any formal way, and what I was taught I already knew. By then, English was irremovably entrenched as the language of imagination. Nothing supposed, daydreamed, created, or invented would enter my mind by way of French. In the paper-doll era, I made up a mishmash of English, French, and the mysterious Italian syllables in recordings of bel canto, which my mother liked and often played. I called this mixture "talking Marigold." Marigold faded soon, along with paper dolls. After that, for stories and storytelling there was only one sound.

The first flash of fiction arrives without words. It consists of a fixed image, like a slide or (closer still) a freeze frame, showing characters in a simple situation. For example, Barbara, Alec, and their three children, seen getting down from a train in the south of France, announced "The Remission." The scene does not appear in the story but remains like an old snapshot or a picture in a newspaper, with a caption giving all the names. The quick arrival and departure of the silent image can be likened to the first moments of a play, before anything is said. The difference is that the characters in the frame are not seen, but envisioned, and do not have to speak to be explained. Every character comes into being with a name (which I may change), an age, a nationality, a profession, a particular voice and accent, a family background, a personal history, a destination, qualities, secrets, an attitude toward love, ambition, money, religion, and a private center of gravity.

Over the next several days I take down long passages of dialogue. Whole scenes then follow, complete in themselves but like disconnected parts of a film. I do not deliberately invent any of this: It occurs. Some writers say they actually hear the words, but

I think "hear" is meant to be in quotation marks. I do not hear anything: I know what is being said. Finally (I am describing a long and complex process as simply as I can), the story will seem to be entire, in the sense that nearly everything needed has been written. It is entire but unreadable. Nothing fits. A close analogy would be an unedited film. The first frame may have dissolved into sound and motion (Sylvie and her mother, walking arm in arm, in "Across the Bridge") or turn out to be the end (Jack and Netta in Place Masséna, in "The Moslem Wife").

Sometimes one sees immediately what needs to be done, which does not mean it can be done in a hurry: I have put aside elements of a story for months and even years. It is finished when it seems to tally with a plan I surely must have had in mind but cannot describe, or when I come to the conclusion that it cannot be written satisfactorily any other way; at least, not by me. A few times, the slow transformation from image to fiction has begun with something actually glimpsed: a young woman reading an airmail letter in the Paris Métro, early in the morning; a man in Berlin eating a plate of cold cuts, next to a lace curtain that filters gray afternoon light; an American mother, in Venice, struggling to show she is having a fine time, and her two tactful, attentive adolescent children. Sometimes, hardly ever, I have seen clearly that a character sent from nowhere is standing in for someone I once knew, disguised as thoroughly as a stranger in a dream. I have always let it stand. Everything I start glides into print, in time, and becomes like a house once lived in.

I was taught the alphabet three times. The first, the scene with the high chair, I remember nothing about. The second time, the letters were written in lacy capitals on a blackboard—pretty-looking, decorative; nuns' handwriting of the time. Rows of little girls in black, hands folded on a desk, feet together, sang the letters and then, in a rising scale, the five vowels. The third time was at the Protestant school, in Châteauguay. The schoolhouse had only two rooms, four grades to each. I was eight: It had been noticed that I was beginning to pronounce English proper nouns with French vowel sounds. (I do it to this day, thinking "Neek" for "Nike," "Raybok" for "Reebok." The first time I saw Ribena, a fruit drink, advertised in the London Underground, I said, "What is Reebayna?" It is the only trace of that lacy, pretty, sung alphabet.) At my new school it was taken for granted that French and Catholic teaching had left me enslaved to superstition and wholly ignorant. I was placed with the six-year-olds and told to recite the alphabet. I pronounced *G* with its French vowel sound, something like an English *J*. Our teacher pulled down over the blackboard a large, illustrated alphabet, like a wide window blind. I stood in front of the blind and was shown the letter *G*. Above it a large painted hand held a tipped water jug, to which clung, suspended, a single drop. The sound of *G* was the noise the drop would make in a water glass: it would say *gug*.

"The sound of *G* is *gug*. Say it after me. *Gug*."

"*Gug*."

"Everyone, now. *Gug, gug, gug*."

"*Gug, gug, gug*."

"What letter is it?"

"*G*."

"What does it say?"

"*Gug*."

"Don't forget it, now."

Whatever it was, it could never be sung.

Good and bad luck comes in waves. It was a wave of the best that brought me to William Maxwell, my editor at the *New Yorker* who read my first story and every other for the next twenty-five years. He turned away the IOUs I tried to hand him, which announce just simply that I owed him everything. And so I am writing another one here, with no possibility of any answer: I owe him everything. When we met for the first time, in the spring of 1950, I did not immediately connect him to the author of *The Folded Leaf*. He, of course, said nothing about himself at all. He asked just a few questions and let me think it was perfectly natural to throw up one's job and all one's friends and everything familiar and go thousands of miles away to write. He made it seem no more absurd or unusual than taking a bus to visit a museum. Everyone else I knew had quite the opposite to say; I felt suddenly like a stranded army with an unexpected ally. I was about to try something entirely normal and that (he made it sound obvious) I was unlikely to regret.

He seemed to me the most American of writers and the most American of all the Americans I have known; but even as I say this, I know it almost makes no sense and that it is undefinable and that I am unable to explain what I mean. I can get myself out of it only by saying it is a compliment.

There is something I keep wanting to say about reading short stories. I am doing it now, because I may never have another occasion. Stories are not chapters of novels. They should not be read one after another, as if they were meant to follow along. Read one. Shut the book. Read something else. Come back later. Stories can wait.

—MAVIS GALLANT

OTHER NEW YORK REVIEW CLASSICS

For a complete list of titles, visit www.nyrb.com or write to:
Catalog Requests, NYRB, 435 Hudson Street, New York, NY 10014

* *Also available as an electronic book.*